THE FROST WITCH

THE COVENANTS OF VELORA

BOOK ONE

EMBERLY ASH

For the girls who have looked in the mirror and wondered...
No, you didn't deserve it.
Yes, you can heal.
You are worthy.
You are good.
You belong.

CONTENT WARNINGS

The Covenants of Velora is a dark fantasy romance series. While it is not a true dark romance, the themes are heavy and may be triggering for some readers.

Content warnings include: starvation, dystopian world, prostitution, anxiety, murder, profanity, references to past sexual assault (not MCs), acrophobia, ableism, loss of a loved one, explict sexual content, graphic depictions of death, violence, and torture.

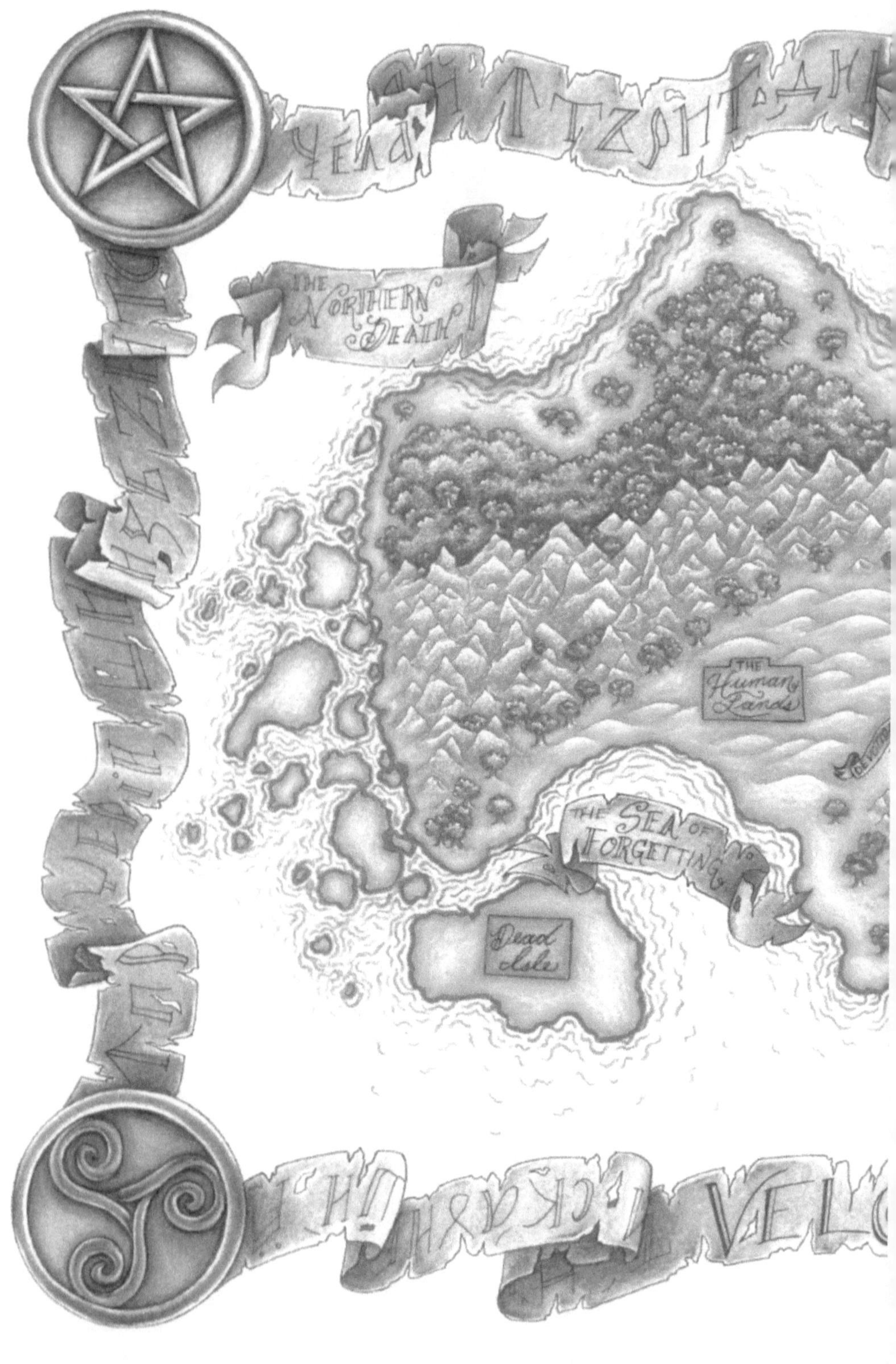

THE NORTHERN DEATH
THE Human Lands
THE SEA OF FORGETTING
Dead Isle

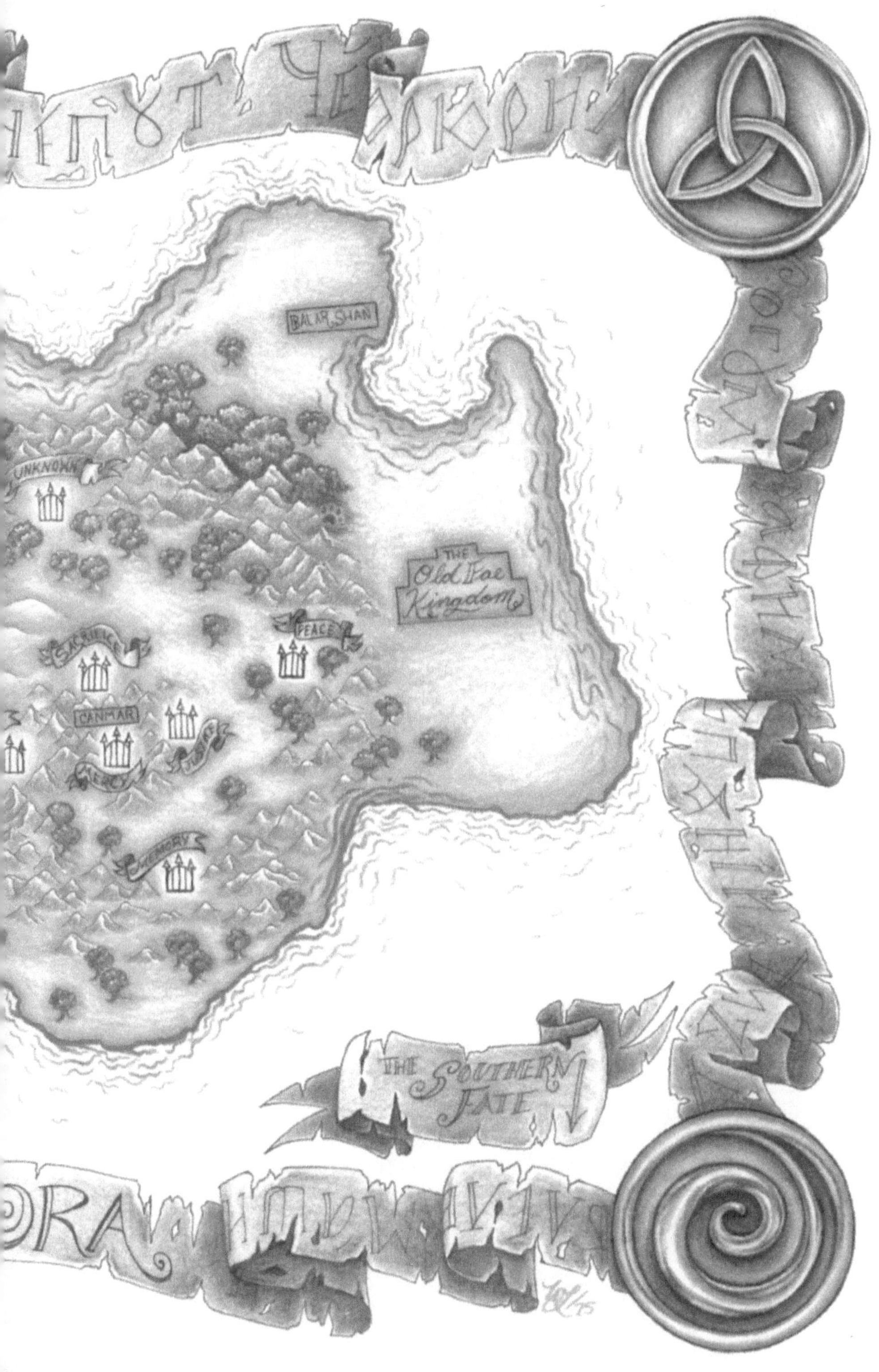

BALAR SHAN
THE Old Fae Kingdom
UNKNOWN
SACRIFICE
PEACE
CANMAR
MERCY
MEMORY
THE Southern Fate

PROLOGUE

I DIED ALONE IN A FROSTBITTEN FOREST.

It was not heroic.

I did not die defending an innocent or hunting to feed my loved ones.

I died because I was reckless and cowardly. I died running away.

Alone, half-soaked in a frigid stream with icicles in my hair, I slowly froze to death. The cold stole my last breath, no more than a wisp of frost in the air as my organs stopped pumping and my eyes turned unseeing.

And that would have been the end of my story.

A selfish girl who died alone in the wood, having spurned those who would have missed her.

Until the witches found me.

I was dead. I did not hear their approach, could not wonder or worry. My soul—whatever fragment of self remains when the body dies—was not aware of itself. I saw no afterlife. Nor did I linger above my lifeless body, contemplating my existence, as the poets would have us believe.

One moment, I existed. The next, I did not.

But then I did again.

Sight returned first. Dark figures lurked on the edge of an even deeper darkness. The only light filtered down from a mostly obscured moon. Yet I could see the outline of each cloaked body clearly.

Next came sound. They chanted, deep and low. Words—words I should have recognized but could not force my mind to parse. I felt the thrumming of my blood in my veins, surging in time with their otherworldly chorus. But how could that be? I'd felt my blood slow and stop in time with my heart...

Blood.

The scent of it flooded my consciousness until the smell was the color and the sound. Red, hot, demanding. I'd never spilled enough of my own blood to learn the scent of it. But as I felt my knees bend beneath me, lifting me out of the frozen creek bed, I knew the tang in my nostrils belonged to me.

It dripped from my fingertips as I stood. There was a cut on my left forearm, just above the wrist. The blood flowed freely, thick and unclotted. Mesmerized, I lifted my fingers, entranced by the pattern of scarlet rivulets that decorated my palm and knuckles. My eyes followed the path—over my skin, down to the snow-covered ground. A thick layer of frost coated the rocks and mud at the edge of the stream. Droplets of fallen blood spread over the ice, their shapes distorting as their warmth melted the thin top layer of ice.

But the blood did not end there. It was all around me. I'd been freezing, not bleeding... so much blood... how was I alive?

The blood was not in a pool around me. It spread out in purposeful, intersecting lines. Five of them. And I stood at the center.

It wasn't possible. Unless...

Unless I wasn't alive at all.

Five lines. Five points. Five figures chanting.

Except they were no longer chanting.

A lone hooded figure approached, walking a straight line from the point where two lines of my blood joined until she stood directly before me.

She. I knew without seeing the face beneath the hood.

A hand emerged from the layers of heavy fabric, its graceful movements at odds with its ten long nails, each sharpened to a point. It took my larger one without hesitation. As if she was entitled to touch me.

I didn't catch her words. The silence around me was too loud. But I watched as her other hand produced a needle and thread and her graceful fingers stitched my skin back together. A few more words and a bandage appeared from the frigid air, winding itself around my wound.

She squeezed my hand, now suddenly clean of blood, before retreating to her point on the pentagram.

Five lines. Five points. Five witches.

And I stood at their center.

Though blood flowed in my veins, it was not my heart that pumped it, but an ancient power. That same power now surged through me, claiming every corner of my being. When I lifted my hand again, frost coated my fingertips where moments before had been blood.

I was not alive. Nor was I truly dead. Not reborn, but remade.

A fragment of memory curled around the icy stalagmites of my mind. An old adage, a line of a faerietale, a whisper of who I'd been before. Uttered by someone who'd loved me, who I'd loved in return.

But new words forestalled the old. The same witch who'd stitched my wound lowered her hood, revealing a riot of black curls and an eerie but alluring countenance that matched her hand. "Welcome, sister."

The words hung in the air. Then more joined them—the voices of the other witches echoing her greeting.

But different words filled my mind. Words that as a child I'd never fully understood. I was little more than a girl now, but I knew their truth in the same way that I knew my name. And knew what I now was.

A witch.

My mother's voice whispered a farewell as the girl I'd been slipped away. *Beware, sweet Koryn. Witches are not born. They are made.*

PART I
MERCY

They bow beneath the weight of sin,
Still mercy's light glows clear—
To lift the low, restore the lost,
An act of faith and fear.

CHAPTER 1

Three hundred and seventy-seven years later...

DESPERATION HAD A TASTE. SOME PEOPLE TRIED TO SEASON IT TO make the flavor more palatable. They spiced it with anger or sadness or bravado. But it was a futile effort. It always tasted the same in the end.

In the last four hundred years, desperation had become the national dish of Velora. Though calling what remained of the continent a nation would be overly generous. Four hundred years ago, the gods sentenced the continent of Velora to death. She'd taken her time about it, but there was no mistaking it now. The once prosperous, viable land was in her final death throes. Those who lingered here were either stupid or desperate. Most were some combination of both.

Not me.

I was perfectly aware of the gravity of my situation. Alone. Abandoned by my coven. Unlike the humans mulling around the dark hovel of a tavern where I'd taken refuge, I would not starve to death.

I forced myself to eat a bit of the gruel that I'd purchased from the gaunt proprietor. His bluster was apparent even from the dark corner where I sat. He wore it like armor, glaring at every person who blew through the door, bringing a gust of frigid air with them. The skin around his face was loose, his neck even worse. The thick woolen scarf he wore wrapped around it did little to disguise the slack skin. Once, he had been a bull of a man. Muscular, strong. Intimidating, even. But the gods had stolen that vitality from him, leaving a decaying husk. It was not even a metaphor; the comparison to the landscape and continent beyond was too direct for poetry.

The gruel stuck in my throat, but I forced it down. Witches needed no such mortal sustenance; we were already dead, after all. My body was sustained by ancient power, not by nutrients. But I could still feel hunger and cold, even if they would not be enough to kill me. The gruel was noxious enough I would have preferred the hunger, but it comforted the humans to see me eat.

It was one of dozens of small adjustments that I'd learned to make. My hair was braided instead of loose around my shoulders, the way I'd prefer it. No part of a witch was meant to be constrained. My nails were trimmed to points, but they did not curl around to kiss my palms, like the witches of the ancient covens. I'd even softened my coven mark—though too soon, it would begin to fade. My connection to my sisters was weakening.

I forced down another bite of gruel, studying the other occupants of the tavern. I could tell by looking what most of them would ask for, though who would summon the courage—or desperation—to approach first was not as clear to me. Would it be the young mother in the corner, squalling child at her empty breast? She would ask for a spell to increase the supply of her milk so that her child might live another week. There was a reason so few children were born in Velora. The land could not sustain them, nor their mothers. Perhaps it was a bit of mercy from

Seraxa, that instead of allowing the children to be born only for their mothers to watch them die, the women of Velora hardly ripened with child at all.

Or perhaps it would be the farmer. Two hundred years ago, farmers were easy to spot. They were lean, like all the others as food became scarcer, but they still had muscle. Even as crops declined year after year, they fed themselves and their families. They *had* families. But over the last century, that had changed. The crops dwindled to nothing. With neither crops to tend nor food to sustain them, their muscles disappeared. Their wives were now gone, their children unborn. Stolen by the gods.

A hundred years ago, I'd had a coven around me. My existence had been fraught in many ways, but at least I'd had my sisters. I'd had *something*.

A hundred years could change everything.

The farmer in the corner ordered a watered ale instead of wine. He saw me waiting. He would spend his last coin on a spell in hopes of coaxing some bit of life from Velora's fallow, worthless ground. And I would take it from him.

My shoulder blades drew together, my body protesting the decision my mind had already made. Any kindness died when I did, I reminded myself. My heart was too dead to protest the lies that I told myself in order to keep moving forward.

The fae were the first to leave, retreating beyond the mountains to their walled refuge. No one had seen or heard from them in more than three centuries. Good riddance. All of this was their fault. Not just the curse—*all of it.*

The rich were next, booking passage on ships across the ocean in all directions. Anywhere was better than Velora. That left the middle and poorer classes, those who could not immediately afford to flee, along with those who were stupid enough to hope.

Many covens left, but not mine.

If we had fled to richer lands, where power still grew up from the ground with the crops, would it never have happened? Would I be with my sisters, still?

A useless thought.

I ought to have learned by then that the past did not matter. If I had not learned that lesson by now, maybe I was doomed to never learn it at all.

The mother or the farmer. One of them would be the first to approach me that night.

There were more that would come to me. It was my third night in this tavern on the outskirts of Canmar, what was once a thriving capital city at the heart of a prosperous continent. The old fae palace in the center of the city was deserted, as were most of the larger residences.

Three nights was the maximum, I'd learned. Enough time for the desperate to pass word from mouth to ear and muster the courage to come to me. Any longer and I would attract the wrong sort of attention.

I rolled my shoulders, trying to dispel the tension building in the center of my back. Remorse for what I was about to do, what I'd been doing for months, paired with the flood of sensations that accosted me from every direction.

Even the sparse tavern was almost too much to bear. Wood crackled in the hearth, the warmth spreading relaxation through the haggard patrons. Watered wine and ale were enough to intoxicate these days. Voices grew louder. The heat pressed in. The power thrumming in my veins grew to a rush. I flattened my palms against the table, fighting for control.

I might have been the only non-human in the tavern, but desperation makes humans do stupid things. If I was anything less than the hardened, ruthless witch they expected to see, there was no telling what the desperate patrons around me might convince themselves to do.

I forced myself to continue scanning the interior of the tavern, looking for prospective customers. It dulled the edge of tension, but only slightly.

A prostitute emerged from the shadows at the rear of the tavern. Her rouge was smudged, the kohl that lined her eyes expertly covering the heavy bags that should be beneath them. Comely women were harder and harder to find in Velora. Most of them had escaped with the more affluent, selling themselves as mistresses and broodmares. The ones left behind were those born too late. Unlucky to have been born at all.

She sauntered to the bar top, crooking her finger to call for wine. No man nor woman appeared from the shadows behind her. She must have sent her most recent customer off through the back door. The gaunt proprietor slid her a goblet. There was an arrangement between them. But I did not have any interest in her. She wouldn't seek me out. Prostitution was one of the few professions that continued to thrive in Velora.

A hacking cough filled the close space, reminding me that the patrons I'd marked were far from the only occupants of the desolate corner of the world I inhabited. The tavern was a beacon of warmth, and unlike many such establishments, the proprietor had managed to procure a stock of wine. The price was exorbitant, but desperation… well, desperation and stupidity. Even those without money for the next night's lodging will spend their coin on the escape alcohol can bring.

The door stuttered, protesting against the contrast of frigid cold outside and insulated heat within. It was the only redeeming trait of the dark, noisy establishment—warmth.

But even that might not be enough to keep it full.

As one, the occupants of the tavern held their breaths. I exhaled into the blessed silence, even knowing it would not last.

Sometimes, desperation outweighed stupidity. Instinct took over. The will to survive overpowered all else. Right then, every person in the tavern was calculating the threat posed by the new arrival.

It was not just the greatsword sheathed across his back or the full quiver of arrows, though the weapons said enough. Why carry a bow and arrows when there was so little game to hunt?

There was no doubt this man was a predator. Violence peeled off of him in curls as visible as the cloud of breath he huffed into the cold air he let in.

"Close the door!" the proprietor yelled without looking up to see who he accosted. Desperation and stupidity could look eerily similar.

I braced my hands flat on the scarred tabletop in front of me, a surge of power centering in my palms.

He was massive—tall enough that I found myself trying to pick out his ears in the dim light scattered from the lone stone hearth. I hadn't seen a fae in more than three hundred years; not since they realized that the curse the gods had warned about had truly taken hold. The fae took too much. They set themselves above the gods. Those same gods cursed Velora as punishment. Those same fae retreated to the safety of their walled fortress beyond the mountains while the rest of us were left to die.

Hate curled in my stomach, turning the meager gruel to ice in seconds. The fae had stolen everything from me—my past and my future. I'd never matched myself against one, though the hate for them ran deep among my kind. The witches and fae were natural enemies, both contenders for the power and magic rooted in the land itself. Except one of us had destroyed it and then fled to safety, while the others were left to scratch out an existence from the remains.

I would kill him.

He was handsome enough to be fae. The broad shoulders swathed in fur, the elegant but masculine lines of his face, the hair so blond that it might have been mistaken for silver, if not for the gold tones cast by the firelight.

But amid the tangle of pale hair, the man was just that—a man. Human. There were no points atop his ears, only rounded shells that proclaimed him as mortal as every other person seeking refuge in this particular hellhole.

The power that had overwhelmed me moments before ebbed to a light frost. He would scare away some of the patrons with that grizzled visage and all those weapons, but the most determined would remain. I would still get my coin and eventually get off of this cursed continent. Survive another day.

Though what I'm surviving for...

The thought slid from my mind, replaced by a sharp stab of awareness.

I may have dismissed him, but the newcomer had not returned the favor. Like everyone else who entered, he scanned the occupants of the tavern for predators or prey. He found me.

Even in the low light of the tavern, I marked the way his eyes widened. Recognition shone in the blue-green orbs. Recognition and intensity. The rest of the tavern melted away, the sounds of voices and scraping of metal and wood fading into a blur of indecipherable background noise. He held me in his gaze, his eyes boring into mine, as if he could see past the rings of exhaustion and into the dark power that pumped through my veins.

I dragged in a breath, the air scraping across my throat painfully enough I had to blink back a reaction. A blink was all it took to shatter the connection. He swung away from me, giving me no more heed than the prostitute who was already sidling in his direction. The cacophony of voices and sounds came crashing back in on me.

He pulled out a stool at the bar and put his back to every other occupant in the tavern. A distinct contrast to the approach I'd taken, tucking myself with my back to a wall at a table within an easy run of the tavern's rear door.

Wood scraped across the floor as someone pushed up to stand. More than one someone—the calculus of the tavern was rearranging itself around this new arrival. I exhaled slowly, trying to settle the tempest that raged through my stomach. He was just a man. A well-armed one, but nothing more.

From the stink of unwashed cloaks and the murmuring emerged a slim human figure, hair disheveled and cheeks pale despite the blazing heat of the tavern. And she was coming my way.

The mother. I should have known. Mothers were always the most desperate. And determined.

The child strapped across her chest was as slight as she. He would have been easy to lose in the layers if not for the squalls of hunger every few minutes. The words of a spell danced along my tongue already, but I wouldn't give it to her without payment. I'd made that mistake early in my exile. Word of a benevolent witch had spread quickly, and I'd barely escaped with my life. Kindness was a weakness. Kindness allowed others to take advantage of my gifts. Kindness had gotten me cast out of my coven and set me on this desperate path.

I was not merciful. I did not have pity. Maybe if I said it to myself enough times, it would be true.

"My lady," the mother mumbled. She tried to dip a curtsy but lost her balance, not used to the weight strapped to her front or too weak to execute the movement. She grabbed for the table that separated us.

I didn't wait for her to steady herself. "I am not your lady," I bit back.

She blanched, one hand wrapping around the child protectively. My teeth ground together of their own accord.

Touching the child seemed to give her courage. "I beg your pardon, miss, but I—"

"Call me what I am."

Maybe it was cruel. Maybe *I* was cruel. It would be among the least of the charges leveled at my kind, and believing it about myself might give me the hardness I needed to survive. But in that moment, I needed to hear her say it. I needed to know that she understood exactly who—*what*—she was dealing with. And I needed to remember what I was, even if my sisters had cast me out.

"Witch." The whisper slipped between her lips. An admission and a curse. A plea.

My spine straightened.

"What do you want?"

"My babe." She swallowed, mustering her courage once more. "My milk is drying up. I do not have enough food." She opened her palm, dropping a single sparkling coin onto the table.

If she could not feed herself, then her body would not produce the milk to sustain her child. She was not the first mother to seek me out since I was cast out of my coven, driven to performing parlor tricks in dark, fetid holes of humanity to scrape out an existence. I could practically taste the power that she needed, the words that would give her what she so desperately wanted, at least for a time.

But those weren't the words that came out of my mouth. "Then use your coin to buy a meal."

Maybe I was as foolish as the humans loitering around that desolate place. The woman wanted to give me her coin. I might not technically need food or shelter to survive, but I'd rather sleep in a bed than on the ground. The sole of my left boot was nearly worn through. The leather and expertise to repair it would be dear; there were few animals left to hunt for hides, and most craftspeople had deserted the forsaken continent for kinder shores. The passage off of Velora was even more expensive, and my only real option. If I lingered too long on Velora, in a festering land without my coven to concentrate what power there was and sustain me, I would die.

The young woman's lower lip trembled, but she did not turn away. She used the broken fingernail at the end of a dirty finger to nudge the coin across the table in my direction. "A meal will not be enough. Nor will ten meals. Not when there is no shelter to keep him warm. I do not care for myself. Only for him."

She would let herself waste away for the sake of her child. She would suffer the pangs of hunger, using whatever resources remained to her to give her child warmth. She would die, but he might live. It was a choice I'd seen before, and one I was sure to see again.

This was the curse of Velora.

"It will not last forever," I warned.

The mother nodded. "Long enough."

I did not have the power to read minds. My active power was less useful, particularly in this frozen wasteland. So I could not know what her plan was once she had my spell—and nor did I care, I reminded myself. She had a coin, and for now, I had the power to cast.

I lifted a hand in her direction, although the action was meaningless. It was the words that mattered. But the motion comforted the humans and drew the attention of other potential patrons.

"*By river's flow and rain's sweet song, let mother's milk again flow strong.*"

Once, the spell would have been enough to keep a mother's milk flowing until her child's second name day. But Velora's power was dying right along with everything else.

The mother closed her eyes, her focus turning inward. Her baby squalled again. But unlike before, a wet spot bloomed through the fabric over her breasts. She didn't bother with thanks, too transfixed with her child and the outcome of my power.

But others noticed. The farmer slid off his stool, leaving his empty tankard of weak ale behind. The pale-haired behemoth at the counter leaned on one elbow, his gaze more casual this time, a lingering perusal. Let him look. If he believed I could offer him some solution, he was welcome to part with his coin. But I doubted a man like that would pay for anything he could obtain through violence instead.

The prostitute from earlier was at his side, her laugh echoing off the low overhead beams of the roughshod, single-story structure.

Familiarity prickled my spine. I'd spent too many nights in desolate, desperate places like this. It was beginning to impede my judgment.

An elderly woman leaning on a cane sidled up behind the farmer, a makeshift line beginning to form. I flattened my hands on the tabletop once more and licked my lips.

CHAPTER 2

I LEFT THE TAVERN AN HOUR LATER. THERE WAS A CADENCE TO THE evenings in such places. When the second prostitute arrived and the noise ratcheted up, it was time for me to leave. Once the humans began brawling over their company for the night, it was too easy to get injured and harder to control my power. Best to be gone before desperation took on its more dangerous shades. There was enough coin in my purse to buy a night of shelter—many nights, if I was not too particular about my accommodations. Getting my boot patched would be trickier. Or I could save it all. Not enough for passage out of Velora—not yet. But soon.

The door that stuck earlier gave way to me without a hitch. The walking death threat must have knocked the door into submission. He was still seated at the counter when I left. He did not glance my way, and I didn't glance his. Whether that eerie perusal allowed him to recognize me as the threat I was did not matter. I would never see him again.

The cold whipped in from every direction, pressing against the thick layers of my cloak and in through the leather and wool and linen beneath. There were never enough layers to truly keep out the cold. Not in Velora. Not in the last decade.

I died on a night like this. Back then, such extremes were rare. Now, we went months without seeing the sun.

But I could see just as well in the dark—a gift of the ancient power that moved my blood through my veins. Or more specifically, from the Dark God who created the witches.

I noted the pair of men huddled just within the dark alley that separated the tavern from the boarded-up remains of a general store. They were just that. Men. Too short to be fae, a possibility that had not even entered my mind in years until that huge hulking beast entered the tavern. And they were certainly not witches, for the simple fact that they were not female.

The tiny hairs at the nape of my neck prickled again.

Wearing it like this was driving me mad. I reached over my shoulder, dragging the thick braid forward and dislodging my other hand from inside my cloak to pull out the knot that held the plait in place—

My hands froze, every muscle in my body tightening.

It blended with the snow, white and so finely ground that it was nearly impossible to see. But I felt the impact immediately, as if I'd been punched in the gut, all of the air forced out of my lungs.

Salt.

The two men stepped out of the alley. A smile curved one of their faces—the bigger of the two, his cheeks still full and round. The rich and the evil were the only ones left in Velora with full cheeks. And the former were mostly gone.

"I told you she was real," the slighter man said, rubbing his bare hands together against the cold. He held his place behind the larger man, lingering just over his shoulder as they approached, leaving a trail of shuffling footprints in the fresh snow.

"The salt was worth the price," the bigger one agreed, his smile still in place.

Salt was expensive this far inland even before the gods cursed

Velora. With so few people left on the continent, the once flowing trade routes from the sea had thinned to a trickle. A vial of salt could buy an entire month of shelter. Or capture one witch.

Anger rolled through my veins. This would never have happened if I were with my coven. If I was where I belonged.

You did this to yourself, a voice that sounded like an eerie mixture of Maura's and my own hissed in the back of my consciousness. There was no hint of kindness in either. I could be gentle with others, but never with myself.

I was the one who got banned from my coven. My actions. My choices.

The same choices that had landed me here, trapped by two dirty, stinking men.

My fault.

But what happened next would not be. Men who hurt women all deserved to be punished.

The men moved closer, emboldened by the rigid lines of my muscles where the salt held them in place.

"She does not even try to hide her dark master's mark," the smaller remarked, rising on tiptoes to see over his accomplice's shoulder.

My coven mark, the one that proclaimed me a member of the Midnight Coven, burned on the center of my forehead, protesting the salt that held my power at bay. The paste I'd dabbed across my skin to soften it hours before had rubbed away. I did not need a mirror to verify that the lines were clear and dark now. I could feel each one where it was carved into my skin. I'd thought it was fading as the months and miles separated me from my coven, dwindling along with my power, as Maura had always warned… but maybe this resurgence of power had reinvigorated the mark.

That *was* power crackling in my veins, solidifying within my blood. What these rash humans did not realize was that when they trapped me, they trapped all of my latent power as well. Instead of seeping from my skin with every drop of sweat, pouring from my lungs with every breath, it was trapped within me. Building. Building. Until it burst out.

I may be weakened, like all of Velora. But without realizing it, these two vermin had shoved me into a pressure-cooker of power.

Words formed on my tongue, but without the ability to move my lips, I could not speak the spells into existence. Spells must be spoken to have power. But the power that curled through my body was not bound by movement. I summoned the energy, molding it into deadly shards, waiting.

The smaller, more skittish man halted several feet away, letting the other approach on his own. "How long will the salt hold her?"

"How should I know," the bullish one answered, circling me. He let out a low, appreciative whistle as he inspected my backside, the curve of my cloak where it was belted around my waist outlining my full hips. "That purse on her belt is full."

The thinner man paled. "And it's nothing compared to—"

"Speak for yourself, I'll take every coin I can get for this job."

Do it. All I needed was for him to put one bullish foot out of line, to break the constrictive ring of salt I'd stumbled into, and I would immobilize them both.

The smaller man threw himself into the space between us. "No. We..." his eyes flew around the deserted street. The only eyes watching us belonged to a singular crow, perched on the half-caved in roof of the abandoned general store. It cawed plaintively, hopping from foot to foot. Not much help to any of us.

"We *can't*," he finished, eyes turning up to his partner. The wide shoulders squared in protest.

Yes, I silently urged. My fingers began to tingle.

"Then I'll take what's mine." Spittle sprayed the smaller man's face. But before he could wipe it off, the bigger one spun, reaching across the barrier of salt for the small leather purse tied at my waist.

Mistake.

He hadn't disturbed the ring of salt, but he'd willingly put himself within its power. Within mine.

His hand never made it to my waist. Frost engulfed the tips, spreading up his fingers to his palm before his feeble human heart could pulse a single beat. Curls of sparkling ice snaked around his wrist. He jerked back violently, colliding with the other man, sending them both sprawling in the snow.

He howled, clutching his ruined hand. Already, his fingertips were darkening to black, frostbite setting in.

"We can't touch her," the other one rasped, crawling backward. Realization turned his features paler and paler until they nearly matched the snow all around us.

The injured man huffed, clouds billowing out from his nostrils like an angry bull as he clambered back to his feet. He shoved his ruined hand inside of his overcoat, between the buttons. A soundless laugh rolled through my unmoving chest and throat. Let him try to warm that hand. He would lose the fingers, regardless.

Before, his dark eyes had been filled with greed. Now they gleamed with hate.

Good. Hate was one step away from fear. And fear made men stupid. That was a lesson I'd learned long before becoming a witch.

"We don't need to touch her." He reached inside the pocket of his overcoat with his uninjured hand, digging around even as he kept his eyes firmly fixed upon me.

The smaller man was on his feet again as well, though he'd put even more space between us. His eyes darted from side to side, lingering on the alleyway where they'd lain in wait to accost me. He was going to bolt.

I'd decide later whether to hunt him down and punish him. I kept the larger share of my attention on the wide man in front of me. I knew the moment that he found whatever it was he was searching for. Those eyes, dark and full of malice, shifted to something more than hate.

"What do we do with witches?" He did not wait for an answer

as his lips curved, drawing the device from the confines of his overcoat. "We burn them."

Dark God, be with me.

Even immortality had its caveats.

The skittish one froze mid-step, his eyes flaring as the other clicked the device together. Shiny metal against glittering pyrite. A pale gold spark fell to the ground at his feet, disappearing instantly in the snow.

The power in my veins stuttered. But the thin ring of salt held me in place, so that while my insides recoiled, my body could not.

"You won't get to try that trick again." Click. Another spark fell uselessly into the snow. He was playing with me now, confident that he'd found my weakness even if I could not so much as twitch an eye to prove him right or wrong.

Stupid or desperate. Not the latter; he was well rounded, if unkempt. A man used to doing unconscionable things to keep his belly full. The smaller one was gaining confidence as well, his shifty eyes no longer searching out an escape route, though he still hovered a few steps behind.

They wanted to kill me.

But you cannot kill what is already dead.

"How will you set her alight without touching her?" the other man asked.

Click. Spark. Fall.

"Rip a piece of wood off of that boarded-up building."

Click.

Spark.

Fall.

Each spark that disappeared into the snow brought the brute closer, his confidence growing. The tiny pinpricks of fire disappeared almost instantly, no match for the layers of ice and snow that completely covered the ground.

The second man trotted through the snow with newfound determination. But he lacked the other's brute strength—his muscles were weakened by lack of nutrients and years spent in the bitter cold, like most residents of Velora. He tried to pry off one of the boards covering the general store's doorway, cursing beneath his breath as it refused to give way. He pulled a knife from his pocket and shoved it between the plank and the doorframe, using the blade as a lever.

Click.

"Have you started counting the seconds that remain to you?"

Spark.

The crow cawed again from the rooftop.

"My fingers will heal." *No, they won't.* "But you'll burn until there is nothing left of you but a pile of ashes in the snow." *No, I won't.*

Fall.

He was in my face now, hovering just outside of the ring of salt. He wouldn't broach it again. Even if he could not see the power pulsing within, he felt it. He believed he was smarter than me.

He was wrong.

"I have it!" Footsteps crashed through the snow, but my eyes were fixed on the device.

Another spark fell on the exact spot as the one before it. It disappeared as quickly as every one that came before.

Right on the line of salt.

Salt did not burn. But snow melted.

Click.

"Say your prayers to the Dark God." The lines at the corners of his eyes deepened with his smile.

Spark.

He stretched out one hand to his compatriot, his beady dark eyes never leaving mine. The wood landed in his hand. "Oh wait… you cannot speak at all."

Fall.

A narrow stream of melted snow rolled away in the direction of the messy footsteps they'd made while leaving my circle undisturbed. It disappeared in an icy furrow, swallowed by the power of the cold.

It was not much.

But it was enough.

And it took the grains of salt with it. That tiny crack in the thin circle was all I needed.

I flung my hands forward, unspent power surging from my fingertips. Two columns of frost shot from my hands, wrapping around each of the men. The swirling torrent of snow and ice and frigid air started at the ground, then climbed up around their calves to their knees. The smaller one threw himself backward, trying to run, just as he had before. But the other bellowed with rage instead.

I curled my fingers into my palms, fisting my hands abruptly, closing off the torrent. Only the silence of the deserted street allowed me such control. The power inside of me screamed in protest, clambering to escape after all of those torturous minutes of confinement. But I held it, used it to lift the corners of my mouth in a smile that wiped any remnants of the smirk off my attacker's face.

He fought against the restraint, but the wall of ice and snow held him to the waist, keeping his hands pinned at his sides.

I watched in appreciation as the ice encasing the smaller one turned translucent, temporarily warming as he pissed himself.

The crow that had watched the entire spectacle cawed again in the distance. A chorus of sound leaked from inside the tavern. A brawl, probably. Both heads turned hopefully toward the closed door.

I clucked my tongue. "They cannot save you." As I spoke, tendrils of frost climbed their bodies, like hands stretching out their fingers, up over their cheeks, curling around their eyes. The smaller one cried out again, shivering violently as the intruding cold entered his nostrils and ears.

The other sputtered, shaking his head, choking as he tried

uselessly to dispel the cold that infiltrated his body, freezing him from the inside out.

"You bitch," he managed, spit dribbling down his stubbled chin.

I allowed myself the space of one breath to savor the horror on their faces, illuminated by the glowing blue light of my coven mark.

Then I lifted my hand and uncurled my fingers, releasing the full torrent of repressed power. "I think you mean *witch*."

Whatever unclever retort rose to his lips, the man did not get the chance to say it. The muscles of his face froze in place a second before the rest of him. I watched as the glint of life drained from his eyes.

A sharp pain cleaved into my chest, ripping me from the trance of rage and power.

He was dead.

My power collapsed, the ice that held the two men in place shattering. They both fell. The smaller one tried to catch himself. The other could not.

I lifted my hands from my sides, expecting to see them thick with blood or coated in frost. But my palms were smooth and unremarkable. There was no indication of the power that lurked beneath my skin, the power I'd just used to kill a man.

A man who'd wanted to burn me alive. I'd killed him for protection. I'd killed for less. But the ache in my chest did not particularly care. Three hundred and seventy-seven years, and I'd never gotten better at it.

The accomplice whimpered on the ground.

He'd been just as keen as his companion. I should have killed him, too.

But instead, a single word fell from my lips. "Run."

He could not. He crawled, and then limped, the lower two-thirds of his body still half-frozen from the pillar I'd made him into.

I stayed until he disappeared, until my sharpened senses told me that he was nowhere to be seen or heard or smelled. I fought through the unwelcome torrent of emotions that pulsed through me in waves, trying to focus on what came next.

Three nights had been too long.

From now on, I would not linger longer than two. Maybe it was time to desert Canmar altogether. I'd lingered here out of a sense of familiarity I did not want to acknowledge, moving from one ragged hovel to another. Once, I could have hidden in the city of thousands indefinitely. But now, the population was too greatly reduced.

I already carried all of my possessions on my body, but I sighed as I resigned myself to the fact that I could not return to the deserted attic where I'd lodged the last few weeks. I would spend the night in the cold.

I dragged my boot through the surrounding snow, destroying what remained of the salt circle. I did not let myself look back at the remains of the man on the ground. I could not avoid what I'd done. I could only add it to the litany of crimes I kept in my conscience. The wounds I'd done to the world. I'd avoid them for now, because I had to keep moving forward. I had to get out of Velora.

But there was no avoiding the witch who stepped out of the shadows.

CHAPTER 3

THE PROSTITUTE'S FACE WAS UNCHANGED, THOUGH HER MAKEUP showed the evidence of her evening within the tavern. The smudged rouge from earlier was now gone completely, leaving behind pale pink lips that were just a bit too thin.

A pattern of bruises that looked suspiciously like fingers colored her pale throat. Were they new, or had I missed them in my perusal earlier?

They might not even be real.

I should have realized it sooner. My scalp did not prickle this time; my entire body sang with recognition. "Sister."

Her features shifted as I watched. The heavy kohl-lined eyes flattened, taking on an entirely different shape above her rising cheekbones. The teased brown curls morphed into a curtain of silky, straight black hair. The bruises disappeared as the alabaster of her skin warmed to a pale olive with golden undertones that shone even in the silver light cast by the moon over the snow.

"Koryn."

Her voice remained her own. If I'd heard her speak in the tavern, I would have known instantly. It was the only thing about her that she could not change. Like all witches, her active power was tied to the manner of her death.

Elodie died wearing the face of another, a lowly maid who'd disguised herself as her well-born mistress in order to rendezvous with a man that she imagined loved her. In immortality, she'd learned to wield those many faces and take revenge for the death blow paid to her.

But why was she here? And where were the others? My power churned within me, calling instinctively to my sisters.

No. I am not foolish enough to hope.

I willed my power to quiet within me. There in the deserted street, with the snow deadening all sounds, it actually obeyed. The ice in my veins thawed to match the temperature of my blood.

"Why have you come?" I tried not to let myself choke on the words, but the last one caught in my throat.

Sister—Elodie had been my sister once. Before I'd been cast out from my coven. But I was not certain what that word meant to me anymore… what she meant to me.

Without power and cosmetics distorting her features, I was able to see clearly as she raked her gaze over me in appraisal. And when it flicked over my shoulder, to the wreckage of what I'd done.

"Your power remains," she observed, her voice carefully even.

The muscles in my abdomen tightened, heat rising in my cheeks despite the cold. "Why shouldn't it?" I shot back, even though the same head witch trained us both. Maura had always warned that power faded the longer a witch was separated from her coven.

Elodie's eyes paused at my forehead, in the spot just above my brows. "Your coven mark fades."

My power was tied to my coven and should have faded as well. That was the sentence she did not say.

But minutes before, I'd felt the coven mark burn. I'd seen the reflection of light on the faces of my attackers. My power had surged, answering my call without hesitation or stutter. Was that why she'd come—because my sisters could still sense me, and the strength of my power, even after all these months?

"You should have killed them both." Her dark eyes were once again on the body behind me.

My mouth twitched, my entire being bristling at the suggestion —the expectation—that I follow the norms of a coven that I no longer answered to. That I'd been cast out from, without any chance of ever returning.

Punishment must be absolute. That was the way of the coven.

"I do not answer to the coven any longer," I bristled.

Elodie's gaze rested back on my face, still utterly devoid of emotion. Was that a consequence of having worn so many faces? Was she incapable of wearing her own? Or was she truly that immune to feeling?

That lack of emotion, that evenness, had always bothered me. How could anyone be that controlled all the time? And why couldn't I?

Even before—I was not supposed to think of *before*. That dictate had been beaten into me from the moment of my remaking. For a witch, there is only the now and the future, the concerns of the coven over the concerns of the self. Thinking about a past that is lost was the ultimate form of selfishness.

But I was no longer a member of the coven. Elodie, however, was.

"Maura sent you," I said. My fingers curled at my side, frost tingling at the tips, but I kept myself under control. Barely.

"Yes." Elodie nodded. And waited.

"I have followed all of her dictates." To the letter. As if I actually believed that if I abided by the strict parameters of my banishment, then someday it would be lifted.

Without your coven, you are nothing. Maura's last words echoed in my head as they had every day since my ouster.

Elodie's eyes trailed back over my shoulder. "So I have seen."

I did not bother parsing technicalities with her. Maura had banished me from my coven—from seeking out any member, from attempting to enter the coven lands, or using any of the sacred artifacts. I had not done any of those things. She had said nothing about practicing my active power… probably because she thought it would fade to nothing in time.

It would. Everything in Velora would die eventually.

Which was why I peddled my spells in dark taverns where brutes like the ones behind us could too easily find me. I needed enough coin to buy passage out of Velora. On another continent, one rich with magic and power, I at least had a chance. I could seek out another coven. Other continents had dozens of covens residing on them, instead of just one. Soon, the dying magic and power of Velora would not even be enough to sustain the one that remained—the one to which I belonged. Used to belong.

Grief burned in my chest, where my heart no longer bothered to beat. Still, Elodie watched me with the damned impassive expression of hers.

Dark God, spare me these useless emotions.

Elodie had yet to state a reason for her sudden appearance. Not so sudden, I reminded myself. She'd been watching me in the tavern while disguised as a prostitute for the last few nights. Which meant she probably already knew where I'd been sleeping, too. But where I could not rest tonight, because someone had sent those two buffoons. I would not linger long enough to find out who. There was an abandoned stable three blocks over. The humans had eaten the horses decades ago. It was just close enough to the forest that no humans risked it, empty enough that it hadn't attracted any of the forest's more dangerous occupants.

The hayloft was as good a place as any to pass the night.

Elodie could find me again if she wanted.

But I had not even reached the alley before she spoke. "We are not far from the Mercy Gate."

I turned slowly. "A gate is always near," I recited.

"A god is always watching," Elodie parroted back.

The words had been instilled in me from birth, in every citizen of Velora. It was an invocation. If a gate was near, so was a god. Always watching, always waiting to see the provenance of their punishment.

Most citizens of Velora—were we citizens, if the government had ceased to exist? — lived their entire life in proximity to a gate without ever passing through it. The years of people hurling themselves at the gates in hopes of lifting the curse had long since passed.

Seven gates. Seven gods. And a promise that had never been fulfilled.

But the witches did not answer to seven gods. We answered only to one—the Dark God who'd created us.

Elodie lifted her chin, her curtain of inky hair skimming her sharp cheekbones as it fell back to frame her expectant eyes. I frowned at her. It was late and I was tired. Being immortal was exhausting. Sleepiness settled in my chest, threatening to dull the edges of my reflexes dangerously if I did not find a bed soon. I shifted, trying to dislodge the feeling. This much exhaustion was unusual. I'd only performed a half dozen spells in the tavern. Was it the use of my active power? Still strong, but at a cost?

"If Maura has more to say, then say it," I said, rolling my shoulders. That was why Elodie was here. Her words were not her own, just like her face.

Her impassive fucking face.

"The priests and priestesses offer bed and board to anyone who plans to attempt the gates," Elodie said.

Millions of words—in the language of the Dark God and the common tongue—and never in three hundred and seventy-seven years would I have expected those particular ones to exit her mouth. She could not possibly be implying… no. Impossible.

"Walking through the doors of that temple is a binding promise," I said. Anyone could enter the temple and enjoy the safety, warmth, and food therein. But there was only one way to leave the temple—through the Mercy Gate.

Elodie knew that. She was older than I was, had already been a witch in the Dark God's keeping when the curse was placed on Velora.

A deep, rumbling roar echoed from the woods beyond the city. Gods, it might be in the city itself, now. Without humans to populate the continent, the monsters that dwelled in the mountains had become bolder. Once, I had not given the monsters a second thought. Most of them were created by the witches at one point or another. Spells gone wrong—or horribly right. But I no longer had the protection of a coven.

Elodie did not react to the sound. Her dark, unreadable gaze held mine as she twisted my entire world on its axis. "Pass through the Seven Gates, lift the curse that is killing Velora, and you will be welcomed back to the Midnight Coven."

Welcomed back to the Midnight Coven. The weight in my chest lifted instantly, replaced by something light and shining and impossibly bright. Hope. That was hope.

And I was just as much of a fucking fool as every human in that tavern, because the condition was impossible.

For nearly four hundred years, fools had been passing through the gates in futile attempts to lift the curse. Some made it through one. Fewer still conquered two. There were stories that one person —a fae, before they disappeared—had passed through five gates before meeting his gruesome end at the Memory Gate.

"Maura asks the impossible," I bit out, anger filling my chest, determined to murder that reckless, foolish hope. It was a cruel trick, even for Maura, to dangle the prospect of return before me like this. She'd actually sent Elodie to seek me out and make this impossible offer. "Was my banishment not enough?"

Elodie gave me nothing. Not a quirk of an eyebrow or quiver of her lips.

The anger in my chest burst into a frigid flame of blue and

white that matched the ice in my veins. No sooner I'd thought it depleted than it rose to meet my fury. I didn't pause to analyze that development. I was too fucking angry.

Frost formed at my fingertips, crawling over my skin beneath the layers of my clothing. I felt it lick at my collarbones and then my throat, curling around my ears.

I watched as it drew swirls of sparkling power over my cheeks and framed my eyes—watched—how was I watching?

Elodie.

She'd changed, showing me my own face. Her body was a perfect mirror of mine, her dark blue cloak identical, the same purse tied to her belted waist that now matched the width of mine.

The power inside of me contracted. Elodie's face changed back to her own.

She lifted two fingers, her middle and index, and drew familiar lines in the air. She traced the lines of the pentagram, inverting the symbol so that the tip pointed toward the snow-covered ground. As if I needed a reminder that my spirit was out of control after that horrifying display.

"Pass through the Seven Gates, lift the curse, and you will be welcomed back," Elodie repeated, word for word. Words mattered, and she'd clearly been told to report Maura's precisely.

Crows cried in the distance. Scavengers made to survive in a dying land. Was I really any better, waiting around in a tavern, preying upon the woes of the dwindling, desperate occupants of Velora for my own gain? With my coven, I would live. My power would be restored, rather than dwindling to nothing until my blood ceased to feed my organs and I succumbed to the second death.

I cannot lift the curse. No one can.

No one had ever made it through more than five gates, if the most outrageous of rumors were true, let alone seven. It was impossible.

I opened my mouth to tell Elodie so. To send her back to

Maura with a curse of my own, little power though it would have without my coven to bolster me. But she was already walking back in the direction of the tavern, the curve of her hips no longer her own.

This time when my power rose, it was nothing more than an icicle in the empty cavern where my heart had once been.

Returning to my coven was impossible. My sisters were lost to me, both those of blood and those of power. Anger, hope, they faded away until I was empty. Nothing, no one, alone on a dark street in a dying land.

I'd had everything, and I lost it. Not just once, but twice.

CHAPTER 4

BEFORE

I was born the year of the curse. Not made. Born. To a mother and father, in a stately manor house set close enough to the sea that the sounds of waves breaking against the cliffs were my lullaby. My father certainly never sang me one. If my mother did, I did not recall. The mind keeps very few memories before the age of five, and she did not live to see my sixth year.

In the beginning, no one understood what the curse truly meant. The fae had overreached their power and tried to set themselves above the gods. The curse was punishment—their punishment, not ours. What did magic or its loss mean to humans, when we had none to begin with?

Everything.

For the first few years, humans prospered in the void left by the fae. My first fully formed memory was of a party—a grand gathering that filled our home to brimming before my mother's body was fully cold.

"Stay upstairs," my sister insisted, pushing past me.

I grabbed for the railing but still stumbled. Two hands caught my shoulders and hauled me back, away from the landing.

"You ought to be in bed." Janessa, my other sister. She didn't release her hold until I was fully out of her way, leaving her enough space to stand at our elder sister's side.

Their taller bodies blocked out the light but not the sound. Dozens of voices, laughter, even the hum of stringed instruments. And above it all, one boomed loudest of all. Our father. He laughed and laughed and laughed. How could he laugh like that when all I did was cry?

I pressed closer to my sisters, peering between their bodies to see. But they were arguing and shoving, and all I got were disappointing flashes of color.

"You should not be wearing that," Janessa hissed at Rylynn.

Rylynn tossed her head. She was always tossing her head and throwing her beautiful dark hair over her shoulder. But she'd fastened it up in some kind of intricate coiffure. My mind twisted with wonder just looking at the plaits and patterns. Beautiful. Like my mother. She even smelled like her.

"And her perfume as well?" Janessa huffed, recoiling enough that I caught a glimpse of a servant carrying a tray of petit fours.

My mother made the petit fours. She was a baker. The best baker south of the mountains. If there were petit fours at the party… the physicians must have been wrong.

"I am the lady of the house now," Rylynn said.

"The pendant is fae-made. Father will kill you if he sees—"

Rylynn grabbed Janessa's arm and yanked her close. I slid into the opening she left, unnoticed by either of them. My eyes followed the path of the petit fours across the crowded room.

"If I have it, then Father cannot sell it," Rylynn said, cupping a protective hand over the ornament pinned to her chest.

I clutched the banister, one foot already reaching down for the next step, my little body fighting the forward momentum.

Mother would never let Father sell the brooch. It was given to her by her mother, passed from her grandmother and great-grandmother and great-great-grandmother…

"He wouldn't," Janessa whispered. Her body went limp beside me.

Rylynn sighed, the sound shakier than it should have been, coming from my confident eldest sister. "He would. Mother is dead. He will sell it or gift it to his next wife…"

Mother is dead. She didn't make the petit fours.

Mother is dead.

My hand slipped on the banister. I tumbled down the stairs into the chaos before my sisters could catch me.

CHAPTER 5

THE HAYLOFT WAS COVERED IN BIRD SHIT. I SLEPT THERE ANYWAY. AT least the crows would alert me if anything more perilous came near. But aside from the occasional caw, they let me sleep right through the night and well into the next morning.

Black night gave way to gray day. The sun rarely broke through the clouds anymore, but at least it wasn't raining. Or snowing. The cold couldn't kill me, but it could make me damn uncomfortable.

I planned to get up, eat the heel of cheese I'd shoved into my pocket the night before, and get the hell away from Canmar. Instead, I found myself in front of the temple with Elodie's offer echoing around inside of my head. At some point, the words transformed. They were no longer in Elodie's melodic voice, but Maura's sharp, abrasive one.

In her voice, the words morphed. Not an offer, but a threat.

Go through the Seven Gates, or else.

An unhinged laugh bubbled up out of my throat. Maura had already banished me from my coven and sentenced me to a slow, excruciating demise as the Dark God's power deserted my veins. What else could she possibly do to me?

The snow swallowed my laugh.

Plenty.

She was a thousands-year-old witch in command of the last remaining coven on the continent. The fae were gone. The humans had never had power or magic to begin with. Maura might well be the most powerful individual in all of Velora.

And she'd ordered me through the Seven Gates.

I inhaled an icy breath and refocused on the courtyard sprawled out in front of me.

The stone edifice rose several stories overhead, seven of its faces ornamented with colorful stained-glass windows depicting each of the gods. Even with the rest of the continent in shambles, the temple rose out of the ice and decay, still standing strong. I hadn't frequented temples in life, let alone in death. I could hardly report on whether the inside had changed in the four hundred years since the curse. But while the stones stood strong, the altars beneath each stained-glass window were depleted. No more flowers grew in Velora. Food was too scarce to be left as an offering, candles needed for their meager warmth.

But food and warmth were plentiful within those walls. That, I knew. Everyone in Velora knew. Enter the temple, fill your stomach, rest your head, and pay the price.

Just as I had the night before in the tavern, I surveyed everyone who entered the courtyard. I'd been watching for half the day and only two people had approached the temple. One only made it halfway across the courtyard before veering left and disappearing at a run. The other was unremarkable at this distance. But he entered the temple, so he was desperate enough.

Not much in the way of adversaries.

They'd only be adversaries if I entered the temple. If I accepted Maura's offer and attempted the gates, I'd face not only the challenges set by each of the gods but also the other desperate suppliants trying to get through them.

Death was not certain. Everyone said that. People did survive the gates—for a while. One. Maybe two. But eventually, one of the Gates or their fellow supplicants would kill them. No one was ever going to get through all seven. No one was going to break the curse.

Velora would die.

This was a fool's errand.

I could go without fixing the hole in the sole of my boot. I shifted my weight behind the embankment of snow where I watched, noting the comforting heft of the purse strapped to my belt. Another month and I would have enough coin to buy passage off of this cursed continent. Maura, Elodie, and all the rest of them could stay here and rot.

But I had to get out of Canmar. I would go south. There weren't any cities left, but the villages that remained mostly clung to the coast, scraping an existence from the sea and the passengers buying their way to safety across the water. I'd be more careful this time; no more than one night in a village, and I would move erratically to prevent detection. Smaller taverns, too. Two months, then, to account for the less than direct route. Two months, and I could leave Velora forever.

I shook out my cloak, dislodging the snow from the bank where I'd crouched. The blue and gray stones of the retaining wall at my back kept me relatively camouflaged as I did a quick inventory of supplies.

But movement on the other side of the courtyard froze me in place. Another person approached the temple, and this one did not hesitate. This one, I recognized.

The hulking beast of a man from the tavern.

Everything about this man screamed a warning. The hair that had appeared blond the night before was almost silver now in the grayish light of day. Platinum blond, the rich had once called it, when such precious metals were still traded from across the sea. It was half-tied back, but loosely. Carelessly. Whoever he was, he did not need to worry about impressing anyone.

Leather gloves covered his hands, but I knew they'd be power-ful. Violence wafted off of him as surely as any true scent, discern-able even at this distance. I marked out the weapons strapped to his body the same way I had the night before: bow and quiver of arrows over his back, greatsword at his waist, a bandolier of wickedly curved knives over his chest. I doubted that was the sum of his weapons.

They moved with him as his long strides carried him through the snow and tangled, dead bushes that marked once fruitful garden beds. He walked directly across the courtyard toward the temple.

He can't be... but he was.

He was going to enter the temple.

Why would a man like him, well-fed and dripping with expen-sive weapons and thick furs, attempt the gates?

They'd long since stopped being a source of preening pride. The gates were a death sentence.

He wrenched open the nearest of the double doors. But he paused, looking over his shoulder. Right to me.

I was too far away and too well camouflaged for him to see me easily—unless he'd known I was there all along. Cold that had nothing to do with my power curled in the pit of my stomach.

His eyes lingered. Even at this distance, I could feel the inten-sity of his gaze just as I had the night before. He saw me. Neither of us could pretend otherwise.

But just as suddenly as he'd caught me in his stare, he broke it, swinging away to the nearest corner of the courtyard. My gaze followed his, tracking the crunch of footsteps in old snow. A third person had entered the courtyard.

Positioned as I was, I heard more than saw for the first few seconds. The snow crunched but didn't give way entirely; either a slight woman or an emaciated man. Their steps were steady, but something was different about the rhythm. Maybe they carried a heavy pack of some kind. It could be the mother from the tavern the night before. Surely her milk hadn't run out so quickly that she'd needed to seek out the temple—

I don't care, I told myself.

I pulled my cloak tighter across my shoulders and maneuvered around the snowbank. It was past time to get out of Canmar.

The woman—it was a woman—was halfway across the courtyard by the time I reached the corner. I'd closed the space between us without hurrying. She was moving slower than she should have been. Some reckless, soft-hearted part of me turned. Fucking ironic, considering my heart did not even beat anymore.

If it had still been beating, it would have stopped in that moment.

I recognized the braid. The hitched gait that suggested an injury. But I knew it was a feature she'd carried from birth, born with legs slightly mismatched in length.

Still, my mind protested what my eyes could see clearly in the gray afternoon light. She shouldn't be in Canmar. She lived in a small village on the coast, near the Southern Fate.

She can't be here.

But she was. That was a string of tiny seashells woven into her plait. Her brown hair wasn't just brown. It was a deep umber with strands of chestnut that would lighten to blonde in the summer—a summer that she'd never seen. That she would never live to see if she entered that temple.

The only person on this entire fucking continent who I cared if they lived or died was walking toward the temple.

She can't be here, my brain screamed.

But she was.

And if I don't move now, she will die.

CHAPTER 6

I would never make it in time. The entire courtyard separated us, thick with snow and overgrown brambles crusted in ice. If she went through those doors, that was it. There was no going back. She'd be obligated to pass through the Mercy Gate. She would die.

All things being equal, I could outpace her easily. She'd learned to compensate for her limb difference, but she was also underfed and must have traveled for weeks to get to Canmar. But all things were not equal. She had a head start on me.

She was only a few heartbeats from reaching the door—and that brute of a man held it open for her. My mind did not have time to contemplate why a man like that, armed with weapons and reeking of brutality, would perform such a simple act of kindness as holding open a door for a young woman.

I ran.

But even as I did, I threw out my arms. Frost shot from my fingertips, coating the ground and turning to ice, racing atop the snow toward her. Faster, I urged the power in my veins. I ran harder, my body crashing forward over the ice.

The hulking beast in the doorway offered a hand to pull her in, but my ice was already there, rising up in spikes between them and shoving her to the ground. I urged my feet faster, cursing the frosted ice that both helped and hindered, keeping her from the door but slipping traitorously beneath my feet.

I slammed into her, ice shattering and shards flying. Pain seared across my cheek, but all of my focus went to the slim body beneath me. I pinned her with my superior weight, making out her limbs and core. She was fully trapped. I exhaled a long, shaking breath.

But that was all the reprieve I got. She was already thrashing beneath me, trying to get free. She managed to roll, getting her back to the ground and bracing her hands on my shoulders so she could shove me away.

Her narrow fingers dug into my shoulders. "What the—*you*," she hissed through her teeth. I was too close to get a good look at her face, but I could feel her rage. *Fine, rage all you want. At least you will be alive.*

"Yes. Me." I plunged one hand into the snow, levering my body off of hers but maneuvering so that I was between her and the doors to the temple. The doors—where the man from the tavern stood, watching the entire spectacle.

I gritted my teeth, waiting for him to say something. There was warmth at my back. He was still standing there. Anger swirled in my stomach; we hardly needed an audience, and I was about to tell him so—no matter how fucking handsome and huge he was.

I clambered to my feet, slipping on the ice, resisting the natural urge to reach out to steady myself because he was the only thing I could have used to do it. The reprimand died on my lips. I was too close to him. Standing had brought us chest to stomach, because of our height discrepancy. But I could see his face just fine, and the confusion he wore there as well. His turquoise eyes moved from me to the other woman and then back again. Whatever he saw, the quizzical angle of his brow softened.

Behind me, the young woman cursed. As I turned back to her, the doors of the temple clicked closed, the warm presence disappearing. Our value as entertainment had apparently run out.

The young woman in front of me had also gained her feet, and that was murder shining out of her honey-brown eyes as she stared me down.

"What...in the Dark God's hell..." I panted, shoving out the words between breaths, "...are you doing in Canmar?"

Her anger didn't disappear, but it softened slightly. For several beats, I thought she would not answer. But she finally opened her stubbornly familiar mouth to say, "My father is ill."

"I don't care," I snapped back.

Her father had been a drain on her for years. His obsession with that fishing village had kept her in Velora even when they could barely bring in enough to feed themselves, let alone sell to anyone else.

Her cheeks had hollowed out in the last few months, making her high cheekbones even more prominent. Discomfort settled in my chest. She looked so much like my sister, especially when she glared at me like that.

I could avoid thinking of her name, refuse to acknowledge what she was to me. But the ache spreading into my shoulders and stomach did not care what my mind pretended.

Kyrelle was the last. Every other one of my sister's descendants had left Velora at some point over the last four hundred years. All except for Kyrelle, Rylynn's thirteen times great-granddaughter. She was just as fucking stubborn as my sister ever was.

She did not argue with me. Kyrelle knew exactly what I thought of her father. She tried to shove past me, reaching for the door. But I shouldered her back. She may have a few inches on me, but I was wider and stronger. I was a fucking immortal, and she was a starving human. There was no way I would let her enter that temple.

I rolled my shoulders, positioning myself between the double doors, covering the handles. "I gave you a spell."

"And it wore off."

Of course it did. It had been the first I cast after I was ousted from my coven. Honestly, I was surprised it had lasted this long. Ever since her mother had fallen for her useless father and settled in that fishing village, I'd traveled to the coast every few years to cast another spell that would fill their nets. Then her mother died. I was cast out from my coven, and even the spells weren't enough. I'd spent three hundred and seventy-seven years keeping my sister's line alive in one way or another, only for Kyrelle to try something as reckless as attempting the Seven Gates.

There was no way in the Dark God's eternal, frozen hell that I would let her through those doors. Anger started to replace the ache. Good. Anger was more comfortable than longing.

"I did not save you for this," I seethed.

"I never asked for your help. I do not want it," she countered.

She tried for the doors again. Again, I pushed her back. "How will this help your father?"

"If there is magic in Velora, we will not need your spells to fill our nets. We will be able to afford a healer. The fae will come back, and with them, their healing magic."

I shouldn't have laughed in her face, but I could not stop the cold, acerbic sound. "And will your father still be alive in the time it will take you to pass through all the gates? To save up enough coin for a healer, to summon those mythical fae? The fae have taken everything—and if you are rash enough to seek them out, they will take you, as well. Not that it would matter." Because the gates would kill her well before that.

Kyrelle's face twisted, her beautiful features sharpening with something deeper than rage. "You think I am weak."

"No, I don't," I said. And I meant it. I could not fathom what it felt like to be a human in Velora in the four hundredth year of the curse. What kind of strength it must take to wake up every damn day, knowing that your body was failing because the land itself was dying, minute by minute, day by day.

My power would die eventually, and my body with it. But at least I had a chance; options, meager as they were. Kyrelle was only alive by the grace of the gifts given to me by the Dark God. And the choices I'd made.

I did not lose everything so that she could die for *nothing*.

"If you enter that temple, you will die. Then your father will die. Alone, without ever knowing what happened to you. They don't send word back to the families of those who die at the gates. They stopped doing that a long time ago." There simply weren't reliable mail routes anymore. The population of Velora had dwindled too low to facilitate them. Or need them.

I waited, watching for the surrender on her face. Kyrelle was stubborn, but she was not stupid. She'd let me come year after year to cast my spell, even though she hated the sight of me.

But she did not yield. So I used the wound my words had already created to push deeper. "Your father will waste away, too weak to pull in the fishing nets. He will sit at that window by the road, watching and waiting for a daughter who will never come. He will waste away to nothing, and the entire world will forget that he even existed."

Kyrelle's entire face flushed red. She pulled a dagger from her belt, springing forward and driving it toward my chest. She was faster than I'd expected, but the tip hit my shoulder, encountered the padded leather and ricocheted off, disappearing into the snow at our feet. There wasn't put enough force behind her blow. That was just inexperience. I could see in her face that if she could have killed me, she would have.

How fucking ironic. One family had ousted me. The other wanted to kill me. It seemed that neither bonds of power nor blood were enough to keep someone with me. On my side.

"I don't need you to like me," I said, knowing the words were mostly for myself. "I just need you to stay alive."

Kyrelle's chest heaved up and down, the exertion of crossing through the snow, tumbling with me on the ground, and trying to stab me too much for her weakened body.

I reached for my belt. Kyrelle flinched back. My stomach clenched. I would never harm her—I had done everything, even pushing the bounds of my own coven, to protect her. But still she flinched.

I unhooked the purse of money and shoved it inside the folds of her cloak, out of sight. "Split it into multiple pouches and hide it against your body. Get on a ship and get out of Velora."

It wasn't enough, not for two people. Not even for one. But now that he was ill, maybe her father would finally do the right thing. Maybe he would sell off the remainder of their possessions and make her go.

Kyrelle caught the bag, bending her arm to keep the purse secreted within the folds of her cloak. She stared at the ground between us. When she lifted her head to meet my eyes, relief flooded my senses.

Until she shook her head.

"No. It is not just his body that is giving up, it is his heart. He won't survive a trip across the sea. I have to go through the gates and lift the curse. It is the only way."

She said it with such conviction, such belief and love brimming from every word. She loved her father and would do anything for him, including giving up her own life.

I'd never been loved like that. Or if I had, my mother had died too young for me to remember it. Ever since then, I'd been searching. But to dwell too long on what I'd found—and what I hadn't— was much too dangerous for my fragile psyche.

"Kyrelle—"

"I must do it."

"No."

"Let me go." She ducked under my arm and managed to get a hand on the worn-down door handle. I twisted, grabbing her wrist and wrenching it away. But the door was already opening. Kyrelle threw all of her body weight at it. It wasn't much, but I was off balance.

In the space of an inhale, I made my decision.

She wasn't going through that door. I was.

I shoved her out of the way as I stumbled backward into the temple.

"Go," I could only mouth, all of the air knocked from my chest by the fall. "Go," I tried again and failed. Then I kicked the door closed and sealed my own fate.

CHAPTER 7

Darkness consumed me. My senses welcomed it back as an old friend, my eyes adjusting easily to the lack of light. My other senses sharpened, the gifts of the Dark God thrumming to life in my veins. Frankincense and palmarosa filled my nostrils, burning in the shallow stone altars to each of the gods. Near, something dripped. Far, something different flowed. The dripping came from me, the frost and snow on my clothing melting in the heat of the temple. My sight cleared more with every second, but I didn't need sight to recognize the source of that flowing sound. Too thick to be water. And even the burning frankincense and palmarosa could not cover the coppery tang. At the center of the temple, a single enchanted fountain ran with the blood of those who had come before—those who had attempted and failed the gates.

My hands tightened to fists, my pointed nails scraping across the stone floor before sinking into my palms. But the noise was overshadowed by hurried footsteps.

"Get up," a male voice hissed.

Even with the sparse light creating a silhouette, I was able to make out his features. His thick black curls created a halo around his thin face, a riot of freckles dancing across his golden-brown cheeks and the bridge of his nose. His voice didn't quite match his face—it had dropped into the heavier tones of maturity, while his face remained trapped in the fervor of adolescence. He could not have been more than twenty—so young.

Which must have accounted for his idiocy when his long fingers curled around my upper arm.

"Get your hands off of me," I snarled, ripping my arm away. I was still on the fucking ground, and though he knelt over me, he hardly had the advantage.

The young priest flinched but didn't back away.

"Please, get up." He wrung his hands, whipping his gaze over his shoulder and then back to me.

He was more scared of whatever awaited deeper in the temple than he was of me, I realized. An unhinged laugh bubbled up in my chest.

"Please," he said again, his gaze spearing for mine. His amber eyes were soft, pleading. Begging, actually.

I swallowed as I braced my arms beneath me. What was more terrifying in the temple than a witch?

"Hurry," he urged, checking over his shoulder again.

I'd never seen a priest act so strangely—not that I'd spent any time with one in the last three hundred and seventy-seven years. Most priests and priestesses considered witches a dangerous aberration. The Dark God had broken with the other six gods in creating us.

He nodded and exhaled as I gained my feet, my cold, wet garments scraping uncomfortably over my skin as I straightened and shook loose the remainder of the snow.

"Put your hand out," he instructed. I did as he asked, but I didn't remove the fingerless leather glove that covered my palm. He eyed it, as if he'd ask me about it, but wisely decided otherwise.

"I have to touch you now," he said.

I lifted one eyebrow.

"It is required for the Oath of Atonement." Another furtive look over his shoulder. "It's required," he repeated.

His eyes whipped to the two males I hadn't noticed before, one positioned on the inside of the doors. Muscular, well-fed, and armed to the teeth. The threat was clear enough—offer my hand willingly for this oath or the guards would force my hand. Quite literally.

I exhaled between my teeth but nodded.

If the priest noticed how cold my skin was, he didn't show it. He probably assumed it was from the frigid day outside, not the power that simmered beneath my skin. He did not react to the pointed nails, either. Not that surprising, considering that all the other covens had fled Velora years ago. The odds of this young human male having ever encountered a witch were next to nothing.

He dragged his finger over my palm in a practiced movement, touching seven pre-determined points around the edge before spiraling his fingertip in toward the center.

"Repeat after me," he said. "I offer up this mortal frame, in storm, frost, or cleansing flame. Not for glory, nor for grace, but to purify the past I face."

Both of my brows rose this time. I was no mortal. I guess the gods hadn't expected a witch to attempt the gates, though plenty of fae had in the first century of the curse. But I didn't question him. I repeated the words.

The young priest nodded along with each one, the tension in his shoulders easing as I spoke.

"Good," he murmured to himself. "Judge me, break me, take my breath. Let my sacrifice outweigh my debt. So swear I now, in endless night. My life for balance, wrong for right."

I repeated each word. On the last, a great exhale whooshed from the young man's chest and he released my hand.

"Thank you," he breathed. "I should have been at the door to greet you. It's the job of the acolytes. But I—" He shook his head, saving me from whatever plaintive excuse he'd offer. "No matter. It's done. You've taken the oath."

An acolyte, not a priest, my mind corrected the understanding it was rapidly constructing of the temple, the gates, and their rituals.

The acolytes met supplicants at the door and required them—by force if necessary—to recite this Oath of Atonement. I hadn't felt the burn of power at his words, so it was not a spell. Priests and priestesses did not possess magic or power of their own. Any that was wrought, like the blood bubbling continuously in that foundation several yards away, was an act of one or more of the Seven Gods.

At some point, I'd receive food and a bed. That was the promise made to all supplicants who entered the temple in advance of attempting the gates. This temple belonged to the first of the seven, the Mercy Gate. How long before I'd be forced out the rear door of the temple and through the gate? What other rituals would I endure before? How much rest and food—how much would they fatten me up before the slaughter?

A thousand questions, and yet I asked not a single one.

My stomach grumbled, so I conceded on one point. "Where is the food?"

The acolyte's face broke into a wide smile. Dark God save me. The boy had dimples. And now that he'd accomplished his duty, the worry had melted away. The priest or priestess who oversaw the temple must have been a strict disciplinarian, if the fear he'd displayed moments before was any indication—and such a departure from his usual manner.

He tilted his head toward the center of the temple to indicate I should follow him.

"There are seats around the fountain. The other acolytes will wait upon you." He wrinkled his nose. "Try to ignore the blood. Food isn't allowed by the altars."

The scent of the fountain intensified as we moved away from the burning altars that lined the perimeter of the temple.

"I don't mind blood," I said.

He looked at me again, closer this time. But still, no alarm bells sounded in his mind, the wide smile now softer but completely unconcerned. Most of the supplicants who entered the temple were starving; they wouldn't be much of a threat. I was bigger than most, even with my short stature. My curved hips and soft stomach never seemed to change, no matter what food was available. Another gift from the Dark God, I supposed.

Or would it be a hindrance at the gate? No one knew what the gates entailed. Each was different, and rumors said that some even varied depending on who was attempting to pass through them at any given time.

Still, I didn't ask. Not that the acolyte gave me much of an opening.

"It has been slow the past week, but you are the seventh to enter the temple, so she'll send you through the gate tomorrow."

Not much of a respite for the weary. But I dissected the other information he'd offered up in that singular sentence. They waited until there were seven supplicants before advancing them to the Mercy Gate all at once. I would have six competitors, and all of them had enjoyed more time in the warmth and security of the temple than I had, as the last to enter. At least one had been there for a full week. And *she* would be the one to send us through the gate—the superior who so terrified the acolyte was female. A priestess.

"After you eat, you must visit each of the altars, then you can do what you want until the evening." He leaned in, lifting his hand to cup his mouth as he added a conspiratorial whisper. "Most come back for more food."

A smile tugged at my lips. He was probably this loquacious with every supplicant who entered the temple. But it was so refreshing. I hadn't seen a smile like that in... decades. Maybe even centuries. I did not have a heart to warm, but something in my stomach reacted. It was probably just the hunger.

The gurgling of the blood fountain intensified as we neared the center of the temple. It rose far above our heads toward the domed roof, taller than the height of two men standing on one another's shoulders. Taller even than the massive brute from the tavern—who was somewhere in this temple. He'd entered only minutes before I did.

My eyes snapped down from the flowing scarlet fountain to the ring of stone benches surrounding it. The spindly man who'd entered earlier that morning sat far to the right, stuffing gobs of food down his throat and chewing with his mouth open. His eyes darted between the blood fountain and the wide-shouldered man sitting a few feet to his left. But that man hardly seemed to notice the cowering supplicant on his right. All of his attention was focused on *his* left, on a lithe female who speared chunks of meat with her dagger before bringing them to her mouth. Her dark hair was cut unusually short for a woman, falling in uneven layers that revealed her ears.

Her pointed ears.

Fae.

Rage spiraled through my body, up from the pits of my stomach, through my chest, into my arms as the anger gave way to power and my mouth opened on a spell to freeze the blood in her very veins. But before I could lift my hands or curl my tongue around that first syllable, a dark mass slammed into me.

CHAPTER 8

"Tomin, take her to Pava's altar," a calm voice ordered. The voice belonged to a swirl of deep purple velvet, the same one that had bodily shoved me away from the blood fountain.

She was too tall for me to see over her shoulder, but even those billowing purple robes weren't wide enough to keep me from leaning around her to get at the fae female. A hand shot out. Unlike the acolyte, the priestess did not flinch at my snarl as she grabbed my arm.

She stared down her slightly crooked nose directly at me, her eyes sliding right past the coven mark on my forehead. "Supplicants are protected within the walls of the temple. If you kill another, they will kill you." She nodded to the guards still flanking the doors.

I gnashed my teeth like an animal caught in a snare. "They could try."

She looked vaguely amused. Like she would have enjoyed watching that spectacle. But she merely lifted her shoulders. "The gods will have their due."

I twisted my arm away, and this time she let me go. My ears detected no shift in the sounds of eating and murmuring behind her. The other supplicants weren't paying us any attention.

Good. She'll never see me coming.

But even though she'd released me, the priestess did not move out of my path.

"You have entered the temple and taken the Oath of Atonement," she said, still watching. "Attacking another supplicant in the temple is abhorrent to the gods. You will be in violation of your oath and you will be struck down."

Not if the Dark God has anything to say about it.

But I kept that thought to myself.

The rage that sprang so violently to life didn't die, but it banked. I had to survive the gates. For Kyrelle, who I silently prayed would take the gold I'd given her and run. And for myself. Maura's offer to regain my place with my coven was no doubt self-serving; but it was also my only chance at survival. Maura had never told us precisely how long a witch could survive without her coven's power to sustain her, but it had already been six months. My hope of escaping to another continent and finding a new coven had died when I handed over the gold to Kyrelle. If I did not fulfill Maura's quest, my power would wither away to nothing and I would die the second, eternal death. That was not a path I could allow my imagination to trod.

For the first time in three hundred and seventy-seven years, my duty to my bloodline and to my coven were aligned. *I can control myself.*

"Take her to Pava's altar to pray for guidance," the priestess said to the acolyte. I'd been so focused on the fae female, and the priestess determined to stand in my way, I'd forgotten the young man entirely. He'd paled, his cheeks taking on a greenish tinge beneath his freckles.

He looked from the priestess, back to me, to what he could see of the supplicants seated around the fountain, and back to his dark-haired teacher. "But first they eat."

She rolled her eyes. I blinked—not very priestess-like. I regarded her again, noting each of her features: the rich jewel-toned amethyst of her robe, the olive skin, the dark eyes, and matching hair. Her nose was slightly crooked, as if it had been broken, and in more than one place. There was something eerily familiar about her, too...

My gut clenched. Elodie. Not again—

"She'll eat later," the priestess ordered, and though her voice was melodious, that was its only similarity to my many-faced sister witch.

Elodie could change her face and body, but she could not change her voice. The priestess before me was just that—a priestess. Not my coven sister.

The tide of emotions in the past ten minutes threatened to fracture me from within. I did not even resist as the acolyte, Tomin, finally obeyed the order and led me away from the blood fountain. Witches prayed only to our dark creator, but perhaps the Goddess of Peace would spare a bit for me.

I followed Tomin around the perimeter of the temple, past the altars to the Gods of Mercy, Justice, and Sacrifice. I marked the altar to Ramkael, the God of Devotion and doomed lover of Pava. Then the altar to Memory and finally Peace, Pava herself. Last was the Dark God, his altar shrouded in shadow, no flame of frankincense and palmarosa to light his cold corner.

The order of the altars matched the order of the Seven Gates. If I was going to take up praying to new gods, it would make more sense to start with Seraxa at the altar of Mercy, creator of the gate I'd attempt the next day.

But I desperately needed every one of those steps to steady myself. Fighting off Kyrelle, entering the temple, seeing the fae female—it had unbalanced me. I'd never reached that internal quiet and control that the other witches preached on and on about.

But this… the hum of energy and power under my skin was worse than usual.

As much as I tried to focus on the back of Tomin's deep emerald robes, my eyes strayed back toward the blood fountain. To the shape of the female, now balancing the dagger in her palm.

Tomorrow, I will kill her.

"Here we are," Tomin said, stating the obvious as we arrived before the ornate stained-glass window depicting Pava. Arrayed around her was a kaleidoscope of races and creatures, all staring up at her with love and adoration. There were no witches. Either this temple predated our creation by the Dark God, or we were the one race of beings undeserving of peace.

"You can place anything you've brought as an offering at the foot of the altar," Tomin said, nodding to the rectangular pedestal that held the basin burning frankincense and palmarosa.

I blinked down at the space of stone floor he'd indicated. A half-dead bunch of weeds tied with twine and a singular opal the size of a pea made up the entirety of the offering. I bit back a hysterical laugh. The people of Velora were so destitute, all we had to offer were weeds. The opal, no doubt, had come from the fae female. They still hoarded wealth in their fortress beyond the mountains.

The gemstone could have come from the mountain of a man who'd entered just before me, my mind argued. In sighting the fae, my mind had skipped over him entirely. Had he been there at the blood fountain?

I turned my head to check, only for Tomin to unleash another onslaught of words.

"Your prayers are a sufficient offering," he said quickly. "The gods understand the consequences and trials of the people of Velora. They offer the Seven Gates as redemption so that we may prove ourselves truly worthy. Blessed are they…"

I returned my eyes to him in a hard stare I hoped would shut him up.

It failed.

"…and honor the Seven Gods by conquering the Seven Gates."

I crossed my arms over my chest. "Do you think any of these supplicants will conquer all seven gates?"

Tomin's dark curls bobbed in time with his throat as he swallowed.

I rolled my eyes and turned to the altar. The gods and I weren't on speaking terms, with the exception of one. But I lifted my eyes to Pava anyway.

Before I could come up with some nonsense to utter, footsteps announced the return of the priestess. She ignored Tomin altogether, focusing all of her intensity on me.

She placed a round tin into my hand, showing none of her acolyte's reticence. For some reason, I did not open my mouth to tell her off for touching me. But I did look down at the palm-sized tin with skepticism.

"Cover that mark," she said, her eyes lifting to my forehead.

Her gaze remained steady, but the acolyte at her side paled. His eyes flew from my forehead, down to my hands and the pointed tips of my nails and back again, understanding and something between horror and fear dawning on his face for a fraction of a second before he blinked back to a façade of neutrality.

That was the reaction I'd expected. And the one I planned to use to my advantage.

I shook my head. "I will not hide."

"Then you will die." The priestess did not even blink as she said it. "Even your kind must sleep. And there is no protection offered between the gates. Those guards stay here."

I did blink, processing her meaning. While I resided in the temple, the armed guards would prevent any violence. But while the Mercy and Justice Gates were only a day apart, the others spread out at increasing intervals of distance. And there would be no one to stop the other supplicants from banding together and murdering me in my sleep if they saw me as a threat.

Dark God save me. My best weapon—my only weapon, really—was my power. And I could not use it without sentencing myself to death.

Because even though I was an immortal being whose body would never age nor organs tire, I could be wounded. And unlike the fae, I did not possess the gift of rapid healing. If I received a mortal wound, I would die with all the indignity of a human.

I curled my hands into fists to hide the points of my nails.

"If you cannot control yourself, then stay clear of the other supplicants," the priestess advised. Or ordered. Her tone was unchanged.

No comment on the fact that the fae were the reason all of this had happened. Their greed was the source of everything terrible that had happened in Velora over the past four hundred years.

As if the witches and humans haven't taken full advantage of their absence, my conscience argued.

I wouldn't feel guilty for what I'd done to survive. I refused.

"Pray at each of the altars and then you may eat." By which time the fae female and other supplicants would have left the blood fountain, her order implied. She did not wait to see if I would comply. But the guards on the other side of the temple tracked her every movement, awaiting her orders.

My course was set. What I wanted did not matter. It never really had.

"Acolytes are allowed to accompany supplicants while they pray," Tomin offered.

I hadn't exactly forgotten the boy, but I certainly didn't want him hovering at my side for the next hour.

"No."

His mouth twitched for a few seconds before he plastered his smile back into place. "As you wish." He hurried off after the priestess, presumably back to monitoring the temple doors.

My chest twinged, right between my breasts. I rolled my shoulders to dispel the sensation. He reminded me of someone, too.

But that was inevitable when you'd spent four hundred years walking the same continent, I told myself. It was possible I'd met one of his ancestors at some point. And I cared as little about the acolyte as I did every other person I met.

I did not want or need friends. I had my coven sisters. And I'd pray at a thousand altars if it earned me back my place with them.

CHAPTER 9

BEFORE

MY MIDDLE SISTER CAME OF AGE THE SAME YEAR MY FATHER reached the pinnacle of his power. Human spectacles had become even more opulent since the disappearance of the fae, as if we were determined to prove we were just as powerful and prosperous. No one was more dedicated to this purpose than my father.

"Two hundred and twenty-one guests," Janessa crowed as we waited in the courtyard. The temple was already full to bursting.

I shivered against the cool late spring breeze that seemed determined to hold on, despite the longer days that drew us closer and closer to summer. Janessa had chosen sleeveless gowns for me and Rylynn, her attendants in this inane spectacle of womanhood.

"And I had a hundred. You have outstripped me. Are you satisfied?" Rylynn snapped. She should not have been here at all—only unmarried women were attendants. Having reached her own womanhood three years before, Rylynn should have been long married. Except our father was so drunk upon his own wealth that not a single of the dozen offers made for Rylynn's hand had satisfied him.

"I *am* satisfied," Janessa said. The tallest of us, she looked right down her perfectly straight nose at Rylynn.

I stepped between my sisters before someone got blood on the gowns.

"Isn't it time to go in? We do not want to keep all of the guests waiting. I saw Lord Devlin's son arrive a few minutes ago." An offering to each sister. *So* many people had come to watch Janessa, a young man my father might finally approve of for Rylynn among them.

Rylynn glared over my shoulder at Janessa before turning and gliding through the doors. Despite Janessa's ornate gown and the hours she'd spent perfecting her cosmetics, there was no disputing that Rylynn was the prettiest and most graceful of the three of us. Janessa frowned after our eldest sister—well aware of it, too.

I sighed and took my place between them, as usual.

The heat of the temple pressed in from all sides, the thick scents of burning frankincense and palmarosa mingled with the odor of crowded bodies, sweat, and perfume. Two hundred and twenty-one guests were too many for the dark, close space of the temple. We walked in procession around the perimeter, stopping at each of the seven altars to place a bloom at the base before spiraling toward the center.

Guests crowded into whatever space they could. They lined the stone walls beneath the windows behind each altar and crowded the spiraled path that we followed toward the center of the temple. They watched from every angle as Rylynn and I took our places a few paces from where my father and the priestess who would conduct the ceremony awaited Janessa.

The young woman of the hour made her way through the crowd slowly, watching every footstep. She may not boast Rylynn's natural grace, but she'd practiced for this moment for months. When she finally arrived at the center of the temple, her curtsey before the priestess was as elegant as any our elder sister had ever executed.

I watched in silence as the ceremony unfolded.

There was a lot of praying. A song I didn't like that my father had selected. There was a bit where the priestess cut into the fleshy part of Janessa's palm and said something about the lifeblood of mothers. I paid all of my attention to my sister and none of it to the words.

The hours she'd spent in front of the mirror were not in vain. Her golden-brown hair, lighter than both me and Rylynn's deeper umber, caught and reflected the flames burning in sconces and candles all around us. The pale green gown she'd chosen brought out the celadon stripes in her hazel eyes. I was a bit sad that none of her freckles were visible. I'd always admired the way they danced when she smiled and laughed. But Janessa complained they made her look childish, and she'd covered them with paste and rouge.

My head began to swim, my attention slipping away in a thick cloud of frankincense and sweat and chanting.

Rylynn refused to look at Janessa, staring at the ground instead.

The boy who'd come to see her was frowning.

The people were swaying.

No, that was me swaying.

I forced my spine upright, discreetly peering left and right to see if anyone had noticed. But all eyes were fixated on the trio at the center of the crowd, where the priestess had just revealed the showpiece of the ceremony.

The diadem was fae-made, just like everything my father collected. He'd bought the treasures for cheap when the fae were fleeing, and now sold them off to the humans, all desperate to elevate their status by acquiring one of the rare heirlooms. Some were followed by whispers of magic, but I'd never seen one of the artifacts do so much as sing, let alone ensure fertility or multiply wine, like my father alleged.

The ceremony of womanhood always concluded with a crowning. The circlet could be made of anything. Less affluent families wove together lilies and roses. The poorest of all would craft a tiara of twigs and wildflowers.

But not even gold and diamonds would do for my father. He'd saved this spectacular fae heirloom not for his daughter, but for himself.

My father nudged the priestess aside, taking the diadem from her hands. Her dark eyes flashed, her lips drawing together, but she let him take it. The priests and priestesses would not reach the zenith of their power for another century, when the crops failed and desperation reached a crescendo.

Janessa's eyes brightened as she focused on the diadem. Ornate whorls swirled from the sides, hundreds of tiny gemstones in every shade of blue creating an effect that could be waves or clouds, depending upon the viewer's imagination. At the center, a translucent stone unlike any I'd seen before reflected the light around us. In one blink it shone red, then it caught the green of Janessa's dress and then the deep plum of the priestess's robes.

A whisper of awe rolled through the crowd. I looked to Janessa —this was exactly what she'd always wanted, to outshine our perfect elder sister—but her eyes were transfixed, focused on the diadem.

I glanced around me. No one had noticed me almost passing out because all of them were equally transfixed. Even Rylynn, who'd been looking on with such apathy... her mouth hung open in unmuted anticipation.

A shiver of awareness snaked down my spine. It hadn't been like this, even at Rylynn's ceremony. My stomach lurched, my heartbeat accelerating into an erratic, painful beat that pushed me forward, demanding I take a step toward the center of the temple as Janessa kneeled and my father stepped forward.

But there were so many people that the motion didn't stand out. No one noticed me, they were all in thrall to the diadem. They did nothing as my father lowered it to Janessa's head, setting the intricate platinum confection atop her crown of golden-brown hair. For one long heartbeat, my sister shone brighter than any star, as glorious as any of the goddesses we worshiped in temple, more beautiful than Rylynn could ever hope to be.

Then she started screaming.

The trance broke. Around me, the guests jolted back to awareness, some swooning while others recovered faster and held their neighbors up. Their movements were awkward, their voices muddling together as they tried to grapple back to reality. But all of it was drowned out by Janessa's horrid screams.

She clawed at her hair, tearing at the perfectly arranged curls as she tried to pull the diadem from her head. But it wouldn't budge. Her fingernails dug into her scalp, ripping away chunks of her golden hair as she desperately tore at the metal.

My father stood over her, blinking in confusion. She stumbled forward, pain etched in every feature as she fell hard on her elbows, unwilling to release the diadem enough to catch herself before she hit the hard flagstones. Rylynn rushed forward; my feet pulled me along with her.

Rylynn grabbed Janessa's arm, pulling her up and cradling her in her lap. I reached for her wrists, trying to pull her hands away from the diadem. Tears tracked down her cheeks, but they'd mingled with the blood from where she'd ripped out her hair and clawed at her scalp.

"It burns!" Janessa wailed, fighting against my hold.

"It's the diadem," Rylynn realized. "It's cursed."

With fae magic. The same magic that had held two hundred and twenty-one guests in thrall was now burning my sister alive.

Rylynn tightened her hold on our sister as she turned her head up to our father, still standing helplessly in the center of the temple. The priestess had disappeared entirely.

"Help her!" she demanded.

But my father only gaped like a fish, staring not at his bleeding, keening daughter, but at the diadem that crowned her head.

"It burns!" Janessa screamed again. She wrenched her hands

free of mine, reaching for the diadem. The scent of burnt hair and flesh overpowered the frankincense and palmarosa.

What was left of her hair fell away in golden ribbons. The skin of her scalp blackened and began to melt. My stomach turned, but Rylynn grabbed me before I could flinch away.

"Help me pull it off!" We twined our fingers around the diadem, cool to the touch even as my sister's hot, melted flesh seared my arm.

But it would not budge. We pulled together. Again and again and again. Until it was no longer Janessa's flesh, but her skull there beneath the ornately wrought diadem. Until Janessa's screams stopped. Until my sister died in my arms.

CHAPTER 10

I HAD A KNIFE, BUT PULLING IT OUT TO TRIM THE POINTS FROM MY nails seemed unwise with the armed guards looking on. My teeth had to do the job instead. I kept my eyes down as I moved from altar to altar, but none of the other supplicants approached me. By the time I reached the blood fountain to eat, they were nowhere to be seen.

I hadn't been in a temple since Janessa's death.

They were all roughly the same—an entrance at the front, an exit at the rear, and a wall with an altar to each of the gods. The blood fountains were unique to the temples that preceded each of the gates.

I could still remember the scent of my sister's blood as it coated my hands. More than three hundred years had not been enough to dull the memory. Her screams pierced my ears, overtaking the bubbling of blood as it fell from one tier of the fountain down to the next. I blinked, and I did not see the fountain at all, but my father, standing there presiding over the gore, gaping and fucking useless. He should have been the one to die that day, his obsession with the fae bringing nothing but death and—

"Your meal."

I blinked. The memory was gone, replaced by a trembling acolyte who stood between me and the blood fountain, a tray balanced across her forearms.

Garbed in the same emerald-green robes as Tomin, this acolyte avoided my eyes and hurried away as soon as I accepted the platter of food. Good. I wasn't in the mood to chat.

My mind blanched at the prospect of eating with the memory of Janessa's death so fresh and visceral. But by the time I balanced the tray across my lap and picked up a utensil, my stomach was already grumbling traitorously. It had been months since I'd had a full, rich meal, and the array spread out before me was nothing short of magnificent. I might not need food to survive, but it made life a lot more comfortable.

Thick pats of butter melted atop three slices of crusty brown bread, the edges sopping up the red wine sauce that bathed a cut of meat the size of my hand. And along the other edge, sliced and roasted to perfection, were *vegetables*. Thick asparagus, vibrant orange carrots, seasoned purple potatoes... fully colored, fully mature, and fucking delicious... not the stunted, pale versions that popped out once out of every hundred sowed in the farmers' fields.

I hadn't even realized food like this still existed in Velora. The gardens of the temple must be exempt from the gods' curse. Or maybe they were imported from across the sea... I didn't care. I ate.

I was taking my last bite when the others began to appear.

More acolytes in emerald, taking up places at even intervals around the perimeter of the fountain. They remained standing. I kept my seat on the stone bench and chewed slowly, drawing out the pleasure of every dash of salt and drip of butter.

When one of them took my plate, I sighed but didn't resist. Not because I was above sopping up the remains with my fingers, but because the first of the other supplicants had arrived.

A young woman about my height appeared. Pretty, her gold hair was pulled back in a tight braid that made her large, doe-eyes appear even bigger. Those eyes darted around the circle, widening at the blood fountain, landing on me, and then flinching away to stare at the ground.

Not much of an opponent. Unless she was putting on a ruse. She continued to stare at the ground. I stared at the blood fountain, but every other sense was attuned to her, making mental notes.

If I was going to masquerade as a human, then I could not use my active power. That left me with spells, but I'd have to be very careful and judicious with how I used them. Spells had to be spoken aloud, so I would have to be out of hearing range of the other competitors; not impossible, given how poor human hearing was. But the fae would be trickier. And I could only use spells when their consequences could be attributed to something else, like the gates themselves.

Quick footsteps and another supplicant appeared—another woman I'd peg in her mid-twenties, dressed in worn homespun clothing but neat and upright. Unlike the doe-eyed girl, who had taken a spot on the opposite side of the fountain, this one took the space directly to my right, with only a singular acolyte separating us.

She leaned forward, looked at me, then turned to the acolyte. "When will we begin?"

The acolyte shook their head, keeping their eyes fixed forward.

The new supplicant frowned, shook her own head, and then pushed her gaze past the acolyte to me. "I don't think they'll talk to us."

I kept my eyes from rolling upward. Why was everyone in this cursed place determined to talk to me?

"It appears not," I said.

"There are more women than men." As she spoke, she scanned the perimeter of the fountain, pausing for only a moment on the girl before deciding I was more interesting. "Is that usual, do you think?"

I had another weapon at my disposal—nearly four hundred years of experience with life. They would never know me, but I could learn as much as possible about them. And I supposed that started with the nervous-talker to my right.

"I don't think desperation discriminates based on gender," I said, softening the syllables of my voice from their usual sharpness. Covering another part of myself, just like I had with my coven mark.

"No, I don't suppose it does," the woman hummed in agreement. "I am Nimra. I don't know if they will introduce us." She didn't offer a hand, which I was grateful for, but I couldn't very well keep staring straight ahead.

I bobbed my head, taking in more details about her appearance. Her clothing indicated she was familiar with struggle—like everyone else in Velora—but her upright stature and the ruddiness in her cheeks indicated general health. She was a bit thinner than the width of her shoulders might have called for were food in abundance, but her eyes were clear. She'd fill out nicely—if she lived through enough of the gates to take advantage of the food the temples offered.

"Koryn," I offered, and no more.

The corner of Nimra's thin lips quirked, but she didn't push for more. We turned in unison as the third and fourth supplicants arrived. First, the thin man who'd cowered while eating. Then the fae.

The blood in my veins chilled, my rage frosted with ire and a cold burn as deadly as any flame. I clenched my fists at my side, determined to keep my power in check. The woman at my side— Nimra, my mind filled in—was still babbling on. I should be listening to her observations; she'd been here longer than me, days, perhaps; who knew what information she could offer on the other supplicants, including the fae female.

"Garrick the Red is here."

That earned her back my full attention.

"The bounty hunter?" I asked, managing to close my mouth after the question left it. But there was no disguising the surprise in my tone.

Nimra nodded, her mouth flattening into a grim line.

My mind flashed to the man with the wine-red hair who'd been busy staring down the fae female. The lanky man had flinched away from him. He must have already learned who he would be facing in the gates.

Not that supplicants needed to take one another out, really. The gods would do it for them at the gates. But what did I know? Each of the gates represented a different god. Pava, the Goddess of Peace, would hardly require murder to pass through her gate. But Edravos, the God of Justice? Or even the witches' own creator, the Dark God? Who knew what price they would demand.

My gaze swept over the supplicants arrayed around the fountain. The thin man, the doe-eyed girl, the fae female, Nimra, and me. Five. That left two—and I already knew both of their faces as they appeared one right after the other.

The hulking beast of a man from the tavern the night before, who'd almost pulled Kyrelle into the temple instead of me. My stomach turned, the rich food inside of it threatening to revolt as I realized how close I had come to losing her. Even as I looked over his shoulder, past him, I felt his eyes land on me. Less intensity than before, but why me? I was the shortest female, the softest and roundest. I bore no visible weapons.

But he'd seen me in the tavern the night before, when I'd been selling spells. He knew I was a witch. *Dark God, be with me.*

Before I could come up with a solution to that, the other man appeared. Garrick the Red. If his deep scarlet hair had not been enough to convince me, the expression on his face would have. He looked around the group of supplicants like a vicious mountain cat ready to pick off a human who'd wandered too close to the village's edge.

He was smaller than the man from the tavern, several inches shorter, not quite as wide. But still taller than me. And unlike the brute from the tavern, whose face was unreadable, Garrick the Red did nothing to hide his ruthlessness. His dark eyes paused on each of us in turn, his grin growing a bit wider with each supplicant he appraised.

This was the man who'd gained such notoriety over the past twenty years that even my coven stayed clear of him. A man who had come to Velora, rather than fleeing from it. Where others had run, he'd seen an opportunity. If a tenant farmer fled his lord after failing to pay his tithe, Garrick the Red was happy to hunt him down. If a lordling needed to find his wayward daughter, running away from an arranged marriage for the farce of true love, Garrick the Red would locate her and escort her home. And he'd kill anyone who delayed him for sport. There were even rumors he'd been a guest at the fae fortress beyond the mountains.

What reason could a man like that have for attempting the Seven Gates?

When that cruel smile landed on me, I believed every word and rumor I'd heard.

I shivered despite the cloying heat of the temple.

He saw it, his mouth stretching over his teeth. They were crooked, but all there. And it looked like he'd sharpened a few of them to points. I wished my power was earth-based. I could have whispered a spell to make every one of his teeth fall out. But my active power was water-bound. Without access to my coven sisters to share power, any spells I cast on my own would have to draw on the water that in my veins took the form of frost and ice.

I will get as creative as I need to. For Kyrelle. And for myself.

The debates I'd had with myself back in the courtyard outside the temple did not matter now. I was in the temple. There was no alternative but to attempt the gates. I would get through them, and

I would get back my coven. My sisters. I would protect my power and myself.

And I'd pray to the Dark God that the gates took out Garrick the Red before I had to.

Nimra exhaled slowly beside me as Garrick the Red took his place between the last two acolytes. The familiar footsteps of the priestess approached.

"Better pick a god and start praying," Nimra said quietly.

My coven mark burned on my forehead. I hoped the paste was thick enough to cover it. I did not look at her as I said, "I already have."

CHAPTER 11

THE CEREMONIES HAD NOT CHANGED MUCH IN THREE HUNDRED
years. Chanting. Call and response. An offering of blood directly
into the fountain. Though it ran so continuously, I doubted those
few dribbles from each of us were enough to sustain it. It would
take our blood as we died in the gates, too.

"You will enter the Mercy Gate at dawn," the priestess said once
we'd all made our final bloody offerings. "By entering the temple,
you have pledged yourself to the Seven Gates. The only forfeit is
death. If you have a query, speak it now."

"I have heard that you can walk away between the gates."

Every eye in the circle swung to Nimra, including the acolytes.
Apparently, the supplicants did not usually take the priestess up on
her offer.

The priestess inclined her head. "For a time," she confirmed.
"But the gods will demand their due. Should you not return in a
timely manner, they will punish you."

I nearly snorted at the rhyme, unintentional or not.

Nimra appeared unphased by the attention now focused on

her, though her left hand did tap out an unsteady rhythm on her thigh. "What is a timely manner?" she questioned.

"That is up to the gods." The priestess bowed her head. "A gate is always near."

"A god is always watching," Nimra murmured back. Her eyes had glazed over now, some calculation happening behind them.

The priestess did not linger; too bad if any of the rest of us had queries. The acolytes filed out behind her, Tomin included. He winked at me before disappearing in line. This time, I didn't hold back the impulse to roll my eyes.

The thin man bolted, following the train of acolytes. Nimra stepped into the now empty place at my side, mouth already open. A headache began to form at the base of my skull.

"That skittish one is called Rilk," she said, crossing her arms over her chest. "I doubt he'll make it through the Mercy Gate. I cannot see him caring about anyone other than himself."

I let the laugh bubble out of me. *I* did not care about anyone but myself. At least, not anyone else within the walls of this temple. To do so was naïve. I opened my mouth to say as much to Nimra, then closed it. She was a friendly fount of information and nothing more.

Besides, I had two hulking men to deal with. The first was approaching me with a glint in his eye I wanted nothing to do with —whatever Garrick the Red had seen in his appraisal of me, he wanted a closer look.

But the other had moved into the semi-darkness at the outer edge of the temple. The altars provided scant light, and now that evening was falling outside, the ornate stained-glass windows provided almost nothing. My eyes adjusted easily to the darkness. I could see his outline between the altars to the deities of Sacrifice and Devotion.

I had to get to him before he could spill my secret. And before Garrick the Red could get to me.

"Don't let him get you by yourself," I whispered over my shoulder.

I did not wait to see how or if Nimra would heed my warning. She seemed astute enough on her own, if a bit too talkative. I did not care about her wellbeing for her own sake, but my own. She was already proving a valuable source of information on the other supplicants. It was not kindness that had me uttering the warning. Witches were not kind.

I moved quickly despite my size, several lifetimes of maneuvering my wider-than-average body working to my advantage as I used the doe-eyed female as a shield to exit the ring of stone benches and avoid Garrick the Red.

I only had a few yards to consider. The man from the tavern already knew I was a witch. I'd given all of my gold to Kyrelle, and he boasted more weapons than I'd ever seen on a single person. He certainly wouldn't want the meager dagger I carried. So I'd offer him my power. A spell of his choosing, but I'd put limits on it. It couldn't reveal my secret, and it could not directly kill one of the other supplicants. Power and magic were always enticing to humans, the only race born on the continent without a scrap of either.

Only a few steps to go. I didn't try to quiet my steps; I was close enough that he wouldn't be able to flee. His shoulders tensed as he turned. He'd left off the thick cloak I'd seen him in before, clothed now in a black linen shirt that was too thin for the cold outside the temple walls and a well-worn leather vest that fit him to perfection.

Dark God spare me, I will not lust after a man who holds a dangerous secret about me.

I'd been so concerned with getting enough gold to get out of Velora that I hadn't taken anyone to my bed, man or woman, in months. I may not have a beating heart, but I certainly had a fully functioning female body otherwise. Later, I promised the tingling in my stomach. Alone in the dark, I'd see to my own physical needs. Not when it made me vulnerable. Not when—

He turned to look at me, his turquoise eyes darkening a full shade. But that was not what turned the heat in my belly to icy flame. It was the fae female standing behind him.

CHAPTER 12

"You already have the women flocking to you. How irritatingly predictable," the female said, her dark eyes flicking over me from crown to toe and then dismissing me entirely.

The icy flame solidified. My fingers began to tingle with cold. I curled them into fists, stuffing down the power so I would not slaughter her then and there. For my mother. For Janessa. But mostly for myself.

The man kept himself angled between us, not so quick to dismiss me. Satisfaction bloomed in my chest. I'd fooled the fae female, even with her supposedly superior senses. But he *knew*.

"You will not consider what I said," this directed to the fae female, though he did not phrase it quite as a question.

The corners of her mouth slid up her cheeks in a smile that lacked all joy. It was a challenge, and one she did not even bother leveling at me. It was all for the man between us. "Save your offers for others who need them," she said.

She deigned to flash that menacing smile at me for half a heartbeat before she turned and strode away into the recesses of the temple. Yet another reason to be wary of the behemoth before me.

I needed to learn his damn name. My mind wasn't particularly creative with the adjectives. He watched the female go, though it was only his eyes that followed her. He did not turn his back on me.

Then, just as quickly, he caught me in his gaze, just as he had in the courtyard hours before. "What do you want, witch?"

The offer I'd been about to make froze in my throat.

A smirk tugged at one corner of his mouth.

"Let me guess. You'd like me to keep that bit of information to myself." His distinctive turquoise eyes flicked up to my forehead. "You've covered your dark master's mark."

"No one is my master," I breathed, and I even half believed it. Maura might have given me the charge to pass through the Seven Gates, the Dark God might have resurrected me, but I was making these choices all on my own. For better or worse.

He huffed out a laugh. Damn, he was attractive. No wonder the prostitute had been so interested in him the night before. Elodie, I reminded myself. Not a real prostitute. But even one putting on an act would always approach the most attractive man in the tavern in the hopes of passing a more pleasurable than usual night. And there was something about the slash of a smile on his face that made me think he was capable of delivering on that prospect.

I bit down on the urges swirling through my body. I could use him as a fantasy in my mind later in the night, but right then I needed a clear mind. I stepped into the space between us, only then realizing just how vast the discrepancy in our size really was.

I was a short woman, but not a small one. The leather belt at my waist did nothing but accentuate the width of my hips. Beneath the corset that held my considerable breasts in place, my stomach was soft and ample. Those soft curves could not have been more opposite to the hard lengths of the man before me. He stood easily a foot above me, perhaps more. As he crossed his arms over his wide chest, the linen of his shirt pulled tight over his fore-arms and biceps, outlining the corded blocks of muscle beneath.

I had to summon my frost to cool the heated desire that roared to life in my veins. I had to learn some control. Before, I'd had my coven to protect me from poor choices. Now, I was on my own with everything to lose.

I lifted my chin and prayed it didn't quiver with nerves—or worse, lust. "I have come to offer you a bargain."

"So, you are afraid I'll turn you over to the other supplicants." His eyes sparkled as he said it, that smile dangerously sensual. He was enjoying himself, I realized. He was actually deriving pleasure from watching me grapple with the fact that he had this sort of power over me.

"I understand that you could use what you know about me to your own advantage." I gritted my teeth. "So, I'm here to offer you an alternative."

He looked me over slowly, taking his time, letting his eyes linger on the spot between my eyes where I'd covered my coven mark. "And why should I trust you? There is no such thing as a good witch."

The temperature around us dropped. "You trust the fae bitch."

I watched the gooseflesh rise on his forearms where the cuffs of his sleeves had ridden up. But he didn't move to cover himself against the cold. "Talking to her and trusting her are different things. I am not foolish enough to think that Alize won't shove a knife into my back the first chance she gets."

I flinched at his casual use of what had to be her name. "You know her." Yet another reason to be wary of this man. How had I wandered into such a deadly coterie of supplicants? Maura… she couldn't have known… could she? But the thought disintegrated as quickly as it formed.

"We've met," he said. He didn't bother to deny it. "But she is not your problem, is she?"

I exhaled through my nose. If I'd died in a fire, I had no doubt that smoke would have poured from my nostrils. I'd rarely had occasion to thank the gods for the manner of my death, but in that moment I almost did. The last thing I needed was this man seeing how easily my emotions got out of check.

I would make myself the fae female's problem. Alize. Now I had a name to add to my prayers of misfortune.

One problem now. One for later.

"A spell for your silence," I said before I gave him any other bits of information about myself.

He tilted his head, the moonlight that cut through the stained glass turning the platinum blond to silver. "Why keep your power a secret? You could use it to your advantage."

The way he watched me with those turquoise eyes was as forceful as a physical touch. At a distance, the intensity had been noticeable, but close like this, it was almost painful. An itch that demanded to be scratched. One that should have been easy to ignore, given the irritation the man was determined to stoke.

"I don't need Garrick the fucking Red painting a target on my back."

The light in his eyes shifted into something new. "I see."

"He'll be coming for you, too," I pointed out. The sooner I had his agreement, the sooner I could find a bed and sate both the exhaustion building in my shoulders and the ache low in my belly. "A well-placed spell could disable him long enough for you to neutralize him."

Was that a twinkle of amusement I saw in the corner of his eyes? Did he actually find my proposition laughable?

"And what spell will you save for yourself?"

I exhaled more steadily this time. He was going to accept my offer and keep my secret. "None. I've met enough of his kind over the years. I will stay well away from the bounty hunter."

The corner of his eye crinkled in time with the tilt of his wickedly lush mouth. "Too late for that, witch." He leaned down, closing the space between us too quickly for me to step back. "*I am Garrick the Red.*"

CHAPTER 13

THE DARK GOD MUST HAVE BEEN LAUGHING FROM HIS OBSIDIAN throne. Hell, we were in the first temple of the Seven Gates. After all the chanting and praying, all seven gods were probably looking down on us right then. And laughing hysterically.

At least the lust burning beneath my skin had banked, stifled by pure humiliation.

I put one hand on my hip, closer to my little dagger. Though I doubted I'd get the chance to draw it if Garrick the Red decided to attack me. But a bounty hunter who'd made a fortune on a desolate, dying continent would not be stupid enough to attack me in a temple where it was expressly forbidden.

I was not defenseless. I was never defenseless. Even without my coven to bolster my power, I had killed the man who'd attacked me outside of the tavern. I could hold my own, even against Garrick the Red. He had twenty years of killing for hire? I'd been resurrected nearly four hundred years ago. Let him try me.

Never mind that he'd made a career out of killing, and I'd flinched away from it at every turn. It was not the moment to dwell on my failures as a witch. There was always plenty of time for that in the night, when I ought to be sleeping.

This man was used to intimidating people wherever he went. I'd watched it happen in the tavern the night before. But now we both saw each other for what we were. His reputation may precede him, but that did not mean he scared me.

I cocked my head to the side. "Who would have guessed— Garrick the Red is blond."

His own head tilted to match the angle of mine. "The red refers to the blood."

I snorted. "Congratulations. That is the bare minimum to keep you alive."

He uncrossed his arms, the action shrinking the space between us. He could have touched me as easily as I could have stabbed him. And damn it all to the Dark God's coldest, cruelest hell, but there was that flare of desire in my stomach again.

"Not the blood in my veins. The blood on my hands."

My eyes snapped down to those very hands. Huge—they were ridiculous. They should have been out of proportion to the rest of him. But *he* was huge, especially in comparison to my short stature. He wouldn't need one of the weapons strapped to his body to hurt me. He could rip me apart with his hands alone.

Blood on his hands, indeed.

I bit my tongue before I could say something worse. I still needed him to keep my secret. I was supposed to be bribing him.

I forced my arms down from my waist to hang at my side. Garrick tracked the movement with his eyes, his lids lowering a fraction as my thick cloak fell back into place around me, hiding my body.

"My offer stands," I said.

He at least did me the courtesy of looking at my face as he denied me. "Keep your spells for yourself, witch."

The word bristled against me like wool on bare skin. I'd forced the mother in the tavern the night before to call me what I was.

But from Garrick's lips, it rubbed wrong. Maybe because he did not say it with even the slightest hint of fear—but plenty of derision.

"I have a name."

"I've already told you mine."

And looked so fucking smug while doing it.

I wanted to withhold my own name just out of spite. But unlike his, there was no prowess or gravity associated with mine. Once, I could have said Koryn, daughter of Gallatin of Crenmea. Or Koryn, frost witch of the Midnight Coven. In their own times, both would have meant something. But not now.

Now, I was just — "Koryn."

"Koryn," he repeated, rolling the syllables over his tongue. "Koryn, the wicked witch of Canmar."

I hissed through my teeth. "Two spells—"

"Keep your spells and I'll keep your secret," he interrupted.

The hairs on the back of my neck rose. "Why would you do that?"

He shrugged, a truly ridiculous gesture from someone his size. "My reasons are my own."

I did not have much height, but I had plenty of indignation. "And once they no longer apply, you'll tell everyone I'm a witch so they can band together and kill me."

He shrugged again.

My hands curled underneath my cloak, frost cooling my palms. "*You* think you can kill me." That was why he didn't care about my spells or my secret. Because he did not see me as a threat.

The rest of the world thought him a predator. Yet the feeling swirling in my chest was not fear but impudence. How dare he reduce me to a triviality. The power of a thousand generations of witches hummed through my blood. *Fuck him.*

But by the time I opened my mouth to hurl those words at him, his swirling turquoise eyes were fixed firmly back on my face with that intensity that froze me as effectively as any ice.

"What sort of witch makes friends with human competitors?"

He could only mean Nimra. He'd noticed us speaking before the ceremony. That was hardly noteworthy. I doubted that Garrick the Red had made his fortune on Velora by being blind to his surroundings.

She is not my friend, I almost said. *I don't have friends,* close behind. "I do not have to explain myself to you," I went with instead. He might know things about me the others did not, but that did not entitle him to any more secrets.

He continued as if I had not spoken at all. "You warned her to get away, instead of sacrificing her."

For a moment, I did not understand what he was saying.

He'd done more than watch. He'd heard my whispered warning to Nimra before I'd approached him, while he was yards away, at the edge of the altars, speaking with the fae female.

My head whipped over my shoulder. They were gone, both Nimra and the dark red-haired man I'd mistaken for Garrick the Red.

I had warned her not to let the man get her alone. Even now, knowing that he was not Garrick the Red, my instincts told me he was dangerous.

But Garrick should not have been able to hear any of it. My gaze slid upward, toward the sloped ceiling with its pitched vaults and ornate carvings. The acoustics of temples were always strange, sound traveling in unexpected ways. That must be how he'd heard my whispered words. There was no other way, with his human ears, no other reason for him to have paid such close attention to me.

I turned back to him, startled at the sudden closeness. The space between us had closed so gradually I had not realized it until I could feel the warmth of his body.

"I don't need to kill you," he breathed, returning to our earlier conversation. He took another step forward. One more, and we'd be touching. I'd be close enough to shove a dagger between his ribs. Though I wasn't arrogant enough to think I'd manage that before he gutted me. I'd be much better off loosening the frigid power building beneath my skin.

I refused to give an inch of the space he took. "And why is that?"

"Because the gods will do it for me," he said with a soft chuckle. That close, I felt it against my skin, smelled the faint traces of cinnamon and wine on his breath.

I did not step back, even as the feel of that warm air sliding in between the folds of my cloak did things to me. Inconvenient things.

A few heartbeats—his, not mine, because I could hear those, too—and his lips flattened into a smirk. He broke the tension, stepping away. He did not bother with a farewell, but I could not let him have the last word. I should have kept my mouth shut. But maybe I was as stupid as the humans in the tavern the night before.

"I'll see you on the other side," I said to his retreating back. Because I assumed he would make it through, damn him.

He paused, but did not look back over his shoulder.

"We'll see." Because he assumed I would not.

THE DORMITORY COULD HAVE HOUSED ten times our number. I remembered those days, when men and women of all ages had entered the temples and attempted the gates with glory on their minds and foolishness in their hearts. A century later, the temples were still busy, but the air of excitement had worn away. Supplicants entered out of need and hope, rather than glory.

As I lay silently and made my supplications to the Dark God, glory was the furthest thing from my mind. For so many months, since I'd been ousted from my coven, I'd had only two goals. Preserve my power and stay alive. But in a blink, it had all changed.

Get through the gates, lift the curse on Velora, and be restored to my coven. To sisterhood and safety and true power.

Get through the gates, or Kyrelle would make one reckless, self-sacrificing decision after another until both she and her father were dead. I'd known, even when I gave her the gold and entered the temple in her stead, that she would never leave her father. I'd seen the love between them, year after year, even as their already meager circumstances deteriorated.

I had never loved another nor been loved like that.

And after the pain I'd seen in Kyrelle's eyes? I never wanted to.

I rolled over in the lumpy bed and fell asleep. By some blessing of the gods, my night was dreamless.

CHAPTER 14

THE ACOLYTES CAME FOR US AT FIRST LIGHT. I WAS ALREADY AWAKE.
Judging by the surrounding sounds, most of the other supplicants
were as well. The man I'd mistaken for Garrick the Red might have
been the only one who'd slept well. I'd listened to him snore loudly
most of the night from four beds down.

They lined us up in the dark. I was placed fourth, between
Nimra and Rilk. Garrick was at the back, his looming presence
impossible to ignore, though I did my best. He created a solid wall
that separated me from the fae female who came last. At least if he
was close, he'd have no chance to whisper my secret without my
realizing it. I trusted his vow to keep it about as much as I did the
cowering man behind me not to shove a dagger into my back. The
cowardly could be just as dangerous as the cruel.

I scanned the acolytes as they led us out of the dormitory and
into the temple proper. But they all had their hoods up and heads
bent. I was only looking for Tomin because I wanted any last-
minute information he might impart about the gate. I certainly
was not looking for a friendly face I did not need.

We circled the perimeter of the temple, passing each altar as the acolytes began to chant. I sighed. My headache from the night before had only just faded.

"I was wrong," Nimra whispered over her shoulder. "The red-haired one is named Nash."

My gaze snapped to the front of the line, where a head of wine-red hair was easily visible over the hoods.

"I tried to stay away from him, but," Nimra paused, looking away. "But he was insistent."

So far that morning, my emotions had been limited to grim exhaustion and mild dread. But as suddenly as a lightning strike, rage unfurled in my stomach, sending icy spears of power shooting through my veins.

"What did he do?"

Nimra's head whipped back over her shoulder. Her eyes widened enough that panic surged up alongside the rage. If my coven mark was glowing, even the priestess' thick paste might not be enough.

But her attention focused on my eyes—and the dagger that was suddenly in my hand. I did not even recall pulling it from the sheath at my belt.

The procession slowed to a shuffle as the violet-clad priestess paused to perform some religious nonsense at each altar. Nimra's eyes jumped between me, the acolytes on either side of us, and then ahead.

Human senses were too weak to smell fear. But I was not human. When she looked to the front of our line, it peeled off of her in waves. The warmth of the temple, the chanting of the acolytes, the scent of her fear… they pressed in on me, taking over my too-sensitive senses, making it hard to think, but too easy to feel.

I grabbed her arm. "What did he do?"

Nimra bit her bottom lip, but she did not flinch away. She might be scared, but she was far from a coward. She glanced over her shoulder to make sure she would not trample on the person in front of her before looking me directly in the eyes as she said, "He told me that if I came to his bed last night, he'd make sure I made it through the Mercy Gate."

Every flame in the temple went out. The temperature dropped quickly, too fast to attribute to a passing draft. Power was thick in the air.

The acolytes went silent, the emptiness made even more stark by the sudden lack of chanting. Behind us, a low chuckle slid over my senses. I did not turn to look at Garrick the fucking Red.

I crunched my hands into balls, fighting for control.

A voice boomed in the dull light of dawn leaking through the stained-glass windows.

"The gods have made their presence known," the priestess decreed, drawing every set of eyes to her even in the dim light. I could see her clearly, standing directly before the altar of Seraxa, the Goddess of Mercy.

"Darkness consumes Velora," she continued. "Yet Seraxa compels us to remember that even a single act of mercy can be a light in the darkness." As the last word left her lips, she relit Seraxa's altar.

Whispers of awe rippled through the acolytes. Slowly, so slowly, I uncurled my fists. The air around us warmed, but neither the priestess nor the acolytes moved to relight the remaining altars.

"If I hadn't believed before…" Nimra whispered.

I watched the clever priestess, reassessing my estimation of her. She'd given me that paste and suggested I cover my coven mark. She had not so much as glanced in my direction, but I would have gambled a spell or two that she knew the real source of the power still fading from the air around us. But she'd attributed it to Seraxa before anyone could even wonder otherwise.

Why? To elevate the gods? To bolster her own prestige? Or to help *me*? Why?

The word echoed around in my head as we resumed our

procession. But when Nash turned back, looking over the supplicants behind him with lazy perusal, my stomach turned. He found Nimra and a smile crawled up his face, a smile that I recognized easily.

Men had been looking at women like that far longer than my four hundred years. Suddenly, it did not matter that Nimra was neither my coven sister nor a descendant of my long-dead sister. She was a woman, and that was enough.

"You turned him away," I said, already knowing the answer.

Nimra nodded but said nothing more. The procession began to move again.

Nash's eyes found mine. I kept my frost in check, but barely. I let all of the rage flood my gaze. I held it as I sheathed the dagger back at my waist.

He laughed soundlessly before turning back to follow the priestess out the rear entrance of the temple. He had no idea that he'd just made an enemy of a nearly four-hundred-year-old frost witch. But that did not matter.

My power would kill him just the same. And this time, I would not let myself hesitate.

Warm breath lifted the hair from the back of my neck, the looming wall behind me moving closer.

"I won't even have to spill your secret. You seem determined to reveal yourself all on your own," Garrick said, his cinnamon and wine scent overpowering the altars of burning herbs.

"I can manage myself just fine." A lie, most likely. I'd struggled to manage myself even with the help of six powerful witches. In fact, I'd done the opposite of *manage myself*. I'd lost control and gotten myself cast out from my coven.

But I'd rather spend the next three gates listening to my own stomach growl from hunger than admit that fact to him.

"There won't be a priestess in the gate to pass off your power as an act of divine intervention," Garrick said.

I stumbled over his words, the toe of my boot catching on the hem of my cloak as we moved to the next altar in procession. But before I could hit the ground, a hand caught my shoulder. Engulfed it.

That first touch was as intense as his gaze and more than I'd imagined lying alone in my bunk the night before. But it was his words that had tripped me up.

His tone was acerbic, but the thrust of the words themselves... they sounded like a warning, not an admonition. That was almost as unsettling as the warmth radiating from where his hand still gripped my shoulder.

Thanks to the Dark God, he removed it and I was able to breathe again. But thinking still eluded me. That could be the only explanation for the words I let slip.

"Sometimes the use of power is justified," I said over the rush of my own blood in my veins. I could not stop my gaze from lifting with the words, my chin with it, until I found the back of Nash's head.

Garrick shifted behind me. I hadn't realized how close he'd gotten, moving in so that no one else could hear our whispered words. Even though he was no longer touching me, the weight of his presence was inescapable.

The heat from the night before returned, hotter than before, kindled with the anger already simmering in my veins. But if Garrick felt that same burning attraction, he gave no sign I could detect, even with my heightened awareness. I allowed myself to look over my shoulder long enough to confirm that his gaze had followed my own.

He glanced from Nash, to Nimra, and then back to me. The grim tilt of his mouth told me that he'd heard Nimra telling me about Nash's threats.

"A witch with a functioning heart. Who knew such a thing was possible," Garrick said.

I opened my mouth to tell him that he clearly knew less about witches than he believed. But I doubted Garrick the Red would have made such a mistake, which was even more unsettling. My heart was nothing more than a decaying, atrophied organ in my chest. To believe anything else went against everything Maura and my coven had taught me. To wish anything else was doom.

"I like it better when you do not speak," I hissed between my teeth.

Again, his warm chuckle filled the space between us. "What you like does not concern me, witch."

I could not keep his mouth shut, but I was done running mine. I pressed my lips together and spent the remainder of the procession imagining possible ways to stage Nash's death without revealing my power to the other supplicants.

I was so busy plotting that I almost missed the incongruity before me. The Mercy Gate was located in the heart of Canmar, the capital city of Velora. There were very few humans left to populate it, but most of the buildings remained.

What certainly did not exist was a fifty-foot wall of ice that expanded as far as I could see in either direction. A single, precarious-looking rope ladder ascended up the sheer face before disappearing over the top.

We'd reached the Mercy Gate.

I had no doubt my muscles would be screaming for mercy by the time I hauled myself up that ladder. Beside me, even Nimra was speechless. Whatever I'd imagined… it was not this. And I doubted the gate required nothing more than climbing a ladder.

"You will ascend in the order you now stand," the priestess said.

I glanced side to side and over my shoulder. We'd maintained the same order since leaving the dormitory—Nash, the doe-eyed girl, Nimra, me, Rilk, Garrick, and Alize.

None of us moved toward the ladder. The priestess looked up and down our line, but she offered no final prayers or hints about what awaited us atop the wall of ice.

"Surviving supplicants should proceed to the Justice Gate," she instructed. "Begin."

The acolytes moved swiftly, forming a pathway around us, their green robes lining either side. At the end, the rope ladder swayed in the breeze. It was not even affixed to the wall. Fuck. This was going to hurt.

Nash threw a malicious grin over his shoulder and started climbing. I counted under my breath as he rose, rung over rung. He never paused to catch his breath, and he did not slip. The highest rungs were difficult for even me to see, but as he climbed over the top of the wall, his pace remained steady. He'd reached the top without injury.

But instead of disappearing over the edge, he reached into his cloak, withdrawing something in his hand. Then he crouched down and cut the rope ladder loose from the wall of ice.

So much for mercy.

CHAPTER 15

THE LADDER *WAS* ANCHORED—AT THE HALFWAY POINT. MAYBE IT WAS Seraxa intervening, but the first twenty-five feet of the rope ladder remained intact. But the final stretch was nothing but bare ice.

The girl at the front of the line turned. We all did, finding the dark-haired priestess behind us. She stood between the last set of acolytes, closing the channel they'd formed with their green robes. Behind her, the armed guards from inside the temple stepped into place.

We were trapped. The only way out was up.

Tears broke free from the girl's round eyes, spilling in rapid streams down her sunken cheeks. I did not need the Dark God's gifts to see her hands shake as she reached for the ladder.

She was petite, which gave her less weight to haul up using her non-existent muscles. I cursed the hearty meal I'd eaten the night before. I wouldn't have that advantage.

But too soon she reached the midpoint, where the severed ropes fell away to dangle uselessly. We all watched in agonizing silence as she remained frozen.

"Begin."

Again, we turned as one to look at the priestess. Everyone except Garrick. When I turned, he was looking straight at me. His unsettling turquoise eyes made no effort to pretend otherwise. But like nearly every time before, they were inscrutable in everything but their intensity.

I forced myself to look past him. Whatever he did or thought now, whatever attraction I'd felt for him, they were distractions that would get me killed.

The priestess stared back, her expression completely unchanged—brow smooth, eyes expectant, and a menacing guard at each shoulder.

The gods will have their due.

"Please start moving," Nimra said under her breath as she stepped up to the ladder.

She began to climb, but slowly. Slower than her healthy body should have allowed, slow enough to give the petrified girl a chance to get herself off the ladder and up the wall—before Nimra reached her and was forced to choose.

An act of mercy.

Nimra could have overtaken the girl easily. But she moved up the ladder with purposeful slowness.

Would I have given the girl the same chance? My throat tightened. That heart that Garrick thought still worked said yes. But the determination to return to my coven, to save myself and Kyrelle... I did not have an answer.

Something that couldn't have been relief seeped into my chest cavity as the girl reached up past the end of the ladder, found a handhold in the ice, and pulled herself up. She was painfully slow, but by the time Nimra reached the midpoint of the wall, the young girl was well out of reach.

Nimra did not hesitate, finding her own path and starting up the ice wall with impressive speed, given her humanity. I stepped forward, expecting the priestess to direct me to begin immediately.

But she remained silent. Nimra reached the top. The girl was still only three-quarters of the way up and barely moving.

"Begin."

The climb was every bit as torturous as I'd expected. My own body worked against me, the thickness of my thighs painfully apparent as I dragged them up rung after rung. My weight had often been a hindrance in a world built to honor waifish figures. But for centuries I'd had my power to bolster me. I'd become dependent on it, and it was too fucking late to do anything about it. My biceps and thighs screamed, and I hadn't even reached the midpoint.

I cannot die here.

Not alone, without my coven sisters. Not so pitifully close to the beginning, as useless as Kyrelle had accused me of being.

Rilk started up the ladder as I reached the midpoint. I doubted he would show me the same mercy that Nimra had the young girl.

I assessed my options. The girl was about twenty feet above me but several yards to the left. Her path of hand and footholds had taken her off course and prolonged the dangerous climb. I could not make the same mistake. I needed to go straight up.

I allowed myself one glance down at Rilk. He was closer than I'd have liked, but I had to risk it. If I attempted the icy expanse on my quivering muscles alone, I would fall to my death.

I did not waste time looking for a handhold. I summoned my power, and when my hand touched the wall of ice, I created one of my own. It was still slow, and I still had to drag my body upward foot by agonizing foot. But at least I did not have to worry about slipping. I was far enough away that none of the supplicants waiting below could see what I was doing. The girl to my left was too worried about herself. The only danger was Rilk, and he was gaining on me.

I rallied my power, but it could do nothing for my tired muscles or the breath scissoring in and out of my chest. My lungs burned, but I forced myself up another foot. I was almost even with the girl, who'd stopped climbing completely.

I swung another arm up, channeling my power to form another handhold—

Something caught on my foot, ripping it loose of the foothold and tugging my entire body down. I kicked wildly, my other foot coming free so I was dangling all of my weight by one hand. My body slammed into the wall of ice, knocking all of the air out of my already searing lungs.

Ice scraped across my face as my body twisted, pain shooting through my wrist as I tried to see what had caught me up.

Not what. Who.

Rilk.

He'd used a dagger to anchor himself into the wall of ice. The other hand clung to my booted foot, wrapped around my ankle with strength that belied his thin frame. Strength born of desperation.

I will not be felled by a man.

Both of my feet were dislodged. Instead of trying to find another foothold, I used the one he wasn't holding to kick him directly in the face. The scent of blood filled the air in time with the crunch of his nose breaking. He released my foot, and that was all I needed. I kept climbing.

"I will kill you, fucking bitch!" he roared below me.

Bitch. Why were men all so disappointingly unoriginal?

I kept climbing. My cloak snagged. I didn't stop to see if it was the ice or Rilk that had gotten ahold of it. I ripped open the clasp and let it fall away. I could not die of the cold, but if he got that dagger into an artery, I'd bleed out as uselessly as a human.

Ten more feet to the top of the wall. Nine. Eight. Tears of relief threatened to overwhelm me, but I froze them before they could fall. I did not know what—or who—waited on the top of the wall. Four feet. Three.

A scream.

I forced myself up another foot before allowing myself to look.

Rilk had given up on me, but he had not given up altogether. He'd set his sights on the young woman who'd preceded Nimra.

Two feet.

With the next swing of my arm, I grabbed the top of the wall. My power froze my palm to the perpendicular surface, making it impossible for me to lose my grip.

I looked again.

Just in time to see her fall.

CHAPTER 16

I DID NOT LOOK DOWN.

I could assume that Garrick was already climbing and that the fae female, Alize, was behind him or soon would be.

I could not look down at the girl's shattered body. I could not risk losing my nerve. People died attempting the Seven Gates. No one had ever passed through all seven. Which meant that every single person who had attempted them in the four hundred years since the curse had died. Hundreds, maybe even thousands, had fallen to their deaths just like that doe-eyed girl.

But I would not be one of them. I could not.

I forced myself to turn and face what remained of the gate.

In the distance, I could make out another wall of ice, but instead of a ladder, there was a rectangular opening carved into its base. That was the real Mercy Gate. Whether everything we'd done since climbing that ladder was a test as to whether we were allowed to pass through, or simply reaching it was the task... I'd find out when I got there.

But between me and that gate stretched a hundred yards of ice.

Ice fields that I should have run over without incident. Except that I could not use my active power without revealing myself.

It looked innocent enough, that expanse of white and blue. But I knew the same thing that everyone in Velora had learned since the curse settled the continent firmly in its grip. Ice was more dangerous than any flame.

I counted at least a half dozen crevices between me and the gate, but those were just the ones I could see. The deep, crystalline blue cracks could appear out of nowhere, hidden beneath a drift of innocuous-looking snow. One unfortunate step, and you'd fall down only to be impaled on spikes of icy death.

Ice crackled in my veins.

If I could stay far enough away from the other supplicants, perhaps I could use my power sparingly.

Nimra was already halfway across, but Nash lingered atop the wall. Was his plan to throw us off as we reached the top? But Nimra had gotten past, and he did not approach me, either. Though that could have been because of the deep crevice that cracked the ice between us. Though he'd been up there long enough to go around if he really wanted to target me.

What is he waiting for?

A few seconds later, I had my answer.

He reached down and hauled Rilk up over the ledge, and clarity shot through me. He'd tried and failed to align himself with Nimra. Rilk was his second choice. He had purposefully waited and pulled the other man up the last few feet. An act of mercy. A twisted one—but Seraxa would be the judge, not me.

But that mercy apparently ended right there. Nash left Rilk panting on the edge and started running. He'd had plenty of time to regain whatever breath he'd lost in the climb, and his approach to the ice field seemed to be to move fast enough that he was over any crevices before they opened up beneath him. Not a terrible strategy if one had the endurance to make it straight across the ice field, which I did not.

I couldn't stay and think it over. Rilk had made it to his knees. Garrick must be close behind. Two slender, golden hands gripped the edge a few feet to my right. Alize. The urge to drag my dagger across her knuckles screamed through me. But I fought to control it the same way I did my power—with middling success.

My own sense of self-preservation got me moving. I'd never best Alize without using my active power. I kept the first crevice between me and Rilk and started at a jog that I hoped I'd be able to maintain.

Without the priestess to direct the supplicants, the sprint across the ice field was a free-for-all. Ahead of me, Nash stumbled but didn't fall. Nimra reached the gate and disappeared through it. I kept Rilk in my periphery. We were both moving at the same labored, slow pace.

A blur of earth tones flashed by on my right. I blinked, sure the gate was playing some trick on my vision. It was not possible for a human to move that fast. But it was Garrick, not Alize, who surged past me first, closing so fast that Nash looked like he was hardly moving.

Garrick came from my right, Nash had started from my left, but their paths were converging, the pattern of crevices they dodged pushing them closer and closer together. Nature or a trick of Seraxa, it didn't really matter. Their intersection was inevitable. Nash looked over his shoulder, and for the first time that self-satisfied, malicious grin was nowhere to be seen.

He'd heard about Garrick the Red, too. I hoped he was regretting cutting the rope ladder. I hoped Garrick would reach him and punish him.

Nash was in shape, but Garrick was a honed hunter, and the extra few inches of height gave him an even bigger advantage. No wonder he'd refused my spells and any type of obligation between us. He was so strong and so fast that he did not need them.

Nash was almost to the gate. He leaped the last few yards, hitting the ice with an impact that reverberated across the ice field.

A sapphire blue crevice opened behind him, and even Garrick was not fast enough to avoid it. Nash careened through the gate, disappearing from view.

Garrick disappeared, too. Down into the crevice.

My stomach tried to drop directly out of my body. Garrick the Red. That quickly, he'd been claimed by the Mercy Gate. What chance did I have? Panic bubbled through me, fighting with my power, fighting to take control.

The number of crevices had doubled. Tripled. More opened with every footstep. I'd pulled ahead of Rilk, but just like Nash and Garrick, we would eventually collide. I forced myself forward, tracking the crevices as they yawned open one after another. My tired muscles moved me around and over, slower with every step, but still moving.

I maneuvered sideways as yet another new crevice opened, throwing all of my body weight to the side and hitting the ice with an ominous crack. A golden blur approached, moving in an unnaturally straight line. *Alize.*

I braced myself, power surging to my fingertips. I did not care what it would reveal to the other supplicants. If she tried to take me down, I would use every bit of power at my disposal to destroy her.

The fae had stolen everything from me. They would not get my life as well.

The ice beneath me shifted. I didn't have time to get to my feet. I tucked my arms into my sides and rolled, praying to the Dark God that I'd be able to stop myself before I reached the next crevice.

Alize darted past me, dodging the spreading crevice easily. Her feet hardly touched the ice—no, they did not touch the ice *at all*. They moved as if she was running, but made no contact with the ground, the air itself providing traction to her steps.

She was wind-gifted.

Even as my mind struggled to understand the implications of

her magic, my instincts buried the thoughts. I could worry about that if I survived to the next gate. I shoved my hands underneath my shoulders and pushed up. My thighs roared at the demand to bunch and strain and take my weight.

Ahead of me, Alize dashed past the crevice that had claimed Garrick. She did not pause; did not look back; did not say a word, unless she carried that away on a magical wind as well. If she said a prayer for the man she'd known, however they were connected, I could not hear it.

She disappeared through the gate.

Rilk and I were the only ones left. My fall had cost me. He'd closed the gap between us, the crevices driving us together for a second round of what had begun on the wall. Except now we were both more exhausted and more desperate.

I pushed every bit of stubbornness and anger into my legs and lungs. Kyrelle would not die because my body was not strong enough. Maura would not get the last laugh, sentencing me to death in the gates. I deserved more and I would take it.

I will fucking take it.

But my foot stuck in the first crack of a new crevice, sending me sprawling across the ice. I scrambled for purchase, trying to slow my slide, but the ice was so slick. What was left of my fingernails ripped, blood leaked down my cheek, the cut from earlier ripping even further.

Dark God, save me.

By his gift or some other, my belt snagged on an uneven chunk of ice. My body jerked back, the inertia of every pound protesting the yank. A sound perilously close to a sob broke from my chest.

My right arm dangled over the edge of a crevice. But the rest of me was on solid ice, for the moment. For a half second, I contemplated just letting the ice have me. The bravado of a few seconds earlier was gone. It would be so much easier to just stay there and give in to the exhaustion. The cold had already claimed my life once before. It was a fitting end.

I felt that dangerous numbness of disassociation begin to spread through my body as I stared over the edge into the abyss.

From the deep crevice, a pair of blue-green eyes stared back.

"Hello, wicked witch."

"You're alive," I rasped, the words scraping over my throat. Even that was raw—which reminded me of every single place on my body that was, as well. So much for giving in to the numbness.

An ominous groan echoed from the depths of the crevice.

"Not for long," Garrick said.

I almost laughed. Which would have been cruel. But it was Garrick's fault, because he was right. He dangled from a ledge about two feet below the top of the ice where my body lay, ignoring my directions to get the fuck up. If I did not manage to get myself moving, either Rilk or the ice would claim my life.

Knowing all of that, there was no accounting for what I did next.

I reached down my hand.

Garrick didn't give me time to second guess myself. He swung up one of his arms, latching on to my wrist with his much larger hand. His fingertips dug into my arm so hard I could not have released him if I'd wanted to.

I thought my muscles were screaming before? Garrick had a foot of pure muscle on me. Even with him clinging to the side of the crevice, trying to help haul himself upward, every muscle and joint in my body protested.

"You're too fucking heavy," I groaned. I wasn't going to drop him. He was going to rip my arm right off.

"Brace your shoulder so it doesn't pop out of the socket," he demanded.

Demanded, as if he was not the one dangling over a certain death, and me, his savior.

The ice groaned again. We were out of time.

I just was not strong enough, at least not physically. But another part of me was.

I freed my other hand from bracing my shoulder and threw it down, nearly colliding with Garrick's face. But he did not flinch as power filled the air. A ledge of solid ice formed beneath his feet. Then another, six inches up. And another and another. I built him a staircase, and he climbed right out. Most importantly, he did not rip my arm off.

Nor did he release it.

He pulled me to my feet, head whipping side to side as he assessed our situation. Even that was too much time. The ice beneath our feet splintered. "Run."

My body obeyed his command without question.

Even so, it wasn't fast enough.

He had every reason to release my hand and run on. I'd seen him before his fall. He'd have made it easily without me slowing him down. We weren't allies or friends. I'd pulled him out of that crevice, but he did not owe me anything. Getting me moving from that ledge was surely enough of an act of mercy to appease Seraxa.

He did not let go.

"Faster, Koryn," he demanded.

I couldn't go faster. I was going to get us both killed.

I looked back. Rilk was only a few yards behind, but even that would be fatal. The entire ice field was disintegrating.

We weren't going to make it.

I threw out the hand that Garrick did not hold. Bright power so cold that it burned flowed from my veins, but to me it was not pain. It was release. It was right.

Frost solidified into a thick, solid layer of ice, creating a path to safety.

Rilk was close enough for me to hear his gasp.

But I let the consequences roll past me. Life, first.

Another few yards, that was all that stood between us and the gate. My legs pumped beneath me, mustering the last dregs of life-saving energy.

We slid through the gate as the path of ice I'd created crumbled and a crevice opened beneath our feet. We were too late. I was certain we would die. I'd risked it all—my chance to return to my coven, my quest to protect my sister's legacy, my own life—for a bounty hunter who'd imagined me dead as easily as breathing.

My last thought as the ground fell away was that maybe Seraxa would take mercy on me before the Dark God got ahold of my soul. I fell and fell and fell. An eternity of falling. Then my back crashed into the ground.

CHAPTER 17

I lay blinking up at the sky for more minutes than I cared to count.

My senses picked up on the other supplicants. Rilk's wheezing breath came from somewhere to my left, but far enough away not to be an immediate threat. Somehow, he'd made it through. If my body was wrecked, I could only imagine the state he must be in.

Of course, the Gates would require physical strength and endurance. And without my power to bolster me, I was too fucking vulnerable.

Not that it mattered anymore.

Rilk had seen my power. He'd already shown himself to be a snake by making a deal with that monster, Nash. Soon, he'd spill my secret to the rest. I lacked pointed ears, so there was only one other thing I could be. So much for that tin of paste still tucked in my pocket. Covering my coven mark was now the absolute least of my worries.

I couldn't keep laying there so openly exposed. I would be too easy to pick off once the others recovered. Dark God, spare me. The fae female didn't look like she needed any recovery time at all.

Every muscle screamed, but I forced myself to sit up. I shivered and moved to pull my cloak tighter around me, only to remember ripping it from my shoulders on the ice wall. Fucking great. I might not technically be able to freeze to death, given that frost ran through my veins, but I could still feel the cold.

Steps crunched in the frost, someone else dragging themselves up to stand. My power rose despite the exhaustion. If there was anyone I could muster the energy to kill, it was that fae bitch.

But the weight of the steps was too heavy, and I knew exactly who it was that stopped a few feet short of me. I could already feel the bruises forming around my wrist from where his hand had gripped mine as I dragged him up over the ledge.

I did not waste any more time panting on the ground. I would not give Garrick the Red the satisfaction.

The ground was slick and my muscles so tired, I stumbled half a step as I dragged myself up to stand. I lurched forward into his space, but he didn't so much as flinch. When I lifted my head so I could glare up at him, the corner of his mouth had quirked upward.

I glared harder.

His eyes raked over me for half a second before he shrugged. "You're alive."

"That is all you have to say? *You* are only alive because of *me*." I could practically feel my eyes bugging out of my head. But the bastard was completely unruffled. He looked like he might have rolled out of a particularly rough romp in bed—pale hair slightly mussed, lower lip swelling, buttons on his leather vest torn askew.

I was *not* picturing Garrick in bed. Not after what he'd just put me through.

He rolled his neck along the back of his shoulders, giving me the absolute bare minimum of his attention. "Did you expect a thank you?"

Frost curled around my fingertips.

"I expect nothing from you," I said through gritted teeth. "Get yourself into a situation like that again, and I will happily let you die. There is only one Mercy Gate."

His eyes paused on mine, and for a fleeting moment, the turquoise almost seemed to glow. My stomach lurched in traitorous response. I blinked, and he wasn't even looking at me any longer. It was nothing but a ridiculous trick of the light.

I forced myself to look away from him. The gate had dropped us into a snow-covered meadow. Garrick and I were near the southern edge, the rest of the surviving supplicants spread out across the clearing. I counted quickly—six remained. Everyone but the doe-eyed young woman who I'd seen fall—the one that Rilk had thrown to her death.

How was that mercy? What had Rilk done to prove himself to the Goddess of Mercy? I'd saved Garrick, but the fae female he'd been so chummy with the night before hadn't stopped to help him. Nimra had let the girl get away, for all the good it had done her. Nash had given Rilk his last arm up over the ledge. But what about the others? What had Seraxa seen that had proved them worthy?

Fuck, I was spiraling. I could not let that happen—not with that behemoth of a man looking on.

A cramp burned in my side as I tried to take a deep breath. Maybe the true mercy would have been if *I'd* fallen down into that crevice. My coven sisters wouldn't be sent on hopeless treks to give me even more hopeless challenges, and Kyrelle wouldn't have to deal with my twisted loyalty anymore.

A growl of surprise echoed from above me—just as a cry peeled from my own lips to match.

My arm burned, a plume of fire from my shoulder down to my fingertips. I ripped off my fingerless glove, expecting to see my skin searing red. But my palm was pale, and the sizzle disappeared as quickly as it had come on, narrowing to a single point of familiar burning pain.

My stomach dropped to the icy ground.

I'd felt that burn once before in my life—or rather, in my death. Power and magic always came at a price.

With my glove gone, I could see it clearly. There, inked on the inside of my wrist, was a new tattoo.

"The Lifebind."

No, it was not possible.

"Most consider it a blessing from Seraxa," Garrick said, lifting his own arm to the gray light overhead to examine the mark closer.

Most. *Not him, and certainly not me.*

"Most people save the life of someone they actually care about," I bit back, snatching the edge of my sleeve and dragging it down over my wrist. Unlike Garrick, I had no desire to examine the new brand inked on my skin.

That was what it was, a brand that declared two things—the favor of Seraxa, and the new bond between Garrick's life and mine. My stomach flipped; I wasn't sure which would be more dangerous. The gods were jealous beings. But now there would be no escaping him. No avoiding him.

"Why? Why?" I yelled, first to him, then up at the sky as if the Goddess of Mercy could hear me. "It was the Mercy Gate! Saving him was an act of mercy! It was the bare minimum, not deserving of this!"

Garrick's brows, two shades darker than the pale hair on his head, lifted in amused unison. Unlike me, he apparently did not feel the need to yell.

"You exposed yourself for my sake," he said. "They all know your secret now."

I knew that. But I followed his gaze, tracking Rilk, who'd recovered enough to crawl across the meadow to his new master, Nash.

I should have let Garrick die, I realize. That would have been the best thing for me. My secret would have died with him, and I'd have eliminated a dangerous competitor. He'd boasted that the gates would kill me. But if at any point he'd seen me as a threat, I knew he was more than capable of doing the job.

But none of that had entered my mind when I offered him my hand or when I'd used my power to help us reach the gate.

How many times would I play out this same series of disastrous decisions? Had my death not been enough? My banishment?

Offering him your hand was a decision made by your heart, not your mind, a barely remembered voice whispered from the recesses of my consciousness.

My heart was dead, the one part of me that had not been resurrected. I had to stop pretending otherwise.

Garrick jerked his sleeve back down, covering the Lifebind tattoo.

"Congratulations, Koryn. Now you have a protector and you can use your witch magic freely." The way his eyes narrowed kept me from correcting his words. Witches were gifted power by the Dark God. Fae were born with magic. I expected someone who'd made a life off of Velora's misfortune to know that key difference.

A knot formed between his brows as he looked me over, considering. "Perhaps it was not such a merciful act, after all."

He was more than just a hulking behemoth with a reputation for violence. He was an absolute ass.

Frost leaked from my hands, spreading across the already ice-drenched snow at my feet. "I did not ask for this."

I'd saved his life and been *rewarded* with a *Lifebind.* Which meant that until he repaid the favor and saved my life in turn, his life depended upon mine. If I died, he died.

That sounded a lot more like his problem than mine. I whipped away from him—wishing I still had my cloak for dramatic effect— and stomped toward the edge of the meadow. The Justice Gate was northeast. Time to start walking.

"You didn't choose the gift from your Dark God, either."

Three hundred and seventy-seven years of mostly-failed practice in self-control was the only thing that kept my hand at my side, instead of lifted to my forehead. Or swinging around to connect with his face.

No. I had not chosen to be resurrected as a witch. But Garrick-the-fucking-Red was not entitled to any of my thoughts or feelings on that.

"This," I scowled at my wrist as I shoved my glove back over the blasted mark, "changes nothing. Stay away from me."

He was behind me too fast, his movements over the snow so quiet they defied reality. His fingers curled around my wrist, pain searing up my arm as he tightened his grip around the bruises he'd left behind when I'd foolishly saved his life.

I thrashed against him, but he spun me easily, dragging me up so that my face was mere inches from his and we were forced to share breath.

"On the contrary, Koryn. I think you will find that this changes *everything* for us."

PART II
JUSTICE

They walk the path of pride to wrath,
But justice does not sleep—
For every act, a price is set,
For every wound, the judgment deep.

CHAPTER 18

MORE THAN HALF OF THE DAY HAD ALREADY ELAPSED BY THE TIME I exited the frozen meadow and started northeast. The gates distorted time. Another new fact that the rumors had always missed. If we'd set out early enough, we might have made it to the temple at the Justice Gate by nightfall. As it was, we were all stuck spending the night in the dark, frozen wood.

Maybe the cold night would do me a favor and pick off another one of the supplicants. Rilk had been in bad shape before the Mercy Gate. If I was suffering, so was he, and I had a lot more meat on my body to keep me warm.

Even though I'd been the first to start out, I let all the other supplicants pass me early on, Nimra included. She gave me a wide berth and avoided meeting my eyes. I'd revealed my power. That was enough for even the friendliest of the others to keep their distance.

More than fine with me. I would rather keep them in my sights than risk someone coming from behind and stabbing a knife into my back. Even if it meant I was the last one to arrive at the temple.

Garrick surprised me when he passed me by, just like the

others. He disappeared into the woods ahead of me, seemingly unbothered by the exertion of the Mercy Gate. Bastard. Maybe my power had been enough to unnerve him, too, despite his dramatic threats.

I pretended that the bruises he'd left on my arm didn't bring me right back—not to the Mercy Gate, but to the moment he'd dragged me up close enough to share breath. I also spent most of the afternoon ignoring the heat that had coiled low in my belly in that moment, with his mouth only inches from mine.

But as I settled myself into the hollow created by a tangle of tree roots, I let the memory come back.

The barest stubble kissed his chin, so pale that it could have been a dusting of my frost. What would it feel like against my skin? Would it be warm like the heat that spread from his hand through my arm, or cool from the frigid air around us?

The Mercy Gate had claimed my cloak. The cold would keep me from sleeping well, and I'd need all of my strength to face the next gate. Bathing in the memory of Garrick's breath skittering across my cheeks and into the sensitive space where my ears met my neck was an act of self-preservation. It would keep me warm.

Maybe I should have let Garrick protect me. That was no doubt what he wanted—to keep me alive, now that his life depended upon mine. *A Lifebind.* In four hundred years, I'd never met someone who'd received one. They were as much a thing of legend as the gates themselves.

But the legends of Velora were becoming more real with every passing breath.

It was not Garrick's protection that flooded my mind as I settled deeper into the hollow. I imagined the hard curves of wood were the rigid lines of his body, wrapping around me. Not just protection, but warmth. Safety. Things that had eluded me for a very long time.

Things that I certainly would never receive from Garrick the Red, or anyone else. But in my mind, I could live out whatever fantasy I wanted. Especially if that fantasy would keep me warm in the cold, dark night.

Overhead, a crow cawed, its cry echoing among the trees. But I kept my eyes closed, determined to stay in the fantasy my mind was busy constructing.

I remembered to throw out my hand, sending a ring of icy spikes around me to deter any intruders. I mumbled a spell just before I lost the battle against my own exhaustion and impossible fantasies.

CHAPTER 19

BEFORE

"Where are you taking me, lovely?"

The hairs on the back of my neck rose, an accompanying shiver sliding down my spine.

"Just a little farther," I said without turning. His hold on my hand tightened. I tried to ignore it. We were almost there. But his touch turned insistent. He tugged me back, and though I could have fought him, I turned instead, letting him pull me flush against his body.

"There you are," he said a second before taking my lips. I opened under his touch, letting him into the warmth of my mouth. The heat between us was a nice contrast to the cool midnight air. Sultry summer nights were a thing of the past, of the years before the curse. But I found comfort in the cold, and I hated that sticky hot feeling.

"Oh, lovely," he groaned against my lips. He took the hand he held and slid it between us, taking hold of my wrist and rubbing my palm against the bulge in his trousers.

I hated nicknames. They'd always felt infantilizing. I'd spent my life confined to the role of the childish, forgettable youngest sister. A nickname was the last thing I wanted to hear from a lover's lips.

Almost the last thing, my mind corrected, still irritatingly sharp when I should have been pulled under by lust.

He rubbed my hand back and forth, even began thrusting his hips forward into it. When his hand finally moved away, a trickle of wetness finally broke loose between my legs. At last, I was going to get some attention.

But his hand went to the buttons at the top of his trousers, not to me.

Men were too predictable. This one was no different. A year older than me, but still a boy. Maybe that was the problem. I was wasting time with boys my own age when I needed a more experienced man who thought of someone other than himself.

Before he could shove my hand into his trousers, I caught his and brought it up to cup my breasts. Men loved my breasts—full and heavy, large enough to fill their entire hand. Overflow, really, but I was not about to complain. I loved having them touched. So at least I would get something out of this exchange.

He pawed at the fabric of my dress, trying to get to my skin. I obliged, shrugging my shoulder forward so he could pull my breast out. He pulled his mouth away from mine and dropped it to my breast, going straight for the nipple without any preamble. How original.

Maybe Rylynn had the right of it, shutting herself in her room instead of chasing boys down dark alleys in search of a distraction.

She was still unmarried. The horror of Janessa's womanhood ceremony had seen to that. Soon, they would begin to call her an old maid. Jealous words from younger women who were angry that a woman nearing thirty was still more beautiful than any of them.

I curled my fingers in the man's hair, pressing him harder to my breast. His mellow suckling was doing nothing for me.

"Tell me your name, lovely," he said, peeling back his mouth. Typical, doing the opposite of what I needed.

"We don't need names," I said, tugging his hair to get his mouth back up to mine and to cut off any more nonsense before he could spout it. Less talking, more touching. I had not approached him for his rapier wit.

"But how can you scream my name if you do not know it?" he panted into the night, his breath wet and heavy.

I threaded my fingers with his and slid them down between my legs. My other hand took care of lifting my skirts. "This is how you make me scream," I breathed against his mouth.

He pulled our hands away in a sharp jerk that freed his cock. "You first, lovely."

The last of my lust burned away, replaced by the sharper edges of temper.

I shoved him off of me.

He stumbled backward, tripping over a heavy wooden crate. "What is wrong with you?"

"With me?" I threw back my head and laughed at the ridiculousness of it. How dare I ask for my pleasure to be considered.

"You dragged me back here," he spat.

His cock still flopped around outside of his trousers, softening by the second.

"Get out." My hands curled into fists at my side. I would have no problem swinging one at his face. He stared me down, chest heaving, contemplating his options.

Options? I was not a fucking option. I'd already said no. If he came at me again, I would punch that pretty face he was so proud of. I would claw out his eyes. I would make him pay for thinking that I belonged to him, that he was entitled to any part of me. Even my name.

"Get out!" I screamed, rage billowing out of me.

He shoved his cock back into his trousers and took off down the alley, not quite running. But not strolling easily, either.

My breath moved in and out of my chest in time with the ferocious beat of my heart. I took a few steps back until I could lean against the wall on my side of the alley. I let my head fall back to rest against it.

I'd have to choose my distraction better next time.

Why wait until next time?

It was past midnight, but the city was still wide awake. No one at home would miss me. Rylynn would have to come out of her room to notice I'd left at all. My father had not really looked at me since my mother's death.

But my feet didn't carry me to a tavern or a dance hall. They took me home, because no matter how foolish it was, I still had hope that someone might care.

CHAPTER 20

A WARM HAND SLID UP THE INSIDE OF MY THIGH, INCREASING THE pressure of the touch with every upward inch. My hips lifted of their own volition, desperate for the contact, urging it higher. It had been so, so long. I needed that pressure at my center, where the ache built with every heartbeat—

My heart doesn't beat.

I startled awake to the crack of ice.

One crack was an animal. A crow landing. A wayward squirrel.

Two cracks were an attack.

And even the squirrels were dead in Velora.

I opened my eyes as the two figures crashed through the spiked stalagmites I'd created around me. The ice barely slowed them down. But that hadn't been the reason for it. It had been a warning system, and that had worked. Somewhere in the distance, a crow cawed.

I braced my feet in the snow and ground my back into the tree roots, pushing myself up to stand. Two shapes came into focus as my eyes blinked, the Dark God's gifts sharpening the details. But even before I could make out their faces, I knew my attackers.

Rilk dodged to the side as Nash swung his massive sword wildly, searching for me in the dark. But Rilk couldn't see either. He howled with pain when Nash clipped his arm.

"Shut up," Nash hissed—as if every one of the other supplicants could not hear them.

But I kept my mouth shut. They couldn't see me. I was not going to give them a hint by opening my mouth, no matter how tempting it was to mock their incompetence.

Rilk got his screams down to whimpers. Nash did not bother to stop and check on his accomplice. He edged closer, swinging his sword in front of him with every step.

"We know you're here somewhere," he called into the darkness. "We mean no harm. We want to invite you to join our alliance."

Alliance. I choked on an involuntary laugh.

No wonder none of the humans had ever successfully made it through all seven gates if this was the sort of nonsense they engaged in. We did not need to take one another out; it was a waste of energy. As Garrick had pointed out the night before, the gods would do plenty of damage on their own.

But people like Nash… I'd met plenty of men like him over the centuries. He could not handle the idea that there were people stronger than him, worthier than him. He needed to cut down his opponents before the gods could confirm that fear.

The scent of blood began to flood the clearing. I couldn't quite make out the blood from their dark clothes, but Rilk's wound was substantial. I could use that. Too bad he wasn't the primary danger.

Every instinct screamed at me to move. Another yard, and the end of that pointy sword would reach me. But a layer of ice had formed over the top of the old snow. Any attempt to move would only bring them closer faster. I had to trust in my—

"Argh!" Nash's rage ripped through the clearing, every pretense of quiet and comradery gone. "You bitch," he swore, writhing in place to try and break his legs free.

Sweet, familiar power filled the air between us. The spell I'd muttered in my last throes of wakefulness had done its job, the water on the ground soaking into their boots and pants and then instantly freezing. It wasn't particularly clever, but it was sufficient.

The spell held them in place, but it wouldn't last for long. My power to cast was weakened by the lack of connection to my coven. While my active power did not yet seem to be affected, I was not going to take a chance on the efficacy of my spells.

This was my opportunity to get away. I clambered over the tree roots, not caring about how much noise I made. I had to put as much distance between myself and my attackers as possible.

My muscles groaned, still not recovered from the Mercy Gate. But once I was free of the tree roots, I could run. Run where, I didn't pause to think. More ice cracked and in the next second, a huge mass fell upon me, crushing me to the ground.

I braced myself for the pain, expecting the sword to pierce my flesh at any second.

Nash's fetid breath clouded my senses, but then I felt it, pressed not to my side, but to the back of my neck where he'd pinned me down in the snow. The threat was clear, but I had no choice. I could not get my hands free, but I could still speak. I turned my face up so I could watch while my spell eviscerated him.

"Where you stand upon the ground, let water—"

He slapped me across the face, knocking the words of my spell loose before I could finish.

"I said—I don't want to kill you." So much for *we*. I could still hear Rilk a few yards back, free now of my spell, but making no attempt to join us. Nursing his wound, most likely.

"Then get your blade off my neck," I hissed. His hand remained poised above my face, ready to hit me again. Even if I tried, I would not be able to turn my face away into the snow fast enough. And I'd never get an entire spell out.

"Soon." He shifted his weight above me. "Rilk, get over here."

Dark God spare me, he stank. When was the last time he'd

cleaned his teeth? Ever? When I was human, the rich had prided themselves on extensive, expensive bathing rituals. Things could not have changed *that* much in three hundred years.

"What do you say," he said, shifting again. This time, an elbow landed hard in my back.

"I say get the fuck off of me," I bit out. There had to be a way to get him off. Spells spun through my brain. If I could get him talking, maybe I could whisper one beneath my breath. Or if he turned again, I could get a hand free.

"Such a vicious mouth," Nash laughed, leaning in closer. My stomach turned at the rancid stench of his breath. "But that's what I like about you. I want to see just how good you are with it."

Cold shot through me that had nothing to do with my power.

"I want one of those clever little spells—well, not just one," Nash said. He shifted so that his knees bracketed my waist. My left hand was underneath my leg. If he leaned forward just a bit more—

Metal sang through the air. Instead of moving, Nash froze, as surely as if he'd been turned to ice.

A voice just as cold spoke from the darkness behind us.

"Your friend is dead. And if you do not do exactly as I say, you will be, too."

CHAPTER 21

RILK WAS DEAD. I HAD BEEN SO PREOCCUPIED WITH MY OWN survival, I had not even noticed. I certainly shouldn't care. I should have killed him myself. Instead of running, I should have sent spears of ice into their hearts. Tendrils of frost through their mouths and noses to freeze their blood in their very veins.

I'd done it before. I would do it again.

But my stomach twisted once more, and this time it was not from the stench of Nash's breath.

"Release her."

Nash hissed through his teeth, the metal of his sword still flush against the back of my neck. But Garrick must have had his own blade pressed somewhere vital on Nash because he withdrew. I did not take another full breath until both his weight and that sword were gone; I did not trust Nash not to accidentally stab me with it and kill all three of us.

I hardly felt the burn in my tired muscles as I got my knees beneath me and pushed up to stand. The relief of freedom was so heady it wiped away everything else.

Until I caught sight of the two men behind me.

Garrick had grabbed one of Nash's arms, twisting it behind him. Nash's sword stuck out of the snow several feet away. One of the curved blades from Garrick's bandolier pressed into Nash's jugular. It was hard to tell over the flood of Rilk's blood, but I thought I detected the hint of a different tang. Garrick had already drawn blood.

Something I did not want to acknowledge as admiration spread through my chest. Garrick the Red was human, but he moved faster than any being I'd ever encountered. I was an immortal, and despite my active power and a thousand spells, I had never felt as powerful as I sensed him to be in that moment.

There was no indecision in the rough lines of his face. He was going to kill Nash without a second thought.

I envied that, too.

"I released her. Now you release me," Nash demanded.

Unwise to risk moving his throat at all with Garrick's blade that close, but I couldn't say that I would have been able to keep my mouth shut, either.

Garrick twisted his arm tighter. Nash's face contorted as he struggled to keep in the cry of pain.

"I made no such agreement," Garrick said. His face was unmoved. His expression had not changed at all in the last minute. The night turned his turquoise eyes to a sapphire so deep it was almost black. The line of his mouth, which had quirked up into a smirk more times than I could count in our short acquaintance, remained flat.

The lack of affect shouldn't have been menacing; it *should* have been neutral. But my stomach clenched… and my thighs squeezed together. *For fuck's sake,* I chastised my body.

"You can't kill me," Nash bit out.

"You probably shouldn't tell him what he can't do when he has you stuck like a pig for slaughter," I said. Nope, definitely could not have kept my mouth shut. But at least talking served to distract me from my body's very inconvenient reaction to Garrick.

"You're a bounty hunter. I can pay you," Nash said, trying to twist away from Garrick's blade. But Garrick was exactly what Nash had pointed out, and he was far too comfortable holding someone at knifepoint to allow them such an easy escape.

Garrick chuckled. I could not help but mark the difference from the sound that had caressed my senses in the temple. There was no humor here. No amusement. Only threat.

But Nash pressed on. "I have gold." No response. "Land. My father has plenty of it that he will cede on my behalf. Anything. Name it, and it is yours."

Garrick worked his jaw, slowly distorting the line of his mouth. Then again… as if he was actually mulling it over.

I did not consciously decide to make the sound low in my throat. But there it was, nonetheless. Garrick's mouth curved, just for me, before he shifted his eyes back to his captive. "There is nothing you have that I want badly enough to alter my course."

I blinked in the darkness. What the fuck did that mean?

"We weren't going to kill her," Nash insisted. He struggled again. He was stupider than even I'd estimated. I heard a faint crack. Any tighter, and Garrick would snap the bones in Nash's arm.

"What you wanted was worse than death," Garrick said. "To enslave her. Belittle her."

"Nothing is worse than death." The words slipped from my mouth unbidden, a whisper in the darkness.

Garrick's gaze remained on Nash, but a muscle tensed in his jaw. "Then death shall be his punishment."

"Don't!"

Garrick's head snapped up, and that smooth affect was gone. He looked right at me—because I was the one who'd screamed the protest. Not Nash.

A deep divot had taken up residence between Garrick's brows. Tendrils of pale hair fell forward to frame his face, a face that was ruggedly handsome but just then contorted into surprise and disbelief. It was still handsome, even so. Irritatingly so. But most marked was the intensity in his eyes. The same intensity I'd felt before now bored into me in a way that should have been impossible to detect in the darkness of midnight.

I could shape my frost into ice, but I had not used my power to freeze the three of us in the clearing.

Even Nash had stopped his squirming, staring at me in disbelief. At least, what he could see of me in the dark. I relaxed a bit. He could not see my face. With his human eyes, the best he could make out would be my silhouette. The uncontrollable emotions playing across my face were safe from both men.

"He was not going to kill me," I said. I was just as stupid as every human in the tavern, every human who attempted the gates. So fucking stupid. "He understands now. Let him go. The gates will kill him for us."

Us. That was the weapon I chose to wield.

I thanked the Dark God for his gifts, which allowed me to see how Nash's eyes widened when he realized the implication of that word. That from now on, I was not alone. A witch and Garrick the Red. He would not attack again.

Still, his heartbeat thundered in the night. For several beats, I thought Garrick would ignore my request. I understood that for what it was. Garrick could ignore me and kill Nash. For more than one of those heartbeats, I thought he would. Then his hold eased. He shoved the other man to his knees in the snow but did not restrain him any longer.

Nash swiped up his sword and clambered to his feet. The glare he cut in my direction was anything but grateful. But then he disappeared into the night and that was all that mattered. The ice I had not even noticed forming in my veins slowly began to thaw.

Garrick sheathed his blade, his head tilted ever-so-slightly in the direction that Nash had disappeared. Listening, I realized. He was determined to protect me even now, when the danger had passed.

Even when he no longer needed to. He'd saved my life, I realized.

That *us* I'd used against Nash was pure bravado, the Lifebind between Garrick and me was done. So quickly. Then why didn't I feel relief?

Still, I took a few steps closer so he could see me easier in the darkness and inclined my head. "Thank you."

His expression was anything but neutral as he turned and glared at me. "I don't want your thanks. I want you to stop being so naïve and thoughtless that you get both of us killed."

Naïve. I had walked this continent for nearly four hundred years, and this human had the audacity to suggest I was naïve? He could rot in the Dark God's hell.

"You saved my life, we are done." I reached to pull my cloak around me as a shiver of cold prickled my neck. But I did not have my cloak. Rilk had seen to that at the Mercy Gate. He could go to the Dark God's hell right along with Garrick the fucking Red.

He already has. Rilk is dead.

I could not bring myself to feel anything but relief about it. If I'd had a beating heart, it would have clenched and twisted at that moment. My stomach did the job instead.

I squeezed my fists at my sides and tried to ignore the shivers making themselves more demanding with every passing second. We were approaching the deepest, coldest part of the night. Without a cloak, the next two hours would be torture. But first I had to find another place to sleep. Rilk's reeking body was not the sort of bedtime companion I enjoyed.

I turned north, lifted my hand to harden the snow and make walking easier, and left Garrick the Red to his own problems. I was not one any longer.

"Check your wrist."

My feet stilled. Even my hand flicked, as if it too wanted to obey his command. What was it about this man that made all good sense desert me?

Whatever it was, I fought it hard. I refused to lift my arm, even as I realized that there had been no burn of magic or power. The dissolution of the Lifebind did not have to feel the same as the forming of it, I reasoned. The workings of the gods were rarely logical.

Garrick closed the space between us in two easy strides, grabbing my forearm with one hand and tugging off my glove with the other. Even without my stronger sight, I could see that hateful tattoo on the inside of my wrist. The lines of the rune were straight and true. A single line branched into three two-thirds of the way up. Then, alongside it, the same shape was copied in inverse. Garrick did not bother to pull down his own sleeve to show me that his was still intact as well.

"You saved my life for no purpose other than mercy, when doing so put you at greater risk by exposing yourself as a witch. You would have been safer to let me die. A true act of mercy," he breathed. He'd gotten so close to me that I could see every detail of his face. Not just the broad features, but the intimate ones as well. A half-moon scar no bigger than a fingernail that framed his right eye. The flecks of pure, clover green in his eyes that must be responsible for the turquoise they appeared to be at any distance other than this. The moonlight changed them even more, making it seem like the ring of slightly lighter blue around his pupil was glowing.

He released my arm, increasing the space between us enough that I could actually breathe as he exhaled and added, "I cannot say the same."

Right. He'd only saved me because it benefited him—because if I died, so did he. That wasn't mercy.

"There is no escaping the Lifebind until its terms are satisfied." His words were heavy—disturbingly so. They lacked the intensity or the menace that I'd come to expect from him.

"I could kill you, and then I would be free." I thrust my chin out in challenge.

"You could try," he said, the corner of his mouth quirked upward, that smirk back in place. "You'd risk the wrath of Seraxa after she's shown you such favor."

He emphasized the last word, infusing it with sarcasm. But his heart was beating faster than before, faster than it had been even when he'd held Nash at knifepoint. Despite the dark, I could see that the divot between his brows had not entirely smoothed. For once, my heightened senses provided me with an advantage rather than overwhelming me. They told me that Garrick the Red was hiding something.

I folded my arms beneath my breasts. "Why didn't you accept his offer?"

Garrick huffed a soundless chuckle. "I do not need gold or land."

How much of that acerbic humor was genuine and how much of it was a front?

"This is Velora. Those could be the very things that keep you alive from one week to the next—"

"He tried to kill you," Garrick said. "He does not deserve redemption."

The biting edge of humor was still there, but so was something else. Something that I could not quite account for, but I could read just the same. The way his jaw worked around the words, the rough sound of him clearing his throat of unnamed emotion.

"And that would kill you, by extension," I said slowly.

His smirk faltered.

He shifted forward, old snow crunching beneath his boots as he moved closer, trying to see me better in the dark with his human eyes. I did not try to disguise my face. I let the confusion show, my lips parting slightly, my eyes widening, as the full force of him flooded over me. The height discrepancy between us should have afforded more space, but his mouth seemed to hover mere inches from mine.

"You believe that our two lives are the only ones that hang in the balance," Garrick said.

I swallowed. His eyes slid down, watching the movement of my throat. He could not see me clearly enough for that, I reminded myself. But he must have heard the sound.

If I died, Kyrelle would as well. That was the only other life I cared about, I told myself.

But who did Garrick care about?

He had to mean Velora's citizens, didn't he? But Garrick had built a life by exploiting Velora's curse and those living under it. What reason could he have for wanting to lift it now? Yet he'd entered the temple and taken the Oath of Atonement, the same as every other supplicant.

What we did next, whether we survived the gates and lifted the curse, it was bigger than just the two of us. I could not deny that, but nor could I let the weight of all of Velora sit on my shoulders. If Garrick could, I pitied him.

Maybe that was how my coven sisters had always felt about me. It was too dark and cold to explore that line of thinking.

I sighed, my breath creating a cloud of mist between us as the world claimed the warmth my body surrendered. The sight of it sent another shiver through me. The layers of wool and linen and leather I wore just were not enough in that hour of cold.

Garrick moved again. Before I could make sense of it, a wave of pure darkness flashed before my eyes and something heavy settled over my shoulders.

It took me several seconds to comprehend what warmth felt like again. The scent of cinnamon and wine clung to the thick fur lining that brushed against my cheeks. The heat from his body still warmed the cloak as it settled into place around me.

I opened my mouth to thank him, but his words from earlier weighed my tongue down and kept it from forming the words. He did not want my thanks. Fine. That would not stop me from appreciating the warmth of his cloak. It dragged on the ground, but if he noticed, he did not point it out.

While I'd been busy reveling in the warmth, he'd already turned and taken a few steps, aiming slightly east of the direction I'd taken. Maybe he'd found a better place to sleep. Anywhere was an improvement on the stink of Rilk's blood. I did a quick sweep of the area with my eyes, looking for anything that I might have dropped in the attack.

Garrick was already halfway across the clearing when he turned back, smirk nowhere to be seen. "Let's go. We are not skulking around in last place."

I frowned, considering the meaning behind those words. He could not be implying that we keep walking, in the middle of the night. After the day we'd had at the Mercy Gate. And the attack I'd just survived.

"It is not a race," I huffed.

Garrick turned and kept walking. "Says the loser."

I stomped after him. "Is this a game to you?"

"These gates are dangerous. If you lose, you die. I would have thought you'd learned that lesson in the last day, if not the last hour. The sooner we get to the next temple, the more time we have to eat, rest, and avail ourselves of their healers. If you've failed to notice, I have not. You are a mess."

Any gratitude I'd felt for the cloak evaporated. The sooner we got to the temple, the less time he had to babysit me. That's what he meant.

I *was* a mess, but I hardly needed him to point it out. And I certainly did not need to be minded like a child. I was the senior here. I'd put his age at thirty or forty years; a man in his prime. But at three hundred and seventy-seven years since my resurrection, I was a witch in her full power. Or I would have been, if I had not been ousted from my coven.

Which Garrick had no way of knowing. Humans did not know the ways of witches. He could not know that my power was diminished, my very life in jeopardy the longer I remained on this desolate, cursed continent without my coven's communal power to sustain me.

Which meant he said all that just to irritate me.

I thought I had ice in my veins, but Garrick the Red made my blood *boil*.

Had I admired that smirk on his irritating face? Maybe I was naïve, though not for the reasons he'd insinuated. His life depended on mine, but Garrick did not like me. We were not friends or even allies. We were prisoners in the Lifebind.

Any smiles or smirks he directed my way? They were to serve whatever twisted purpose he had for attempting the gates in the first place.

I pulled the cloak around my shoulders and stomped off through the snow. "Let's go."

That was when an ominous thought occurred to me. I had my reasons for attempting the gates. But I still had not heard Garrick's. The more time I spent in his company, the less I was certain I wanted to.

CHAPTER 22

THE SECOND TEMPLE WAS JUST AS ORNATE AS THE FIRST. PER Garrick's insistence, we arrived first—even ahead of Alize, who'd cracked open her eyes to watch us pass her in the night before turning over in her bedroll and dismissing us entirely.

My legs hurt, my feet hurt, my ankles hurt, all from the never-ending, brutal task of keeping myself upright in the deep snow.

Garrick watched every agonizing, humiliating step. He hung back behind me, only entering the temple once I'd passed safely over the threshold. *Bastard.*

Once we were inside, he went straight to the blood fountain, waving down an acolyte to call for food. I muttered a spell under my breath, and the water and ice clinging to my clothing evaporated. I did not extend the courtesy to my new bonded. I'd already wasted my power on him once.

Without any of the other supplicants to watch me, I rolled my shoulders and stretched my arms overhead, trying to appease the aching muscles. Eat, and then sleep. The sun was well over the horizon now, but surely the priest or priestess who attended the Justice Gate would not force us through until the next day.

A plate of food arrived for Garrick. Maybe I would sleep first, just to avoid having to spend one more minute in his presence. I rolled my shoulders again, satisfied with the relief compared to the tightness of minutes before, and scanned past the altars in search of the entrance to the dormitory.

"You made it through!"

It took me a few seconds to place the voice. There had been so many new faces and names in the past few days, and this time I'd actually tried to remember most of them.

Tomin's name came to me as he pulled down the emerald hood, revealing his deep brown skin, riot of curls, and honey-gold eyes. The disappointment or other feelings he'd experienced at my harsh dismissal in the first temple were either forgotten or forgiven.

"You are probably wondering what I am doing here—"

I wasn't.

"—since acolytes are assigned to specific temples, while the priestess or priest moves along with the cohort of supplicants—"

Totally new information to me, and almost everyone else in Velora, I'd have wagered.

"—but Varian asked me to accompany her, since I am close to my final rites."

Varian. I assigned the name to the dark-haired priestess with the unnerving eyes who'd overseen the supplicants at the Mercy Gate. But two other words snagged in my mind.

"Final rites?" That was not possible. He could not be more than twenty years old, and acolytes spent at least a decade in training, sometimes as long as two.

I knew I was bad at hiding my emotions, but my surprise must have been even clearer than usual.

Tomin shielded his reaction much better than me, just as he had at the previous temple. He had not quite mastered the unshakable composure of Varian, his teacher, but it was still impressive. Especially when he explained.

"I was dedicated when I was five. My mother had another child and could not afford to feed us both. She kept the baby. It was a girl. She wished I'd been a girl. I have been here a long time." Tomin's throat bobbed, but he kept most of the emotion confined to his eyes. With such soulful golden eyes, I doubted he'd ever fully master Varian's mask of complacency.

"You must be talented to have advanced so quickly," I said.

Once, I'd been a young and eager newcomer. But that sort of energy and dedication came at a price. Something was always lost in the giving over of oneself fully to another entity, be it temple or coven.

Tomin inclined his head. I thought I saw a flash of thanks there, before his gaze dropped to the floor. An emotion he intentionally let through—for me. An offering I did not deserve.

"You must be hungry," he said.

I nodded, not trusting myself to talk. I had always been the youngest—sister, coven member. I saw too much of myself in Tomin, and that was dangerous. I had priorities already—protect Kyrelle, get back to my coven. Both of those depended upon me conquering the Seven Gates.

"You two arrived earlier than expected. No one will notice if you eat before you give thanks at the altars," Tomin explained, nodding toward the blood fountain. When he turned back, his eyes lingered between mine. The paste must have worn away from my coven mark. I had not bothered to reapply it. There hadn't been much point after the Mercy Gate. "Rest. I will get your food myself."

I wanted to protest the act of kindness. Insist I did not need it. Growl or hiss or do something to put distance between myself and the young man. But I was so tired. I let him lead me to the blood fountain. And when he appeared a few minutes later and sat down beside me while I ate, I did not protest.

CHAPTER 23

"STAY CLOSE," GARRICK SAID AS THE ACOLYTES SHEPHERDED US INTO line in a dark hallway identical to the one we'd occupied a few days before. If they wanted us to maintain our order, none of them dared argue with Garrick as he inserted himself behind me.

"You stay close," I bit back. It sounded childish even to my own ears. Despite a full belly and the warmth of Garrick's cloak, I had slept poorly in the temple. The brand of the Lifebind on my wrist itched like a healing wound, even though my skin was smooth.

"I have nothing to lose if you die," I reminded him.

"Except your protection."

I held open my hand between us, thankful for the darkness and relative quiet, which allowed me to focus my power until a dagger of ice formed in my palm, its hilt perfectly suited for my grip. "I can defend myself."

The corner of his mouth lifted. Whether that was approval at my weapon or amusement at my arrogance, either way, it annoyed me.

"That is not what you said the other night."

Alize laughed, the sound echoing through the darkened hallway.

Nimra looked over her shoulder, unable to ignore us any longer. The implication was enough to make me consider stabbing him with my new icy weapon.

The most irritating part was that I *had* been thinking of him when I fell asleep that night in the snow. It was his impossibly large hand I'd dreamed of sliding up my thigh in the moments before cracking ice had awoken me to the attack.

In the dormitory the night before, I'd tossed from side to side, sleep forestalled by the thoughts that refused to quiet. Was Garrick as conflicted as me? Who or what had compelled him through the gates? The more I thought on it, the more certain I was that the wellbeing of the continent of Velora was not sufficient motivation to force someone like Garrick through the gates. He had someone or something he cared for enough to abandon a life of abundance, albeit fraught with danger. It was just possible that there was more to Garrick than hulk and sarcasm and the next bounty. The empathy I tried not to feel for him, the connection… that was just as dangerous as the attraction. Intensified it, really.

Even in the dark corridor, about to walk out to the Justice Gate and whatever fresh horrors awaited, I wondered what he would taste like, if I could reach his lips if I stood on tiptoe, or if I'd have to thread my hands into his hair and tug him down…

A low chuckle filled the heavy air between us. The thought of stabbing him sounded better again. But if I had his protection, I'd be foolish not to take advantage of it.

So I hissed through my teeth instead.

Garrick stared down at me, pinning me in place with that intensity that I still had not found a way to escape. He didn't flinch away. His pupils widened—because the corridor was dark and his eyes were adjusting—not because of any rush of feeling or attraction. Despite the traitorous responses of my body, Garrick had shown absolutely no indication that the physical feelings were reciprocated.

And there was more than a little bite to his tone as he leaned into my space, completely unintimidated by me, and said, "Charming."

I gave him the back of my head.

Which earned another infuriating chuckle so low, I was certain I was the only one who could hear it.

Varian appeared at the front of the line, which acted as some sort of silent signal to the acolytes. We all moved out the door, the walls of green cloaks on either side guiding us. Tomin winked from my left before putting on his composed mask of neutrality.

I pulled my cloak—Garrick's cloak—tight over my shoulders as we exited into the frigid morning. At the Mercy Gate, we'd emerged into a different world, the buildings of Canmar wiped away by the gods. The Justice Gate did the same. Gone were the woods we'd trudged through the day before. The acolytes took up places behind us, forcing all the supplicants to turn and face the rising edifice.

The stone wall was unremarkable. Unlike the wall of ice, it did not expand outward endlessly in either direction. There was a round tower at each corner, crenulations overhead. A perfectly ordinary curtain wall in the standard configuration of a stone fortress. The Justice Gate was even wide open, the portcullis pulled up to allow passage. But I spotted easily what the others, with their human eyes, could not.

Dangling just inside the gate was a noose.

CHAPTER 24

"You enter as one."

That was all the direction Varian gave us before turning back toward the rear entrance of the temple. Unlike the Mercy Gate, she did not wait to see if we complied. Two guards—different faces but the same in every other measurable way—watched from a few feet behind the line of acolytes.

I avoided Tomin's eyes as I turned back to face the gate. I could not risk seeing whatever emotion he allowed to seep into those big, golden eyes.

I'd have hung back, watching the others approach and assessing my chances, despite what Varian said. But Garrick did not allow that. He cupped my elbow. I shook him off, but either way, we started forward.

"I bet we get to pick one of us to hang," Nash said as we passed beneath the portcullis.

"This isn't the Sacrifice Gate," Nimra bit back, but the rest of us remained silent.

Daylight brightened as we emerged into the courtyard of the fortress. Velora was lucky to get one day of sunshine in a month. It shone down on what we hadn't been able to see before. Not one noose, but five. One for each of us.

"Care to take another guess?" Nimra prodded, glaring at Nash. He gnashed his teeth at her.

Something more had happened between them since the Mercy Gate. But Nimra had not spoken directly to me since I'd revealed myself as a witch. The enmity was still there between the two of them, but Nimra's fear had transformed into something sharper. I hoped Nash had a bruise or wound somewhere as evidence, even if I couldn't see it.

The nooses dangled in an evenly spaced line. No platform was necessary. A wide trench cut into the ground on the other side of the wooden structure that held up the nooses. Beyond that, five chairs stood empty. Waiting.

Besides the five of us, not a single person was in the courtyard. No priest or priestess, no acolyte, no gods given form. Just us, five nooses, and five chairs.

Nooses or chairs. It was not a difficult choice.

Only when the last of us sat—Nash, unsurprisingly—did the courtyard spring to life. Doors on either side of the inner bailey opened to a flood of people. Women, men, children... dozens of children. I had to stop counting, the number of people growing too fast. More than a hundred, maybe two or three times that number. There were babes in arms, toddlers atop their parents' shoulders, boisterous boys, and preening teenagers moving between the adults. They filled the courtyard around us on all sides, their round faces smiling and laughing.

Round faces. Children. Mirth.

"They aren't real," I said softly, the realization twisting my breakfast inside my stomach.

"No, they couldn't be," Nimra said. For a brief second, our eyes met, sharing in the devastation of that realization. But that was it, all she gave me, and all I deserved before turning away.

"Be glad they aren't real," Garrick said from my other side.

I blinked, waiting for the others to react. But he'd said it quietly, for my ears alone. A private reassurance.

Because whatever the crowd had to do with the Justice Gate… it would not be kind.

A door I had not noticed before slammed open in answer to Garrick's prediction. Directly across from our chairs, on the other side of the trench and line of nooses, we had an unobstructed view as a new group of humans appeared. None of them smiled.

I'd assumed the five nooses were for us. But the new arrivals disabused me of that notion. Ten people emerged, walking in two paired off lines of eerie similarity to the one we'd formed exiting the temple. Five prisoners. Five jailers.

The prisoners wore little more than rags despite the cold. I counted off the other details, determined not to miss any more. Three men, two women. They ranged in age, from an elderly man at the rear to an adolescent girl who looked no older than Kyrelle. A middle-aged man bent in a terrible, hacking cough, his entire body spasming with the motion. His jailer showed no mercy, driving him on with a thick whap of his baton across his back. This certainly was not the Mercy Gate.

This was about justice. As the scene fell into place, the hairs on the back of my neck rose.

They aren't real, I told myself as the jailers positioned their prisoners, one behind each noose. But the longer I looked, the more horror dawned in my stomach.

Unlike the crowd of people around us, the prisoners were thin and ragged. I could count every one of the old man's ribs through the shirt that hung off of him in shreds. The girl at the front of the line now stood directly in front of Alize, shivering violently.

Shivering. Unlike the crowd of people around us, now moving to fill in behind the prisoners so they could watch the spectacle from every angle, the five people awaiting justice were very real.

I looked to either side, trying to see if the other supplicants had come to the same conclusion. On the far end, Alize's face was impenetrable. The sharp laughter from the corridor was completely gone, replaced by a mask of beautiful silence. Anger rallied the ice in my veins. Of course, this would not faze her. She was fae. Her kind had sentenced an entire continent to death. What were five more lowly humans?

Beside her, a slow smile grew on Nash's face. He realized what was about to happen and relished it. I let the frost loose; couldn't help it, didn't want to. I sent it crawling across the compacted dirt ground, wrapping around his ankles and snaking beneath his trousers. He jerked violently, leaning down to rip at his pants and find the source of instantaneous pain.

"Do not antagonize him," Garrick ordered from my other side in that harsh, low voice just for me.

I ignored him, and the slight tingle in my limbs in reaction to the way his voice scraped over those syllables.

Nash forgot himself, forgot the others around us. He tore at his boots, trying to undo the laces and rip them away to find the source of pain, those icy daggers of cold I drove into his ankles and calves.

"Koryn," Garrick said. "You let him live. Now you must pay the price."

My palms flattened, my power melting away. Nash cursed under his breath. On either side of him, Nimra and Alize stared at him like he was having a fit.

But my eyes met Garrick's, could not resist lifting and finding that intensity that I was coming to expect. It had been a long time since I'd met someone who looked right into my eyes, knowing what I was, without a drop of fear. Maybe that was the reason I could not keep my mouth shut.

"He is enjoying this," I hissed between my teeth.

"Aren't you, wicked witch? Don't your kind delight in torturing the unsuspecting humans who wander into your clutches? Those who seek your power but are unwilling to pay the price?"

Yes. The cost for crossing a witch or her coven was a painful death. But it was more nuanced than that. At least, it always had been for me.

I was spared having to explain myself by the first jailer, who banged his baton on the wooden structure beside him and called the crowd to attention. An excited hush settled over the not-real-humans around us. I turned forward with the rest of them. But beside me, Garrick was not so quick to move. I felt that intensity, still focused upon me, for more seconds than seemed necessary. Did he feel it too, the magnetic pull between us? It could be the Lifebind, the goddess-made tether. That was the safest explanation. The one that did not involve emotions and internal conflict and the tangible relief of finding someone who understood.

Relief eased through my muscles when he finally turned to join the rest of us.

It lasted mere seconds as the guard on the far left stepped forward, shoving his charge ahead of him. Last to enter, now first to face judgment.

He rammed his baton into the old man's back, sending him stumbling forward. He reached for the noose by reflex, a withered hand closing around the loop like it was a lifeline, not a threat.

Nimra lurched forward in her seat as if she would intervene, but she stilled the impulse.

The guard spat on the ground, narrowly missing the old man, before turning to us.

"This man is convicted of raping a woman who took shelter in his stable. He demanded payment in gold and having none, she could not help but refuse. Instead of offering her mercy, he took his payment by force."

In a few sentences, the prisoner before us was transformed. I no longer saw a weak, suffering old man. Instead, I noticed the deep scar that ran down the side of his face, still red and puckered and healing. Had the woman left it behind as she clawed at him to protect herself? He limped slightly, favoring his left leg. Another wound his victim had managed to get in?

In front, behind, all around us the crowd yelled and jeered. Fathers screamed justice for their daughters, women for themselves. How many of these women had suffered similar abuse at some point in their lives? Too many, I knew. Too many women were the victims of men.

They are not real.

"Dispense justice. The majority will determine his fate." The guard did not step back, but he lowered his head. A clear sign of deference to us, the decision-makers. Mere supplicants no longer.

Beside me, Nimra blinked in stunned silence. She'd sunk back fully into her chair. On my other side, Garrick remained upright and unmoved. His characteristic smirk was nowhere to be seen. Something inside of me released. He was not enjoying this any more than I was. Which did not quite fit—Garrick the Red was a bounty hunter renowned for his viciousness. He would take any contract so long as it paid.

And I was a witch, who'd stood by as her coven tortured humans for no crime worse than wandering unbidden into the coven lands. But I'd hated every moment of it. I could recount every death I'd been party to over the past three hundred and seventy-seven years.

Did Garrick keep his own mental tally?

I wished I could hide the revulsion that built inside of me. Not because the old man did not deserve to see it, but just because I wondered what it would be like, just once, to be fully in control. If Garrick felt any of that internal conflict, he masked it brilliantly.

"He dies. That is my vote," Alize said from the other end of the row of chairs. Her face, like Garrick's, was a study in immovability.

"Do it," Nash agreed. He kicked out his feet in front of him and crossed one ankle over the other. Regret turned my stomach. Maybe I should have let Garrick kill him. Not because I did not think the rapist deserved to die, but because Nash was so openly enjoying it.

But was I really any better? Because in the next second, I opened my mouth. "He hangs."

The roar of the crowd pitched even higher at my decree.

I could have waited. With Alize and Nash's decisions already made, I could have let Garrick or Nimra cast their votes. Mine might not have mattered at all. But I wanted my word to be the one that sentenced this man to death. He'd violated a woman. It was the next thing to murder, and I believed that he deserved to die. Even if I hated myself a little for it.

"Agreed," Garrick said from beside me.

"Yes," Nimra nodded.

Neither of them needed to say it. I knew neither of those votes had been cast for my sake, but I was thankful for them either way. The old man would have died, no matter what I had to say about it.

Before us, the old man transformed again, though this time it was not just in my imagination. His hateful face contorted with rage. "How dare you! You will all rot in the pits of hell—"

He never got to finish the threat. The jailer slipped the noose around his neck and kicked him forward over the trench. For a brief second, the crowd around us quieted. The old man sputtered, jerked, clawed for his throat, and then died. When that final spasm of life released, the people roared their approval.

His life force fled, a wisp of power that only I felt. The rotting pits of hell where his soul would dwell belonged to my Dark God. I could not see souls, but I felt their presence in the moment when they fled their fleshy bonds. For what was power, at its deepest definition, but life?

My heart did not beat, but I could still feel the rush of blood in my veins as the excitement of the moment ebbed. The sounds of the crowd dulled to anticipatory whispers while the second jailer nudged his charge forward. A pretty woman who appeared to be in her mid-twenties, her cheeks high with color despite the cold. Her mass of hair was matted, but I could see that the clothes she wore had once been opulent. A woman who came from means.

"This woman is convicted of crippling her sister's betrothed out of spite," he said to the group. "She saw that her sister had happiness within her grasp, and she ripped it from her because she could not have it for herself."

Tears spilled out of the woman's eyes, but she did not stumble like the old man before her. She kept her chin high as she stared us down.

Something colder than ice overtook me—veins, organs, skin. I might as well have turned to a block of solid ice as the other supplicants began to talk around me. I could not hear them, trapped within my own mind.

Maybe the woman standing there facing judgment and death had committed that crime. But so had I.

CHAPTER 25

BEFORE

"You cannot be here," Aurienna whispered, the words cushioned by the foliage all around us. It was unnecessary. The thick brick walls of the guildhall kept noises out as well as in. I could not hear what was happening, but I could see it through the windows.

"I am breaking no laws," I said without looking at her.

Despite the cold of midwinter outside, the guildhall shone with golden light. I'd never seen it decorated like that, with every chandelier alight, and all the sconces on the walls, too. Candles were becoming more and more dear. The expense to light the massive space so fully must have been exorbitant.

"You answer to no laws," Aurienna reminded me. She sighed, looking from side to side to make sure we were unobserved. But the wall of ivy she'd built up around us did its job well. We could not see out and no passersby would have any idea that two witches were concealed within the briar.

I ignored her. I had not broken the habit of thinking of myself as human, answerable to the laws that governed the human lands of Velora south of the mountains. And I'd been chastised about it enough.

"But you are breaking the covenants of sisterhood," she lectured, leaning into the brick wall beside the window, careful that she could not be seen by anyone within.

I had no such worry. They had hardly noticed me in life. They would not begin now, when I had become a nightmare.

The covenants of sisterhood. How many times had I heard those words in the past year? At least once per day, often more. Five hundred, conservatively. Five hundred reminders to abide by the covenants and rules of the sisters who'd resurrected me from death, who'd saved me from a meaningless afterlife and granted me great power.

Maybe if I'd ever experienced true sisterhood, the words would have had more meaning to me. But even before my mortal life was cut short, I understood that I was alone.

It was my death date. One year since my resurrection. And tonight, on the winter solstice, instead of mourning the sister she'd lost, Rylynn danced with her betrothed.

After Janessa's horrific death, she'd retreated into her bedroom for years. She'd ignored me, like my father had done since my mother's death two decades before. Maybe I would have been able to forgive her and move on, eventually. I was an immortal now, after all. But instead of mourning me as she had our sister, my death brought her out of her seclusion.

And instead of visiting my grave, she was in the center of the guildhall, arm in arm with a handsome man who matched her own eternal beauty. I did not recognize him, though that did not mean much. The family estate was not far from the sea. Though trade had slowed since the curse, with Velora's exports less predictable, there were always new faces along the coast. Especially with the fae gone. More human settlers had arrived from other continents, eager to farm the land and take over the cities the fae had abandoned.

That wouldn't last. One of my coven sisters had the active power of foresight. Killed by her own folly when she ignored her parents' warnings and snuck from her bed to meet a man, she now possessed the power to see into the future. She'd seen what the next hundred years would bring to Velora.

Standing there, watching Rylynn laugh in her betrothed's arms, the first thing I felt was pleased. Not that she was happy—but that her happiness would be short-lived. She would be old, but she'd live long enough to see Velora spiral downward into ruin.

"By clinging to your mortal life, you prevent yourself from fully accessing the gifts given to you by the Dark God," Aurienna said. She'd pressed her back flush against the brick wall now, her eyes scanning the darkness. Supposedly, she could hear and see what no one else could. One of those gifts she spoke of. But while I'd noticed some improvement in my hearing and sight—and I could certainly smell the refuse bins we'd had to climb past to reach the window—I did not see or hear whatever it was that caught her attention.

She lifted a finger to her lips.

I rolled my eyes and turned back to the window. What did I care if I was caught? I was nothing but a forgotten woman looking in on a world that did not belong to her. And, as I'd pointed out before, I broke no laws by watching.

The music stopped. How did I know that? Maybe my senses were sharpening more than I'd realized.

Because they stopped dancing.

The swirling pairs slowed, then moved to the edges of the hall to make room for the couple of honor. Rylynn glowed in a gold and green striped gown. The bodice cut low to show off her breasts, then cinched again at her tiny waist. Even a year on, she remained the perfect specimen of womanhood. Her breasts were generous but not lascivious, her waist trim instead of thick. Her delicate, pointed chin was the opposite of my round face. The only feature we shared was our lustrous dark brown hair. But while mine was loose in thick waves around my shoulders, Rylynn's was twisted into an elegant chignon at the nape of her neck. Jeweled clips decorated the coiffure. At least she had not allowed my father to crown her with another fae heirloom.

Or maybe I was wrong about that, too.

I'd expected to find my family in silent vigil beside my grave. Instead, my father stepped up to the young couple. He cupped Rylynn's face. Shook the gentleman's hand.

My stomach twisted in anger. I still expected to find my heartbeat thundering in my chest. But instead, a rush of cold power suffused my body. It poured into my veins and clouded all of my senses.

Aurienna sensed the shift. She straightened, her focus divided between me, the image through the window, and the wall of ivy that separated us from the rest of the world.

"They do not need you," she said, pitching her voice low. No one could hear us, but there was a gravity to it. It was anything but accidental. "They do not need you," she repeated. "But we do. Your sisters do."

"My sisters are gone. One is dead. One..." *has forgotten me altogether.*

Aurienna shook her head fervently, tendrils of blonde hair flying forward across her face. "Your sisters wait for you to join us. To claim your full power."

I could feel that power inside of me, waiting to burst free. The ice was thick in my veins, sharp. I wanted to let it out, to feel the world around me tremble for all that had been taken.

"I want it."

Aurienna exhaled, her face settling into certainty. Not quite pride, but satisfaction. She'd been the one sent after me when I tried to slip away from the coven, foolishly running back in search of my mortal life. And she would be the one to bring me back—not just back, but forward.

A tendril of ivy snapped free, its curved end flattening to point to the scene still unfolding through the window. My sister and her betrothed held court like a prince and princess while well-wishers approached them, embracing and smiling, laughing. More laughing than I'd ever been privileged to in the twenty-three years of my life and one of my death.

Aurienna's gaze followed the tendril of ivy. "Sever the bond."

I understood what she meant. Sever the bonds that held me to my family. Cut out the festering wounds of my humanity.

Light caught on one of the jewels in Rylynn's hair, reflecting through the window and catching me in the face. For one second, I was frozen. Unable to move, to think, to be. And then the ice broke free.

It shattered the window, sliced through the wall of ivy my coven sister had created as if it had not been there at all. But it did not stop there. Icy power exploded out of me in shards. The frost had claimed my life. Now I claimed my power.

The candles in the guildhall extinguished at once, their flames suffocated by a frozen wind. People jumped out of the way of the glass from the window that shattered inward, avoiding the worst of it.

But not my sister's betrothed. He jumped in front of her, protected her. The way no one had ever protected me. My power responded to the rage I felt for the girl I'd been, who died alone in the woods. My frost slid not just into his skin, but into his veins and then his very bones. I crushed them, twisted them, held them immutably in place. He crashed to the ground, his knees unable to catch him, the bones in a state of permanent frozen fracture.

Aurienna's hand closed around my wrist. "We must go."

The torrent of ice stopped as suddenly as it had begun. I had only seconds to blink, to take in the damage I'd wrought. But even though the power no longer flowed from me, the frost and ice remained.

Aurienna pulled harder. She muttered a spell beneath her breath, and suddenly my feet began to move without my permission. But she could not stop my head from turning, from looking back over my shoulder, or hearing Rylynn's scream as terror unfolded behind us.

I did not know how to pull it back. I would not master that skill for decades. So, his spine remained permanently frozen in place. His legs remained unmoving. I stole the happiness my sister had found. But instead of keeping it for myself, I drowned us both in misery.

CHAPTER 26

"Dispense justice. The majority will determine her fate."

The crowd jeered, though the pitch was distinctly female. The men were persuaded by the woman's beauty, convinced by the show of remorse.

I looked at her again, trying to make sense of what I was seeing. Maybe the prisoners were all illusions, created by Edravos, the God of Justice, just like the crowd. If that was true, there was no risk in assigning every one of the five to death.

But I'd felt the old man's life force flee his body.

Or was that another clever bit of work from Edravos?

"Just kill her and be done with it," Nash said, waving his hand over his still-crossed feet. He looked like he ought to be drinking a glass of wine or a pint of ale. Snacking on grapes. Casual, where Nimra's posture was tense, Alize's carefully upright, and Garrick… I avoided looking his way at all.

"Isn't that excessive? She hurt someone. She did not murder them," Nimra argued.

My eyes went back to the woman who'd been charged with my

crime. Whether she'd actually committed it or not, we would have to judge her. That was what the Justice Gate required.

But if she'd been charged with my crime... who had committed the rape we'd just punished the old man for?

Nash.

Every muscle in my body tensed, ready to spring forward—when a hand landed on my arm.

"Do not move."

The effort I'd made to avoid looking at Garrick evaporated. I swung back around, tried to rip my arm free from his grasp, and failed utterly. My power immediately flared in response, my skin turning cold enough to burn. But he did not even flinch.

"You do not command me."

His hand was burning. I knew it was. It would start off pink, then deepen to red. If he was stubborn enough, the skin would turn black and start to flake away and die. He could lose his entire hand to his effort to keep me in that damn chair.

"If you want to survive the Justice Gate, you will stay in that chair."

He wasn't afraid of Nash, I realized. He worried about the wrath of the gods if I tried to walk away. *A gate is always near. A god is always watching. Especially now.*

Nimra raised her voice behind us. "I will not sentence her to death."

"Hang her," Alize's cold voice said from Nash's other side. All three of them turned their eyes to Garrick and me.

He made no rush to take back his hand. He let the others see how he held on to me, see that I did not push him away. Then he leaned back in his own seat and crossed his arms over his chest. He may as well have stamped the word 'mine' across my wrist along with that damn Lifebind.

If it kept that rapist away from me, then I wouldn't even protest. Much.

He shifted his gaze to the woman standing beside the noose,

awaiting her fate. Behind us, the bystanders closest leaned in so they could hear every word we uttered. It had felt so refreshing to see so much life when the crowd first flooded in. Now, every face I saw felt like a needle jabbing into my skin. They were a reminder, meant to make this worse as we judged others for the crimes we'd committed. And made an irrevocable choice for justice.

If Garrick understood or suspected what was really going on, he gave no outward sign. Nash was reveling in the spectacle, Alize was above it, and Garrick looked like a man who was comfortable with it. At home with brutality. Not enjoying it, but unmoved.

That was all a part of the curse of Velora.

"Let her go," he said.

Two votes for freedom. Two for death. A tie was impossible. Hundreds of pairs of eyes swung to me.

I'd had three hundred and seventy-six years to think about what I had done to my sister. There was no doubt in my mind what justice meant in that moment.

I balled my hands in my lap and prayed to the Dark God. "Hang her."

THE MIDDLE-AGED MAN with the cough was next. He was convicted of stealing bread when the baker stepped away to care for a sick child. If Nash was the rapist, me the terrible sister, it was an easy guess that Nimra was the one who was guilty of this crime. In comparison to the first two, it barely registered. Everyone but Nash voted to release the prisoner.

Which left Alize and Garrick. The crimes were too specific to be coincidental, which meant that Nash, Nimra, and I all understood that each of the crimes belonged to one of the five supplicants sitting in judgment.

I stared straight forward, trying my best not to look at the others, to ignore the crowd, to not remember what the weight of

Garrick's hand on my arm had felt like. I hated the commands he issued with such pugnacity. But for the minutes his hand had laid on my arm, holding me in place, I had not felt alone.

A guard urged forward the adolescent girl. Her face had turned an indelicate shade of green. I braced my hands against my thighs.

"She is convicted of attempting to murder her infant sibling in their cradle."

Nimra choked. Everyone around us screamed for the young woman's death. At my side, Garrick gave nothing. He did not reach for me, he did not smirk, his eyes did not take on that strange glow I'd noticed from time to time. On the opposite end of our row of chairs, Alize was as aloof as ever.

I'd crippled my sister's betrothed in a fit of jealous power. But this…

The crime was particularly heinous given the nearly non-existent birth rate in Velora. But it was only an attempt. No actual murder had been committed.

Nash voted for death. Nimra did, as well.

They both looked to me, expecting the two possible perpetrators on either end to keep their silence. But before I could speak, Garrick did.

"Release her," he said. His eyes were not on the girl who'd committed the crime, but on Alize. That heavy gaze meant something, but his face gave no clue as to what.

Alize lifted her chin. "Release her," she echoed.

Again, the vote came to me.

What did Edravos want in this moment? I had not spent much time paying homage to the God of Justice, in life nor in death. It was possible that my task had already been completed when I passed judgment on the prisoner accused of my own crime. But maybe this decision was just as important.

But Edravos was not what swayed my vote. It was Nimra. She watched me, as did all the others, but her eyes held more. I sat in judgment of the young girl, but Nimra sat in judgment of me. She was trying to decide if I was as wicked of a witch as every story she'd been raised on… or if the kindness she showed me before the Mercy Gate had not been misplaced, after all.

That made my decision. "Release her."

Disappointment pulled Nimra's brows together, tugging down the corners of her lips.

I did not need friends. I was already saddled with Garrick. Proximity to me would just get Nimra killed sooner. I did not need that on my conscience, whatever was left of it.

I told myself I would not look in either direction during the next vote.

The last prisoner dragged forward was tall and slight, not unlike Rilk had been. It was the first thought I'd had for the supplicant who'd tried to kill me not once, but twice. Thankfully, it did not elicit any emotion that I would have struggled to hide.

The convicted looked left to right, eyes widening as he took in the crowd and his jurors. The not-really-humans around us had become restless with the whole spectacle. They hadn't appreciated our release of the young girl. They began to jeer before the man's crime had even been stated. They wanted to end on blood.

The black-clad jailer elbowed his charge forward. The man swerved to the side, trying to avoid touching the noose. But his jailer jerked him back into place, so that the loop of rope circled his face, resting against his chin in ominous promise.

"This man is convicted of the death of a family of seven. He poisoned two parents, a grandfather, and their three adult children, one of whom was with child. All died."

The roar of the crowd turned deafening.

I resisted the urge to look to either side. Neither Alize nor Garrick would show any clues. I wondered if the others had narrowed down the possibilities for the perpetrator among us, as well. Maybe that was part of the challenge. We would carry this knowledge with us beyond the Justice Gate.

I kept my gaze carefully trained on the man. His throat bobbed up and down, his jaw working, eye twitching. I could easily imagine him as a poisoner.

Gender was not a clue. The man we'd let go free had committed Nimra's crime. So it truly could have been either of them. Neither spoke to motive, not really, not in a way that fit with what I'd experienced of either of them so far.

But Garrick had to be the poisoner. He was a bounty hunter. We all knew it. He must have committed all kinds of sins in his jobs for hire. Though maybe that was a trick from Edravos, as well, to assign a crime that we would all naturally attribute to one supplicant but that truly belonged to another.

None of that changed the crime of the man before us. An entire family was dead by his hand. The members of the crowd were not the only ones desperate to conclude the ordeal.

Nimra— "Hang."

Nash— "Hang."

Alize was already halfway to her feet. "Hang."

My vote was immaterial.

In the space of an exhale, the guard tugged the noose tight and shoved the man out over the trench. My hands balled into fists, bracing for the scream of the crowd.

But none came. In a blink, the crowd had disappeared. The jailers, too. The courtyard of the fortress was entirely empty except for the three bodies dangling over the trench, and the five of us that had condemned them.

I could not help looking around at the others. Nash was already halfway to the gate, an open portcullis that had appeared in the solid stone wall behind us.

Alize stood, peering down into the trench as if checking that nothing was going to leap out at us when we tried to walk away. Garrick had taken a similar stance, though he scanned the perimeter and the crenulations on the curtain wall, checking for a last-minute twist.

"None of us died. We weren't even injured or in any real

danger. I do not understand," Nimra said, now avoiding my eyes, speaking to no one and everyone.

Her crime was stealing bread. Of course, she did not understand. The person convicted of her crime was released. It was an easy decision.

But for the rest of us, the Justice Gate was meant to inspire terror. To force us to reckon with the darkest parts of ourselves and pass judgment that would be inflicted not on us, but on another—

Guilt washed through me, so powerful I nearly fell from my chair as the true gravity of what I'd done hit me. I had not sentenced a woman justly to death.

I'd punished her for my crime. Not her own. I had no idea what context surrounded her actions. I could have shown mercy. But this was not the Mercy Gate, and I'd shown none. I'd sentenced her for the crime that *I* committed, to the fate I believed that *I* deserved—but had been too cowardly to bestow upon myself.

I deserved to be punished for the happiness I'd stolen from my sister. Instead, I'd lived for nearly four hundred years. Instead, I'd sentenced a woman to death to assuage my own guilt.

I turned my head and emptied my stomach into the dirt.

I left my head hanging there, accosted by the scent of my own sick. Waiting, hoping that there was some twist of fate. That there was a final punishment the gods would inflict for the crimes we had all committed. But they'd already played their game, and now I understood just how truly I'd lost.

Death was too good a punishment for me. Living with the guilt was what I deserved.

"Not all wounds are physical," Alize said.

Nimra did not have the same scars on her soul as the rest of us. For her, the Justice Gate had been unpleasant. For me, it was devastating.

PART III
SACRIFICE

They chase their will beyond all bounds,
And reap the debt they sow—
In loss they find the cost of pride,
To sacrifice the soul.

CHAPTER 27

The acolytes sent us on our way with a small parcel of food each, enough for four days' worth of meals between the Justice Gate and the Sacrifice Gate. Hopefully, the packs would get larger when we reached the later gates, where weeks of travel would stretch between one gate and the next. If we had to hunt or depend upon our own resources, the gates might not be the thing to kill us.

Garrick moved easily with his pack attached to his back. I was slow. He did not seem to care. He set a grueling pace as we turned northwest, following the curve of the mountains toward the Sacrifice Gate. The forest thickened as we moved into the foothills, providing cover from the falling snow that started midafternoon. At least it did not add to the deep layer that already covered the ground.

"You could use your power to make it easier for yourself," Garrick suggested about midday.

"You could keep your mouth shut about things you know nothing about," I shot back.

I could have used my power. But touching it felt abhorrent.

After everything I'd put my sister through, after the death I'd condemned that woman to in the Justice Gate, I did not deserve to have things easier.

My own misery kept my mouth shut for the rest of the day, even when Garrick pushed us through dusk and did not stop to make camp beneath a knot of evergreens until the sun was well below the horizon.

Garrick made a fire. I created a bed for myself using the thick cloak and the pack of food. My muscles ached, but not quite as badly as they had before the Justice Gate. I settled into my nest and told myself I was watching Garrick to judge his reaction to what we'd endured.

He moved with precise movements that spoke of experience. He'd built a thousand fires. His pale blond hair had come loose over the course of the day. Once the kindling had caught, he paused to loosen the knot at the back of his head and retie it. He left half of it loose, as usual, falling just to his shoulders. Despite the fact that we'd both spent the day hiking into the mountains, those shoulders were solid and moved steadily. No quakes of tired muscles for him.

I cursed my immortal body.

Fae could live for nearly a thousand years. Not true immortals, but for that span of time they enjoyed unnatural strength and speed, heightened senses, and swift healing abilities. Witches could live forever. True immortality. Our organs never wore out, our faces did not age from the time of our resurrection. But while the Dark God gifted us with power and sharpened senses, we could die as easily as humans. We suffered their ailments as well—sickness, exhaustion. Because while fae were born with their gifts, witches carried a curse of our own — the legacy of humanity. We were all born of woman and man.

I was so busy watching Garrick's mortal body and lamenting the faults in my immortal one that I did not actually track what he was doing until he shoved a bowl into my hands.

The confusion must have shown on my face.

"You have not eaten at all today," he said, crossing his arms over his body. He stared down at me expectantly. Like a child.

And like a petulant child, I placed the bowl untouched in the snow beside me. "I am not hungry."

For once, it was true.

Since heaving my breakfast on the ground of the fortress, the thought of food was impossible. Even if a headache was beginning to form at the base of my skull. I sipped some water instead.

Garrick turned that intense stare at me, like he was trying to see into my soul. Which he could not do, I reminded myself. Even if he could, my insides were in such disarray even I could not make sense of them.

For once, though, I stared right back. He'd been at the Justice Gate, too. He'd heard the crimes. No matter which one he suspected belonged to me, they were all heinous.

But one of them belonged to him. Maybe he felt as turned around as I did.

The longer he stared, the more I doubted it. Despite my earlier ruminations on the state of his soul, the events of the day had me wondering if Garrick the Red felt anything—except annoyance with me.

He was the one who broke the stare. He picked up the bowl from the snow and walked back to where he'd set his things on the other side of the fire. But instead of sitting down to eat, he swiped up the bandolier of weapons he'd dropped to the ground earlier and buckled it across his chest.

"What are you doing?" I asked as he returned to my side of the fire, dragging his foot through the snow in a wide arc.

"If you are not hungry, then you will work up an appetite." He stood at the edge of the circle he'd drawn in the snow. "Get out your knife."

He wanted me to fight him. After a day of trudging through the snow, after the hell of the Justice Gate, with only breaks to relieve myself? Not fucking likely.

"I have plenty of reserves," I said. Without thinking, I rolled my shoulders, putting my full breasts on display. As if they could be hidden.

Garrick shifted his weight, looking away quickly. The firelight reflected off of his hair, turning the blond nearly silver, and into his eyes as they scanned the clearing he'd selected. I'd never seen a color like that, where the turquoise almost glowed when in the right light.

If I did not know how much he detested being saddled with me, I might have mistaken that glint for interest, especially given how quickly he looked away. You could be attracted to someone and still detest them. The way my stomach flipped as he reached his arms overhead, the muscles of his chest shifting beneath his shirt and vest, was an infuriating example.

"You should learn to use your size to your advantage," he said, selecting a curved blade the length of my forearm from his bandolier.

I actually laughed aloud. But I also came to my feet.

"I barely reach your shoulder." I stepped closer to him to prove the point.

He did not move, nor lift his blade from where it hung in a deceptively loose grip at his side. "Opponents will underestimate you because of your height."

I'd been underestimated my entire life. Human, woman, witch.

"Use your weight as a weapon. Put it behind your punches and your stabs, and you will be able to take down opponents much taller than you."

My fingers tingled with power, but I did not reach for the dagger tucked into my belt. "Like you?"

His eyes narrowed, the turquoise flaring impossibly between cerulean and emerald. "The day you can take me down is the day your Dark God walks upon Velora."

I forgot that I was determined not to use my power. It was so much a part of me that I summoned it without thinking, letting it form the dagger of ice in my hand from just that morning. How had so little time passed, and yet so much occurred?

I let the hilt melt just a little, reforming around the shape of my palm. "Cocky words for a human."

That infernal smirk curled the corner of his mouth, lifting the little half-moon scar near his eye as well. "You have not yet shown me a part of yourself that I fear, witch."

He swiped up with his blade, catching my wrist and knocking the ice dagger loose with ease. I cursed, jumping backward just in time to prevent that dagger from coming down on my shoulder.

I did not have time to create another before he was on me again. I sidestepped, but Garrick used his height to yank me back by the neck of my leather tunic. I was so grossly overmatched that it was pathetic. Unless I was willing to unleash my full power, he would always best me.

He might even then, a small, hateful part of me whispered.

I had already proved myself a coward once today. What did it matter if he thought me one now? His next jab skated off my cheek. I'd barely tried to sidestep it.

Garrick pushed into my space, annoyance building on his face. The tightening of his jaw. The flicker by his eye. I did not even flinch as he pulled another blade from his bandolier and pressed it into my palm. "Fight me like you mean it."

I curled my fingers around it because I was afraid that if I didn't, it would fall to the ground and stab me in the foot. Not because I liked the way it felt to have a blade that close to him.

I should have been cold. I'd barely moved, and the fire wasn't throwing off much heat. But my entire body tingled with awareness. Another natural reaction. And instead of hating myself, I turned that hate back on Garrick. How dare he make me feel alive when I'd sentenced that woman to death?

"I don't want to fight you at all," I hissed, my breath clouding the cold air between us.

He did not retreat, lifting his curved blade so that it was positioned just beneath my ribcage. With one shove, he could have hit a vital organ that would have me bleeding out in the snow.

"Because you blame yourself for their deaths?" he pressed the tip of his blade into my tunic along with his words.

I did not move. Let him fucking kill me. He'd die, too, thanks to the brand inked on the inside of our wrists. And maybe the world would be a better place because of it.

But Kyrelle would die. The curse would linger over Velora. I would die a disgrace and disappointment to my coven.

When that wound did not work, Garrick pressed against another. He understood perfectly what Alize had meant. "Aren't you afraid? You're too clever not to have figured out that those crimes belonged to the supplicants."

He should be scared of me. I'd ruined my sister's life—a sister who'd ignored me for years, but who had lost just as much as I had. Rylynn had not been innocent, but she certainly had not deserved the life I'd condemned her to. A man she married out of love, who would forever blame her for what had happened to him. A marriage that turned to duty and then to something much darker.

"You cannot kill me," I reminded him, even as he pressed the tip of his knife through the first layer of clothing with precise pressure.

Past the leather, then through the wool underdress. "The other supplicants can."

I shoved him away, two fists to the middle of his chest. He moved quickly enough to avoid the end of the dagger he'd placed in my hand. I tucked it into my belt. I did not need a blade to do damage.

I ripped off my leather gloves, throwing them down into the snow. I did not technically need my hands bare to access my power, but it always felt more real, more visceral. More powerful.

I threw my hands out, plumes of ice flowing from my palms to encircle his legs and hold him in place. But Garrick moved quickly, anticipating the move like he'd seen it before. He shifted his center of gravity lower to keep his balance and used the same ice I'd laid down to increase his speed, sliding toward me with inhuman speed.

He wanted me to fight? Fine. I'd fucking fight. If it could wipe that self-satisfied smirk away from his face, I'd drive one of my ice daggers into his gut. But before I could summon one, he'd reached me, delivering a punishing blow to the back of my knee. My leg gave beneath me. I did not even have time to soften the ice on the ground, pain screaming as my full weight landed on the joint.

But now I had rage to fuel me. I did not aim for his feet, but his chest. A blast of frigid wind knocked him back long enough for me to invade *his* space. He recovered too fast. I swiped the new blade from my belt, determined to draw blood. But Garrick grabbed my belt with one hand, dragging me forward and throwing me completely off balance, while his other hand swung up and caught my wrist, holding it tight over our heads.

I hadn't even noticed him dropping or throwing or sheathing his own blade. He had me, one arm pinned between our bodies, the other overhead. Fury raged through me, ice cold. I tried to rip my hands free, but he held me tight.

"That is what I meant," Garrick breathed, our faces too close for the words to form a cloud of condensation. The fury inside of me threatened to melt with the heat of his body, flush against mine. "Good girl."

My blood thrummed wildly through my veins, my pulse points pounding with a new, hotter fire than the cold power that had hummed through them seconds before.

Garrick's eyes flared wide, his mouth curling upward. Not a smirk, but a smile. The first genuine smile I'd seen on his face. His fingers were folded right around the pulse point on the inside of my wrist, right beneath the tattoo that marked our bond.

"Good to know," he murmured.

For a second, I considered closing that space between us. I'd challenge that infuriating smirk. I'd take what I wanted from him—his mouth, his touch, to have him as out of control as I was. I would drive him there, make him experience all of the agony I did. But... why? What would I gain? What would I do, other than make the impossible situation between us worse?

I ripped my arm free, and this time he let me go. "What is the point?"

Without asking, I knew that he understood the question was bigger than this moment of ill-conceived training he'd tried to force upon me. He didn't answer, and he did not try to regain the space I'd put between us. He reached down, retrieving his curved blade from the ground and tucking it back into place across his chest.

"You will die," he finally said, dropping down on his side of the fire and picking up the bowl of food I'd turned down. "We will die."

I watched him eat through the flames. My stomach rumbled, but I had no desire to feed it. The weight of the day pressed in on me, making even sitting up too painful to bear. "You were at the Justice Gate. You heard the crimes," I said as I settled in, pulling the fur-lined cloak up over my shoulder. "Maybe we don't deserve to live."

CHAPTER 28

HE WAITED UNTIL I'D BEEN ASLEEP FOR WELL OVER AN HOUR. I DID not know Garrick well enough to detect his tells, if he had any at all. But that disadvantage worked both ways. He did not realize I was feigning sleep. Not because I did not trust him, but because I couldn't handle another argument. All I wanted was silence.

As for the existence of trust between us… I trusted that Garrick cared about his own life enough to protect mine. Whoever or whatever had pushed him through the gates only bolstered that motivation. If he was feeling reckless with his life, there were easier ways to die in Velora than the Seven Gates. But apparently that feeble trust was not returned, because once he felt certain I was asleep, he snuck away into the woods.

And because the Dark God had a well-known appreciation for torture, he started hiking up the mountain, rather than down it.

I dragged myself up, leaving the thick cloak behind. Its heavy layers caught too easily on the forest brambles. My body protested the exertion as we hiked up the mountain, reminding me rudely that I'd hardly eaten in the last day. Despite my boasts to Garrick earlier, the only reserves I had when I got hungry were temper and sass. A winning combination.

But I pushed on, moving as quickly as I dared. Little puffs of snow softened my footsteps, a slow but steady release of power that actually felt soothing rather than draining. I used my power only because without it, Garrick would have caught me in a second. We climbed for nearly an hour. I was ready to give in and start the trudge back down the mountain when I heard voices.

Garrick had snuck away to meet with someone.

A few careful steps to conceal myself behind a tree later, and I recognized the voice. He'd gone to all this trouble to meet with Alize.

Fae bitch.

CHAPTER 29

BEFORE

A WITCH'S POWER ORIGINATED FROM TWO SOURCES—THE DARK GOD and her coven. Her active power, derived from the manner of her death, was a gift directly from the king of hell himself. But her ability to cast came from her coven. Their collective power fueled every spell, whether uttered by one or all.

A witch is nothing without her coven.

She may utter the words, but the power would be weakened and temporary. The coven itself was only as strong as its weakest member. Its rules must be obeyed at all costs, or the power of the whole would suffer.

A witch is nothing without her coven.

Maura drove those words into me night after night. They were my new lullaby, the only prayer I said to the Dark God that had subsumed all others.

When my thoughts turned to my past, to the family I'd left behind, the sister whose life I'd ruined, Maura had an answer for that as well.

"You have true sisters now," she murmured, catching a lock of my dark hair and pulling it free from where I'd tucked it behind my ear. "Sisters who truly understand you, as your others did not."

Witches, who'd suffered violent or brutal deaths like me. Whose veins flowed with ancient power. Who had all managed to master their power. All except for me.

"Control will come," Maura said, sitting back and nodding.

With a flick of her wrist, Aurienna transformed the singular stem on the ground between us into a beautiful, vibrant flower. She never spoke of what death had given her such extensive power over plants. I never asked.

Maura made no secret of hers. With a tilt of her hand, the bloom turned to ash.

Maura had been burned at the stake.

"Focus," Maura breathed.

Weeks had blurred into months and then years, every single one of them narrated by Maura's commands. Control. Sisters. Coven. Focus.

I focused my attention on the bare space between us, attempting to block out everything else around me. I told my ears to ignore the whispers of my sisters, sitting at each point of the pentacle around us. Ordered my eyes to see nothing but the bare patch of stone. But the details seeped in. Elodie's hum of disapproval from behind me. The scent of the pine soap Maura used to wash her springy black curls.

Focus. Control.

A trail of frost spread from my fingertips, coating the ground in a thin layer of iridescent sparkle.

"More," Maura urged.

The frost thickened, turning to ice.

The murmuring from my sisters increased.

"Now shape it." Maura's voice rose with excitement.

I'd spent hundreds of silent dawns alone, practicing this exact exercise of power. I'd formed lethal daggers, soft snowballs, delicate wine glasses, and more. But only when I was alone. Only when I could maintain control.

Wood snapped somewhere to my left. A swish, and then the scent of wine. Tiny cracks started to form in the layer of ice.

"Your power answers to you. Control it." Maura's voice had taken on a harder edge.

I dug my teeth into my lower lip, trying to center every sense on the frost and ice in front of me. But I could not keep everything else from pressing in.

Someone cracked her fingers. The ashes of the flower Maura had burned stank of brimstone. It was going to rain soon. That was petrichor pushing in with the fog—

The ice shattered, tiny shards flying out in every direction. My coven sisters dove out of the way or threw up walls of power to counter mine. Maura did no such thing. She let the icy needles pierce her skin, drawing blood at her temple, chin, and collarbone. Little streams of scarlet opened up as the shards melted against her burning skin.

I could feel the heat of her anger. She did not bother with words. Maybe she knew that nothing she said could be worse than the litany of disappointment I would heap upon myself.

I'd known it would end this way. But I'd dared to hope this would be the day I was something other than a disappointment.

I should have known it would end this way. It always did.

CHAPTER 30

"Where have you left your little witch?" Despite the query, Alize's tone was bored, each word punctuated by the rhythmic *thwap* of a blade being sharpened across a leather strop.

"Somewhere safe," Garrick bit out. I was coming to recognize his tones of voice, I realized. Especially the annoyed ones.

Alize kept sharpening. "Learned to set wards, have you?"

No response.

The magic of ward-weaving had left Velora along with the fae. But Garrick was not from Velora. Garrick the Red had only been a name of note here for the past fifteen, perhaps twenty, years. I'd never heard the name of his land of origin. Perhaps he came from a place still rife with magic, where the fae still ruled on high. Maybe he'd bartered for some of their secrets before coming to seek his fortune in Velora.

"You went to all the trouble to track me up the mountain. I assume you have something to say or do other than glower at me."

"You know what I am going to say." This tone was similar to the one he'd used when urging me to eat. I pictured his face in my mind—jaw locked, a slight flicker in the vein by his temple.

"Then save us both the time, and yourself the wasted exertion, and say something else." *Thwap. Thwap. Thwap.* She repeated the movement again and again. How much sharpening could her fancy fae-made blade really need? Unless she was honing more than one.

"Walk away."

Alize sighed. "Sticking with that, are we?"

"I am not telling you to return to Balar Shan, Ali," Garrick said. Heavy footsteps moved through the snow. He approached her as he spoke. "I know what awaits you there. I understand your reticence to return. But you can walk away from the Seven Gates without going back."

For a time, my mind added.

Even as another part of me screamed.

She was more than an acquaintance. If the content of his words had not revealed it, the emotion behind them did. That was a tone of voice Garrick had never directed at me.

Metal sang in the air, the unmistakable sound of a blade leaving its sheath. "I pledged my life to the Seven Gates, just as you did. I cannot walk away."

Whatever emotion lined Garrick's voice, there was no mistaking the anger in Alize's. It had not ended well between them.

Had Garrick entered the temple to protect her? Had he come to Velora… and fallen in love with a fae? I dug my fingernails into the tree bark that held me upright. No wonder he was so surly and annoyed with me. He'd come for a beautiful fae female and ended up saddled with a witch.

The tree behind me shook violently, suddenly, a sharp thud reverberating through the forest and echoing off of the sheer stone cliffs that rose overhead. Someone had driven a blade deep into the wood.

"You cannot be here," Garrick growled behind me.

The blood in my veins turned to ice.

Following him had been a mistake. He may be human, but he

was still Garrick the fucking Red. He'd killed witches and fae alike, if the stories were true. The longer I knew him, the less I doubted. He could not kill me for following him and learning his weakness, but he could make my life torture—

"It is my birthright!" Alize yelled.

Garrick was not the only one whose impenetrable composure had cracked.

The ice in my veins thawed. They did not know I was there.

It was past time to go. I needed a significant head start on Garrick, plus time to cover my tracks. I did not need to hear any more of their lovers' spat. I slipped away as silently as I'd arrived, frost power cushioning my footsteps.

Garrick had banked the fire before he left. The embers still glowed to welcome me back just under an hour later.

My power buzzed beneath my skin, but my muscles nearly gave out at the sight of my cloak and bedroll.

Exhaustion was my only excuse. My eyes were already half closed as I dropped down into my makeshift bed. That was the only way I could have failed to realize.

"Eavesdropping is rude, Koryn."

Dark God fucking spare me. How had Garrick beaten me back? How had I failed to notice him passing me in the snow? I'd under-estimated his skill and cleverness, taken in by the sarcasm and ever-present smirk. They were facets of his personality, but they conveniently obscured the other parts. The quiet observation, the random acts of caregiving. He'd noticed me lost in my own thoughts and tried to draw me out through fighting. He'd given me his cloak when I shivered and cooked for me when he noticed I had not eaten.

He'd risked my life, and his own by extension, to trek up the mountain and try to convince Alize to abandon the gates for her own safety.

I was not the only beneficiary of his attention.

"So is abandoning your bonded in the middle of the woods on a mountainside so you can go argue with your fae lover." As usual, the words were out of my mouth before I could stop them. But I was too fucking tired and hungry to moderate myself.

The expression on Garrick's face was worth the embarrassment from what those words revealed.

For one second, his face went totally blank. Devoid of feeling, maybe even understanding. Then his brows shot up—panic, maybe. The firelight reflected the turquoise as he pushed to sit up from where he'd reclined on the other side of the fire. Then that mysterious glow was gone, and his features settled into a smirk I wanted to slap right off of his handsome face.

Or kiss.

One or the other.

One was definitely more disastrous than the other. Especially given the quarrel I'd just witnessed.

I'd been a burden my whole life. First, as the youngest sister always tagging behind my elders. Then, as the youngest, most intractable member of my coven. And now, bonded to Garrick the Red. Continent-famous bounty hunter. Lover of a fae female who looked like something out of a faerietale. Who represented everything I hated in the world.

"You were perfectly safe."

"I do not need you to be responsible for my safety." I dug down into my furs, pulling them over my shoulder and rolling away. Even if for a few hours, I'd allowed myself to think that maybe, just maybe, I was worth protecting.

"So I am learning. But that doesn't mean I do not want to be."

My head jerked back over my shoulder, certain I'd imagined that last sentence. But Garrick had already laid back down, his back to the fire and to me.

CHAPTER 31

The next three days were progressively worse. Garrick woke me earlier and pushed me faster. And he fucking smirked when I threw myself down on the ground on the second day and ate an entire day's worth of food in one sitting.

There were no more midnight trips to visit Alize, nor attempts to teach me to defend myself. We did not see the other supplicants at all, though it did not take much reasoning to puzzle out that the only one who could be ahead of us was Alize.

Occasionally, I caught Garrick watching me with that intense gaze. And just as occasionally, I gave him my back. The less I had to talk with him, the less I was reminded that I was deficient in every way describable.

Without my coven, my power was fading. I had barely made it through the first two of the Seven Gates. My inability to defend myself in hand-to-hand combat made me a liability to the man whose life I'd saved, only to saddle him with mine. And my body had the audacity to be attracted to him, while he lusted after a female whose race was responsible for the destruction of my family.

On the fourth day, we climbed. Each day had boasted an elevation gain, but this was by far the worst. The cold air burned my throat as it entered my body, then scraped like a knife on the way back out. I was a fucking frost witch, and still I could not breathe steadily enough to appreciate the icy beauty of the mountain we climbed.

Crevices like the ones we'd dodged at the Mercy Gate traced patterns of cerulean death up the glacier. A fresh dusting of snow coated the treetops, but this high it hadn't accumulated because of the brutal wind that whipped between the peaks at night.

I was about to yell up to Garrick to ask how much longer before we reached the gate when the temple appeared like a ghost from between the trees. The first two temples had been impressive, but this one made the others seem like feeble attempts at grandeur. This temple had been crafted by the gods themselves.

It was carved directly into the mountainside, dark slate-colored stone forming shining faces that reflected the morning sunlight. Instead of seven stained-glass windows, effigies of the Seven Gods towered over the arched entrance.

Seraxa, the Goddess of Mercy, was draped in voluminous robes. Then came Edravos, holding the scales of justice. A pair of nooses would have been more appropriate. And then Xyta, the Deity of Sacrifice, twin to Ramkael, the God of Devotion. My eyes slid to the end of the line, to the uncarved face of the Dark God. When I was a child, they'd called him the Unknown One. There were no hints as to what his gate, the final of the seven, might entail. No one had ever made it far enough to find out.

Maybe, if I made it that far, I would have some advantage. I'd prayed to him for three hundred and seventy-seven years. The witches were his creations.

But I would never make it that far.

It had been just over a week since I entered the temple at the Mercy Gate. In that time, I'd nearly died in one gate, gotten myself bonded to a deadly bounty hunter, and proved how unsuited I was to the mental and physical demands of the Seven Gates.

I would not survive the gates.

But Varian, the priestess, had said that we could walk away from them for a time. Nimra had asked specifically. She had a family that needed her, I guessed. Why else would a young woman like her attempt the Seven Gates?

If I could walk away long enough… maybe I could leave Velora altogether. That had been my plan since I was first cast out from my coven. I'd pledged my life to the gods by entering the temple… but maybe there were different gods on different continents. Maybe the Dark God would protect me from the wrath of the others. I could do it.

I could run.

Garrick was nearly at the doors. Just like before, he would not turn to check on me. We were the only supplicants for miles, thanks to the grueling pace he had set. We might even get two nights to rest, depending on what had happened to Nimra and Nash over the past few days.

I would use my power to cover my tracks more carefully than I had a few nights before. Maybe he would not follow me at all. I was his bonded, but Alize was his love.

I can run.

I took one step backward. Then another. A few more, and I would fade back into the shade of the tree line. Garrick reached the doors, yanked them open and—

Turned.

Found me at the edge of the clearing that spread out in a semi-circle in front of the temple. Pinned me with his gaze. Even at that distance, I felt its burning intensity.

"Come inside, Koryn."

His mouth barely opened, yet it felt like he'd whispered the words directly into my ear. They were not sarcastic nor lined with dry humor. They were warmer and softer than I deserved. I felt them deep in my stomach, then in the center of my chest where the dead organ of my heart had once beat so painfully.

My feet started moving again. Garrick did not enter this time, instead holding open the door for me as he'd done for Kyrelle all those days ago. Before I could account for it, I'd stomped past him and into the temple.

CHAPTER 32

THERE WAS NO SLEEP QUITE LIKE THAT OF PHYSICAL EXHAUSTION. IT was still fully dark when I awoke. Or maybe it wasn't. Even with my heightened sight, it took me several blinks to clear the sleep from my eyes enough to make sense of my surroundings.

The dormitory was smaller than the first two we'd slept in. The beds no longer had bunks above them. That was ominous, considering the temples dated from the original date of the curse, four hundred years ago. Even then, there had been no need for as many beds by the third of the Seven Gates.

The long room was mostly silent. None of Nash's loud snoring. I scanned the rest of the beds, finding two occupied. The one right beside mine—Garrick. And on the far opposite side of the room, Alize. None of the others had arrived while I slept the day away.

My body creaked as I sat up. I just managed to clamp my hand over my mouth before the groan of pain left my lips. The last thing I needed was Garrick awake and irritated that I'd woken him. His eyes had lingered a little too long as I'd walked past him into the temple hours before. Like he suspected the thoughts that had run rampant through my head in those moments of frozen indecision.

My thick leather tunic lay over the foot of my bed. So did the wool overdress. I'd managed to peel down to just my linen gown and stockinged feet before falling into bed. But with everyone else asleep, I did not bother reaching for the other layers. I had my power to protect me...

I took two quiet steps toward the door before turning back and cinching on the belt that I'd tucked beneath my pillow. Something about the weight of the two blades on my waist felt better, even if I was useless at wielding them.

Garrick rolled over in his sleep as I snuck past but did not rouse. There was every possibility he was feigning sleep, as I had that night on the mountain. It would account for the sense of awareness that prickled through my shoulders. Also, for the heat that spread through my stomach and up into my chest... and lower.

I swayed my hips a little, just in case he was watching.

And then cursed myself. Lusting after a dangerous human was imprudent. Lusting after one who was in love with a fae? That edged toward desperate.

Awake or not, he did not stop me from slipping out of the dormitory.

The door swung free with blessed silence, allowing me to make my way into the heart of the temple without notice. I passed the bathing rooms where I'd only stopped long enough to relieve myself. In the morning I would take the time to bathe properly and wash my hair. The temples had hot water—a luxury I had not enjoyed since being cast out from my coven.

All of the candles in the temple were extinguished except for the offerings of frankincense and palmarosa that burned at each of the seven altars. The blood fountain gurgled in the darkness.

I had no destination in mind. Food, maybe. But there were no acolytes in sight, and my feet carried me toward the center of the temple, to that coppery tang.

In the muted light, the blood appeared almost black. I watched as it bubbled out of the top of the fountain, a feat of power bestowed by the gods. It fell in a circular sheet down to the first pool. Then a few seconds later, over the edge to the next, larger pool. Was my blood already here? All of the supplicants had made our offerings before the Mercy Gate. Was our blood still there, or had it been magically transported, mingled here? Or maybe this fountain ran with the blood of all those who had died at the Sacrifice Gate over the last four centuries.

The minutes ran together as I watched. The scent of blood filled my nostrils, my mouth, and then my lungs. I ought to hate it. But some part of me savored the idea of the blood of thousands of supplicants mingling with my own. I was a creation of the Dark God, and those were his gifts that allowed me to sense the warmth that wafted from the blood in the fountain, as if it still belonged to the living. I lifted a hand to my mouth expecting to see my fingertips coated in that thick red blood—

But they were bare. Pale, rounded nails touched my lips.

"You made it."

I startled out of my reverie.

It felt like waking all over again, blinking my way back to consciousness as I tried to make sense of my surroundings. I stood in the temple before the blood fountain. My hand... seconds before it had been coated with blood. No, that was a vision. An imagining. Maybe I had dreamed while waking. I'd never been physically exhausted like this before.

Steps echoed across the stone floor, the sound amplified by the emptiness of the temple. About the time his face came into view, framed by an emerald green hood, my mind placed the voice.

"Tomin," I said, dropping my hand to my side. "Yes, we—I made it."

His eyes crinkled at the edges, but that was all the question he let show. "We do not know until you arrive at the next temple. At least, the acolytes do not. Varian has not told me otherwise."

I turned, sweeping the temple for what I might have missed in my earlier stupor. I was not afraid of the priestess. But her dark eyes were too watchful for me to feel fully comfortable. I still had no reason I could place for the help she'd offered me. That alone was enough to keep my senses on guard around her.

"She is not here. Not in this part of the temple," Tomin amended. "She is seeing to the other acolytes, the ones stationed here."

Because the acolytes remained in the temples, and the priest or priestess traveled from gate to gate. That was what Tomin had said earlier. Another thought occurred to me. "How do you get from one gate to the next?"

"The same way as you," he said. I knew he could have hidden his frown, but he let the distaste show on his face. He leaned down and pulled up the hem of his emerald robe, revealing a leather boot with a hole in the sole. "One painful step at a time."

At least I was not the only one who found the journey agonizing. There was a strange comfort in that. Garrick made climbing through snowy mountains look like an afternoon jaunt to the sea. *Bastard.*

"Don't they let you sleep?" His eyes were lined with the same exhaustion I knew must mar mine. Thankfully, mirrors were not in abundance in the temple.

"Someone must be here to greet arriving supplicants, no matter the hour." Tomin nodded back toward the doors. For the first time, there were no guards.

I swallowed down that information. I truly could walk out those doors, and no one would stop me. It would be between me and the gods.

"I volunteered," Tomin said, interrupting my thoughts. "I like the temple best like this."

I lifted my brows, looking pointedly to the ominous, bubbling blood fountain. "Creepy?"

Tomin's face remained neutral. For half a breath, I thought I'd offended him, a feat I'd previously thought impossible. I didn't want or need friends, I reminded myself. But on my exhale, his mouth slashed into a wide grin, his freckles dancing in the low light.

"You are a witch," he laughed. "Isn't creepy your purview?"

I rolled my eyes. "I don't have a coven to cast any powerful spells," I said. My chest tightened. Witch ways were not to be shared.

But Tomin merely shrugged.

"You are not afraid of me," I said softly.

Again, a shrug. The nonchalance of youth, I realized. And mortality. In some ways, things mattered more, with so little time, but in others…

"You have never threatened me," he said. "You are a supplicant, the same as the others."

We stared into the darkness of the blood fountain. This time, I kept full control of my mind. Even so, it was only the night and the darkness that allowed me to admit, "I do not want to be."

I felt Tomin nod beside me. "Few do, anymore."

"I want to leave." Admitting it out loud made it sound every bit the pitiful plea that it was. I could not leave. The gods would punish me with death. Kyrelle would die in that seaside town, the gold I'd given her wasted on a father who would never do what was best for her. Wasted for love.

Tomin did not argue one way or another. He stood with me in silent understanding. He was young, but age could mean so many different things in a world of immortals and gods. Perhaps I'd misjudged him. He was not a newly minted acolyte, but one nearing his final rites.

He only spoke when I turned to look at him, wearing my confusion on my face. "I cannot offer answers. But I can try to help quiet your mind."

I did not laugh at him, though the impulse was there. It would have been easier than accepting his offer.

"Are you allowed to help me?"

He shrugged. "There is no specific provision against it. The acolytes have two roles—assist the priestess and serve the supplicants."

That did make me smile. "What about serving the gods?"

He grinned again, bright despite the darkness of the temple. "That, too. By serving the supplicants on their quest to prove themselves worthy and lift the curse, I serve the gods as well. Satisfied?"

"I am not the one you need to convince." I looked pointedly at the altar over his shoulder.

His smile softened as he held out his hand.

Only days ago, he'd reached for me at the Mercy Gate and I'd angrily shook him off. Now, he extended his hand to me. Me, a witch. One who'd been unkind and cranky and downright murderous.

What must it be like to have that kind of goodness inside your soul and actually be able to act upon it and fulfill it? To have suffered, like Tomin had, like I had, but instead of turning to... whatever I was... remaining whole?

I could not help myself. I wanted to know. I took his hand.

Tomin led me away from the blood fountain, outside the ring of benches, toward the perimeter of the temple lined with altars. Unlike the other two temples, this one boasted no windows. Carved directly into the mountain, the only light came from the flames burning on each altar. Instead of stone bowls on pedestals, the altars were carved into the walls of the temple itself, a shallow depression at the bottom housing the flames. There were no offerings at the foot of the altar. Few supplicants made it far enough to leave them.

But around each inset altar were intricate stone reliefs carved into the mountain. I'd barely looked at them when I first arrived. In the low light, they were difficult to see. Maybe that was part of the trick, to draw you in closer to the altar.

"You choose the god," Tomin said from my side, still holding my hand.

There was no spark of heat like when Garrick's skin touched mine. But there was a low, humming warmth. A comfort. What I imagined friendship might feel like.

I traced my eyes over the altars, considering.

"Xyta," I decided. The ungendered Deity of Sacrifice. Beside me, Tomin lifted his brows. Without his hood up, his dark curls visible and wild, he looked even younger than he was. I let my lips curve, an action that was so rare it felt foreign. But right. "You expected me to choose the Dark God?"

"It is believed that the witches worship him exclusively." But even as he said so, Tomin steered me toward Xyta's altar.

"He expects a certain amount of homage, as our creator," I agreed, the curves at the corners of my mouth deepening. "But I already know he is on my side. It's Xyta that I am currently worried about."

"Fair enough." Tomin's smile faded as he reached for my other hand, positioning us on either side of the opening carved into the stone. His expression softened into the mask of neutrality I'd seen him wear so many times in the past week. "Close your eyes."

I was certain the doubt showed in my eyes as I closed them. But there was no one else around to witness whatever religious nonsense I'd just agreed to. If only Maura could see me now. The head of my coven, most adamant in the separation and superiority of witches above all other beings—humans, priests, fae. The one who had sent me into the Seven Gates.

"Focus first on your breathing. Feel each inhale and each exhale."

With my eyes closed, it was easier to focus on the physical sensations. I supposed that was the point. But my other senses were still as sharp as ever. I could hear the gurgle of the blood fountain, the soft whoosh of Tomin's breath, the echoes of wind howling through the mountains outside.

"Notice the way your chest moves, then your stomach." My stomach growled. Not helpful. But I tried. I noted the concavity of my chest and shoulders when I inhaled, the fullness of my stomach as I exhaled. I still smelled the coppery tang of the blood fountain, felt the cool rush of air from beneath the doors of the temple. But they were less fierce.

"Think of a place where you have experienced peace."

My eyes snapped open. "Xyta is the Deity of Sacrifice." Not peace. Even if we'd been at the Peace Gate, I would not have chosen Pava's altar. Not when she'd ignored me for my entire life.

"Xyta will guide you," Tomin soothed. His eyes were still closed. I stared at him for several inhales and exhales, but the constant pressure of his hands on mine finally convinced my eyelids to flutter back down.

Despite his methodic words, my mind resisted. Flashes of memory accosted me as I searched for something like he'd described. *Peace. A place you felt safe. Peace. A sense of stillness. Peace...*

CHAPTER 33

BEFORE

As a human, I'd always struggled to rouse in the morning.
My earliest memories were of Janessa's voice, chastising me for
still not being dressed for breakfast. But as a witch, I found solace
in the dawn.

Our power was strongest at night, with the moon high and the
Dark God reigning. When all of my sisters retired, their power
spent, I ventured out.

The coven lands held on to life longer than the rest of the
continent, drawing on our vestigial power. But the curse tightened
its grip with every passing year. Autumn was harsher than I
remembered, the frost holding on longer into the day. But on that
morning the sun gilded everything in gold tones as it slipped
above the eastern horizon.

It was not a long walk to the glade, but I took the steps slowly,
savoring the quiet. Within me, my power found stillness as well. I
knew if I opened my hand, I could have summoned anything my
imagination could fathom. Only when I was alone, without my
senses invaded by the sharpness that was supposed to be a gift, did
I feel a true sense of control. My coven sisters spoke of their

heightened senses with reverence, used them to enhance their active powers. They'd all adjusted to the change from human to immortal without difficulty. But for me, everything was too loud, too bright, too tactile. My enhanced senses created a cacophony of sensation that overwhelmed me to the point of near helplessness.

But in the dawn, everything softened.

I reached the glade just as the sun's lower curve crested the eastern mountains. I slipped between the trees, following the bubble of the natural spring hidden in the copse of alders. The tall, straight trees created a near-perfect circle around the spring, leaving space only for the wide, flat rock on the edge of the spring that was my favorite seat.

But it was already occupied.

A lithe figure crouched on the flat rock, her fingers threaded around a bow with an arrow already notched in place. I froze between the alders, holding my breath so that not a single sound could escape my lips.

She was not a witch. There were still a handful of covens in Velora beside my own, but they were scattered to the west and north. One had taken over a section of land abandoned by the fae in the far east. But all of them knew where one another's coven lands were—and what the punishment was for entering them uninvited.

There was a familiarity to the lines of her body and the tilt of her head as she peered past the spring to the thicket behind the alders. I had not interacted with humans in decades. Maura had confined me to the coven lands, citing my struggles to control my power. I knew it was because of that ill-fated flight to my family home all those years before. My sister was long dead now. There was no family for me to return to.

Perhaps it was her youth that was familiar, so different from the trenchant immortality of my sister witches. Though our faces and bodies reflected our age at death, there was an acute difference to the way hundreds-year-old witches held those bodies. An assurance and a resignation. None of the hopeful spring that characterized the young woman's crouch or the eager twitch of her fingers on her bow.

Neither would remain once we were done with her.

But the others still slept. For this brief moment in time, we were alone. I could spare her.

I stepped into the glade. "You cannot hunt here."

She did not move at first, holding that impressive stillness as if hoping that I was speaking to someone else. As if she was not fully exposed there on the flat gray rock where she'd perched.

I moved further into the glade, feet close to the edge of the spring. I either had to step into it or onto the rock. I did not want to risk her bolting deeper into the coven lands. The cold water stung, but I'd survive.

She shifted her stance quickly, spinning on her heel but remaining in that crouch with her arrow notched.

"I saw a boar," she said, though she pointed that arrow at me.

"Then it belongs to the coven lands." She needed to understand the danger she was in. Her brown eyes were unflinching in their intelligence as she took me in. She still did not lower her weapon.

Death might be a mercy. But an arrow to the chest was a painful way to die.

"My grandmother told stories of your kind."

"Then you should know that my power could destroy that arrow before it ever reached me." Not quite the truth. Though without the overwhelming sensory input of my coven and the weight of Maura's toxic expectations, there was a chance I'd manage it. But I did not want to kill this girl. "You should have heeded your grandmother and stayed away."

Finally, she lowered the bow. "We need to eat."

I considered her again, noticing that the high cheekbones were made sharper by the hollowness in her cheeks. She was muscled but thin. A huntress who never had quite enough to build anything beyond the essential layers of muscle. Not starving—not yet. But eventually.

"Entering the coven lands is death to mortals," I said, trying to steel my voice. Sympathy would only get her killed. The longer she lingered here, the more danger of her discovery. If my sisters found her, there would be nothing I could do. Nothing except... a new thought occurred to me.

"Unless you are willing to pay the price."

The bow notched up a few inches. "What price?"

"The price is determined by the witch, not the mortal. If you are willing to pay my price, then you may walk away unscathed." Maura had been drilling the covenants into me for decades. I'd never imagined I would exploit this one. I had little interest in torturing humans the way some of my sisters did.

"What price?" the girl repeated, her mouth curling into a sneer that looked just like—

No. It can't be.

"Who are you?" My throat tried to freeze around the words, but I managed to force them out.

"I should not tell you," she said, lifting her chin in a subconscious act of defiance. Because her grandmother had told her stories, and many humans believed that telling a witch your name gave her power over you.

"That is my price," I said. For once, my power was quiet. A frozen weight sat in my chest, colder than the spring water that had begun to freeze around my toes.

The girl considered, her eyes appraising. She looked past me, to one of the gaps in the alders. Her escape route. But she also must have seen that she'd never make it past me without some kind of intervention. She could shoot me with that arrow. I could use my power against her.

She straightened, letting the bow fall to her side. Preparing to run.

"I am Rowellyn, daughter of Karlyn, granddaughter of Rylynn, of the House of Gallatin."

The House of Gallatin. She had not needed to list my father, her great-grandfather, as one of her ancestors, because he'd renamed the entire family line after himself.

Rylynn's granddaughter.

It was a miracle. After what I'd done to my sister, to her fiancée… still, she'd managed to have a daughter and then a grand-daughter. A granddaughter that she warned about witches.

Rightfully so.

Rowellyn was already springing past me, her price paid. I should have been thankful—Dark God, I *was* thankful that she was finally heeding my warnings and getting the hell out of the coven lands. But—

"Wait." I spun to face her, already slipping between the trees. Her brown eyes collided with mine, and I recognized why she'd felt so familiar. They were my sister's eyes. I'd damned Rylynn to a life of misery. But I could offer something to her granddaughter. "When bow draws near to water's edge, let creatures heed this silent pledge."

Whenever she hunted with the bow near a body of water, animals would be drawn to take a drink. She would find enough prey to feed herself and her family.

For a brief second, Rowellyn's bow glowed with soft blue light. Her eyes widened, a million questions in them. But I shook my head. The sun was tracking higher overhead with every passing second.

"Go."

Rowellyn did not ask any of those questions. Nor offer thanks, though I could not have accepted them. This was the least that I owed to my sister.

I started the walk back to my sisters, my feet heavier than before, my chest, too. I would never return to the glade. There was no peace to be found there anymore.

CHAPTER 34

"Are you all right?"

I blinked through the weight in my chest, the block of ice that had formed the first time I'd met Rowellyn somehow present once again, as real as it had been that day in the glade. *A place where you have felt peace.*

Peace was not among the Dark God's gifts to the witches. Nor had the gods gifted it to me in the twenty-three years of my mortal life. If I'd had any as a child, it died with my mother before my sixth birthday.

I refused to feel sorry for myself. But Tomin's golden honey eyes shone with emotion he did not try to shield. Pity. Sadness. Even in the darkness of the cave-carved temple, it was impossible to miss them.

The scrape of his palms against was mine too intense to bear. The walls of the temple themselves pushed in on me, the darkness that was supposed to be a witch's solace caving in until it threatened to crush me.

I jerked my hands from his grasp. "Keep your tricks for the fools who need them."

The pity in Tomin's eyes did not shift to hurt. He saw me pulling away, pulling into myself, and he felt bad for me, still.

He did not need me as a friend. I was a supplicant, he an acolyte. He had entire temples full of companions. Before long, he would be a priest in his own right and have a bevy of acolytes at his command. He did not want *me* as his friend.

I was alone.

I ran back to the dormitories, too deep in the torrent of my own emotions to care about how much noise I made. I wrenched open the door and threw myself into my bed. Across from me, Garrick sat up.

I buried my face deeper into the cloak that I'd layered atop the blankets and sheets. I would freeze the sob in my chest before I would let him or that fae bitch hear it. After several minutes, the mattress groaned. Garrick laid back down. But neither of us pretended to sleep for the rest of the night.

CHAPTER 35

"No," I groaned at the hand shaking my shoulder. I'd only just gone to sleep. And by some mercy from Seraxa, it had once again been dreamless. Actual sleep, not the charade that Garrick and I had put on the night before.

Someone whispered, and there was that bony hand again.

"No," I growled, rolling in my bunk and throwing an arm over my shoulder. The back of my hand connected with someone's face, a yelp echoing off the carved walls. No one was grabbing my shoulder anymore. That was all I cared about.

I started to roll back to my stomach—

A strong hand caught my wrist. I recognized the size and breadth of that hand, even half-asleep. Which meant I wrenched away harder, even as my back arched in a completely involuntary and wholly humiliating attempt to get closer to him.

"It appears our first sacrifice is sleep," his voice rumbled, still husky and rough from slumber. My stomach flipped over inside of me. Is that how he would sound—

"Stop!" I screeched, to no effect.

Garrick dragged me upright and to the edge of my bed. I was so disoriented, I did not fight him half as hard as I should have. But reality was slowly sliding into place. The other supplicants already stood at the door of the dormitory, each flanked by an acolyte in their customary emerald robes.

Nash had arrived in the late afternoon, Nimra an hour after him. The time of making small talk had passed. We all kept well clear of one another. Except for Garrick, who lurked behind me like a shadow.

Garrick only allowed me to shake him off once I put my feet to the stone floor and started dressing. A mass of green hunched over the end of the bed, rubbing at their eye. I recognized the other acolyte, rubbing the injured one's back and murmuring something about Xyta. But this time, Tomin did not look at me and wink. He did not look at me at all.

I am alone.

Which was exactly what I deserved.

I begrudgingly joined the procession of supplicants, Garrick at my back. There was no parade around the temple this time and certainly no breakfast. Varian and her minions marched us out of the dormitory and into a dark hall that challenged even my heightened senses. I reached out a hand to find the wall that I could sense but not quite see. Like the rest of the temple, it was roughly hewn. I kept my hand there, letting the solid rock anchor me as we walked deeper and deeper into the mountain.

Eventually, we started to climb. The ancient power in my veins increased the flow of blood to my organs, but my breath was still coming fast by the time the path leveled out. At least it did not burn like it had when Garrick dragged me through the mountains.

Twin pinpricks of golden light appeared before us. They grew with each step until I could recognize two torches burning, an expanse of dark stone about the length of a man between them. Varian led us directly to them, the acolytes guiding us into a line.

The emerald robed acolytes turned as one to Varian. She

bowed her head, "The Sacrifice Gate awaits. Only the supplicants may pass."

We all turned back to the torches, expecting something to happen. But it remained a wall of solid stone. Retreating footsteps told me that Varian, as usual, would not be any help. I glanced over my shoulder, noting Tomin at her side. He did not look back.

"What now?" Nimra wondered aloud.

Alize was already at one of the torches, examining the flame and where the metal bracket anchored into the stone.

Nash yelled back at the retreating parade of acolytes. He had his greatsword out. I wasn't afraid of him, exactly. Wary, certainly. But with Garrick at my back... and that sound...

That sound. It was fuzzy and indistinct, hard to detect over the voices of the others. A low hum that lurked beneath everything else. It set *me* buzzing, the combination of voices and the pulsing sound grating against my sharpened senses. The need to make it stop overwhelmed every other thought.

The wall.

Alize manipulated the flame of the torch using her wind magic. But she was wrong. I felt it in every bone and every thrum of power in my body. The humming came from the wall.

I laid my hand against the stone. Everything went silent. For one blessed moment, my senses were not accosted by what the Dark God called gifts.

Then a collective gasp of awe echoed behind me. It took me a few beats to understand. I was too distracted by the flood of power inside of me, yawning awake after a night of slumber. But it was not just flooding inside of me, it was flowing into the wall itself.

Cool blue light spread out from my hand across the wall, etching patterns that had been invisible before. I recognized the curved lines and geometric shapes. Runes. I'd been thrice marked with them.

But the others...

"What is she doing? What are those markings?" Nash snarled. "She's trying to bring down the wall on us!"

I felt the shift in the air as his greatsword moved, but I could not pull my hand away. A wall of strength and menace solidified at my back. Garrick.

If he killed Nash for his threats, I was powerless to intervene. All of my attention and power focused on the wall, on the still spreading runes. The mountain itself pulled the power from me, demanding it as the price of passage. I was nothing more than a conduit.

As suddenly as the flow of power had begun, it stopped. A border appeared, a limit. I stumbled backward, but Garrick was there. He caught my elbow, just enough to steady me.

I straightened, coming back to the world around me. Garrick's hand lingered on my upper arm, his warmth pressing in at my back. I took another step backward from the wall to get a better look at what my power had wrought.

Garrick did not anticipate the move. He remained in place, the curve of my bottom and the softness at my sides pressing against his hard lines. Another hum, so low I could barely hear it, slid past my senses. Almost a groan. Almost certainly Garrick's.

I found myself turning away from the wall—less impressed by its strange power than by the change in the man pressed against me.

Garrick's face was nearly impassive. He had not exclaimed with the others. But he wasn't smirking either. He watched me with... expectation. His eyes had narrowed ever so slightly, and his usually decadent mouth settled into a straight line. And that muscle in his jaw ticked.

For once, the intensity in his turquoise gaze did not overwhelm me. For once, it felt like I was the one holding the power, holding him in place with my own intensity.

I felt his chest move as he breathed in and out, and the softer lift of a soundless chuckle as the corner of his mouth curled up in that infernal smirk. "Well done, witch."

My eyes followed the angle of his mouth up to his eyes, still expectant and fully focused on me. "You knew."

He lowered his chin a fraction of an inch in acknowledgment. "Power calls to power."

We were too close. My backside was no longer pressed against him, but my front. The curve of my breasts against the hard muscles of his chest and abdomen. My stomach pillowing out beneath the edge of my laced bustier, rubbing against—more hardness.

Before I could process that, Garrick's hands landed on my shoulders. Even through my cloak, I could feel the interminable heat of him. But he did not give me long to savor it. He turned me around to face the glowing wall of runes and then pulled his hands away.

The runes spread out from where I'd laid my hand in a spiraling pattern. The golden spiral. I recognized it instantly, even etched in blue rather than gold. Alize skimmed her fingertips over the pattern, but she said nothing. She must recognize it. She was fae.

Nimra moved closer, leaning in to examine the runes, though neither she nor Nash made any move to touch them.

I began to pick out shapes I recognized. There were the symbols for earth, air, fire, and water, the four bounds of the witches' power. My eyes found one that appeared to be a corruption of the mark now tattooed on the inside of my wrist, the symbol of Garrick and I's Lifebind. And there was the same rune that was tattooed upon my forehead, though in this context it took on another meaning.

"They chase their will beyond all bounds, and reap the debt they sow…"

"In loss they find the cost of pride, to sacrifice the soul," Alize finished.

Our gazes collided, her magic, my power. For a single beat, I forgot to hate her. I was too distracted by the overlap, the congruity between us when none should exist.

But the sound of stone scraping against stone dissolved the moment.

The wall before us shifted, the runes hollowing out, rocks the size of my fist falling to the stone floor of the tunnel, until nothing was left but an arched passageway with a single glowing rune at its apex.

The message was clear—step through.

CHAPTER 36

JUST LIKE EACH OF THE PREVIOUS GATES, WE WERE TRANSPORTED. There was magic and power at work here, too. I turned, looking over my shoulder and then up, up, up to the craggy mountain peak that rose overhead. The archway sealed behind us, leaving the five remaining supplicants standing on the side of a frozen mountain, with matching peaks in every direction. The sky overhead was a cloudy white that matched the snow-capped peaks. It was a wonder of nature, and the frosted power within me reveled at the brutal beauty.

But there was nothing natural about what spread out below us.

Just as the temple had been carved from the dark stone of the mountain, so was the arena. Multiple tiers descended, each about the height of my waist. Seats for viewing whatever was about to take place. My skin crawled with dread at the prospect of facing another crowd of not-real people.

There were no nooses at the center of the area, at least. It was totally bare, except for a singular round table carved of the same dark gray stone as the arena and the mountains. The table looked eerily like an altar. And this was the Sacrifice Gate.

Nash began climbing down. Going first had given him an advantage at the Mercy Gate.

Alize and Nimra followed.

But I found my eyes straying away from the arena to the passes between the mountains. They would be difficult to navigate, but I had my active power to help me. The temptation to leave was nearly as powerful as it had been outside of the temple two days before. If I made straight for the coast, I could be there in less than a week. I had no money for passage, but I could wait until night and sneak aboard a ship. Use spells judiciously to keep myself hidden. I might exhaust what remained of my power, as Maura had always warned, but if I got away, I would pray to whatever new gods awaited on a different continent...

Except Garrick would never let me go.

And with the curse still looming, Kyrelle would die.

Garrick reached for my elbow again, but I jerked forward, avoiding him. I was afraid if he touched me, I might shatter.

Nash was almost to the center of the arena, just one level of seating left to climb, when the air around us heated suddenly. A pulse of power rolled through the air. A singular figure appeared at the center of the arena, along with two chairs on either side of the stone table.

The dark-haired figure tilted their head back, scanning each of us with their gaze. And then settled, a smile curving the pale face.

"Alize."

We all stopped exactly where we'd been. All except for Alize, who climbed gracefully down with sure, unhurried movements. Nash glared at her as she moved past him, but made no move to reach for the greatsword he'd sheathed at his belt.

The moment her feet touched the stone center of the arena, another pulse of power moved outward and over us. I braced myself against the stone, but none of the others reacted. Was I the only one to feel it? Because I was an immortal?

The dark-haired figure motioned for Alize to sit, taking the other chair for themselves. The shape of her body declared her as female, well-clothed in a rich copper gown and matching mantle trimmed in white fur. Her dark hair was loose around her shoulders, but sections were braided back from her crown. My sharpened eyes allowed me to judge her as somewhere in her thirties, even at this distance. But I could not hear what she said.

Her mouth moved, but the sound did not reach us.

That second pulse of power had been some sort of a shield going into place. Or maybe a ward… though the female did not have the pointed ears of the fae. Maybe it had been Alize who set the ward, or some nuanced use of her wind magic.

Beside me, Garrick sat on the stone, his legs reaching the ground easily. I mimicked the movement, mine dangling. I drew them up beneath me instead, irritated by the comparison.

Garrick's mouth quirked, but he said nothing.

Neither Nimra nor Nash spoke, though each eventually sat. The conversation between Alize and the female stretched on.

Usually, I found silence a relief. The lack of input to my heightened senses was a rare balm. But this silence was too charged to be calming. The pull of the mountains and the escape they offered… the weight of what awaited in the arena when the female called my name… the heat of Garrick just a scant foot to my right. It was as oppressive as any sound. I rolled my shoulders, trying and failing to dispel the tension building there.

"Is this it? Just talking?" I said, quietly enough I could have been talking to myself.

But Garrick responded, just like I'd secretly hoped he would. Damn my nerves and the lurch in my stomach when he did.

"Would you prefer hanging or running over ice fields?"

My hands curled at my sides. "I would prefer to know what I am facing."

"Then watch long enough to find out."

Frost spread along the stone despite the heat that lingered over the arena.

Garrick chuckled, the sound so low and deep I felt it more than heard it. "Patience, witch."

But he was right, Dark God damn him. A few minutes later, Alize stood. She inclined her head to the female as a passageway appeared to her right, carved right into the stone of the levels where the rest of us sat. Alize walked through it, and then the stone stairs reformed, the exit gone.

The dark-haired female reclined in her seat. If it wasn't so far-fetched, I'd have described her expression as bored. She twirled her hand, and a golden wine goblet appeared in her grasp. She took a long, unhurried drink before finally deigning to turn her gaze up to those of us waiting in the upper levels of the arena.

"Nimra."

Nimra kept her gaze forward and focused as she climbed down from her seat about halfway from the base of the arena. The series of events repeated itself. The female motioned her toward the empty seat, Nimra took it, and the two began talking. Again, we could not hear what they said. So, the silence was endemic to the gate.

Even so, I found myself bracing my hands on either side of my wide hips and leaning forward. It was difficult at this angle to see Nimra's expression, only that her mouth moved every now and again. The female across from her, however, I could see clearly. And she was no longer bored.

My family briefly kept a cat in the aftermath of my mother's death. Janessa found it outside, and my father had been too distracted with building his own wealth to bother telling her not to bring it into the house. Once it started catching mice and leaving them on her bed, my sister's interest in the animal had evaporated.

The expression on the female's face reminded me of that cat, one paw holding the tail of the mouse, the other pawing at the poor creature as it tried to squirm away.

Nimra's mouth hung open. The angle was wrong. I could not tell if it was shock or anger or something else.

But when she pushed out of her chair and started climbing, I knew what emotion it was that had my own mouth dangling open.

The passageway did not appear. Instead, Nimra climbed the oversized stair levels of the arena. We all watched, even Nash, as she crested the top level. She paused, looking not at us but back at the female still seated in the pit. The gold-clad figure lifted her wine glass in silent toast.

Nimra turned away and started hiking for the nearest pass between the snowy peaks. Her shoulders were shaking.

My own quivered as a shiver snaked down my spine. "Why would she leave?"

Garrick's voice was grim. "Xyta asked for something she was unwilling to sacrifice."

Xyta.

The dark-haired female at the center of the arena was not a female at all. And not a make-believe creation of the gate, like the human crowd from before, but the *creator* of the gate. It was Xyta, the Deity of Sacrifice. Twin to Ramkael, the God of Devotion. Their gates were one after the other, the siblings never truly separated.

If that was Xyta... a form of Xyta. The gods were too big, too expansive to be contained in a single form, mortal or immortal in frame.

Xyta themself was there in the arena, speaking to each of the supplicants in turn. Not just speaking... but asking for the sacrifice that would allow them to pass through the gate. Whatever it was, it was not pain—at least not physical, visible pain. Whatever the sacrifice was, Alize had been willing to make it.

But Nimra had not.

What would be such a sacrifice that Nimra was unwilling to make it? She had not told me her reason for attempting the gates during our brief stint of pseudo-friendship. But it was not so difficult to deduce that she must have been motivated by the needs of a loved one. She was relatively healthy, clothed in worn but lovingly crafted garments. She came from a home with others who cared for her. Those people—her family—had to be her impetus for attempting the gates.

What sacrifice could Xyta have possibly asked for that was monumental enough for Nimra to forsake her family? A family where true love was present, like that between Kyrelle and her father.

Kyrelle.

My blood pounded in my veins. The power that I'd thought exhausted by the runed wall roared back to life.

There was only one sacrifice that would have made Nimra walk away from the Seven Gates. Her family. Xyta had asked her to sacrifice the very thing that had driven her to try to lift the curse on Velora in the first place.

I dug my fingernails into the mound of my palm, trying to hold back the torrent of power that fought the meager restraints within me.

"Koryn." Garrick's voice cut through the fog of fear, the thick beat of my own blood in my ears, the weight of the ice forming in my chest.

"I am fine." *I am fine. I am fine.*

But I wasn't. Frost spread across the stone, then thickened into a layer of ice. The temperature dropped.

I could not do it. I would be doomed, just like Nimra. I could not sacrifice Kyrelle, not after all of these centuries, all of these mistakes.

Power flowed through me, the ice spreading. Garrick cursed but remained at my side, even though I knew the ice must be touching him now, too.

Xyta sat up in their chair suddenly. Their eyes speared across the arena, searching out the source of that power, finding me.

"Shit," Garrick cursed again.

But instead of doing the smart thing, which would have been to put as much distance between us as possible, he moved closer. He did not even flinch from the ice as it cracked beneath and around and over him.

His dark clothing was coated in a thin layer of frost. But when he pressed himself against me, so that his thigh ran parallel to mine, he was all heat.

He lifted my hand, slipping his fingers between mine and urging my fist to unclench. I was so surprised, so uncomprehending, that I did not even protest.

He pressed his palm flat against mine, the warmth of that huge expanse melting the burst of frost that coated my skin. His fingers intertwined with my own, then curled around to press into the back of my hand. He enveloped me in his warmth. And slowly, ever so slowly, like a limb waking up after the blood flow is suddenly restored, my power receded. The ice around us melted, yielding to the unnatural heat of Xyta's arena.

Xyta, whose eyes were still upon me even as my power ebbed.

Garrick's hand tightened over mine and it felt like more than just the protection of our Lifebind. It felt like safety.

Xyta's posture eased. On another face, their smile might have been called soft. But on Xyta is sent a shiver down my spine. They were going to call my name next, I knew it. This time, it was my hand tightening around Garrick's, my mouth whispering a prayer to the Dark God, begging for a stay of execution that would last only minutes.

But just as suddenly as Xyta had found me, their gaze shifted away.

"Nash," they said.

The last vestiges of frosty power melted in my veins. My power was still there, humming through my body, but it did not try to rise up and overtake me. The warmth that flowed steadily into me from Garrick's hand allowed me to hold my power in a place of neutrality, a place I'd never quite found before.

The shock of that must have been what delayed the realization.

But as Nash took his seat and Xyta began speaking, Garrick's hand squeezed mine, and that was when the reality of my current situation began to take shape.

Garrick the Red was holding my hand.

My power was under my control.

And in a matter of minutes, Xyta was going to ask for the one thing I could not sacrifice. Cold shot through me, but the warmth of Garrick's hand around mine met it, warmed it, shaped it into something less dangerous.

I stared at our joined hands in shock. How was that possible? How—

Garrick's eyes met mine. We were so close, the patches of clover green inside of the blue were visible. How many people had Garrick the Red, legendary, ruthless bounty hunter, ever allowed close enough to see that detail?

"What are you afraid of, Koryn?"

I did not ask how he knew I was afraid. I'd shown him with my inability to control my power. But I could not quite bring myself to answer his question, at least not directly.

"Why would Garrick the Red attempt the Seven Gates?" It was the question that had haunted my dreams, the one that kept me from trusting him fully. Or at least, as far as I had the capacity to trust anyone.

"Why would a witch?" he countered.

It was a sloppy retort, but I'd wanted him to ask, because I'd wanted to answer. I wanted some sort of solution to the impossible situation that my repeatedly terrible choices had gotten me into. I could not walk away from the gates, or Kyrelle would die and eventually, so would I. Nor could I sacrifice Kyrelle or my coven to Xyta.

"Because I was cast out from my coven," I said. Garrick still held my hand. As I spoke, he swiped his thumb along the curve between my index finger and thumb. "It might seem like nothing to you, who has spent your entire life alone. But a witch is nothing without her coven."

I let that information hang in the air between us. But there was not much of it, not as close as we suddenly were. Garrick just watched me, waiting.

"If I remove Velora's curse, they will welcome me back," I said softly. Why did it feel like admitting it would make me less in his eyes? Why did I care?

Garrick showed no reaction to my words. He turned over our hands, lifting them from the stone to rest on his knee. "You fear that Xyta will ask you to sacrifice your chance to return?"

"That. Or… there is someone I care about. Someone whose life is my responsibility. If I do not lift the curse, she will die." I could not bring myself to use Kyrelle's name. Not because I feared him knowing it, but… it felt like exposing myself. Making myself too raw, too vulnerable to a man who I was already allowing to hold my hand. Whose life was bound to mine by Seraxa herself.

"The woman from the first temple," Garrick guessed. "You argued, and then you entered in her place."

I blinked up at him. "I thought you had already gone inside."

He smirked that infernal, irritating smirk. "You were not being quiet."

"I know what Xyta will ask for. My coven or my… person." Just like her name, I could not tell him exactly what she meant to me. It would mean admitting what I'd done. He likely already knew, after the Justice Gate. But still… "Why would Garrick the Red attempt the Seven Gates?"

Garrick turned away, looking down to where Nash and Xyta were engaged in a heated exchange. The deity leaned forward in their chair, eyes glinting with excitement. The back of Nash's neck flushed red. I was not even able to enjoy the sight.

I wanted to know Garrick's motivation. I'd given him mine. It only seemed fair. We were connected by the Lifebind, for the Dark God's sake. Whatever his views on witches, hadn't I proved myself… I was not quite sure what I had proved about myself. That was a thought I could not linger on, so I pressed him instead.

"You have wealth. You are healthy and strong. Does it have to do with you fae lover?" Bile tainted the last two words, but I still said them.

Garrick's hand loosened on mine, as if the words made him forget to hold on. His blue-green eyes were wide when they swung to me. "Alize? She is not my lover."

"You sounded quite familiar." Dark God save me, I hated how choked those words sounded. I had enough hate in my heart for the fae. I would not allow myself to be jealous of one. But the way that Garrick held my hand even after my power had quieted…

"I…" Garrick cleared his throat. "We are familiar. But she is not the reason I entered the temple."

"Then what is?"

He did not try to avoid my gaze. He let me catch his and attempt to turn that intensity he wielded back around on him. But the only emotion I saw in those luminous orbs was resolve. He would not tell me why he had entered the temple. Which was as good of a reminder as any. There was a Lifebind between us, but that was not the same thing as trust.

I disentangled my fingers from his and shoved my hands deep inside my cloak. The one he'd given me. Fuck.

Garrick let me go. He watched the space grow between us as I shifted my weight away. He'd offered no solution for facing Xyta, and I realized I did not truly expect him to. He'd listened to my concerns, and that was something. I'd never had anyone to tell them to. A benefit of the Lifebind, I supposed. He was forced to listen to my complaints.

"I met Alize in Balar Shan many years ago."

My head snapped up. I'd looked away, but Garrick had not. His gaze was as intense as ever as he stared straight into my eyes, as if he could see past them into the twisted soul beneath.

Balar Shan—the walled city beyond the mountains, in the far

northeast of Velora. The enchanted, shining city of the fae, where they had retreated after the gods had cursed the entire continent for the fae's overreaching attempts to gather more magic than had already been bestowed upon them.

Garrick held my gaze, not even blinking as he spoke. "My mother sent me there so that I could meet my father."

The unnatural speed. The sheer size of him, compared to even Nash, one of the strongest humans I'd seen in decades. My eyes strayed to his ears, half-covered by the thick, pale hair he always wore half-pulled back. But they were rounded. Not fae... not wholly.

"You are half-fae," I breathed, even though we were alone. I'd asked for one secret and received another, a different one.

"I am half-human," Garrick corrected.

My mind spun as I tried to make sense of what he had told me. I'd never met a half-fae, though I knew they existed. They were rare, even before the curse had driven the fae into their reclusive city. The fae considered humans to be below them. Cross pairings and marriages were unheard of, the mixed children resulting mostly from—

Oh.

I am half-human, he'd corrected me.

He hated what he was. And I... I understood that on a deeper level than I'd ever admitted, even to myself. Garrick was a prisoner to a fate that he had not chosen, just as I was.

"Koryn."

Xyta's summons echoed through the arena, whatever magic they used to contain the sound of their conversations temporarily dampened. I jolted upright, icy shards immediately starting to form in my veins.

Nash was gone. He must have disappeared through the passageway the same as Alize.

Garrick had managed to distract me from the dread, had used his hand in mine to help ease the tidal wave of power that rolled out of my control. But there was no escaping the deity below with that feline smile curving their mouth.

"Koryn." Not Xyta this time, but Garrick. I turned back to face him, expecting worry. If I bungled this, his life could be in danger, too. But his face was inscrutable once again.

"Xyta is a bored immortal. All they want is some entertainment."

What in the Dark God's frigid hell that was supposed to mean, I did not know. But I committed every word to memory as I climbed down to my doom.

CHAPTER 37

"A witch. It has been many years since one of your kind made it to my gate." Xyta rose for me, which I did not consider a good omen. They looked me over with as much interest as that cat once had its mouse, as if deciding which part would make for the most succulent first bite.

I willed the ice in my veins to hold me still, to keep me from twitching under their gaze. "You are Xyta."

Their smile deepened until a dimple appeared in their right cheek. Right, but not left. A tingle of awareness started in my chest, directly between my breasts, where my heart had once beat.

Xyta motioned to the seat across from them. I moved toward it but waited until they took theirs before lowering myself into the chair. Like so many I'd encountered, it was too narrow for my frame. The stone arms clung to my hips uncomfortably. I tried to keep my face neutral, but from the sparkle in Xyta's eyes, I guessed that I had failed.

I did not want their attention on me, not like that. Not reading me. They were a deity; for all I knew, they could read every thought in my head. But that did not mean I had to make it easier.

"Why this form?" I asked, stilling the impulse to shift in the chair to try and make myself more comfortable.

The deity shrugged their delicate shoulders. "I take whichever form pleases me—which is usually the one that will most unnerve the person sitting across this table."

I blinked. They had taken this form... for me?

I looked over my shoulder to where Garrick waited near the top of the arena, watching me intently. Did he... did he see a different form of the deity than I did?

"Do you not recognize your mother's face?"

I turned back slowly, certain I had misheard them. Xyta waited, legs crossed beneath the golden velvet dress, a warm smile on their face.

A smile I remembered so vaguely, I could not have put a name to it. But that dimple... Janessa had had the same one, just on one side, just on her right cheek. And the dark hair that hung in loose waves, not straight but not quite curled, was a very particular shade of dark brown. The same as Rylynn's had been, and then Rowellyn's, and now Kyrelle. The same as mine.

"She died when I was very young," I said.

"And you have walked this continent for many centuries."

You have forgotten your own mother, Xyta's cat smile said. *You should be ashamed.*

And I was. "I have."

Xyta's eyes lit with the victory. "Perhaps I should have chosen this form instead." They waved their hand, and instead of my mother's middle-aged form, now Rylynn sat before me, as lovely and beautiful as she had been on the day of her betrothal celebration. "Or this? She scares you, though you would never admit it to yourself or any other." Rylynn's skin paled to an unnatural white, the texture and color of her hair changing and darkening until an unmistakable face looked back at me. Xyta even got the condescending tilt of Maura's mouth right.

I looked back over my shoulder. Garrick had not shifted, his expression unchanged. He watched me intently but showed nothing else. No flicker in his jaw, no lift to the half-moon scar by his eye. He had not seen Xyta's change. The spectacle was for me alone.

Who did Garrick see? I could not let myself wonder. Not when everything I cared about hung on the next few words.

"Take whichever form pleases you," I said, training my eyes forward. I would not let myself look back at Garrick again.

Xyta uncrossed their arms. This time, I stared down the thick form of my father.

Mistake.

What I felt for my father was the least complicated of the visages they'd shown me. I had nothing but hate for the man who had sold my family to the fae. The father who had abandoned his children after the death of their mother, more concerned with fortune than any of the three daughters left in his keeping.

But I did my best not to let Xyta see any of that. I let the hate shine out, they would expect that. But everything else, I kept at bay by folding my hands together in my lap. I told myself that it was not my own hand gripping the other, but Garrick's. I imagined warmth instead of cold.

It worked well enough to cause the deity to sit back in their seat and reconsider me.

"You had two reasons for entering the temple," they finally said.

"Yes." I grasped my hands tighter together in my lap. The conversation with the Deity of Sacrifice was proceeding exactly as I had expected and feared.

Xyta shrugged as if our conversation covered nothing more controversial than the weather, and then said simply— "Choose."

My stomach jolted. I'd expected them to tell me which one they expected me to sacrifice. They were the Deity of Sacrifice. They must know which would hurt me more to lose. But they twisted a different knife instead.

For a little more than a week, for the first time in nearly four hundred years, the two competing interests in my world had been aligned. And just like that, Xyta set them against each other once again.

"I cannot," I choked out. There was no hiding my distress from the deity, no matter how hard I clasped my hands. My hands weren't even clasped anymore, I realized. They gripped the dark stone arms of the chair, and that was frost climbing down the legs, spreading across the ground. I was perilously close to losing control again. "I... haven't I already... didn't I when—"

"When *what*, Koryn?"

Haven't I already chosen? My mind screamed. *When I—*

I slammed a dagger of ice down on that thought. I could not even think it, it was too dangerous. Whether Xyta had some special power that allowed them to see supplicants' history or they were looking directly into my head, I could not let them have that memory. There would be no coming back if they did.

Xyta watched from their chair. Reclined, but carefully noting every movement I made. When I did not answer, they shrugged their shoulders again. Strange, their mannerisms overlaid on the face and body of my father. It was enough of a distraction that I reclaimed a bit more control over my power.

"If you will not choose, then you are free to go," they said. They looked up toward Garrick, already considering their next victim.

"Where?" I asked, even though I suspected the answer.

"I do not care. Follow your blonde friend from earlier as she bumbles her way through the mountains, back to her precious village. So precious, not even the fate of Velora was worth its destruction." Nimra. She'd refused to make the sacrifice Xyta required, just as Garrick thought.

But... "You let her go."

Xyta pretended that they were not paying attention to our conversation, but their smile deepened. "For now."

"A gate is always near," I whispered.

Xyta was not looking at Garrick any longer. "A god is always watching."

"You will come for her."

"She made her choice."

Did Nimra understand? Even though Xyta had allowed her to walk away unharmed… it was temporary. No one could walk away from the gates. Xyta had gotten their sacrifice either way. By refusing to sacrifice whatever—or whomever—Xyta had demanded, Nimra was sacrificing herself. But it would not get her through the gate and onto the next. She would just be dead.

It was not just a choice between my coven and Kyrelle that Xyta had presented to me, but between those and my own survival. I could try to get off of Velora before they came for me. But this encounter had solidified in my mind what I'd been foolish enough to forget in my misery and desperation—there was no escaping the Seven Gates. Not for the residents of Velora. We either lived under their curse or we died trying to break it.

The gods ruled us all, fae, witch, and human.

But who ruled the gods? Or *what*?

My tattoos burned. I knew what I had to do next, dangerous as it was. Garrick had the right of it. Xyta was a bored deity. Now was my chance to be entertaining. I leaned forward in my chair, unflinching. I would have to be made of ice in order to brazen this out.

"I will make you a bargain."

Xyta's eyes shone. The pupils—my father's pupils—dilated in his hazel eyes. The rough flesh of his cheeks flushed to a ruddy, excited color.

"You have dealt with my kind before," they said, leaning forward to match me.

"As you said, I have walked this continent for hundreds of years. I have learned a few things." I did not dare tell them how I knew. I would take that knowledge with me to meet my Dark God when my end finally came.

"If I allow you to pass through my gate now," they said, tapping a finger against their lips, "I will demand two future sacrifices in return."

I exhaled slowly. I should have had terms ready. But the idea hadn't formed until I was there before them. I'd have to do what I could with what they'd presented.

"But neither of those sacrifices will be my coven, nor my… Kyrelle." I did not have a word for what Kyrelle was to me. Ancestor, relative, not sister or niece or—it did not matter. So long as neither she nor my coven could be taken from me, I would manage. There was nothing else that mattered to me.

Xyta nodded, though their muddy blond brows drew together. They'd hoped I would not figure out that loophole. "And what shall your punishment be if you refuse either of the future sacrifices I demand?"

I knew there was only one answer they would accept. "My life."

Xyta's smile made my stomach turn. Not just because it belonged to my father, a man I'd longed for in life and hated in death. But because of the joy they found at the prospect.

Even in the rage I'd felt after maiming Rylynn's betrothed, I had struggled with the covenants of my kind. The revulsion that filled every pore of my being proved that, even now, I was less than. I might gain my place back with my coven, but I still would not fit with them.

Garrick was right. My heart still ruled me, even if it did not pump the blood through my veins.

It did not matter.

They were the only sisters I had left. There was no place for me but with my coven. *A witch without her coven is nothing.*

Xyta licked their lips. "Do you agree to my terms? Even knowing the price will be twice as painful?"

I did not tell them that nothing could be more painful than what I'd already endured. That this bargain saved the only two things left on this cursed continent that I cared about. If they could not see that in my mind using whatever power or magic they possessed, I would not give it freely.

"I agree."

Xyta waved their hand, and the passageway opened.

I braced my hands on the arms of the chair, shoving it down past my hips as I stood. I finally let myself look to Garrick. He was closer. When had he gotten closer? How had I not heard it?

He waited just above the lowest level of the arena, his intense gaze focused wholly on me. I tried to reflect back the words he'd give me. *Xyta is a bored immortal. All they want is entertainment.* I'd given it to them in the form of a bargain. I hoped for Garrick's sake that whatever they asked him to sacrifice, he could give it.

Then I turned and walked through the passageway before the bloodthirsty deity could take back the bargain we'd made.

I WAITED in the darkness on the other side of the passageway. I could see the light at the other end, smell the cold mountain breeze that beckoned me to freedom. A false freedom, at that. It would take at least a fortnight to reach the Devotion Gate, but reach it I must.

Garrick would appear. If there was anyone suited to go through the gates, to conquer all seven, it was Garrick the Red. The legendary, *half-fae* bounty hunter.

I'd asked for his motivation for attempting the gates, and he'd given me a damning secret instead.

Alize no doubt knew about his birth. He'd been sent to Balar Shan so that he might know his father... a father who had done unspeakable things to his mortal mother... a new rage formed in my veins, as bright and sharp as any frost I'd ever shaped for myself.

I was not the only one in Velora who blamed the fae for the death of the continent and loved ones. If the world knew of

Garrick's parentage, he would be killed. If Nash learned of it… Garrick could take Nash. He'd proved that again and again.

But Nash had also shown that he was able to convince others to join his cause. If he could convince Alize to ally with him, it might be enough. Enough magic, enough malice, to kill a witch and a half-fae bounty hunter.

The odds were infinitesimal. Alize did not like Garrick, that was clear from their exchanges, but she'd never shown any violence against him.

And yet.

I would keep Garrick's secret.

There was more at play here than I was able to fully comprehend. The gods themselves had a stake in whether a supplicant made it through the Seven Gates. If I was playing games with the gods, then it was possible the other supplicants were as well.

I leaned my head back against the dark stone, letting my eyes fall closed as I waited.

A minute or an hour or an eternity later, the stone shifted and heavy footsteps I would have recognized anywhere approached.

Any softness or concern that had been in Garrick's face before was gone, the cold mask back in place. He'd retied his hair, the pale blond now tight where earlier the tendrils had fallen forward to soften the severe lines of his jaw.

Not blond, I realized. Silver. Like a fae.

I swallowed the observation.

"What did they ask for?" I said instead.

Garrick paused only long enough to look me up and down, the way he did each morning before we started out. His customary check that there was nothing about me that would slow us down. The acolytes must be waiting somewhere ahead with our provisions for the next stretch of the journey.

He did not meet my eyes before turning away. "We've told each other enough secrets for today, Koryn."

PART IV
DEVOTION

CHAPTER 38

I could not believe that I had ever entertained thoughts of goodwill toward Garrick the fucking Red. If the man had ever slept, I would have contemplated killing him just to free myself of the Lifebind between us. But if he did sleep, he never let me see it. When my eyes opened in the morning, he was there, cooking breakfast over the open fire. When I fell into my bedroll at night, too exhausted for even verbal sparring, he was there, banking the flames to see us through the night and ward off any of the mountains' more aggressive occupants.

I couldn't even call him a bastard anymore. Not even in my mind. It was too damn derogatory now that I knew about his parentage.

It was only a few hours past midday, and already I was about to collapse. The first half of the day had been a brutal upward climb. When we'd started downhill after our midday meal, I'd almost wept with relief. Only to remember that going down was just as punishing when you had to keep a body as considerable as mine from tumbling head over ass straight down the side of the mountain.

"You do not need to sigh louder to get your point across. I have excellent hearing."

I had not even realized I was sighing. Though the way my breath came in and out of my chest, with significant weight, suggested I had been doing exactly that. Even my subconscious hated Garrick the Red.

"Of course you do," I shot back. The fae had heightened senses, just like witches. I fixed my eyes over Garrick's shoulder. If I looked right at him, I was liable to freeze him where he stood.

He turned to face me, hands braced on the straps of his pack where they rested over both of his impossibly wide shoulders. "Do you want to rest?"

I walked right past him, determined not to admire those shoulders. "Not if you don't."

"Stubborn little witch, aren't you?"

The woods were thinner up here in the mountains, the air as well. It made all of our words sound longer, stilted.

"Do not call me that," I said between gritted teeth.

Garrick had stopped walking. For fuck's sake. If I stopped, I seriously doubted my ability to get moving again.

"It is what you are," he said.

"I am not little. I am a witch. Call me that if you must. But don't saddle me with an infantilizing sobriquet to entertain yourself." I was sweating everywhere. Despite the cold that held Velora in its perpetual grip, despite the frost that ran in my veins, I was so fucking hot. I unstrapped the cloak from my shoulders and tugged at the buckles that held my leather vest in place atop the wool overdress. Cool, brisk air found the triangle of my chest that I'd exposed, and I could have wept.

Garrick made a distressed sound in his throat. My eyes fell closed as I savored the bliss of the cold air snaking between the crevice of my breasts. I did not open them to see if he was choking on his water.

"Nicknames do not have to be infantilizing. They can be endearing," he said, his voice still gruff.

I sighed—loudly, just as he'd said. "And I am supposed to believe that when you call me a *stubborn little witch*, it is a term of endearment?"

"Yes."

I was going to murder him. The conscience and indecision that had plagued me for centuries were quickly evaporating. Fuck my supposed gentle heart and its refusal to die within my chest. I dragged my hair forward over my shoulder with one hand. "You are the most infuriating man—male—"

"I am a man."

Because he was half-human. That was the side of himself he chose to identify with. I might loathe and lust after him in alternating breaths, but I could respect that choice.

I snapped the cloak from my shoulders, draping it over my arm. "You are the most infuriating *man* I have ever had the displeasure of knowing."

I still had to carry the weight of the cloak, but the cool air around my shoulders and on the exposed back of my neck was divine. I could even feel the faintest breeze tickling the nape of my neck as I started forward again.

"I thought we were resting."

I spun without thinking, shards of ice flying from my palm as I swept it behind me. The daggers embedded in the ground several feet short of Garrick.

Pity.

"You want to fight, witch?"

Damn him. On his tongue, it did sound like an endearment. I could not even chastise him for choosing to use the epithet, because I'd approved it. Not a nickname, but a statement of fact. I was a witch.

Garrick's eyes were doing that thing again, where they caught the light and seemed to glow. His canteen was nowhere in sight to account for his gruff voice. But he could have stowed it in his pack while my back was turned.

He stared me down, one hand hovering near the hilts of the blades in his leather bandolier, waiting for a response. Apparently, I did not give him one quickly enough for his liking.

"The sooner you learn to defend yourself, the sooner I can actually get some restful sleep," he taunted.

"I am exhausted. If you want to keep hiking, then let's go. Never mind that we could be walking along the base of the mountains, rather than trudging through them." A point I'd made a dozen times in the eighteen hours since we'd left the Sacrifice Gate. To the north of the mountains were thick forests—and the coven lands. But to the south were the once-fertile valleys of the human lands. We could be walking through rolling hills instead of trudging up and down literal peaks.

The corner of his mouth quirked into a smile. Not a smirk. A fucking smile. "But you are not as exhausted as you were a week ago."

"What in the Dark God's frigid hellscape do you mean by that?" I enunciated the last few words carefully, each one laced with an unspoken threat that I would make good on, reckless or not.

"You are getting stronger every day. Initially, I was worried it would diminish those delicious curves of yours, but your body seems determined to hold on to them."

Had Garrick fallen down and hit his head? If he had, how had I missed it?

The man had taken complete leave of his senses. He could not actually mean that the reason he was dragging me through the mountains was to build my endurance. Just like there was no plausible way that he had just used the word *delicious* to describe my body.

I'd seen myself in a mirror plenty of times. *I* knew I was

fucking delicious. But it was something entirely different when Garrick said it.

I had two choices. I could either drop my pack, strip off my clothes, and take up the implied offer in those words. Or I could pull one of the daggers from my waist and stab him with it.

I sucked in a breath, decision made.

I dropped my pack.

CHAPTER 39

"YOU WANT TO TEACH ME TO FIGHT?" I KICKED THE PACK TO THE side, tossing my cloak over it as I palmed the dagger Garrick had given me. "Fine. Do your worst."

His brows drew together, an almost imperceptible sigh slipping from his chest. He could not be disappointed that he'd finally gotten what he wanted. I braced my feet, readying my stance as best I knew how as he selected a blade from his bandolier and started circling.

I rotated with him, determined not to allow him any unnecessary advantage. He had plenty already. But he simply circled, pausing now and again to test the terrain beneath his feet before continuing on.

When he spoke, his voice was smoother than it had been before, but there was an undertone that had not been there before. "Attackers will not care if you are sleeping." Nash. "Or if you are tired." Rilk. "You have to be prepared to defend yourself in every scenario."

"But isn't that why I have you?" I said with mock sweetness.

He was halfway back around the circle when he charged. I held my stance, meeting his first blow with an offensive of my own. But he seemed to expect that and swiped with his other fist even while I held off the hand holding the blade.

I dodged backward, which gave him space to bear down with the curved knife again. Fuck. I swerved to the side—

The entire world slid sideways, my feet churning in a deep divot that had been covered by a bed of pine needles. Garrick stepped back, letting me flounder around to find my feet again.

"First lesson—use the terrain to your advantage."

I was going to fucking kill him.

Garrick the Red. Renowned bounty hunter. Half-fae bastard.

I was going to kill him, and I would fucking enjoy it.

"You knew the hole was there," I growled, like an animal. That's what this man turned me into—a feral beast. A pit viper ready to strike. One of the atrocities that lived deep in the very mountains he insisted we traipse through.

"Of course I did," he said. "Second lesson—know the terrain better than your opponent."

Which he did, because I'd given him the time to reconnoiter it while he walked in literal circles around me. I gritted my teeth and sprang forward before he could.

He was ready for me, catching the downward swing of my knife against his own. I tried to replicate the maneuver he'd used against me moments before, swinging my other fist at his stomach. But I was weaker with my left hand than my right and he did not even react to the blow.

He caught my left hand, encircling my fist with his hand, and twisted. My body bowed with the pain, twisting with my arm to try and relieve it. Garrick hooked his other arm around my neck. With one swift movement, he had me pinned against him, my back flush with his chest. My knife was still in my hand, but it was useless.

I struggled against him, but that was useless, too. A low, self-satisfied chuckle caressed my exposed neck. I forced myself to be still so he could not enjoy my struggling, and so that I could try to break down the series of maneuvers that Garrick had used to get me there.

But thinking analytically was next to impossible with my body pressed up against his.

Garrick was as hot as I was. Hotter, maybe. I wore multiple layers of wool and leather, but I could feel the spot where his hand gripped my forearm like a brand. Except that it was a pleasant heat, a heat that ignited an answer low in my stomach.

He leaned in, his lips brushing the shell of my ear. "Third lesson —use what you know about your attacker."

The ice in my chest from earlier melted. My entire body was liquid.

"And what is it you think you know about me?" I gasped out.

"I know all sorts of things about you." He leaned in lower until his mouth was at the delicate intersection of my ear and my neck. "Witch."

Dark Lord, save me. On his lips, it did sound like an endearment. The kind that was whispered in darkened bed chambers between lovers.

I jerked out of his grasp. He could have held me in place if he'd wanted, but he let me go. I spun, wary to expose my back, and retreated quickly until there were several steps between us.

Garrick tracked every movement with those infernal glowing eyes.

"You should train with your left hand, as well."

"Maybe I should get better at my right hand, instead of being painfully incompetent with both."

A bead of sweat rolled down his temple, catching on the half-moon scar on the outside of his right eye before sliding the rest of the way to his jaw. I wanted to trace that exact path with my tongue. I wanted to be the one to make him quiver, to have the advantage over him just once. What would it feel like, to have power over Garrick the Red?

More intoxicating than any wine or liquor.

But allowing myself to give in, even if he wanted it, was dangerous. Foolish. He was my Lifebind. If Xyta had proved anything, it was the mercurial nature of the gods. The Goddess of Mercy might never consider the debt between Garrick and me satisfied. We might be stuck together through all seven gates. Or until one of us died. Or both.

As much as I hated to admit it—and certainly wouldn't to him—Garrick was right. I needed to learn to defend myself better. I no longer had a coven to protect me, nor the safety of the coven lands. Thus far, my power had remained strong. But when it began to fade, I needed to know how to wield the daggers in my belt for more than just slicing food.

I shifted my stance and threw myself into my next attack.

I WAS TERRIBLE, and it was not just the exhaustion. Even as I got better at anticipating his next move, I was not adept enough to avoid it. And for every parry or spin I did anticipate, he revealed another. Garrick's well of fighting tactics seemed to be endless.

"Your attackers will not give you time to catch your breath," Garrick said.

I braced my hands on my hips and ignored him. I hunched forward, struggling for every breath. Whatever improvements in endurance he imagined I'd gained, an hour of sparring had eviscerated them. I was sweatier than before, thirstier than before, and angrier than before.

"I am done," I said between gasps.

"Not yet."

The arrogance of that tone— "You are not my master."

"You are determined to get both of us killed."

I pushed myself up to stand, fueled by righteous rage. "I am doing my best!" I yelled, lifting my hand to throw my dagger at his fucking head. But something flashed behind him. I blinked, trying to see—nothing. There was nothing but a few scant patches of snow that had hidden from the watery sun beneath the evergreens.

"We are not done," Garrick was saying, though he sheathed his blade. "You need to know more than just how to defend yourself. If you need to incapacitate your attacker long enough to obtain information—"

"You mean torture." Ice shot through my veins.

Garrick did not flinch. "Yes."

"Teach me to defend myself. But keep your lessons in torture to yourself." *I already know how.* I did not finish the sentence aloud.

Garrick took several slow, careful steps toward me. I did not protest, but I did not move closer to him, either. I looked over his shoulder, to where I'd seen that strange reflection of light. It was an excuse to avoid his gaze and any questions I might find there.

"If you wish to incapacitate your attacker—"

My stomach tightened and twisted. "I already said—"

"Koryn." Garrick's hands landed on my shoulders. I expected him to pull me to him. I didn't know why. Whatever it was that existed between us, it was all tangled up with the Lifebind. His life depended upon mine.

I felt the intensity of his gaze upon me. But I still could not bring myself to meet his eyes. I kept staring over his shoulder, determined to keep my distance emotionally, if not physically. But Garrick was as stubborn as I was. Finally, finally, I turned my eyes up to meet his.

More than a foot separated our faces, the height difference never more pronounced than it should have been in that moment. But the way that Garrick looked at me, the intensity, the way the clover green brightened and melted into the blue... I felt impossibly close to him. Foolishly close.

He spoke softly, without breaking the eye contact that seemed to anchor me to the ground. "I understand your wish to live in a world where such things are not necessary. But this is not that world."

I swallowed hard, emotions I could not name nor restrain playing across my face for Garrick to see. He watched them all, unflinching, unafraid. He may call me a witch. But he saw what I was beneath that. He saw things that I was not quite sure I wanted to see for myself.

He tilted his head, just the barest fraction of an inch. Almost imperceptible. But I perceived it—an invitation.

I scraped my teeth over my bottom lip, then my tongue over the tingling sensation they left. Garrick made a low sound in his throat. The blood rushed through my veins in silent demand. I lifted myself up onto my toes, leaning into him to steady myself—

A flash of light flickered over Garrick's shoulder, moving quickly between the trees. Not light, but a creature with shimmering scales.

I rocked back on my heels. "Is that... is that a dragon?"

CHAPTER 40

BEFORE

I was jolted awake by the sounds of pain.

Not screams, not yet. But whimpers and groans, the sounds of someone who'd been injured badly enough that every movement was agony, but they could still move. They were the least terrifying of the sounds I'd heard in the ancient structure where my coven made their home.

After nearly a century, I ought to have been able to sleep through it. But after a hundred years, I still struggled to parse the never-ending input that my heightened senses delivered in a ceaseless barrage. The warmth from the fire that Maura always kept burning pushed against my power. I could counter it with the ice in my veins, but it required conscious effort. The sounds of my sisters moving about their daily routines echoed off the slanted stone walls, assaulting my ears. Although we could have crafted anything using our combined power, we lived in a communal structure. A constant reminder that the coven was a whole, not a collection of individuals.

I slept lightly, my too-sensitive ears hearing every sound.

The tread of footsteps. The scrape of a body dragged over stone.

I roused myself from a restless sleep, dressed only in my linen shift. My sisters rose around me. Most of them had been sleeping, as well. Only Elodie was fully dressed, her red and black velvet gown trailing across the ground as she walked. A thick fur mantle fell from her shoulders. Of all my sisters, Elodie was the only one who dressed this way—like a high-ranking noble, rather than the servant she had been in life.

The soft lines and shimmering velvet accentuated her sharp features and the razor-straight cut of her black hair. My sister could take on any face she pleased, but I'd always found her own the most terrifying. The complete lack of emotion—be it anger or excitement or sadness—was more eerie than any mask.

Like the lady she played, she did not drag the man herself. I recognized the spell that she used to haul him along, one in her repertoire as an earth-bound witch.

Our active powers were determined by the manner of our death. But unless we had our sisters' chanting along with us, the spells we cast must belong to our sacred bind. I'd frozen to death and been gifted with frost I could mold into ice and snow. I was a water-bound witch.

When she reached the center of the cave, she released her prisoner.

The man's face was covered in scratches that still oozed. One of his legs stuck out at an unnatural angle. A fragment of bone was visible through one of his battered fingers.

Without speaking, the rest of us fell into place. There was no need for discussion. One of our sisters had brought this man to us for judgment. His crime would be heard, and the coven would punish him. We each took our spots on one of the points of the pentagram etched into the stone in lines of solid gold.

Aurienna had woken from slumber as well. She caught my eye

as we took our positions on opposite sides of the pentacle. Her red hair hung in loose curls past her shoulders, nearly to her waist. She, too, wore a loose linen shift and bare feet. She was even close to my age, dead in her early twenties, resurrected only a decade before me.

But the chasm between us was immense.

Aurienna had mastered her power quickly. She controlled the vines and the pines with equal ease. Could whisper a few words and turn an otherwise innocuous tea deadly. She did not hesitate to use her power for the good of the coven.

She controlled the gifts the Dark God had given her.

She was not controlled by them.

Maura appeared last. She wore black, as always, accented with bits of gold. A black linen shift embroidered with gold thread. A black brocade overdress trimmed in decadent black leather and fastened with gold and mother-of-pearl clasps. Every piece was carefully chosen to accentuate her harsh natural beauty. The black she wore matched the lustrous cloud of tight black curls that just brushed her shoulders. The warm gold contrasted the cool undertones of her porcelain-white skin.

A beautiful nightmare.

Elodie waited only for Maura to step into place before speaking. "I found this man filching berries from coven lands. When I confronted him, he attacked." I searched Elodie's face and body for any indication of injury and found none. "And then he tried to run."

With those few words, she'd laid three crimes at the man's feet. The punishment for each was the same. My stomach clenched. I hated being woken from sleep, but in that moment, I was grateful I had not yet eaten breakfast.

In a hundred years, I had seen this scenario play out dozens of times. But still it had not become routine.

Elodie threw back her fur mantle, freeing her hands to accept the dagger that Maura had ready. Elodie had caught him, so his life was hers to take. We all must stand witness, but she would do the task. And she preferred it bloody.

Her expression remained blank as she approached. I felt the ice begin to form in my veins. I tried to soothe it back to sleep, forcing deep breaths in and out of my chest.

But when Elodie brought the point to the man's chest, just below the clavicle, something inside of me snapped free.

"Maybe he is willing to pay your price."

It was the only escape. The same one I'd offered to Rowellyn in the glade all those years ago. The price was Elodie's to set. But if the man was willing to pay it, he could walk away. Few humans knew the covenants of witches. They did not know to ask for this stay.

Every one of my sisters looked at me. I'd felt the weight of their gazes so many times before. Their disappointment.

Maura's mouth twitched into a frown. The others spanned a mix of confusion and disbelief. But Elodie, as always, was unruffled. She stared at me for several seconds, the point of her knife still pressed against the trembling man's chest.

"Maybe he is." With a single quick movement, she took the man's hand and pressed the dagger into it. She did not step away. Despite the earlier *attack*, she did not distance herself from the man she'd now armed with a knife. She gestured downward. "Cut it off."

He shook his head, not understanding. His entire body shook, even as he clung to the knife like the lifeline it was. "What? I..."

Elodie gestured again. This time, there was no confusion. "Cut it off."

Horror stole the man's features, distorting them until they were unrecognizable. "No," he cried, tears pouring down his cheeks.

Elodie had died for the love of a man. Betrayed by one.

I should have known better. I should have known this would be her price.

Elodie curled her fingers around the man's hand, pressing the blade downward. "Cut it off."

The man's cries devolved into shaking sobs. The knife hit the ground. Elodie bent to retrieve it, to begin her bloody flaying. She'd remove his manhood anyway and make sure he was still conscious to see it.

"No." Maura's voice echoed through the stone chasm. "Our sister has not yet had the pleasure."

If I'd still possessed a heart, it was by then a shriveled, useless thing. It had not pumped my blood for nearly a century. But the pain in my chest convinced me for half a second that there was still something alive in that cavity of darkness.

"Koryn," Maura said. "What is the punishment for entering the coven lands uninvited?"

"Death." Cold spread through my veins, pumped by the ancient power of the Dark God.

"For stealing the Dark Lord's bounty?"

"Death." It coalesced in my fingertips, frost beginning to coat my skin in silvery whorls.

"And for trying to flee our justice?"

"Death." My pointed fingernails grew, tipped with shards of ice.

"Elodie, Koryn will take your place."

The desperate man at the center of the pentacle was not the only one being punished. Maura knew it, I knew it, and so did every single one of my coven sisters.

Killing was as natural for a witch as breathing. More, if the faerietales the humans told their children were believed. I'd chanted spells with my sisters that had resulted in death. But I had never done it myself.

In the beginning, Maura did not allow me the honor because of my lack of control over my power. That is what it was, to my kind —an honor. A perfect execution of the Dark God's gifts. He presided over hell, did he not? We were his vessels, were we not?

I thought I'd been careful, sneaking away over the years to gift spells to Rowellyn and then her daughter. But when Maura fixed her gold-flecked eyes at me, the pupils rimmed by a brown so dark it was nearly black, I saw the warning she did not try to hide.

Disappoint her again at my peril.

Disappoint my coven again and I might find myself an outcast. Alone in death, just as I had been in life. A disappointment in death, just as I had been in life.

Elodie obeyed Maura's order without question. If she felt anything about it, she did not allow it to show on the perfectly honed blades of her face. I took her place at the center of the pentacle, my shift brushing against my hips, the hem against my calves.

Aurienna began to chant. In temple, it might have been considered a hymn. But here in the cave where the Midnight Coven dwelled, it was an invocation of the Dark God, spoken in his ancient tongue.

I did not have Aurienna's effortless control over her power, nor Elodie's perfect composure. But I had learned much since that disastrous night outside the guild hall. I breathed in and out slowly, letting the icy power in my veins have its way. The silvery whorls on my skin brightened, my forearms gilded with shimmering rivulets of ice.

The man's eyes widened as he watched, as he felt the cold that overtook the warmth of the ever-burning fire and the frost that spread across the stone floor.

I had to kill him. He had broken the covenants. He had attacked my sister.

I would do anything to protect my sister. To protect my coven. To protect my place here.

I will make it quick, I promised him silently, willing him to see the words in my eyes. But I knew all he saw was the glowing coven mark on my forehead.

I lifted my hands. My frost climbed up his body.

The chanting around me grew louder. A blast of heat from my

left—Maura had broken away from the group to throw another log onto the fire.

I tried to breathe, to slow the thrum of power in my veins. I had to strike quickly. A dagger of ice would do the job. I faced my palm upward, trying to focus all of my power.

It spiraled out of me, an icy fury that grew with every passing second. I could not disappoint my sisters.

Sweat slid down my temple. The heat was overpowering my frost. I needed more power. But the chanting was so distracting. The hem of my shift had come loose, the threads dragging across my calves. The damn chanting.

Ice began to form in my palm.

Just a little more power, another surge to form the dagger. Aurienna pitched her voice higher, louder, and all of my sisters joined in—

My power accelerated in a torrent I could not control. Instead of forming a dagger in my hand, frost shot from my fingertips, coating the man's body, piercing into him through his nose and mouth. I could feel the blood in his veins freezing, the organs going cold.

He screamed in pain, fell down, and writhed on the ground. I had to stop it, had to pull it back, but I couldn't. I'd gone too far already. He would die from the damage my frost and ice had wrought.

I had to kill him.

I had to harden that ice.

I channeled every fear, every agony I'd felt in the past hundred years into the ice that fanned out through his weak, mortal body.

He rolled to his back, one final scream echoing back and forth against the walls of the cave. Then he was silent.

I felt the life force leave his body. All of my sisters must have as well. They stopped chanting.

I fell to my knees. The layer of ice I'd formed on the ground cracked under my weight. My breath came in painful gasps. One by one, my sisters returned to their activities. I did not let myself look up to see Maura. Whatever I saw there, disappointment or pride or something else, it might very well break me.

Ruby velvet swished along the ground.

Elodie hummed pensively. "Who knew you would enjoy drawing it out as much as I do, Koryn."

CHAPTER 41

I'D SEEN MY SHARE OF MONSTROUS CREATURES DURING MY TIME IN the coven lands. But I'd never seen anything like her. Her scales were a lavender purple so light that it almost appeared white, with a pale green shine to them when she moved. The iridescent flashes were her, moving between the trees.

A dragon.

And she was watching us as closely as we watched her.

Garrick moved to my side, one hand going to the small of my back, the other casually fingering the line of hilts that crossed his chest. "There are many strange creatures in these mountains."

"What do you expect me to say to that?" I breathed. The dragon cocked her head to the side, as if listening to us even though we whispered.

She was the size of a large dog—or what I remembered of dogs. The humans had eaten those not long after the horses. But with her tail and neck stretched out, I guessed she would be as long as Garrick was tall.

"Many of them are the creations of the witches, if the legends in Balar Shan are true," Garrick said. He was close enough that I felt the words against my skin. But for once, I was too transfixed to do more than note the little flame that licked to life in my belly.

"Spare me your fae legends," I said.

"Even if they are true?"

I shook my head, both to clear it and to dismiss his line of thinking. "Witch spells have wrought all manner of intentional and unintentional consequences over the millennia. But not the dragons. They predate even us."

And they were exceedingly rare. To my knowledge, one had not been spotted in Velora since shortly after the curse. They were creatures who fed on the magic and power of the land. With Velora's slow death, it was believed that the dragons had sought out a new home. They were not stupid enough to die on this continent with the rest of us.

She walked around the base of a tree, her tail curling around the trunk as she did. The muscles beneath her scales bunched as she moved, four legs working in a graceful symphony with the shimmering wings tucked in against her back.

"What do you want to do?" Garrick asked.

As if I had any idea.

Was he deferring to me because I was a witch, an immortal being like the creature before us? Or was it my experience? Despite his accusation of my naiveté, four hundred years had passed since my birth. Or was it something else? Did the half-fae part of him sense the thrum of power in the air, the taste that now rode on the slight breeze?

I watched the little dragon as she moved to stand between two trees. Two delicate horns twisted back from just over her eyes, framing the line of spikes that ran down her neck and back all the way to her tail. They bore a startling similarity to the curved blades that Garrick wore in the bandolier strapped across his chest.

But it was her eyes that gave me pause. They gleamed a bright yellow-green that I had not seen in the forests of Velora since my childhood. The color of new life.

"She's a baby," I said softly.

Garrick's hand tightened on my waist, pinning my side against his. "How can you possibly know that?"

I ignored him. If she was a baby, then her parent must be around here somewhere. Waiting around for that reunion seemed likely to get us burned to death before we even reached the Devotion Gate.

"We have to go," I said, slipping free of Garrick's grasp. I moved slowly back into the trees, keeping the little dragon in my sight as I retreated. Garrick mirrored my movements without question.

It was a damn good thing my heart was long dead, because leaving behind that beautiful, wondrous creature made something inside of me ache.

I awoke to a warm body pressed to my side.

I'd gone to sleep shivering every night for weeks. What had made Garrick change his mind now? He'd already given me his cloak. We'd sparred in the woods yesterday, and he'd said… he'd complimented my curves. He'd been so hard against me.

I had told myself that this was a terrible idea again and again. Giving in to the attraction I felt, and now suspected he returned, with the Lifebind still in place between us…

But he was so warm, curled around my back like that. He'd even nudged apart my legs, sliding his own spiked calf between mine—

Spiked. Calf.

I sat straight up, swallowing my scream for fear that if I woke the creature curled on the ground, it would try to swallow *me*.

But the little—not so little—dragon was already awake. She shook her head from side to side, the same way I did when I tried to dislodge the last vestiges of sleep. She stretched out her neck and flared her wings, reminding me of a child stretching their arms overhead.

"Koryn." Garrick's voice floated across the fire, which was nothing but smoldering embers. "You need to move very slowly. Our friend from yesterday is here."

"I have eyes, you idiot," I hissed through my teeth.

At my side, the dragon cocked her head, then opened her mouth and bared her fangs at Garrick across the fire. It seemed she was a good judge of character. I was not certain I wanted that judgment pointed in my direction, even if she had decided to sleep curled around me.

I inched away from her, curling my legs under me and rising to stand with deliberate slowness, even though it aggravated the perpetually aching muscles in my calves and thighs. She turned her elegant head, well aware of every movement. She watched as I slowly walked around the fire, coming to stand by Garrick's side.

And then she stood up and followed right after me.

I completed the circle, moving back to where I'd slept, where my cloak and pack were still laid out as a bedroll. The dragon followed, circling wide enough to avoid Garrick, but arriving right back at my side.

"Why is she following me?" I whispered—useless, considering she was two feet away from me. But I couldn't help the impulse.

Garrick cocked an eyebrow, the corner of his mouth turning up in his characteristic smirk. Apparently, now that he'd decided the dragon was not about to kill me, he found this whole scenario amusing. "It couldn't be your winning personality."

I hissed at him. To my utter shock, the little dragon opened her mouth, leaned forward, and replicated the sound. With a few more fangs.

Garrick's blasted smirk transformed into an unrestrained grin. "If he gets big enough, maybe you can ride him," he said, taking a cautious step back and looking at us again. *Us. Dark Lord, help me.*

"Though I doubt he will grow soon enough to help you in the gates."

I rolled my eyes. "Stop being ridiculous. Dragons are not for riding." Not to mention those lethal looking spikes that ran down her back. They'd be the size of swords by the time she was full grown, if the legends were true about dragons' size. "And *she* is a baby."

"She?" Garrick chuckled.

The block in my chest eased a bit at the sound, my legs clenching together ever-so-slightly so that I could ignore it.

"Don't ask me how I know," I added. I could not have explained it. But just like I'd felt that thrum of power on the breeze the day before when we'd first encountered the little dragon, I could feel the rightness of my understanding of her.

"Of course I am female. A witch would never accept a male as her familiar."

"How do you know about familiars?" The words were out of my mouth before I realized it was not Garrick who had spoken.

He straightened slowly from where he'd bent to repack his belongings. "I do not know anything about familiars." His eyes slid from me to the dragon, her bright yellow-green eyes now staring up at me expectantly.

"A man who acknowledges what he does not know. I approve. He may stay." And then she nodded her head, dipped her rounded snout a few degrees, and eyed Garrick across the camp. A little huff of frosty air puffed out of her delicate nostrils.

"Good decision. He is impossible to get rid of," I said.

Garrick crossed his arms over his chest, a frown replacing his smirk, his pale brows knitting together. He looked at me like I was losing my mind, and in that moment, I was not entirely sure that I wasn't.

"You are perfectly sane. I already said, I am your familiar. That is why you can hear me and he cannot." Her spiked tail swished danger-ously close to my legs. I did my best not to flinch.

"I do not have a familiar," I said aloud. Could she hear my thoughts?

"You do now." She nudged her snout at my pack, flipping it over easily even though it must weigh half as much as she did.

"What is happening?" Garrick asked.

If only I fucking knew. "She…"

"Isanara," she inserted.

I cringed but adjusted. "She is called Isanara. And she has decided that she is my familiar. Which apparently means she can speak directly into my mind."

"I am also not a baby. A hundred years have passed since my hatching."

"And that makes you…"

"An adolescent."

"Even better." I sighed heavily, the motion lifting my entire chest. "A teenage dragon," I said for Garrick's benefit.

"That dragon," Garrick lifted his hand to point, seemed to think better of it, and inclined his head instead. "Is speaking into your mind."

Another sigh. "Yes."

"They did not mention that in the legends at Balar Shan."

I did not admonish him this time. References to his years in the fae court were the least of my worries at the moment. As if I had not had enough before. *"Stop rooting around in my pack."*

Isanara's head snapped up, her viridescent eyes blinking at me. *"Well done. You are learning quickly. I chose well."*

Familiars chose their witch, that much I remembered from the covenants. But none of the witches in my coven had ever had one, not in the nearly four centuries since my resurrection. Maura had implied that it was because there were so few animals left in Velora. The bond between a witch and her familiar was sacred. Tantamount to her duty to her coven.

But I'd never heard of a dragon choosing a witch. The dragons were powerful in their own right. Familiars were usually less powerful creatures that allied themselves with the witch in order to share her power. But Isanara…

"*Where are your parents?*" I asked.

I did not know her well enough, but I imagined that was sadness that dimmed her bright eyes to a muted celadon. "*My family is lost to me. Just like yours.*"

How she knew… I sighed again. Three times in the space of as many minutes. I expected Garrick to be impressed. But when I looked up, he was watching me with an expression I'd never seen on his face before. Not the inscrutable mask, nor the smirking smile. His mouth was softer, his forehead completely smooth. It almost looked like affection.

The knot at the back of his head had come loose, so that most of his silver-blond hair skimmed his shoulders. It always seemed to be coming loose. Was it because the strands were as silky-fine as I imagined in my fantasies?

"We should get moving," he said. "Am I protecting two temperamental females now?"

"*I withdraw my earlier approval,*" Isanara hissed into my mind.

"*Unfortunately, we are stuck with him.*"

"*I do not need to be protected. Familiars protect their witches. Not the other way around.*"

Except to the best of my knowledge, familiars were either raised from infancy or came to their witches in maturity. Isanara was neither infant nor adult.

And the last place she ought to be was tethered to me. Garrick could defend himself—and me, if it came to that. But Isanara, despite her protestations, would be a glimmering lavender target if she stayed with me.

Garrick watched us from the other side of the fire, but he did not move to intervene. I understood the message he sent without words. The little dragon was my decision. Why, when he'd been so fucking opinionated about everything else?

The ability to make my own decisions had only led me to disaster. It had led to my death in a frozen riverbed and banishment from my coven. It had resulted in a Lifebind to a bounty hunter who was a lot more complicated than rumors had led me to believe.

But my decisions had also kept Kyrelle and all of her forbearers alive.

Maybe I could make this one, too.

I exhaled slowly, trying to ground myself within my own body like Tomin had attempted to show me. But I felt my power rising in time with my emotions.

"Isanara," I paused, weighing my words and their likelihood of getting me incinerated by a moody teenage dragon. *"You should not be here."*

She paused in her perusal of my pack. What was she looking for? *"A familiar's place is with their witch."*

The words echoed with the same power that Maura's always had. *A witch is nothing without her coven.* The covenants were all about sisterhood and community, the basis for the communal power we shared.

But they were covenants I'd broken. *"I am a witch without a coven."* I was not worthy.

The words, even spoken within the confines of my mind, were physically painful. Even before she'd declared the bond between us, I'd felt the connection. There was an irresistible pull, stronger than any I'd ever felt to the sisters of my life or my death.

She was beautiful, but it was more than that. She was young and, despite the length of her fangs, vulnerable. Could she even fly yet? Breathe fire?

She needed protection.

But I could not even protect myself.

Isanara stared at me with a look that was not the same as the one Garrick favored, but equal in its intensity. While Garrick's turquoise eyes lit a heat low in my stomach that always spiraled lower, Isanara's yellow-green gaze spoke directly to the power in my veins. Not calming it, like Garrick did, but singing to it. A rightness I'd never felt with any of my coven sisters.

But that changed *nothing*. I could not allow it to.

"We are bound to the Seven Gates," I said.

Dark God, she probably did not even know what the Seven Gates were and what that meant.

"Do not offend me with such thoughts. Dragons are not bound by the limitations of your puny human minds."

She could hear my thoughts even when I did not direct them to her.

I did not point out to her that I was not human.

"It is not safe." My last appeal and the most honest.

Those yellow-green eyes rolled skyward. *Dark God, help me.* It should not even be possible for a creature to roll their eyes.

"Dragons were not made for safety."

Made like the witches. I could not begin to unpack the meanings she'd couched in that statement.

The only adolescents I'd spent any significant time with were my elder sisters. As much as I tried to forget my past, both at Maura's urging and for my own welfare, I knew that arguing with one was the ultimate exercise in stupidity.

She'd get her way—for now.

I nudged her head away from my pack. She snapped her fangs. I hissed through my teeth. I pulled the pack on and then layered my cloak over the top. "She is coming with us."

Garrick watched the interplay with raised brows. "To the Devotion Gate?"

"To the Dark God's frigid hell, if it comes to that, which seems inevitable given my current luck. She has made it clear that wherever I go, she goes."

Before the Mercy Gate, I'd been alone.

I am still alone.

In my heart, yes. But the number of beings following me around was growing at an alarming rate.

CHAPTER 42

"Not all of us have wings," I said aloud. Garrick might not be able to hear Isanara's never-ending commentary in my head, but I was done being the only one tortured by it.

Especially because Garrick the Red seemed intent upon torturing me.

The mountains between the Sacrifice and Devotion Gates made the ones we'd trekked through after the Justice Gate look like glorified hills. I'd only ever passed through them, never spent time in them.

"I bet the others are walking the base of the mountains," I grumbled, under my breath but loud enough for Garrick to hear, especially with his fae lineage.

"Maybe that is why your bonded chooses the mountains instead."

"You will not take his side." And I was certainly not speaking that aloud so that Garrick would know it.

Isanara walked at my side, sometimes wandering between the trees or bounding off to investigate a sound in the distance. But she never strayed out of my sight and she never took flight. It was hard to guess the width of her wings, as I'd never seen them fully extended. But either the trees were too close together to allow her to fly, or she had some other reason for staying on the ground. If it was pity for me, I might be sick. But, unlike the unlimited access she seemed to have to my mind, I could not peer into hers.

"Our interests are aligned. We both seek to protect you," she said, snapping her jaws in Garrick's direction.

"Then go be his familiar."

Garrick glanced over his shoulder. Like Isanara, he was tireless despite the incline. "Trouble in paradise?"

"I have nothing but trouble," I grumbled. We'd been climbing for days. Every once in a while, there was an intermittent plateau or downhill segment. But what went down must eventually go back up. My muscles ached and my clothes were laced with the sweat of exertion, despite the frigid temperature of the air. I needed a day to wash my damn clothes.

"Have or are?" Garrick quipped, falling back to match pace with me.

"Dark Lord, spare me." I avoided his eyes, unable to deal with their intensity. "I have an adolescent dragon in my head and a half-human bounty hunter at my side. And they seem determined to compete with one another for who will have the honor of driving me mad."

Isanara was suddenly at my side, nudging my pack again. "What is it you want out of there?"

"Maybe she's hungry." Garrick smirked. It was my stomach that had rumbled a few minutes before.

"She is more than welcome to take a bite out of you."

Garrick caught my chin with his hand, stopping me mid-step and bracing the weight of my body against his. "I was under the impression that you were the one who desired a bite of me."

Damn it all to the Dark Lord's frozen hell. He caught me with those glowing turquoise eyes and my insides instantly turned liquid. I had only one defense against that.

"You arrogant bas—"

Garrick clapped his palm over my mouth, stifling the words. I reacted on impulse and bit him. He did not even react. He'd turned away completely, the glow of his eyes flattening to a dark teal as he scanned the forest ahead of us.

I yanked my head to the side, freeing myself from his grip. "What in—"

"Stop talking."

My mouth froze at the demand, the weight of those two words settling in my chest as heavily as any block of ice ever had.

"There are strangers ahead," Isanara hissed.

She was no longer rooting around in my pack. Like Garrick, her eyes were fixed ahead. Her head bobbed in a serpentine motion as she assessed the threat. Were her senses as sharp as mine? As the fae? Or more?

"I have already told you that dragons are not bound by the limitations of humans," she growled into my mind. *"Or witches."*

She had heard my thought, earlier.

"How many?" I asked. I could sense the movement ahead now, the rustling of pine needles and crackling of old snow that was too concentrated to be a single wayward beast.

"Two humans."

I held up two fingers to Garrick. He nodded his understanding, and then inclined his head, but his eyes went to my hands.

I nodded, inhaling slowly and then letting the exhale out through my nostrils. The quiet of the forest helped me throttle my power, smoothing the ground ahead of us with a sheet of ice. Garrick started forward, but I stopped him with a hand on his arm. He froze as suddenly and completely as I had at his command a minute earlier.

I flipped my palm over, swirling my fingers through the air. Technically, I did not need to move my hand to summon my power. But it had always helped me shape it to see my hand in motion as the power flowed from me.

A thin layer of snow formed above the ice. It would provide just enough traction to allow us to walk without slipping, but was not so thick that it would slow us down if we needed to retreat.

Garrick's eyes flared, the pupils blowing wide in time with a smile that was nowhere near a smirk climbing his face. I might have called it a look of pride, if such depth of feeling existed between us.

We all moved forward by silent accord. Or at least, Garrick and I did. Isanara kept up a running commentary inside my head.

"Humans are weak. One well-placed bite is all it takes to fell them. I will go ahead," she said as she wove between my legs, the tip of one of her spikes catching on the leather strap of my boot. It sliced directly through the strap and did not slow Isanara at all.

"You will wait until we know what we are facing," I ordered. I expected the plumes of heated air from her nostrils as she whipped her head back around to face me, but the fangs were closer to my hand than I'd anticipated.

I managed not to flinch back, but only barely.

She would not hurt me. I knew that instinctively. In the same way that I'd known the frost that spread from my fingertips after my resurrection belonged to me, so did Isanara. And it was unnerving as fuck, both times.

Garrick moved in silence at my side, lethal with every step. I waited for him to reach for the arrows and bow strapped across his back. He'd worn them ever since that first night in the tavern in Canmar, but I'd never seen him wield them. But if there was ever a moment for a weapon of distance, this was it.

Instead, he drew the shortest blade from his bandolier. It was smaller than one of Isanara's adolescent fangs.

We were too close for me to challenge him aloud. He was the trained killer.

And what am I?

A killer. A dangerous disappointment. A—

"Witch," Isanara interrupted the spiral. *"A male and a female,"* she added, her attention still firmly focused on the threat ahead.

As mine should be. The heightened senses bestowed upon me by the Dark God felt more curse than gift, but now was the moment to use them. The sound of shuffling footsteps grew louder with each of our own silent steps. We were moving, but the pair we approached did not. Humans, I reminded myself. They could not have outpaced us if they tried; at least, not Garrick. Though I was getting faster, after weeks of him driving me through these blasted mountains.

There were very few reasons for humans to venture into the mountains of Velora. It was too cold for them to survive long, with so little meat upon their bones. Desperation and stupidity. Desperate enough to think they might find game in these untouched peaks, stupid enough to believe that they would not become the game themselves.

But the smell that flooded my senses when the wind shifted was not the stench of unwashed bodies nor the tangy odor of desperation. It was ashes and frankincense and palmarosa. A smell that had become as familiar as my own over the past weeks.

Garrick's entire stance changed as he, too, recognized the scent. A moment later, we were close enough to hear the distinct voices.

"Place the altars at even intervals."

Isanara wove between my legs again, her tail curling around my leg as she did. This time, she missed snapping a leather strap. But most shocking was how easily she matched her movements with my steps. I did not stumble over her, nor did a single part of her get underfoot. *"I will take the female. She looks meatier."*

"We do not eat our..." I paused.

Friends was the wrong word. So was allies. And there were certainly some acquaintances that I would not stop Isanara from taking a bite out of. Nash's face flashed in my mind, hateful and malicious. I banished it as quickly as it came.

"Dragons do not eat humans." A deep, disgusted growl rumbled from Isanara's chest.

"Good," was all I had time to say. We no longer needed the path of ice. Although I could not call the two humans friends, I knew they would not harm us.

Even so, Garrick stepped forward when my feet paused, positioning himself just ahead of me. Isanara held her place between my legs, a low growl hissing out from between her bared fangs.

I rolled my eyes and pushed past them both.

Varian stood beside the small fire, her arms tucked inside a thick black cloak embroidered with violet thread that matched the robes layered beneath. She'd braided back her dark curtain of black hair, though fine wisps had come loose at her temples and the nape of her neck. She regarded us with her customary composure, her dark eyes sweeping over our newly comprised trio—but they lingered on Isanara.

I shifted to the side, putting her more firmly behind me.

Which, of course, she countered by moving to my side and flaring out her wings, taking up twice as much space as before.

Fucking. Teenagers.

Tomin, however, did not assume the mask of quiet unreadability that I'd been so continually impressed with. His mouth hung open in absolute, unabridged shock, his dark curls bobbing with his chin.

He held a stack of flattened stones, the altars that Varian had referred to. Four were already in place in even circular intervals around the fire in the small clearing where Varian and Tomin were making camp.

"What is… is that a dragon?" His throat slid as he said the last word, as if he was not sure he should have said it at all.

Isanara snapped her wings closed, the sound echoing through the trees.

I rolled my eyes again, but they paused halfway to the sky. Tomin jumped backward, the stones in his hands toppling. They slid to the ground, vertical missiles. One hit his foot before bouncing to the ground. He hopped sideways, biting down on a cry, only to slip on one of the others and tumble in the opposite direction.

A gargling sound filtered up from Isanara's throat. It sounded suspiciously like the dragon version of laughter.

A thousand sarcastic comments jumped to my own mind, but after how I'd treated Tomin, I forced myself to swallow them down.

Varian ignored her acolyte entirely. I was not surprised, exactly. The first time we'd met at the Mercy Gate, Tomin had rushed to perform the Oath of Atonement with one eye fixed over his shoulder, watching for her. The relationship between priestess and acolyte could hardly be characterized as warm. But the complete lack of regard was also unnerving. Tomin had been an acolyte for nearly twenty years. I'd assumed that meant he'd forged relationships within the temple.

But maybe he was as lonely as me.

Which made my treatment of him even more abominable.

Varian finally lifted her gaze away from Isanara. "You have taken a familiar."

"As if I had any choice in the matter."

"You did not, and that is precisely how it is meant to be." Isanara did not snap her wings again, but she did that strange serpentine thing with her head as she returned Varian's stare in force.

"Yes," I said aloud.

"That is a dragon," Tomin exhaled, his voice still disbelieving. He'd collected the altar stones he'd dropped, but unlike Varian, who held her ground, he'd retreated several steps.

"The beasts that roam this continent are older than some of the gods themselves," the priestess said. She made no move to come closer. "You need not fear them, Tomin, only respect them."

Then she bowed her head to Isanara.

My eyebrows shot up. Beside me, Garrick made a low hum in his throat.

Varian merely turned back to her fire, withdrawing a small leather pouch from within her cloak and sprinkling herbs over the flames. Another pulse of frankincense and palmarosa filled the air.

"You are welcome to share our evening meal and make camp here," she said without looking up again.

Tomin managed to tear his eyes away from Isanara, but when they landed on me, they clouded instantly. He turned back to placing the altar stones.

Garrick moved again, angling his back so that neither Varian nor Tomin could see his face as he leaned in to speak.

His mouth lingered near my temple as he spoke. "You decide."

I snorted. "Trusting my judgment? I knew humans had short memories, but—"

"What is your point, witch?" My blood surged in my veins. My movement had brought his mouth even closer. I could feel the caress of his lips against the fine hairs on my skin.

"Mere weeks ago you called me naïve." My breath caught in my throat, but I managed to get the words out.

Garrick's low chuckle knocked loose the strands of hair that I'd tucked behind my ear. "And you will never let me forget it."

"The privileges of being female," I sassed back. "And having the memory of an immortal." The sass covered the panic that bloomed in my stomach at being given yet another choice to make, another opportunity to direct events. Another chance to fuck everything up.

He drew back enough that he could look down into my eyes. My body mourned the loss of him, of the closeness. But his open hand brushed against my fisted one. My fingers uncurled instantly.

"You do not trust the priestess," he breathed, his voice pitching even lower than before.

I swallowed, keeping my eyes on his instead of darting over his shoulder. It was easier than it should have been. "Do you?"

The corner of his too-luscious lips curved. "I do not trust anyone."

I rolled my eyes. "She helped me. At the Mercy Gate, first to hide my coven mark and then when I lost control of my power during the procession."

The half-moon scar beside his eye crinkled. "And I thought Seraxa had truly blessed us all. How dare you spoil my faith." I recalled his low chuckle when I'd extinguished all of the candles and torches in the temple in a single breath.

I scraped my teeth over my lower lip. "I don't know why."

Garrick did not ask for clarification. "Could it have been an act of mercy?"

It was the easiest explanation. Varian had made every demonstration of being a devout priestess of the Seven Gods.

But now it was my turn to smirk up at him. "You don't believe that, and neither do I."

The clover green flecks around his pupil seemed to shimmer, contrasting sharply against the outer ring of cerulean. But then he nodded. "Then we go."

My tongue darted out between my lips. A shaft of evening light broke through the trees above, gilding the green in Garrick's eyes to a shade so bright it almost glowed. His fingers curved around mine.

"No, we stay," I said. "We find out more about her."

We'd drifted closer together as we spoke. Our hands were the only part that touched, but a long exhale was all that it would take to bring our bodies together. His cinnamon and wine scent had long since faded from the cloak he'd given me, but here it was renewed again by how dangerously close we stood. Dangerously close to giving in to the pull between us. Nothing like the instant connection I'd felt to Isanara. This current between Garrick and me was not rooted in power, but something else. Something that felt just as dangerous.

Something that I wanted just as much.

"You won't find out much about anyone else if you're busy staring into each other's eyes."

I jerked back, the little dragon weaving between my legs as I did. It was a miracle from the gods that we did not go tumbling as Tomin had moments before.

Tomin, who jerked his gaze away the instant my eyes found him. He nudged the last altar stone into place and then gave me his back.

I managed not to cringe, but cool power swirled in my veins.

"We will stay," I announced.

"Good. Maybe they have something I can actually eat."

CHAPTER 43

"You may avail yourselves of the altar stones whenever you
wish," Varian said as we unpacked our bedrolls.

I rolled my eyes skyward, only to find Garrick waiting. He'd
never shown any indication of piousness. But I did not actually
know much about him. We had traded precious little personal
information. Yet the curve of his mouth was so familiar as he met
me with that knowing smirk. And I knew from experience that he
cared deeply. Not necessarily about me, but about whatever had
propelled him through the gates. It kept him unflinchingly at my
side. A loyal bounty hunter. The prospect was almost as far-
fetched as a witch with a functioning heart.

It was unusual to be laying out our furs beside one another
instead of on opposite sides of the fire. But without a verbal agreement or direction, I'd set my pack beside Garrick's and he'd
unfurled his bedroll alongside mine.

Isanara was already scraping out a patch of snow on my other
side.

I hated that they felt I was so helpless I needed their protection.
But the feeling that settled in my shoulders and chest wasn't hate

or even discomfort. It was soft and new. Maybe it was not just about protection. I could hate being protected… and appreciate being cared for. No one ever had before.

As I adjusted my furs, my sleeve pulled away from the edge of my glove, revealing the Lifebind inked on the inside of my wrist. The comforting weight I'd felt a moment before turned to ice.

Garrick was bound to protect me. As was Isanara. One by the gods, one by choice. But Isanara was an orphaned adolescent dragon in a dying land. Her decision to bond as my familiar could very well have been one of survival rather than preference.

I wanted to shove away the ice-cold burn. I wanted the softness I'd felt moments before.

Garrick straightened, a parcel from inside his pack in hand. I did not let myself turn to face him. Relief mingled with disappointment when he finally moved away to the other side of the fire.

"I will help you prepare the meal," Garrick announced, adding our own provisions to the meat that Varian prepared.

We received enough food from the temple to sustain us between gates. But the Seven Gates followed the curvature of the mountains, which meant that each one was further away than the last. There was no way we'd be able to carry enough food in a pack by the time we reached the final stretch after the Peace Gate.

Varian accepted Garrick's help without a word, moving over to share the workspace she'd set up.

If I'd been in charge, we would have eaten cheese and bread for every meal. Maybe I would have managed to chop up one of the apples that the acolytes included, the fruit so bright and juicy I hadn't seen its equal in hundreds of years. With the same cache of ingredients, Garrick had prepared dishes ranging from apples poached in wine and tarragon to a bacon, cheese, and apple jam sandwich that had earned a place of honor in my nightly dreams.

"He does not have to put in the effort, you know."

"I am not taking romantic advice from a child." Fuck. Since when was this thing between Garrick and me romantic?

Thankfully, Isanara was too busy being offended to latch on to that particular slip-up. *"I am over one hundred years old."*

"And I have walked this blasted continent for four hundred years. Go flaunt your age to someone else."

Of course, my familiar decided to do precisely as I suggested. She snapped her wings and walked past me, past Tomin kneeling before Seraxa's altar stone, and shoved her head into his traveling pack.

"Isanara!" I stomped after her but stopped short of actually reaching down and yanking her head out of Tomin's pack. Those spikes that ran from the crown of her head to the base of her tail were sharp. I'd seen them slice through leather like it was nothing. I did not fancy losing a finger.

Tomin managed not to jump away from her this time, but his lips continued to move in fervent, silent prayer. I hoped the Goddess of Peace was listening, because thus far my familiar had proved wildly unpredictable. And moody.

Not unlike her witch. "I'm sorry about her. She's still learning her manners."

"I am not a child." But even spoken mind to mind, the words were muffled as she buried her head inside Tomin's pack. What in the Dark Lord's hell was she searching for?

"Then stay out of people's packs without me having to remind you."

Tomin rocked back on his heels, dividing his gaze equally between me and my little dragon. "And you are going to be the one to teach them to her?"

My stomach tightened painfully. But I deserved the barb, and more.

"Probably not," I admitted.

My mouth opened and closed in an embarrassing approximation of a fish as I searched for the right words. Before I could find them, Isanara emerged from the recesses of Tomin's pack, a chunk of brassy-yellow stone clutched between her jaws. The warm tones contrasted with the lavender hue of her scales, as did the sharp, angular edges.

To my utter and complete shock, she flared her wings, slid her forelegs out in front of her, and crunched down on the chunk of stone. It disintegrated between her jaws as she chewed and then swallowed.

"What… what is it?" I stammered.

Tomin's honey-gold eyes were as round as I imagined my own must be. "Pyrite."

"Your familiar is sustained by the magic and power of the land itself," Varian said. She still crouched before the fire, an array of food spread before her, but she watched Isanara with the same fascination as the rest of us. A little thrill of triumph bubbled in my chest. It was my dragon that had finally broken the priestess's impenetrable composure.

But discomfort quickly replaced it.

The mysterious priestess knew more about my familiar than I did.

"Gems will sustain her longest, and then pure ores," the priestess continued. "Even soil and stone will pacify her, though not for long, mixed and diluted as they are."

You could have told me this. I sent the thought in Isanara's direction, but she was too busy chewing to bother with a response.

But my stomach dropped as my mind made sense of Varian's words. "The magic and power in Velora are dying, just like everything else."

Varian's mask of composure was back in place as she inclined her head. She could not argue with my statement. "And yet she is here."

I can go weeks without eating, Isanara added in between mouthfuls.

The crunch of the pyrite in her jaws grated against my senses, overwhelming my ability to think or moderate myself. My power surged in response and all the energy I could muster went to holding it in check rather than my tongue.

"How do you know so much about dragons? You said yourself that they predate the gods." The words came out like an accusation. I supposed they were, in a way. Varian was more than she appeared to be and had motivations that could not be explained by or attributed to her status as a priestess of the Seven Gods. I was fucking sick of being the last to know everything.

Her dark eyes did not waver. "I am the keeper of the Seven Gates."

Whatever the fuck that was supposed to mean.

Varian clearly did not feel she owed me an explanation. She turned back to her meal preparations. I avoided Garrick's gaze entirely, though I felt the weight of it. He'd been noticeably silent during the exchange.

Back at Seraxa's altar, Isanara had finished the chunk of pyrite she'd extracted from Tomin's pack. The acolyte was already digging and a moment later, pulled out another chunk of ore the size of his palm.

"You do not have to give that to her," I said, planting a hand on each hip.

"Speak for yourself." She snapped her jaws toward Tomin's hand —which promptly started to shake. But he held out his offering, still.

"I will find you something else to eat. We have caused Tomin enough trouble," I said aloud.

"You have caused him trouble. Not me." Her head darted forward, snatching the pyrite from his palm without touching a single fang to his shaking hand.

"She can have it. All of it," Tomin said, slowly lowering his hand to his lap. He grasped it with his other, trying to quell the shaking. But his eyes never left Isanara. "I still cannot quite believe that she is real."

I tried to see her the way he might. I'd encountered a few

dangerous creatures over the course of my hundreds of years in the coven lands. They'd all been creations of the witches and more or less bowed to our power, unlike Isanara. Dragons predated the Dark God's creation of the witches. I'd never seen one myself, but the power within her spoke to the power in me. Maybe it was because she'd bonded herself to me as my familiar, but I suspected it had as much to do with the fact that we were both immortal beings. Both tied to the power of Velora itself. I was awed by her, but I did not fear her.

Her pale violet scales reflected the light as she moved, her sinuous neck and shimmering scales appearing almost white at times. Like the frost that surged in my veins, she was at once beautiful and deadly, the spikes along her spine a visual reminder of the power of her species. Not unlike the coven mark between my brows.

It felt almost as if we'd been carved from the same ancient stone.

"Me neither," I admitted softly.

We watched her in silence, the quiet stretching out between us. It wasn't exactly heavy, but I could still feel the weight of it. The responsibility for lifting it rested solely with me.

I sat down cross-legged on the ground behind Isanara, giving Tomin plenty of space to ignore me or walk away.

"I am sorry for before," I said, forcing my fists to flatten and folding them in my lap. "I am sorry for how I acted and what I said. Not just at the Sacrifice Gate, but before, too. I treated you terribly when all you wanted to do was help me."

Tomin kept his eyes on Isanara. "You are a witch."

A witch does not apologize. Another axiom that Maura had drilled into me during those early decades with my coven. But there was no way Tomin could have known that. Which said plenty about what he thought of my kind.

"As if that is an excuse," I sighed. "It has been my excuse for a very long time." I could so easily attribute every ugly impulse within me to what I was—what I'd been forced to become. Garrick was right when he said I had not chosen to be resurrected. I'd expected to die alone in that frostbitten forest. Maybe I'd even deserved to.

But there I was, with a familiar and a friend.

Tomin nodded his head, as if deciding something, then lifted his chin to meet my eyes. "I accept your apology. But may I ask a question?"

He could ask, but that did not mean I had to answer.

But I would. There was only one query that I was bound to leave unanswered.

I nodded.

"Why did the exercise in the temple unnerve you so deeply?" He leaned forward as he spoke, an errant black curl falling over his forehead. The earnestness in his face, undisguised, made him look even younger than he was.

I'd always been the youngest sister. First in my family, and then in my coven. I'd never been tasked with guiding or caring for a younger sibling. But if I had, I would have wished for one like Tomin.

That had to be the reason that I answered him truthfully. That and the dimple.

"When the Dark God created the witches, he endowed us with certain gifts. Among them is the heightening of the senses. All of them." My eyes drifted closed, needing to cut off one of those senses so that I could continue, so I could try and make him understand. "I can hear your heartbeat, and Varian's. I can taste the dust from the pyrite that Isanara crunches between her teeth, feel the subtle moisture in the air that tells me we will have fresh snow tonight."

"Amazing," he said softly, the rhythm of his heart speeding up slightly. I felt him lean forward into the space between us, the subtle movement of air whooshing over the exposed sections of my skin.

"Overwhelming," I choked out. I noticed every place the syllables scraped over my throat. "Sometimes... sometimes it feels like a physical pain. A pounding in my head, a knife in my chest." *And then my power breaks free.*

I did not tell him that.

I'd never admitted that weakness aloud. If Maura or my other coven sisters suspected, they'd never voiced their guesses aloud. And Garrick... somehow, his warmth calmed my rampant frost and ice. But not even he knew how I lost control.

"I think the meditation could help."

I blinked, my attention refocusing on Tomin. He'd retreated a bit, but there was an eagerness in the set of his shoulders and earnestness in his honey-gold eyes. My stomach tightened, urging me back. Another attempt to control me, the dark voice in my mind insisted. To protect me from myself. Another who found me less than.

No. Tomin wanted to help. That difference was everything.

I laid a hand on Isanara's side below the line of wickedly sharp spikes. Her iridescent wing flared slightly but then settled again as one yellow-green eye flicked around to look at me. I doubted dragons could smile, but there was definitely approval in that glance.

I let her even breathing steady me. "Would you teach me?" I asked Tomin. "I promise not to run away or yell at you this time."

The dimple in his cheek popped as Tomin leaned further forward and offered his hands, palms up. "Of course."

Isanara chuffed when I removed my hand from her side, but she curled her head around and watched as I slid my hands into Tomin's. I told myself I imagined the dip of her jaw in a facsimile of a nod.

Tomin took me through the same steps as he had in the temple before the Sacrifice Gate. First, we focused on breathing, then on rooting myself in a place of safety. This time, the image that came to my mind was drenched in darkness, a lone fire in the forest. On one side, the rhythmic breathing of a dragon, on the other, a set of glowing turquoise orbs.

At some point, Garrick disappeared through the trees, sent by Varian to gather enough firewood to last through the night. I tried to block them out as Tomin instructed, but Garrick was always there, at the edge of my consciousness.

A lone crow cawed overhead, its deep, melodious notes echoing through the trees. The sound was unusually deep and musical.

When Tomin finally released my hands, my power was quiet. Still there, but less demanding, even when the smells of our evening meal mingled with the sharp call of Varian's voice and the crunch of Garrick's footsteps in the snow as he returned to camp.

Hours later, just as I fell asleep with Isanara stretched on one side and Garrick sitting first watch on the other, it began to snow.

CHAPTER 44

"Put your full weight behind your lunge. You are not going to injure me," Garrick said after he put me on my ass for the fourth time.

"Are you suggesting that I am holding back out of concern for you?" I spat as I clambered back to my feet. Literally spat—his last punch had caught my chin and flooded my mouth with the coppery taste of my own blood.

We had parted ways with Varian and Tomin after breakfast, the priestess and acolyte starting a downward path through the mountains while Garrick suggested an upward alternative. Because why the fuck not.

Though I had to admit that the cliffside plateau he'd chosen for our afternoon sparring session had a breathtaking view. I imagined I could see all the way to Kyrelle's tiny fishing village on the shores of the Southern Fate. Of course, I'd rather have imagined it from my feet than flat on my back from yet another punishing blow.

"You are embarrassing us both," Isanara put in from where she dangled her tail over the ledge. I'd taken one look over the sheer

cliffside and made sure that my back was always to the stone face several yards away. My winged familiar took no such precautions.

"If I could kill you, I would," I hissed between my teeth, trying to moderate my breathing the way Tomin had shown me and purposefully ignoring Isanara. "I am not improving."

Garrick did not offer me a hand up. Bastard.

He also did not argue—because he couldn't. Despite nearly daily sessions, I was only marginally better at defending myself. I could force my body through the maneuvers he showed me, but even as they became a matter of muscle memory, they were not smooth or fast. At least, not fast enough to defeat Garrick.

"You've built up your endurance," he said, already circling for his next attack.

That much was true. I wanted to kill him, but the breath scissoring in and out of my chest did not burn anymore, and we'd been at it for nearly an hour. He'd forced me to condition my begrudging body with every upward step.

Instead of admitting it, I lifted my dagger for what felt like the hundredth time.

"Go for the bow. It's his weakness. He'll defend it like a limb."

Three things happened simultaneously.

Isanara flapped through the air—she could, in fact, fly—landing in front of me in a flash of iridescent wings that reflected the diluted gray sunlight and transformed it into a shimmering combination of purple, emerald, and sapphire. She was even more beautiful in flight. But I had less than a second to appreciate it, because at the same moment, I spotted the owner of that haughty voice.

Alize's golden skin should have marked her out instantly. Her fae speed and the wind she commanded were the only reasonable explanations for how she'd managed to get so close. She leaned against a tree where the stone cliff edge jutted away. A good shove, and she'd go right over the edge. Just like she fucking deserved.

Power flowed uncontrolled from my hands, frost coating the slate beneath our feet, reaching for the fae. The frost thickened, solidifying to ice. Spikes rose up, encircling Alize from every angle and penning her in against the tree. She did not flinch at the display of power.

Isanara threw back her head and roared, a terrifying, feral sound much bigger than a dragon her size should have been able to make. *"She is stained."*

"What does that mean?" I took a step to come stand beside my familiar. She countered with one of her own, keeping herself firmly in front of me.

Isanara turned her head and snapped her jaws at me over her shoulder. *"Got it. Stay behind you. Message received."*

"She has committed the ultimate crime."

The Justice Gate. It had nearly driven me to flee the gates to be reminded of my crime. But what of Alize and Garrick? I had been so focused on my own misdeed, I had not dwelled long on theirs. One of them was an attempted murderer, the other a successful one.

The latter had moved slowly but steadily to angle himself between the three of us. One under his protection, one from his past, and one teenager with fangs. Even I felt a bit bad for him. But all other emotions lost out to my anger.

Garrick the Red was a bounty hunter. I'd known from the outset that he had blood on his hands. But Alize was worse. She was fae. Her kind was responsible for every terrible thing that had happened to my family.

I hated her. For my sisters, for my mother, for myself. And even for Garrick. He hated the fae blood in his veins. Why wouldn't he? I understood what he did not say—that his mother had been raped by a fae male, that he was the outcome of that brutality. He had as much reason to hate the fae as I did.

But it was not hate shining out of his eyes. Nor was it the snarling mask he'd tried before. I knew him too well now. I recognized the crinkle around his eyes, the slight divot between his pale brows, and the thrumming pulse in his throat. He was worried.

Fuck. That.

I was through being protected. "Get out of here before I unleash the rest of my power."

A slow smile climbed Alize's mouth, a joyless thing that rounded her cheeks but kindled no warmth in her features. She traced the path of my ice across the cliffside and up to my hands before skimming right over me, past Isanara, shockingly, and on to Garrick.

The frost in my veins solidified into icy shards.

"She is a witch. The Dark God gifted her with power. She should use it," Alize said to Garrick.

"I am right here. Speak to me directly," I seethed.

"Should I burn her?" Isanara growled.

"Can you breathe fire?"

Isanara remained silent. I'd suspected as much from my observations, but it was a little concerning to have them confirmed. She was more vulnerable than I'd realized. *"My fangs will do just fine."*

She snapped those fangs in Alize's direction, advancing several steps. My power moved in tandem, the spikes of ice that encircled Alize lengthening by several inches.

Alize made a show of removing one of her pale leather gloves and reaching out to touch the pointed tip of a spike with her finger. A tiny pinprick of blood formed. She lifted her hand to her lips and sucked the blood away from her fingertip.

The rich, noxious scent of her fae blood attacked my senses, anyway. The wind that swirled around us could not be coincidental. My power surged again in response, and I did not reach for any of the techniques that Tomin had taught me to leash it. I unfurled my palms and let the power—

"Don't." Garrick's hand curled around mine.

My power immediately responded to his touch, even as my mind struggled to catch up. He wanted me to spare her. He'd spent more than a month training me to protect myself, but when I was finally confronted with the opportunity to kill the fae bitch, he protected her.

Not me.

I jerked my hand away.

Alize watched the interplay with cruel amusement etched into her features. "You are blessed to have Garrick the Red bound to protect you, or you'd have zero chance of surviving the Seven Gates."

How did she know about the Lifebind? We hadn't specifically tried to keep it secret, but I hadn't walked around waving the brand on my wrist for the other supplicants to see, either.

"Your scents are intertwined," Isanara informed me. *"She can probably smell it on you."*

Unlike me, she'd been born with her immortal gifts. She probably used her wind magic to carry odors to her so she could scent her opponents. Like the animal she was.

"The Dark God stands at my side. What gods do you have left to defend you?"

"I don't need the gods to defend me, witch."

It was the same epithet that Garrick used, but there was none of the nuance that he lent to the syllables. Alize hated me as much as I hated her.

Good. It would make it even easier to kill her. The remnants of my human heart had nothing to say about this particular impulse. They were the reason for it. I'd held back from killing Nash and that was a mistake. But this would not be. Alize was a threat just by breathing. I could take care of that.

"Stand back. She's mine," I said to Isanara.

"We are one," my familiar answered, her voice different than I'd yet heard it. More distant, mature. But she stepped to the side with a flick of her spiked tail that said what she did not need to.

I moved clear of my familiar and my Lifebind. It was time for me to stand on my own, and they would both respect it.

"Think carefully about this, Koryn," Garrick said. He did not tell me to stop, even though my death meant his and the downfall of whatever had propelled him through the Seven Gates.

"I won't kill your witch." Alize smiled, showing her pointed incisors. "I can teach her a lesson without doing permanent damage."

Fuck her and fuck that.

I shot a look at Garrick, daring him to intervene. But he'd placed his back against the sheer cliff face that rose on one side.

I rolled my shoulders and snapped my fingers to the side. The sharp spikes of ice crumbled to frosty dust.

Alize understood the challenge. For the first time, I saw a genuine smile on her face.

I'd thought Garrick was fast. But Alize was the wind itself. She sprang forward, halving the distance between us in a single bound. By the time her feet landed on the stone ledge, she already had her blade in hand. It sparkled even in the muted light, the blade a swirling alloy of diamond bright metals.

The blade was like her—lithe and punishing. She bore down, not giving me a moment of grace. I did not want her fucking grace, anyway. I wanted her dead.

I threw up a wall of ice between us, thickening it with power that gave and gave without a hint of resistance. But I was too distracted to question that.

Alize drove her entire weight into the wall of ice, crashing through it without any regard for the shards that sliced into her skin like glass. Her fae healing would take care of those minor wounds. But my power surged in victory at the stream of blood that flowed down her cheek.

Janessa's face flashed in my mind. But it wasn't the freckles I'd adored or the beauty I'd admired outside the temple that fateful spring day. I saw the blood as it drenched her face, smelled the acrid burn of her hair and flesh as that fae-cursed diadem killed my sister.

I threw myself into the maneuvers that Garrick had taught me.

Step, turn, stab. This time, I put my full weight behind every thrust.

I am going to kill her. Kill her. Kill her.

The words moved through my veins like the beating heart I no longer possessed.

But for every thrust, she parried. I knew my stabs were well-aimed, but she commanded the air and used it to guide my hand off course.

I dodged to the side, barely avoiding the tip of her blade. My faltering steps brought me to the edge of the cliff. Garrick growled behind me—or was that Isanara and it was in my mind entirely?

Sweat poured from my temples, my power too busy keeping me alive to bother with regulating my body temperature. But before I could get any closer, I collided with a wall of hard air that sent me stumbling backward.

Alize was playing with me.

The realization turned the rivulets of sweat to frost. Between my brows, I felt the burn of my coven mark as cold power seared through me. It coated my skin, spreading in glistening whorls over the backs of my hands. I felt it lick up my throat and curl across my cheeks.

I saw my father, a man drunk on wine and his own ambition. Even in my memory, he never looked back at me. Always past me, always fixated on something just beyond his reach. Fascinated with the fae.

Fae like the one before me, who looked down on humans as if they were nothing. They had ruined an entire continent with their hubris and then left us all to rot. For four hundred years, I'd been forced to live an immortal life, watching my sister's line struggle for life in the barren wasteland of Velora.

All because of the fae.

Because of Alize. For all I knew, she was hundreds of years old and directly responsible, just like the rest of the faceless cowards hiding behind the walls of the fae fortress in the north.

She attacked again and I threw up an arm to protect myself. Her blade sliced through the layers of wool and linen and then skin and muscle. I screamed at the pain. Or maybe that was Isanara. Or Garrick. But I was too focused on myself, on the whorls of frost that covered my hand.

I would never best Alize in direct combat. Not like this. I had to get a hand on her.

I threw my dagger, but only to distract her. It worked marginally well. She turned her head to avoid the blade, but a smile was already on her face. I'd given up my weapon. But she was the one who had pointed out that I wielded another.

I grabbed her wrist, arching my back to avoid the swing of her glittering blade. I braced myself for another blow, for more blood. I could withstand it as long as it was not a direct hit. I just needed long enough—

Alize screamed as the skin around my fingers began to blacken. Frostbite on its own was a slow killer, but I had the power of the Dark God to speed it along.

My mother came to me last. Was it truly her face I remembered, or the one conjured by Xyta? The Deity of Sacrifice had accepted my bargain, and they would make me pay. But not now. They had left me to determine this moment for myself.

The fae bitch twisted away from me, but I refused to let her go. I felt her pulse slowing beneath my fingers as the blood in her arm solidified and froze. Her fingertips were already turning blue. A bit longer, and they'd turn black. I would hold on until her entire body was a wasted husk—

Her knee slammed into my stomach, stealing the breath from my lungs but not the vengeance. The vengeance so singular that I'd forgotten the rest of her. I doubled over, releasing her without even meaning to.

But Alize wasn't done. Her fist connected with my chin, snapping my head back loud enough that it echoed against the stone cliffside. Her final blow sent me to the ground, flat on my back. I got my knees up, curling to protect myself. The dagger was long gone, but I formed one of ice with only a thought, and I would stab it into her black fucking heart if she tried to touch me again.

Instead, I heard the unmistakable sound of her blade returning to its sheath. No footsteps. She sent her words to me on a wind, a whisper delivered straight to my ear. "Next time you push me, I will kill you."

I opened my mouth to return the sentiment, but she took off at a run through the trees.

I rolled to my back and screamed up at the empty sky. I emptied all of the air from my chest, let the waves of rage peel out of me into the world. I wanted every single one of the Seven Gods to hear me.

I screamed until my throat burned and then I screamed some more, until the sound was pitiful even to my own ears.

A few minutes later, a scaled head nudged my hand up. I forgot to avoid Isanara's sharp spikes. But she did not cut me, and for once, she didn't insert a pithy comment.

Several minutes after that, Garrick's face appeared above mine. For a few seconds, I just blinked up at him. I was angry at him for not training me well enough to beat her, even though I knew that it wasn't his fault. He could not make my body move faster. I was pissed that he'd asked me not to kill her. He was my fucking Lifebind. Where was the loyalty that supposedly bound his soul to mine?

But mostly I was fucking tired.

Garrick the fucking Red, however, was smirking.

"What are you smiling about?" I rasped. "You were going to let her kill me."

Garrick did not respond to that accusation. Whatever else was between us, we both knew it was not true.

"We will make a fighter of you yet," he said, offering me a hand. "And now I know how."

CHAPTER 45

BY MY ESTIMATION, WE COULD NOT BE MORE THAN A FEW DAYS AWAY from the Devotion Gate. We'd spent so long climbing through the mountains that it was easy to forget that was our goal—to get to another gate and try not to get ourselves killed.

Maybe we would get lucky. Other than Garrick and me, only Alize and Nash remained. Alize was still alive. But when we sat beside our fire in various levels of tense silence, I indulged in the fantasy of Nash being eaten alive by one of the creatures that my ancient sisters had unleashed in the mountains.

The clearest sign that we neared the next gate was that Garrick no longer drove us upward. We'd been afforded a map, though we rarely consulted it. The mountains were guide enough. I was not looking forward to the temple, precisely. But the prospect of an actual bed and bath was appealing, as was seeing Tomin again.

I did not let myself interrogate that urge. If a temporary friend was what it took to get me through the gates, then so be it. Getting through them was all that mattered.

Of all the gates, Ramkael was the only one I was not concerned about. I'd spent my entire immortal life devoted to my coven and the preservation of my sister's line. I could face the Devotion Gate.

Garrick walked ahead of me, Isanara at my side. The forest had changed as we descended from the mountains. There were fewer straight fir trees, more spindly alders and sprawling maples. They had never seen the foliage of spring. Unless I made it through the Seven Gates, they never would.

My eyes drifted as we walked, scanning for any signs of life. I knew Garrick and Isanara watched as well, but I refused to be helpless. Alize had bested me in the end, but I'd felt her blood freezing in her veins under my hand. I could and would defend myself.

Light flickered in my periphery. It was probably nothing, just the movement of a leaf in the wind catching the light, but I turned reflexively.

"The stained one," Isanara hissed.

Garrick was at my side in the space of a breath, but all three of us came upon the scene at the same time.

The light I'd seen was not a leaf reflecting the watery sunlight. It was a mushroom. Or rather, a ring of mushrooms. They spread out in a near-perfect circle wide enough that Garrick and I could have laid out end to end and still had space within it. Their white stalks nearly blended into the snow, but the tops glowed. Pale blue and green and yellow alternated in a seemingly random pattern.

Alize crouched at the edge of the circle. Her close-cropped brown hair had grown out some since that first day in the temple of the Mercy Gate, the strands curling around her pointed ears. I'd been too busy contemplating her death the last time I saw her to notice. The wounds I'd given her only two days before were fully healed, no scars in sight. My own arm boasted three stitches where she'd sliced it open. Fuck her.

Garrick stepped closer to the ring, but he did not crouch down like Alize. That now-familiar divot burrowed deep between his brows. He made no attempt to hide the worry that creased his face. "Is that a faerie ring?"

"Yes," I said. "I have not seen one…" Since before I was made.

It took me several seconds to realize that neither Garrick nor Alize was looking at the ring of mushrooms. They both stared at me with varying levels of intensity. Alize's hate was mingled with skepticism. Garrick… was that panic lacing his worry?

"My father traded in fae artifacts after they abandoned Velora," I said slowly, carefully. I was not sure what I wanted to reveal. Especially to Alize. I'd decided not to kill her—not because I did not want to, but because I would not let my temper get the better of me until I was certain I could finish the job. And whatever feelings she held for Garrick that kept her from throwing me over the mountain ledge also kept her hand away from the blade at her waist.

When neither of them spoke, I continued. "There were stragglers. We came upon the rings from time to time when we traveled with him to collect his treasures."

Alize's face twisted. "To loot fae relics."

"Not all of us had a walled sanctuary to escape to after your kind sentenced our continent to death."

"The gods sentenced Velora to death," she seethed. "They decided the punishment."

"And you were the reason they felt the need at all."

Alize pushed to her feet. "Teach your little witch some respect, or I will put her on her ass again."

Garrick did not move any closer to me. For once. That faith in me—if that's even what it was—had me lifting my chin in silent defiance. That was why he'd let me fight Alize on the cliffside and why he had not intervened. He needed both of us, her and me, to know that I was capable of defending myself.

"We are not in Balar Shan," Garrick said.

Whatever that comment meant, the significance to Alize was apparent. She straightened, wiping all of the anger from her face and replacing it with the beautiful, cruel mask she wore so well. There was more pink than usual in her golden cheeks, but nothing else to indicate the threat she'd made moments before.

"This was not me." She waved her hand at the faerie ring. "And I assume that it was not you."

"Why should we believe you? You keep turning up wherever we go," I spat.

Garrick might have some reason to trust her, but he hadn't shared it with me, and he had tried to convince her not to go through the Seven Gates. Something about her being here bothered him, even if he wasn't ready to let me kill her.

Alize gnashed her teeth, the pointed incisors flashing. "I thought you knew so much about our kind."

Isanara displayed her own. I'd never been prouder.

Alize wrinkled her elegant nose but kept her pointed teeth to herself. "There are only so many routes through the mountains, witch." Then she crouched down again, reaching out to brush her knuckles across the glowing blue tops of one of the mushrooms. "Faerie rings are left behind by latent magic. Someone with powerful fae gifts performed an act of substantial magic here."

I blinked down at her. What utter nonsense. "In this exact spot? So near the Devotion Gate?"

Garrick and Alize exchanged a look.

"You are keeping secrets." Maybe I should have kept that realization to myself. But the surprise forced the words out. And the self-preservation had me turning inward. *"Can you poke around in their heads like you do mine?"*

Isanara growled aloud, reserving her disgusted scoff for me alone. *"Thankfully, not."*

"So much for not being limited by the bounds of humans and witches." I looked between Garrick and Alize again, but they'd both turned back to examining the faerie circle. *"And fae."*

She nipped at my hand, but we both knew that if she really wanted to hurt me, those fangs would more than do the job.

Alize insisted she had not performed the magic that had caused the faerie ring. Garrick had not been out of my company for long enough to attribute the ring to him. It put the wind magic Alize had wielded in our duel into perspective. While powerful, no mushrooms had sprung up to mark our exchange of magic and power. Which meant whatever had happened here in the forest...

A new thought sprang into my mind. I spun so quickly I might have fallen if Isanara had not twined between my legs, providing a steadying force.

"Do you have magic?"

Garrick's eyes blew wide, the clover green retreating into the cerulean blue and melding into a variegated turquoise.

"None manifested during my time in Balar Shan."

I would know if he was lying to me. *He wouldn't lie to me.*

Neither of us had shared all of our secrets, not by any stretch of the immortal imagination. But I'd never lied to Garrick, and as far as I could tell, he'd repaid that honesty.

"He is fae," Isanara whispered. But even fae ears were not keen enough to hear the thoughts my familiar and I exchanged within the confines of my mind.

"There is more afoot here than we realize." Alize crushed the mushroom she'd been examining under the heel of her boot, then ground it into the dirt a few times for good measure. She wiped her hands on her tawny leather breeches, adjusted her pack, and started off in the direction we'd been heading before the diversion. "The Devotion Gate is on the other side of that pass. I will allow you to follow me and avoid the tavern on the southern road, but don't let me see you again."

The last was directed at me. Isanara let her know for the both of us that the sentiment was entirely mutual.

Garrick stared after her, his mouth moving slightly as if he were counting off the seconds and calculating how much of a head start to give Alize. But my attention had snagged on something else entirely.

"Tavern?" I croaked.

CHAPTER 46

of on the ground."

It had taken me hours and hours to get those words out of him. He'd been in a temper ever since the faerie ring. There were no more lingering touches and no genuine smiles. Whatever that ring meant to the two of them, it had unnerved Garrick.

That should have unnerved me. But the prospect of an actual bed in a room that wasn't shared with Nash or Alize was more diverting than I would have estimated.

I eyed the weapons strapped to him. Greatsword at his waist, bandolier of knives across his chest, and bow and quiver strapped to his back. Plus, the curved knife he currently gripped in his hand —the one with the braided silver handle. His favorite.

Would he count disarming him as getting that knife, or did he honestly expect me to pick off all of those weapons one by one? If so, I might as well start digging down for a bed in the dirt now instead of later.

I had just the two blades to my name.

"Use your power to complement what I've already taught you."

Logically, I knew the only one who could poke around inside my head was Isanara, busy flapping eagerly from side to side at the edge of our makeshift sparring ring—a slightly sloped riverbed that had long since gone dry. But damn if Garrick did not make a good show of it.

"And what in the Dark God's frigid hell does that mean?" I threw the curse into the wind and charged forward, aiming for his knee. He had an easy nine inches on me; it was the most reliable target I could reach.

Garrick deflected me easily, using the weight I'd put behind my attack to send me sprawling. "Alize uses her wind to push aside her attacker's blade and then shove her own into the opening."

I forced myself up, cursing every delicious meal my bonded had cooked over the past several weeks and every bit of muscle he'd forced me to gain with his endless uphill slogs. "Continue comparing me to that fae bitch, and you will see exactly how I can use what you've taught me."

There was another target within easy reach of my height. While I'd spent more hours than I cared to admit dreaming of that particular appendage, I'd happily shove my knee into it if it shut him up.

He held up his hands between us and curled one in invitation. "Please do."

How the fuck was I supposed to beat him when every maneuver I knew he'd taught me? Garrick was not going to let me win. Not ever. I knew that much about him with certainty.

"Go for the bow," Isanara urged from the sidelines.

I refused to take Alize's advice on principle. So, I threw myself forward into another ill-fated attempt. I got my hand around his wrist, but he dislodged me before I could apply enough pressure to dislodge his blade.

I landed hard on my elbow, the impact ricocheting through my bones.

"Your power is part of who you are. Why are you afraid to use it?"

Because I cannot control it! My mind screamed.

Isanara's feet hit the ground, snow spraying across the dirt between me and Garrick. She'd heard what I said even if I hadn't meant it for her.

I glared at Garrick. "We keep our own secrets."

My eyes dared him to call me on those words and acknowledge his own hypocrisy.

"And that need to keep secrets will get you killed, and then me killed. And not only will we be dead, but whoever that woman was who you convinced not to enter the temple—she will most likely die too."

I was less worried by the moment about controlling my power.

He knew my motivation for entering the temple. But he still had not trusted me with his. What were we doing here, really? We would not be together at all if not for the Lifebind between us. I'd attempted the Seven Gates to save Kyrelle and restore my place with my coven. Neither of those goals had anything to do with Garrick the Red.

"By all means, spend the little time we have left before the Devotion Gate digging around in your own insecurities."

I did not think. I threw out a hand, spears of ice the size of my forearm flying through the air in a deadly attack centered at Garrick's chest.

He dodged them with irritating ease.

"You wield the ice easily enough."

"It isn't ice," I said through gritted teeth. Damn it all to the Dark God's hell.

Garrick tipped his head to the side, a smirk tugging at his mouth. Despite his admonition about wasting time, he stared at me and waited.

"My active power is frost," I admitted begrudgingly. "I can shape it as I need. I can soften it into snow or harden it into ice."

I'd give him that much in the interest of self-preservation. He did not need to know that my active power derived directly from the manner of my death.

"And those clever little rhymes you think you're whispering?"

"Spells," I seethed between my teeth.

He nodded, his eyes catching the light between the trees and sparkling. "Like the one you offered me at the Mercy Gate in exchange for my silence." He cocked his head to the side. "Why don't you cast a spell to kill the other supplicants and be done with it?"

"Why don't you kill them with the bow you carry around but never use?"

Garrick's face hardened. Too bad for him, I'd gotten better at reading his expressions. "I have my reasons."

"So do I," I bit back.

"You're afraid to do it."

Wrong. "I have killed plenty." Truth.

"So have I."

I didn't doubt it.

If he had his reasons not to bring the other supplicants down in one fell swoop, so did I. Yes, I'd killed before. But only when my own survival depended upon it. I could whisper a spell that froze the blood in their veins. Without my coven to sustain me and bolster my power, the effort might very well kill me. Or sap me of the ability to use my active power, which was my most reliable weapon. I had to use my power judiciously. The frost would always come the easiest, and it was the gift that belonged solely to me, given by the Dark God himself.

But the uncertainty of my power was not the only thing that kept me from killing the other supplicants. It was my fickle human heart, still in my chest even if it refused to beat. It refused to die. It was perhaps the most stubborn part of myself.

"You can defend yourself without killing anyone," Garrick interrupted.

That would require control. I was not about to tell Garrick that the only times I felt some semblance of control were when I meditated with Tomin and when Garrick himself held my hand and met my frigid cold with his steady warmth.

I'd rather sleep on the ground for the rest of my immortal life.

So, I gave him a truth that cost me less. "There is a price to power. Without my coven, without Velora, I will fade like the land beneath our feet. The longer I am separated from them, the less power I will be able to access."

Except...

That divot appeared between Garrick's silvery brows. "You were just as powerful yesterday as you were a month ago."

Except.

"You extinguished every flame in the temple before the Mercy Gate. You saved me by using your frost to make a path to safety. And yesterday, you would have frozen Alize from the inside out if she hadn't managed to get out of your grip." As he spoke, he moved closer, the intensity of his gaze building.

What he said was true. I'd noticed it but not thought about it. What did it matter, really? Maybe it was the Dark God bolstering my power long enough for me to lift Velora's curse. Maybe Maura and the others had performed some sort of blood spell that worked even at a distance to keep my power strong while she sent me on this doomed quest.

There had to be a reason the coven mark still burned on my forehead, just as visceral as the Lifebind inked on the inside of my wrist.

Wingbeats sounded overhead as Isanara launched into the sky, gliding over our heads and circling around the barren trees, her small size giving her just enough room to maneuver.

My stomach pitched inside my gut. *"Are you the reason my power is still strong? Are you giving me your lifeforce?"*

She did not even pause her circling. *"What a ridiculous question. Of course not."*

"But then... why would you choose me? If I do not make it through the Seven Gates and return to my coven, my power will fade and I will eventually die. Familiars do not choose weak witches."

"Strength takes many forms," she said, her voice taking on that strange gravity that made her seem older than she was. A hundred years might be a short time for a dragon, but for mortals it was more than a lifetime, I reminded myself. Isanara had not shared what the first hundred years of her life in Velora had been like.

If I'd had a beating heart left to me, it would have ached for her.

Garrick had already moved on, unwilling to let me linger in my own insecurities, as he'd so irritatingly pointed out.

"You don't want me hovering over you." He advanced a few steps as he said it. "So learn. Master your power and you won't need my protection."

Master my power. Like I hadn't spent nearly four hundred years trying and failing to do exactly that.

"It is not that simple," I insisted, but he barely gave me time to finish before launching himself over the frozen riverbed.

I got my arm up just in time to deflect the blow, but the fresh stitches in my forearm screamed at the impact. Frost shot from my hand, my power rising to protect me without my calling it. Out of control, again. Damn it all. I was so sick of Garrick being right. I wanted him on his ass, just like he put me on mine again and again.

The frost heard my frustration. It curled around his feet, solidifying into a rope of ice that cracked with his next movement. But it was enough to distract him. I couldn't reach the blade in his hand.

I wanted him on his ass—literally. I pulled the residual moisture from the riverbed, forming a sheen of slippery ice beneath his feet. He tried to use it to his advantage, pitching himself in my direction. But I used my height—or lack of it—to dodge underneath him. My knees screamed as they hit the ice, but I got my hand around what I wanted.

My wrist protested the angle, but I forced myself to my feet and used frost to fuse my skin to the metal hilt.

Garrick cracked the ice with a sharp stomp of his heel, regaining traction as he spun in a graceful arc, his blade swirling with lethal precision. But for once, I was ready.

I had no idea how to wield it. The blasted thing was as long as my legs. But I forced the quivering muscles of my arms to lift Garrick's greatsword into the space between us.

It started as a smirk. Then it curved both sides of his mouth, lifted his stubbled cheeks, and lit his eyes as a true, full smile took over Garrick the Red's face. And took my breath away.

"That's my girl," he breathed.

CHAPTER 47

BEFORE

IT WOULD HAVE BEEN SPRING IF SUCH A SEASON STILL EXISTED IN Velora. Over the past century, marking the change of seasons had become impossible. Maura kept the dates on the cave walls in the coven lands, marking them out for posterity. As a creature of the Dark God, I tracked the cycle of the moon by habit. The priestesses and priests still kept time in the temples, I was certain. They'd be the last of us to abandon their rituals. The religious zealots might be our equal in stubbornness, but witches were infinitely more practical.

It was that practicality that had led Maura to send us further and further afield each year to seek the herbs and ingredients that powered our potions and bolstered our spells. Those quests had allowed me to track Rylynn's descendants when they left the once prosperous town where I'd been born.

Over the past hundred years, they'd all slowly left Velora. Most took the Southern Fate, the closest route to salvation. But a few traveled east or north. None again entered the coven lands, the warning that Rowellyn had whispered making its way through the generations until it became a family legend.

The Gallatins of Crenmea were protected by ancient witch power. Or cursed by it, depending on how fortunes went.

Only one of my sister's descendants remained in Velora. And she was as stubborn as Rylynn had ever been. I'd had to do more than help from a distance. I knew her name, and unlike her predecessors, she knew mine.

"Are you hungry?" Kyna asked as I shed my cloak.

The cottage she'd inherited from her aunt was sparse but warm. The spell I'd left her with two years before kept the water and mist from the nearby sea from seeping in. She started slicing bread without waiting for an answer. She knew I did not need to eat. She knew I would protest that she needed the food more than I did. That would not stop her from spreading precious butter on the slice before presenting it to me.

"I would rather you eat," I said, playing out the script. Shedding my cloak allowed me to access the leather purse strapped to my waist. Without preamble, I dumped its contents onto the worn wooden worktable.

Kyna's hand froze over the brown seeded loaf, her grip on the knife slackening.

Satisfaction rose in my chest—a feeling that had eluded me for a long time, maybe forever. I watched as her brown eyes, twins to my own, estimated the value of the coins I'd piled on the table. The government of Velora had crumbled almost two hundred years ago. But precious metals and gems still held their value, especially when it came to buying passage across the sea.

"It is enough," I said. "We finally have enough."

For the last ten years, since the fever that took her parents, Kyna and I had worked continuously toward one goal—saving enough money to buy her passage out of Velora. I used my spells whenever possible to bolster her, saving her from spending on things like firewood or a new roof so she could save every coin.

She was as stubborn as Rylynn had ever been, but she was also practical. She knew there was no future in Velora, and she wanted to leave. With her departure, the last of my sister's line would be safe.

Kyna did not speak. Her fingers tightened around the knife as she began slicing once again. One slice. Two. And then a third.

"I have invited a friend to join us," she said.

My throat threatened to close. "Who?"

"He is called Merrick." She kept her gaze down, avoiding my eyes as she opened the crock of butter and spread a thin layer across all three slices of bread. The crock was low. Suspiciously low.

"He owns the fishing boat down in the harbor," she added, lifting her eyes over my shoulder.

I followed her gaze to the window, open to let in a slight breeze. The cold did not bother me, but I watched her shiver, the pain in my throat spreading into my chest. From the window, I could see the harbor and the small fishing boat—the only boat—floating there.

A small figure waded through the shallows up to the beach and started on the path that led up the bluff towards the cottage. Kyna tracked him with her eyes. She'd left the window open so she could watch for him. She'd exposed herself to chill, to danger, for him.

The block of ice solidified in my chest.

I forced myself to speak. "A fisherman. You know as well as I that the sea yields less and less with every passing season."

"I am aware."

I forced a swallow and then more words. "You will have to travel a day or two on the southern road to reach a port big enough to buy passage. I cannot go with you, but I can spell your traveling clothes so that they keep out the ice and snow."

Kyna inhaled slowly, her thin chest lifting and then falling. The frame of her body was more like mine than Rylynn's, but where my curves were always generous and full, the lack of food kept her thin. Maybe one day, if Maura eventually let our coven leave Velora's shores, I would get the chance to see Kyna's body reach its full potential.

She set down the knife, no more butter left to spread, and met my gaze with her equally stubborn one. "I am with child."

My mouth fell open. "How can that be?"

She pursed her lips. "I would have thought someone of your advanced age would be well aware of how a woman comes to be—"

"That is not what I meant, and you know it."

"It is a miracle," she said softly.

And it was. Women in Velora so rarely quickened with life. It was the only way I'd been able to keep track of all of Rylynn's descendants for nearly four hundred years. If they'd reproduced at a normal, healthy human rate, I'd never have managed to monitor them all. But then, if Velora was normal and healthy, maybe I would not have felt the duty to watch over them.

If the fae had not overreached their powers, angered the gods, and brought down the curse. If my mother had not died, and my father had not become obsessed with wealth and selling fae objects. Maybe I would have grown up in a loving home. Maybe my sisters and I would have grown close instead of apart. Maybe I would never have become a witch.

But I was a witch, and Kyna was pregnant.

I loosened the strings that held the wrists of my pale blue wool dress closed. They were meant to make it easier for layering in the cold Velora weather. Now they provided me access to shove my hand up past the wrist, past my elbow, to the circlet of gold on my upper arm. It took me a few turns to work it down, but I managed to get it off. A quick glance out the window—the man had disappeared from sight as he followed the curved path around the bluff. We had only a minute or two more.

"Take this. Sell it if the ship's captain will not accept it in trade. With what we already have, it will be enough to buy you passage across the Southern Fate and provide a start wherever you land.

But you must go now, before your pregnancy is apparent, or they will charge you for two fares."

Kyna did not reach for the gold circlet. She showed no sign of recognizing the family heirloom I'd carried with me for nearly four centuries, the one I'd stolen the night I ran away. But her face was far from blank.

Sympathy. That was the emotion lining her eyes. She felt bad for me.

I felt the blow before her words delivered it. "I will not go without him. And he will not leave behind his family's legacy."

"Kyna," I rasped, the ice in my throat making it hard to speak. "You cannot stay here. You will die. Your child will die."

She raked her teeth over her lower lip, but it was not a mark of indecision. She'd already made her choice. Now she was deciding how to deal with me.

"We appreciate any help you can give us. Spells or such. But I cannot take your coin. It would be in bad faith, as I would not spend it the way you intended."

My keen senses alerted me to the man's footsteps. Merrick. A poor fisherman cursed to fish a dying sea and drag Kyna down with him towards its pitiless depths. Anger rose within me, and my power with it.

I could kill him. I should kill him. There was nothing to be done about the child in her belly, but without the man who'd put it there, she would have no option but to flee across the Southern Fate.

I felt the whorls of frost as my power coated my skin. The temperature in the cottage dropped several degrees. Kyna crossed to the window, but she lingered before closing it, listening to her man's footsteps.

We.

It no longer referred to me and Kyna, but to her and her man and the child they'd made together. *We* had always been an illusion. Kyna might know my name, she may welcome my help outright in a way that her predecessors had not. But *we* were a lie.

I was alone, just as I always had been.

I tossed my mother's golden bangle into the pile of coins, so carefully collected. "Keep it."

I could not stay. Maura's orders were strict. Each sister was to fetch her appointed items for the coven and then return posthaste. I'd already diverted to come here, risking dire punishment if the head witch ever found out where I'd been.

If I watched that man walk through the door, I might kill him.

I grabbed my cloak, not pausing to pull it on. "I will return when I can."

"We will be here." I knew she meant it. That scared me more than Maura's threats ever had. "Goodbye, Koryn."

Kyna leaned her head against the window frame, her hand drifting down to caress her still-flat belly. I thanked the Dark God that my heart no longer beat, for I was certain in that moment that it would have cleaved in two as I forced myself to walk out the door.

It was the last time I saw her alive.

CHAPTER 48

The wind kicked up as we climbed down the mountain, the crags giving way to hills until we saw the southern road emerge. Once, it had been a bustling trade route that circled the human lands before curving around the edge of the mountains to the coast. Now it was mostly overgrown. Only the ancient stone wall that ran along one side made it easy to discern, and only then because it was only as tall as my waist. Any taller and it would have tumbled down to the ground a century ago.

When I'd journeyed out from the coven lands, we'd always been instructed to avoid such thoroughfares. If we came across humans, we were to take what we needed and leave no survivors.

Humans had no power or magic, nor could they enhance our own. There was no benefit in keeping them alive.

We followed the road south, the mountains lurking to the east.

When the tavern finally emerged from behind a hill, my feet stilled.

"It is busy," I breathed, my brain struggling to make sense of what my eyes saw.

A half dozen horses were hitched to the post outside, a few of their owners smoking by the door. The structure itself was impressive. Three stories tall, built of stone, with several windows already lit and burning in the falling twilight. It started to snow as I stood there gaping.

"There are so few places like this left that the humans who are still here cling to them," Garrick said, his voice heavy. He must have seen every sort of place Velora had in the time he'd spent collecting bounties and acting as a mercenary. If he was willing to enter, then it must be safe enough.

For humans.

"Maybe you should hide." I had no notion how I would hide a shimmering lavender dragon the size of a large dog. But the prospect of revealing her to so many people—even a dozen— suddenly seemed ill-advised.

"Maybe you should spend another night sleeping on the ground."

We both growled simultaneously, earning a look of wry amusement from Garrick.

"Isanara is refusing to hide," I said.

"Shocking."

I rolled my eyes. I knew better than to waste my time arguing with a teenager, human or dragon. Isanara did tuck herself in close to my feet, weaving between my legs as we walked. The long cloak partially covered her, and Garrick's scowl did the rest. No one disturbed us as we entered the tavern.

Another half dozen patrons littered the inside, along with a burly proprietor who held court over the bartop that ran the entire length of the southern wall.

"Wait here. I'll go see about lodging."

I had no coin to offer him. I'd shoved all of it into Kyrelle's hands before the Mercy Gate. But he was Garrick the Red. Surely two decades of fulfilling bounties had left him flush enough to afford a couple of warm beds for the night.

He returned a few minutes later, the half-moon scar at the corner of his eye crinkling suspiciously.

I planted one hand on my hip. "Let me guess—there was only one room available?"

"I have only been in Velora for twenty years, and even I know that there are not enough people within a hundred miles who could afford and fill all of those rooms," he said. But he held my gaze, and it was anything but soft.

My teeth clenched together as my throat slid, heat rising from low in my stomach. What was it about his eyes that held me so completely? I'd never felt this pull before, not to man nor woman. Not in family, friendship, coven, or lover. Garrick the Red was in a category all his own.

"So I can finally expect some privacy." The words sounded as false as they felt. I hadn't had privacy in three hundred and seventy-seven years, not since my resurrection. Or ever, maybe. I'd been the youngest of three sisters.

And despite the bath I desperately needed, the prospect of privacy from him now seemed foreign. I imagined that the Lifebind on the inside of my wrist tingled, a living thing rather than a damning brand. I hated it, I reminded myself. I was supposed to hate him.

Garrick reached into the space between us. Reached for me. I let him. I leaned into it, into him, unable to separate my body and mind from the primal urges that controlled me. If he wanted to touch me, then I wanted—

He opened his hand, revealing a single key. "There could be a thousand rooms available and we would still be sharing. My place is at your side, Koryn. Or have you already forgotten?"

Any remaining ice inside of me melted instantly, my core turning to a mess of molten desire. I tipped my head back, hungry for every detail of his face. The silken silver strands around his jaw begged for my touch. His eyes burned into mine, intense with a silent demand that my body yearned to answer. His mouth... *Dark God spare me. No man should have a mouth that decadent.*

"And where will I be sleeping?"

I jerked backward, miraculously finding my footing even with Isanara twining between my legs.

"You can sleep in the stables," I huffed.

Garrick's eyes flicked down, clocking Isanara, then back up to me as he realized what had happened.

Or maybe he didn't, because he stepped away and continued as if nothing had happened. As if I hadn't been willing to let him lay me down right there on the ground.

"I saw a vein of coal in the mountainside as we were climbing down. I will go fill our bags."

Isanara snapped her jaws in approval, her tail swishing in a motion I'd come to associate with satisfaction. In contrast to the sharp way she whipped it from side to side when agitated.

Garrick shifted his pack to one shoulder and then reached for mine. I shrugged it loose, suddenly desperate for the moment alone that seconds before had seemed incomprehensible. But Garrick was faster. He was always faster. His fingers closed over mine on the strap, still taut with the weight of the pack on my shoulder.

Power surged inside of me, frost and ice crystallizing in my veins. But as his warmth seeped into me, the rough callouses on his fingers brushing my knuckles, the power did not overwhelm me. It danced. It curled and flurried and moved with... joy.

I jerked away, dropping the pack. Garrick caught it easily.

"Which room?" My voice came out low and rough, but I could do nothing.

Garrick spared me that intense gaze as he dropped the key into my hand. "Top floor."

"Which room?" I repeated.

"There's only one."

I might be a mess, but Garrick was completely nonplussed. As usual. He turned away and left the warmth of the tavern for the billowing storm without a farewell.

"You could go with him."

For a second, I did not realize it was Isanara that had spoken, not the traitorous voice of my own subconscious.

"So could you." And then I might actually have a few minutes alone.

She blinked up at me, her golden-green eyes wide. Expressive. Staring up at me like I'd lost my mind. *"Someone must stay and protect you."*

"Right. Because I am so fucking incompetent that even a baby dragon is more trustworthy than me."

"I am not a baby," she hissed. But she did not correct my other assertion.

"Let's go. Maybe he'll be gone long enough I can at least have a bath. Possibly even a warm one. Do dragons bathe?"

She huffed in disgruntled approbation. *"I feed on the very power of the earth. I am not bound by such mundane mortal tasks. Do you truly know so little about dragons?"*

I sighed as we reached the stairs. I did not dare correct her about my mortality. *"I guess so."*

CHAPTER 49

T HE BATH WAS COLD, BUT AT LEAST THE ROOM WAS WARM. I WASHED myself, then my clothing. After weeks of traveling between the gates and little more than frigid handcloth baths with melted snow, it felt absolutely decadent to be naked. Even in the temples, there wasn't time for much more than the essentials. A quick rinse of body and undergarments, and then out through another gate.

I told myself it was practical to count the hours that Garrick was away.

It indicated how much coal he was collecting for Isanara.

It allowed me to estimate if enough time remained for my clothing to dry or if I ought to use a spell to draw out the water.

It made me start to worry.

The thick flakes that had shepherded us into the tavern turned to hailstones as I stepped out of my bath. The wind picked up, hurling the balls of ice against the window as I finished rubbing the stains out of my leather vest.

"His fae blood will insulate him from the cold," Isanara said, barely lifting her head from where she lounged before the hearth, while I crossed to the window for the fifth time in as many minutes.

"And how do you know so much about the fae?" I shot back, prying open one of the shutters. I'd closed them earlier, afraid the driving ice would shatter the glass. But now I opened them again, standing on tiptoe to peer out. All I could see was a miasma of dark night and swirling white snow.

The cacophony of sound—howling wind, ice crashing against glass—woke my power.

I slammed the shutters closed.

I yanked my linen shift over my head, unable to appreciate the hint of smokiness that had seeped into the fibers as it dried before the fire. The knot in my stomach was too intense.

My wool overdress was still damp to the touch.

"From every corner, nook, and space, draw forth the water, leave no trace."

The water between the fibers evaporated instantly, leaving the garment dry, but the air around me humid. I ignored the sheen of sweat forming on my skin as I searched for the armholes.

A sharp knock reverberated through the room, shaking the spindly chairs at the table and snapping Isanara to attention. I dropped the gown, my curved blade suddenly in my hand instead. I had not even consciously reached for it. Garrick's lessons were having more impact than I'd realized. I'd known where the blade was instinctively. I was more aware of my surroundings. Somehow, I knew that only one set of boots had climbed the stairs. One person waited outside my door.

I certainly wasn't foolish enough to open it.

But I'd been about to leave. Whoever waited on the landing stood between me and finding Garrick.

"Identify yourself," I called through the door, forcing every bit of imperiousness I could muster into my voice. I tried to summon a memory of Maura, thinking of the tone of veiled disappointment and condescension she wielded so effortlessly. But instead, it was Alize's haughty visage that came to my mind.

Isanara growled at my side, though I doubted the sound permeated the door. The volume of the tavern's dining room two floors down had increased steadily over the past few hours.

A loud *thump* vibrated through the door, the sound of a fist landing against the wood and then staying.

"You know exactly who I am, Koryn."

My breath caught in my throat.

Isanara huffed with disappointment and returned to the fire while I unlocked the line of metal stalwarts that sealed the door.

I steeled myself. He'd been out in the storm for hours. He would be wet and irritated and every bit of Garrick the Red. That was good, actually. It was easier to keep my distance when he was snarling than when he smirked.

But I was completely unprepared for the man staring back at me from the other side of the door.

His silver blond hair was unbound, the wet ends curling as they skimmed his shoulders. His bandolier was missing. So were his leather tunic and the wool layers he usually wore. He stood before me in nothing but tight leather breeches and an unbuttoned gray linen shirt that hung loosely over his chest. A sculpted, glistening chest still damp and smelling vaguely of cinnamon.

"You bathed," I rasped, my voice suddenly a hundred times scratchier than before. His skin was not pale and cold from the storm but flushed from scrubbing.

Like mine.

For the first time in our acquaintance, we were not separated by the layers of leather and wool that Velora demanded. Just two paper-thin layers of linen remained between us. I could feel the heat of him from the other side of the threshold. My skin pebbled, my nipples tightening against the linen of my shift.

The firelight over my shoulder reflected in Garrick's eyes, illuminating the ring of green and setting the turquoise aglow.

"So did you." The timbre of Garrick's voice matched my own.

Dangerous. So dangerous.

"I thought you were out in the storm." My pride—what

remained of it—kept me from saying more. From admitting the feelings that had so inconveniently crowded my empty chest.

"I was." He nudged something with his foot.

Our packs, both stuffed with coal. In his other hand, he loosely held the bow and quiver that were usually strapped to his back. Isanara appeared between our feet, muttering something indecipherable as she shoved her head inside the nearest pack.

Garrick's mouth curved in an affectionate smirk as he lifted the bags and moved them into the room. Isanara moved with him, far too busy stuffing herself with ore to bother removing her head or offering a word of gratitude.

"Thank you," I said as I closed and relocked the door behind him.

I had not asked him to venture off into a storm to find food for my familiar. I hadn't needed to ask, because Garrick just *did*. Even when I should have been the one to do it. Even when Isanara, by her own admission, could go weeks without eating. Despite her insistence, she was a child, she was my responsibility, and she needed to eat. So Garrick fed her.

He bent down, spilling several large chunks of coal across the wooden floor. Isanara lunged for them.

"Don't bite the hand that feeds you," he admonished, but I heard the amusement in his voice.

He set the bow and quiver on the table and then turned to face me, the muscles of his calves and thighs bunching beneath the tight leather that covered them. His eyes snagged on the dark blue wool gown I'd dropped on the floor. He swiped it up, weighing the fabric in his hand, then slowly lifted his gaze to me, as if realizing what I wasn't wearing. His throat slid beneath his fresh shave.

"It is already dry," he said. He made no move to hand me the dress.

I raked my teeth over my lower lip. "A drying spell."

His mouth settled into a line. Not firm, not tense. But not

smirking or smiling either. "Convenient. I had to leave most of mine to hang in the other room."

My brows shot up my forehead. "Other room?"

That did earn me a smirk. "I thought you might enjoy some privacy for bathing, so I secured a second room to take care of my own needs. But make no mistake—we will both be sleeping in that bed."

That bed, just to my left, with four spindly posts and a springy mattress I'd refused to let myself lie on until after bathing. Everything about the third-floor room spoke to lost luxury. Once, this tavern had been busy. This room would have been reserved for the wealthiest travelers—government officials, merchants, an occasional fae wanderer. Humans like my father. Now it was dusty and decayed from disuse. Still, it was infinitely better than a freezing forest floor or temple barrack.

But with Garrick's eyes caught on mine, the inner circle of clover glowing within the bed of cerulean, any horizontal surface would have done for me. I'd never found satisfaction against a vertical one, but something about the way Garrick's fingers curved told me he'd know how to coax it from me.

I exhaled slowly, trying to steady myself. For once, it was not ice flooding my veins but warmth. I'd taken lovers over the centuries and blown through them like wildfire in the years before my death. But none had ever kindled this sort of longing within me.

We stood close enough that a heavy breath might bring our chests together. How had that happened? I did not recall moving toward him. But that was how it had always been with Garrick. I was drawn to him by a magnetic force that defied logic. Maybe it was the Lifebind at work. I'd fought it for so long, but the energy and desire to continue were quickly running out.

I took that breath. Long, deep, my chest rising, my breasts lifting until my taut nipples skimmed across the hard planes of his chest. The scrape of the linen between us was exquisite. I had no words for what I imagined it would feel like without it.

Garrick dragged in a breath of his own, the friction pulling an involuntary whimper from my lips. He cursed under his breath in a language I did not recognize. Maybe it was his home tongue, the one he'd known before coming to Velora. Thinking about his tongue was a mistake, because all I wanted was him inside my mouth. I rose onto my tiptoes, leaning into him more fully.

I waited for him to pull back. I was not going to be the one to throttle us, not tonight. But Garrick did not retreat. He reached down with those impossibly large, infinitely capable hands. One curved around my hip, the fingertips digging into the soft excess of flesh to steady me. He cupped my face with the other, his knuckles tracing the line of my jaw before the rough, calloused pads of his fingers stroked the delicate underside of my chin.

We were close enough to share breath, his wine and cinnamon scent dulled by his bath, but replaced by something else that was just Garrick. My insides churned, a molten, needy mess. I'd take everything he would give me.

He leaned in a fraction of an inch that felt longer than the entire distance we'd crossed since the Mercy Gate.

"Are you certain this is what you want?" Garrick said, his lips so close to mine I felt the words as much as heard them.

There was only one answer. I'd never lied to him, and I would not start now. But I did not need words to give it. My entire body ignited as I closed the distance—

"In front of me? Really?"

I jerked backward, grabbing one of the spindly bedposts just in time to keep from falling on my ass. That, and Garrick's hand on my backside. I saw the rejection in his eyes a second before he masked it, but he still did not release me. His hand lingered, his thumb swiping a caress over my plump, rounded curves, as if he could not quite bring himself to let go.

If I'd let him go on a second longer, I would have melted into a puddle right on top of the ancient rug that covered the wooden floors.

"Isanara," I croaked in explanation.

The look he shot at my familiar could have cowed a dozen warriors. But my little dragon, now fully sated from her feast, merely cocked her head to the side and whipped her spiked tail.

If I stayed with him in this room, I might irreparably damage my relationship with my familiar. There was no way I would be able to keep my hands to myself. I did not want to.

I forced myself to look away from Garrick, knowing the danger if he caught me in that intense stare again. My wool gown was on the ground between us, dropped and forgotten. I slid out of his touch and crouched down to retrieve it.

Garrick growled low in his throat but he let me go.

"I am starving," I said. "Let's go find something to eat in the common room."

I savored the emotions that played across Garrick's face. Once, I'd thought him unreadable. To others, maybe. But not to me, not anymore. I did not know the name of his homeland or even his reason for attempting the Seven Gates. But I knew this man in all the ways that mattered. That might prove even more dangerous than the Seven Gates.

Worry caused the divot between his pale, silvery blond brows. Desire was the brush of his tongue over his lower lip, stubbornness that flicker in his jaw.

"As you wish, witch. I would not want you to lose an ounce off of that delectable body of yours," he said.

Isanara groaned in disgust, but I was too busy physically turning my body away from Garrick so I could not watch him watch me dress.

It was going to be an impossibly long night.

CHAPTER 50

Isanara, of course, refused to stay up in the room behind a locked and spelled door. *What if you need my protection?* I needed a moment to catch my breath, but between the broad-shouldered man in front of me and the stubborn teenage dragon winding between my legs *on the stairs, of all places,* I knew that was nothing but a fantasy.

I paused at the bottom of the stairs, ice coalescing in my chest.

The tavern had been busy by Velora's standards when I went up hours before, but the numbers had swelled to at least twice as many patrons in the interim. More than had been in the tavern in Canmar, more than I'd seen in any of the taverns I'd frequented in the months since my ouster from my coven.

I could not recall the last time I'd seen so many humans gathered together in one place.

Garrick paused as well, even with me behind him. Was it the Lifebind that made him so attuned to my movements, or something else?

"This is the road that leads to the Sea of Forgetting and eventually to the Southern Fate," he said.

I knew that. I'd traveled this road to reach Kyna and Kyrelle's cottage a dozen times over the fifty years. Or rather, I'd avoided this road. But that was essentially the same thing in this instance. I'd surely seen this tavern at one point or another, if only from the outside.

"But why is it so busy?"

Garrick sighed, and I recognized the grimness in the sound. "They recognize the death throes of Velora the same way you do."

Desperation and stupidity. That was how I'd come to characterize humanity over the last several hundred years. But what I saw in that tavern… yes, both of those things. There was something else, too. It looked suspiciously like hope. These people truly believed they'd be able to escape Velora's curse. The drinks in their hands probably helped with that.

"Care to peddle your spells for coin?" Garrick smirked.

My hand flew to the coven mark between my brows.

Garrick caught my wrist, his hand encircling mine so fully his fingers overlapped by two full joints. "Do not hide who you are, Koryn. Not a single part of yourself. No one will touch you tonight."

At the Mercy Gate, I'd used my teeth to rip the points from my nails, to hide the markers of my resurrection. They'd grown out in the intervening weeks, but I had not filed them to points. I promised myself that once we returned to our room, I would do exactly that. No more hiding.

I took the final step down into the tavern's common room.

Garrick parted the crowd, leading us to a table positioned along the wall with quick access to the rear exit and an easy view of the rest of the room. The lone occupant deserted their seat without us asking. Whether it was my coven mark or Garrick's stature… more likely the weapons he'd insisted on strapping back on before we came down.

Garrick waited until I was seated with Isanara at my side. She was too large for a chair, though I half expected her to climb up into my lap.

"I would be better placed to protect you if I did," she sassed, listening in on my thoughts.

"You are conspicuous enough as it is." That might be the real reason the crowd had parted. Dragons were creatures of legend and lore. None of the beings in this tavern were long-lived enough to remember when they roamed Velora freely. Hell, neither was I.

Garrick's eyes flicked between me and Isanara. I wondered if we shared some sort of strange, telltale expression when we spoke mind to mind. If we did, Garrick would certainly be the one to figure it out.

"I will order us food," he said before tracing a path back to where the busy barkeep held court.

Sitting on her hind legs, Isanara's head was almost even with mine. I was not sure I enjoyed the experience of having her that close as I methodically scanned the tavern's occupants. I did not plan on selling any spells, but I applied the same skills of observation that I'd honed in the months before entering the Mercy Gate.

There were several prostitutes, probably in residence in the rooms on the second floor of the tavern. All were rail thin. Despite the popularity of this stop on the way to the Southern Fate, the proprietor was not feeding them well. My stomach twisted at the injustice, but I ignored it. The only human left that I cared about was Kyrelle, I reminded myself.

"Maybe I chose incorrectly," Isanara snapped.

"Excuse me?"

"I ought to have chosen a witch less given to delusions."

Before I could argue back, she flicked her deadly tail across the scarred tabletop. I followed the direction of that point, across several occupied tables, a man kissing a prostitute's bosom, until I found Garrick.

I could not even argue back, not with a being who could hear the thoughts in my head.

Instead, I ignored her and continued to examine the tavern's occupants. There were no children, though that was not surprising. They were too precious to be out in public like this. There were families, though. A woman in her twenties sat beside what could only be a brother, while across from them an older couple sipped from a shared glass of wine. Perhaps the old woman's fruitfulness, bearing not one child but two, had convinced them to linger longer in Velora, believing they would escape the ravages of the curse. But here they were, on the road to a desperate salvation just like the rest.

I counted heads, trying to judge their potential paths. This far south, anyone seeking reliable passage out of Velora would travel around the southeast curve of the mountains until they found a port with ships leaving across the Southern Fate. But there were other, cheaper ways off of Velora. For those who could not muster enough coin, the Sea of Forgetting beckoned. The passage required a stop on the Dead Isle, the birthplace of the witches. Not even I had been there, nor any member of my coven. *Tirybas* was a name whispered in our darkest rituals, in the spells that called for offerings of blood.

To try and negotiate the Sea of Forgetting without stopping to pay homage to the witches was to court death. To set foot upon the Dead Isle meant facing whatever horrors remained after thousands of years.

I continued scanning the room. The faces with hope would seek the Southern Fate. Those with only desperation were bound to an even more dangerous fate. And none of it was a concern of mine. If I made it through the Seven Gates, everyone in Velora would be better off.

A knot of onlookers had formed around two men and a woman playing thrall. The triangular board between them was drawn onto the table with chalk, their pieces each unique. Even after hundreds of years, thrall was still a popular game, in part because it could be played using items of little value. Carved rocks or wood could make the pieces. Anyone could draw the board. And playing the game of skill gave the desperate humans of Velora the illusion that they still had some control over their lives.

There wasn't much coin left, so other items changed hands as the onlookers placed wagers. A bit of ribbon, a heel of hard cheese. Two men bickered over the value of a prostitute.

But it was the quiet patrons lurking in corners that worried me more.

"You are a quiet patron lurking in a corner," Isanara pointed out.

"Exactly."

She made her own perusal of the tavern, then finished by snapping her fangs at the woman seated nearest to us, who quickly vacated her chair. I rolled my eyes.

I understood her point too well. Garrick was dangerous. I was dangerous. Even without Isanara at my side, we were conspicuous. I'd learned during the months between leaving my coven and entering the temple that the less conspicuous someone tried to be, the more they tried to hide, the more dangerous they were. The more unpredictable.

My eyes snagged on a head of overgrown wine-red hair framed between two blonde women.

Nash.

"I hate being right."

"No, you don't," Isanara snorted.

We should have stayed up in our rooms. I should never have brought Isanara down into this fray. The handful of people who'd seen her on the way up spreading rumors about a dragon could not be more dangerous than two dozen drunken, desperate humans having confirmation of one.

One of the blonde women threw back her head in an overzealous laugh. Nash watched her breasts bounce, the hunger on his face turning my stomach. I knew his crime from the Justice Gate. I should have let Garrick kill him after the Mercy Gate when

I'd had the chance. Any crime he committed from then onward could be laid directly at my door.

Nash tossed back his red waves and looked past the woman who'd climbed into his lap. His eyes locked with mine. He'd known I was there, had surely seen us enter and now knew we'd taken one of the rooms above the tavern.

Slowly, with malice curling the corners of his mouth, he shifted his gaze from me to my familiar. He examined her with open, deliberate leisure, just to remind me that he could. I'd brought her down here, I'd exposed her to him.

A low, threatening growl rolled out from between Isanara's jaws.

I made a sound to match it.

Garrick emerged from the crowd, two metal platters balanced in one impossibly large hand while the other lingered near the hilt of his greatsword. He only had to look at my face before the implied threat became real and his hand closed around the weapon.

"Back corner, third from the left," I said, forcing myself to stay in my seat. I watched as Garrick found Nash, though his brow barely creased before he turned back and set the food on the scarred table between us. "It seems we were not the only supplicants drawn by the promise of a soft bed and a meal we did not have to cook."

Garrick lifted one silvery brow. "How many meals have you cooked since the Mercy Gate?"

I blinked across the table at him. What a luxury it must be to feel so confident in one's own abilities that the threat of impending death was no more than a nuisance.

He slid a set of utensils wrapped in a threadbare napkin across the table. When I did not reach for it, he leaned forward, bracing his forearms against the wood and crowding into my space so that I could see nothing but him.

"No one will touch you."

Garrick did not touch me, but his words did. I felt them in the crevices of my body, setting the delicate hairs on end, in the recesses of my soul, where I'd only ever been alone.

Beside me, Isanara decided that the occupants of the next table were getting too comfortable. She snapped her tail, swinging the spiked end close enough to take a chunk out of the wood of their table. The woman fainted, her companion gathering her up and dragging her away as Isanara hissed through her teeth.

"You are drawing too much attention." I reached for the bundle of utensils as Garrick settled back in his chair.

Isanara wove her head side to side in a threatening serpentine motion. *"Let them look. If they try any more, I will take their hands and then their eyes for good measure."*

"For someone who does not eat humans, you seem to enjoy imagining how you will eviscerate them."

"Everyone needs a hobby."

I could not keep my exasperated huff inside. Garrick tracked the motion, his gaze lingering a beat longer than was necessary on my pursed lips.

"My promise extends to your familiar," he said, reaching for his own fork and knife.

I paused with a bite of nondescript meat halfway to my mouth. "What happened to proving to you that I can defend myself?"

"Just because you can protect yourself does not mean that you should always have to."

I'd been protecting myself for four hundred years because I had been alone for four hundred years. Even when my family was alive, even when I was dead. I heard what he said, but I was not sure I was quite ready to believe it.

We ate in companionable silence, the din of the crowd more than making up for our lack of conversation. I tried and failed not to watch Garrick, who was busy tracking my every bite. The boiled potatoes and stringy meat were not seasoned or prepared to the standard Garrick had accustomed me to. I did not risk inflating his ego by telling him.

CHAPTER 51

A FEW MINUTES AFTER WE FINISHED EATING, A BARMAID WANDERED by to collect our platters and ply us with drinks. Her gaze lingered on Garrick. Her hand lingered longer. When Isanara snapped her jaws, slicing the woman's apron away from her skirt, I almost leaned over and kissed her shimmering lavender scales.

But I was not the only one with eyes on my familiar.

The longer we sat in the tavern, the bolder the other patrons became. A pair of unkempt men nursing ales took up at the empty table beside us.

Nash held his seat in the far corner, but I could feel his oily gaze on me. I refused to look his way, keeping him in my periphery but not rewarding him with any more than the bare minimum of my attention. He was the sort of man who got enjoyment out of inciting fear in women. I would not indulge his malignant fantasies.

Nor was he my only concern. As the sky darkened beyond the small windows, so did the tenor of the attention we drew.

"We should go back upstairs," I said, swirling the purple wine I'd been nursing for the last hour.

Garrick sipped the dark brown spirit he'd chosen. "You cannot show them your fear."

"I am not afraid." I drained the rest of my wine to prove it. "Not for myself," I amended.

Isanara projected a sound of absolute disgust into my mind.

I ignored her, casting my gaze over the crowd. Almost everyone had a drink in hand, though they weren't flowing freely and hardly anyone was intoxicated. My guess was that most of the common room's occupants could only afford a drink or two and hoped that would be enough for the barkeep to let them pass the night in blessed warmth.

Without more liquor to soften their minds, they turned their bitterness outward. A strapping bounty hunter and a buxom, well-fed witch with a dragon were easy targets for their angry desperation. My power crystallized in my veins, ready to break free.

But Garrick's words anchored me. *Use your power*, he'd urged me, not just on its own, but in tandem with my other skills.

He'd meant my active power, but it wasn't the only one at my disposal. By whatever trick of fate or intervening gods, my power had not faded yet. I would use it.

"I can handle this," I said quietly. *"From deep the well of liquid flame, grant these drinks a potent claim."*

Garrick paused with his drink halfway to his mouth. "You think intoxicating them further is the answer to the problem?"

"I think distracting them is the best of a lot of shitty options," I said, propping my elbow up on the tabletop and nearly upending my glass of wine. Except it was empty now, thankfully. "Now go put down a ridiculous wager on that game of thrall and distract them."

He stared at me across the table for several beats, his eyes reflecting the shimmering light of Isanara's scales. Then he downed the rest of his drink and went to do as I'd asked.

I leaned back in my chair, pressing into the wall behind me. I anchored myself with every point of contact, noticing my body like Tomin had taught me. The wood dug into my shoulder blades. My hair pulled slightly where it was pinned between my body and the stone slab wall. Instead of letting the sensations overwhelm me, I catalogued them one by one, and in doing so, gained a measure of control over them. It was not perfect, but the frost in my veins did not solidify and fracture into uncontrollable ice.

I reached out for Isanara, skating my fingertips over her scales. Avoiding the spikes along her spine had become second nature, just like walking with her constantly twining around my legs. The power of the bond between witch and familiar had our bodies speaking to one another on a level beyond conscious recognition.

The raucous crowd around the thrall game grew. I watched as several onlookers swayed on their feet, the effects of my spell already taking hold. My mind swam with satisfaction, warming my cheeks and chest where I'd left the top of my shift unlaced.

A few minutes more and the tavern's occupants would be drunk enough they would not notice us slipping up to our rooms. I would not even complain about Garrick's insistence that we share the bed. It was practical, for our protection. And if we shed a few layers to sleep in relative comfort, that only made sense. The bed was not nearly large enough for Garrick's long body and my round one. We would inevitably have to touch and if that led to—

"What a lovely companion."

My fantasies ground to a halt, the wine I'd downed turning to acid in my stomach.

Nash slid into Garrick's empty seat. He filled it well, but his shoulders were no match for Garrick's. But the cruelty in his eyes as he openly appraised Isanara... despite the morbid tales that followed Garrick the Red and the crime laid at his feet at the Justice Gate, I'd never seen cruelty in Garrick's eyes.

"Kill him."

As much as I agreed with her, my limbs had taken on a strange heaviness. Maybe my power was fading, after all.

"Haven't you learned your lesson by now?" I croaked, spreading my palms flat on the table between us. I thought about reaching for one of the knives tucked into my belt, but I didn't trust my wobbly hand to wield it.

Nash leaned back, hooking an ankle across his knee. "And what lesson is that?"

"Stay away from me and I won't have to kill you."

He smiled. "Your warden has wandered off. Though your companion… she looks like she could draw some blood with those fangs."

I hated that he knew Isanara was female. I did not want him to know a single detail about her. If I'd had my coven with me, I'd have used our collective power to cast a spell to scrub her from his memory.

"I will draw his blood."

"Do you see that blade at his side? It's a greatsword, and he knows how to use it." I had no doubt Isanara could do damage. But at what cost? She and Nash were roughly matched for size, and though she was an immortal beast of legend, he was a ruthless killer.

Maybe she was, too. But I only had evidence of that for one of them.

"She doesn't like you."

"Excellent retort," Isanara said with such ferocity I could practically taste the sarcasm.

But my mind was as unreliable as my limbs. My power surged to life, responding to the threat across the table.

A full, twisted smile spread across Nash's face. "Once the gates kill you, I'll see that she reaches her full potential."

"Rip out his heart. I can hear its unnatural beat. It's a sickly, twisted thing—"

"*Quiet!*" I screamed in my mind. I imagined a wall of ice solidifying in the liminal space between us where our minds overlapped. It felt like severing a limb, but I had to keep her out. I could not think, not with her voice and Nash's fighting for supremacy.

Nash laughed, the sound intruding on my senses, overwhelming my already fragile hold on my power.

Frost spread across the table. I surged to my feet but the movement was too fast. My body betrayed me. I swerved sideways. Isanara rose on her hind legs as I collided with her. She should have gone toppling over, but her body felt like stone. The impact rattled my bones, but I did not hit the floor.

Nash's laughter ricocheted through my consciousness, the barrier I'd erected between myself and Isanara crumbling.

She waited on the other side, seething mad. *"Do not ever do that again—"*

The laughter stopped. Everything stopped. No more movement, no more sound. The entire tavern froze, fixating on the two men on the other side of the table.

Garrick did not hold a knife to Nash's throat this time. He had his greatsword in his hand, and it was pressed directly against the part of himself that Nash valued most—his cock.

Nash's eyes shone with wrath and cruelty. But Garrick's… the rage in those turquoise depths was the kind to shatter worlds. What little steadiness I'd found holding on to Isanara quickly fled.

"You're in my seat," Garrick said.

A manic laugh bubbled out of my chest.

Garrick did not look at me. "Move," he ordered.

Nash's face flushed. He could not follow that order without risking Garrick's blade severing his manhood from his body. But to refuse it meant he'd be castrated sooner rather than later.

I sank my teeth into my lower lip to keep in the hysteria rising in my chest.

Slowly, Nash unfolded his legs and slid to his feet. Garrick's sword moved with expert, unwavering precision. Every eye in the tavern watched and marked it.

Once Nash was on his feet, Garrick leaned in. He kept his voice low, but I heard every word. "You live because she decrees it.

Touch her again and I will make you beg until she grants you the sweet release of death."

The male occupants of the tavern sighed in audible relief when Garrick lowered his sword. But I saw Nash's face as he walked away. This encounter had been settled, but none of us would forget it. If the gates did not kill Nash, I would have to.

"Or I will," Isanara promised. Warmth surged in my chest—not at the viciousness of that promise, but at the *or*, because it meant she thought I could be the one to kill him, just as likely as her.

"If you keep smiling like that, I will put my sword through his crotch here and now."

My breath stuttered in my chest. "That might be the most erotic offer I have ever received."

The greatsword was still in his hand. His long, thick fingers curved around the blade with an easy competence that turned my insides instantly liquid. Which should have been impossible, because my power was still crackling in my veins. I looked down at my hands, finding them covered with swirling ribbons of frost. Instead of panicking, I was confused.

Garrick sheathed his weapon, then stepped forward and took my hands between his own. It was not until the frost began to recede that I realized he was trying to help me regain control.

But even as my power quieted, he did not release my hands. Instead, he leaned in closer. Or maybe I was the one leaning into him.

The corner of his mouth curved in that smirk. The infernal fucking smirk. I was going to wipe it off his face. Kiss it off his face—

"You are intoxicated."

Had I said all of that aloud?

"That cannot possibly be true," I said, even as I swayed. Garrick released my hands so he could steady me, one taking up residence on my hip, the other settling just above where my belt tried to nip in my waist.

He lifted his brows—another infernal habit. I reached up and pressed my thumb into the divot between them.

"Your clever little spell backfired," he said. Why did his voice sound labored?

"It shouldn't even be this effective, not without my coven's power to ground my own." I shook my head, regretting it instantly. The tavern blurred around me.

Garrick chuckled. I thought the smirk and the eyebrow raise were bad? The sound of that man's laugh, deep and resonant and impossibly precious as it rolled over my senses, did something irrevocable to me, more dangerous than any god or gate.

"Perhaps you are more powerful than you realize," he said. This time, I knew it was him drawing me closer. Probably just to keep me from falling over, but I was not about to complain.

"You think you know everything about me, don't you?" I pouted out my lower lip, hot satisfaction filling my chest as Garrick's eyes lingered on my mouth.

Which made me want to look at his. They were full and luscious, a soft contrast to the hard line of his jaw and the silvery stubble on his chin. I watched in fascination as they formed around his next words. "I can barely begin to fathom your depths, witch. But I want to know them all."

My mind could not process the feeling behind those words. "Are you intoxicated, too?"

"Unfortunately, not. Your spell does not seem to work on those of us cursed with fae blood in our veins."

I wrinkled my nose.

I could not be drunk. I'd finished my wine before I said the spell... right before. I could not even bring myself to appeal to the Dark God. I'd stumbled right into this mess all on my own. But when I considered my current position—Isanara snapping her jaws at anyone who approached, my chest pressed against Garrick's—I could not bring myself to feel any regret.

Though I was parched. I wet my lips but it wasn't enough.

Garrick had finished his liquor. We needed more drinks, though water would be wiser. Maybe it was time to go back upstairs. Or try my hand at a game of thrall. I licked my lips again.

A low groan reverberated through my chest—our chests. It caressed my breasts and sent heat spiraling through my stomach, then lower. "Please stop doing that."

I tipped my head back so I could see the expression that had accompanied that groan. "Why, Garrick? Why should I stop?"

His eyes were actually glowing. Not the illusion of glowing from reflected light. That inner circle of green lit with some sort of internal flame, the edges bleeding into the cerulean blue. It was otherworldly and unnerving and beautiful.

I'd thought his gaze was intense before. But when he leaned down into my space, closing those inches of height that separated us, I nearly melted under the force of it.

"Because if you do not, I am going to lay you down across this table and show you exactly what you do to me with that wicked mouth of yours."

I licked my lips again. "Do you promise?"

He pressed his eyes closed. "Witch."

I took that as an invitation. I lifted myself to my tiptoes, trusting Garrick's solid form to keep me upright, and pressed my lips against his.

His lips were as soft as I'd imagined. But gods, he tasted so much better. There was the cinnamon that always lingered, tinged with the burning remnants of the liquor he'd been drinking earlier. But the taste of him, the unique combination of spice and sweat and heat... I could not get enough of it on my tongue.

I curled my hands against his chest, gripping the leather of his vest around the lines of blades that he wore strapped against it.

The contrast of his soft lips with the urgent demand of his mouth sent my malleable mind spinning. I needed the next swipe of his tongue more than I needed air. I welcomed that bold touch inside of my own mouth, granting him access without a second thought. My only regret was that I'd waited so long, denied myself for so long, when we should have been doing this from the beginning. I should have taken Garrick the Red to my bed that first night before the Mercy Gate—

"We need to stop, witch."

How dare he take his mouth away from mine.

"Or we could keep going." I tugged on his vest, but he did not move, holding himself just far enough away that I could not reach him without his consent. Or without wrapping my legs around his waist and attempting to climb him.

Garrick's eyes flicked over my shoulder. "In front of your familiar…" Isanara made an indignant sound. "And the entire tavern?"

I'd forgotten about both of them. For once, Isanara had stayed well out of my mind. And as for the rest of the tavern… they were as lost to my spell as I was.

"We have two rooms," I reminded him, settling back onto my feet. Isanara could take one. We'd take the other. "What foresight."

Isanara hissed. *If you think I am letting you out of my sight with your mind in shambles—*

I tried to erect that wall of ice between us, but my drink-addled brain could not manage it. I turned my face up to Garrick, writing all of my desire into my face. I slid my hips forward, pressing against him suggestively. He was hard, and though it was difficult to judge precisely through so many layers of clothing, the impressive length of him had a surge of wetness pooling between my legs.

But instead of appreciating the fact that I was rubbing myself up against him like a cat in heat, Garrick released his hold on my waist. He caught my shoulders with his hands, while my body screamed at the loss of his touch where I wanted it most.

"Koryn." His voice shook. My eyes flew open, the weight of his tone permeating my lust and alcohol fogged mind. "When I take you to bed, you will be in full possession of your mind. You will remember every moment clearly, because I will not take you in a drink-addled haze. When you beg for me to make you come, I want you to mean it with every fiber of your glorious being."

My mouth fell open.

Garrick swore in that foreign tongue.

"Get her to bed," Isanara snapped.

I tried to tell her that Garrick could not hear the words she spoke into my mind. But she must have gotten her meaning across just fine, because the next thing I knew, the world went horizontal, and Garrick the Red carried me upstairs.

CHAPTER 52

I COULD HAVE SLEPT FOREVER WITH HIS WARM BODY PRESSED UP against mine. I did not remember taking off my gown. More upsettingly, I did not remember him taking off my gown. But curled in the warmth of the bed, the fire crackling, and Isanara snoring softly by the hearth, I was ready to make a memory I would be able to recall.

Garrick curled his arm around me, drawing my backside flush against him. Even asleep, I could feel the hard length of him nestled between the cleft of my bottom. Slumber became less and less appealing by the moment. I lifted my right thigh, the one resting on top, and slid it backward over his calf to increase the pressure of his cock against me. The hand he'd draped around my waist tightened on my stomach, holding the rounded, soft curve like it was too precious to possibly let go.

I arched into him, hungry for the heat of his breath on my throat—

I leapt from the bed, dislodging Garrick's arm with a heavy thump on the mattress and a mumbled curse. Isanara's claws dug into the wooden floor as she jolted awake. The bed frame creaked under Garrick's shifting weight. But all of those sounds faded into nothing as my awareness honed in on the one that had dragged me from my languid fantasies.

For a moment, I thought I'd imagined it. But then the door creaked again.

I blasted it open, the force of the frost slamming the door into the wall and then freezing it in place.

I wanted to see the attacker who was foolish enough to come for me, a frost witch of the Midnight Coven, Lifebind of the notorious bounty hunter Garrick the Red, conqueror of four Gates, and chosen by the dragon Isanara.

The firelight reflected off of wine-red hair.

I did not stop to analyze how he'd gotten through a door lined with three heavy metal locks. I didn't think at all. I felt. I felt my power rising to defend me and mine. My body began to move, slipping into the choreographed maneuvers that Garrick had drilled into me for weeks and weeks.

My belt was long gone, but I found the knife already in my hand. It had been tucked beneath my pillow. I threw myself at Nash. He'd lost the element of surprise and he did not know the contours of the room. He knew I was a witch, but he understood none of the nuances of my power, nor had he seen the hours I'd spent training with Garrick.

Once, he would have had an advantage. Now, I would punish him for being arrogant enough to ignore both Garrick and my warnings.

He swung the greatsword wide. I threw myself sideways, one hand reaching for the wall to brace the impact. The tip of his sword caught my shift, tearing a wide gash in the linen. He was more than competent with the sword, but it was a large and unwieldy weapon. I shoved myself off of the wall, putting the table and chairs between us. He'd have to come around them to reach me, and those few precious seconds would give me an advantage.

"A table won't be enough to save you," Nash said, bracing his hands on the first chair that blocked his way. "Or your little dragon."

It was the absolute wrong thing to say, and not because of the floor-shaking roar that ripped from Isanara.

"He's mine," I declared to Isanara.

For once, my familiar did not argue.

Nash sprang to my left, going for what he presumed was my weaker side. But my power flowed just fine from both of my hands.

I sent shards of ice at his face with my hands while I kicked out the chair from my side of the table. Nash swiped aside my frozen missiles with his sword but stumbled on the chair. I saw my advantage. Ice spread across the floor, sweeping his feet out from under him as I dove in with my dagger aimed squarely at his chest.

His sword arm tangled in the legs of the chair, but he deflected me with the other, sending me sprawling. I slammed my elbows into the floor beneath me, forcing myself back up, but before I could gain my knees, Nash crashed down on top of me. I thrashed wildly. I had to knock the sword away. If he got that blade against a vital organ or artery, I was dead.

My hand found his arm. I forced all of my power into that one hand, freezing him the way I had Alize. He shrieked, wresting his arm away, but his knees on my chest kept me pinned. He ripped back the sleeve of his tunic to reveal the dark splotch where the skin had already begun to die. "You frigid bitch."

He punched me in the face. Blood flooded my mouth. Before I could react, he'd knocked my dagger from my right hand, leaving me without a blade.

"I spared you," I gasped out between blood-filled breaths. I did not know why I said it; there was no good in him for me to appeal to, no mercy.

"Do not blame me for your foolish mistakes. I thought that witches were ruthless. Then I met you and I realized that was just a tale told to children to keep them in line." He leaned down, pinning an arm across my throat to cut off my air supply. "You are weak."

"Strength takes many forms." Isanara had remained silent, honoring my request to fight this battle myself. But she gave me those words.

"Strength takes many forms," I repeated aloud, letting her strength of spirit meld with my own. "I only have to be strong enough to beat you."

"When you die, your dragon will answer to me."

He'd robbed me of my blade. But I still had a weapon. And he'd assumed that my left hand was too weak to bother pinning.

I formed the ice dagger in my palm, fusing it to my hand so he could not knock it loose, and raked it down his face from forehead to chin. Blood spurted, the warmth of it shrinking the dagger as he rolled away. I released it, letting the chunk of ice fall to the floor, diluting the pool of Nash's blood.

"Dragons answer to no one," I seethed.

I let myself savor the sight of him hunched over on the floor, cupping his face and moaning. But the second he moved to face me, I released all control.

Frost poured from my hands, glowing a faint, pale blue as it swirled around him. It speared into his ears, mouth, and nose. Into the socket where the eye I'd destroyed had once been.

I felt the flakes coalesce inside his lungs and in the arteries of his heart.

In one last moment of lucidity, Nash turned to me. He looked at me with one ragged, murderous eye. I saw only what he'd done to the woman in the stable. What he'd tried to do to me. What he'd promised to do to Isanara.

I turned the frost to solid ice.

His heart stopped. His lungs could not pull air. I stood over his frozen body, holding my power in place until every organ ceased to function and not a single spark of life remained in his body.

The once warm blood on his face and hands sparkled, transformed into a deep, glittering scarlet.

"So, you do know something about dragons."

My gaze snapped to Isanara, her body cast in an eerie silhouette by the flames of the hearth behind her. The spikes on her back stood up, raised like the hairs of a cat when riled. Her delicate snout and curved horns seemed longer, more imposing than ever before. She'd been ready to come to my aid, I realized. If she'd truly thought me in danger, she would have thrown herself between me and Nash. She would have sacrificed herself.

I hit my knees.

My breath came hard and fast, the blood in my veins thrumming wildly. I fell forward, catching myself on my hands. I slid through the frozen shards of Nash's blood, ripping open little wounds across my palms. The blood began to thaw, the scent of it more noxious with every second. My heart was going to explode out of my chest. *No—that isn't possible. My heart does not beat anymore...*

Not my heart. My power. It was going to explode out of me, take out everyone and everything—

"Breathe, Koryn."

Garrick's thigh pressed into mine as he knelt at my side. He picked up my hands, lifting me back to sit on my heels. His hands engulfed my own, his warmth finding the power within me and soothing it back into submission.

It was just enough for me to remember the techniques that Tomin had taught me. I forced my eyes open, scanning the room through the watery mist that clouded them. I counted off items as I saw them. One—the unmade bed, two—the rusted shutter hinge, three—the torn fingernail on Garrick's left thumb. I closed my eyes again, focusing now on the sounds. One—the crackling of the fire, two—Garrick's thundering heart. I opened my eyes and focused on what I could feel. One—the rough callouses on Garrick's hands where they stroked mine.

Slowly, so painfully slowly, I regained control. My power quieted. So did the blood thrumming through my veins.

Tears streamed down my cheeks.

"I killed him." The rough sound of my own voice surprised me.

Garrick squeezed my hands. "You have killed before, and you will kill again. Killing should never be easy. You should feel every single death. Even when it's necessary, and even when you don't regret it."

I couldn't do any more than nod. That was what made me different than the rest of my coven. No matter how long and how hard I tried, killing had never become easy. A witch's duty was to coven above all others, but my heart yearned for humanity and all its messy intricacies.

My shoulders slid and I leaned forward. Garrick met me halfway, pressing his forehead to my own. We stayed there for minutes that might have turned to hours, sharing one another's air, regulating until I could begin to make sense of the hell that had unfolded around me—the hell I'd wrought and that I'd have to live with. In some ways, it was more intimate than the kiss we'd shared hours before.

My breath turned shaky again. I'd kissed him. Dark God below, I'd done more than just kiss him. I'd been ready to let him take me right there on that table, before thirty humans and my familiar. And more than anything, I wanted to lean in and kiss him again.

As usual, I had no control over my mouth. "Earlier, in the common room, I shouldn't have—"

Garrick drew back, breaking the connection. My hands tightened around his, reflexively trying to keep him with me. He did not pull those away, but it was impossible to miss the small sigh that slipped between his lips. "Forget it. You were intoxicated by your own spell."

But I could not forget his words any more than he could take them back. Things had been shifting between us for a while. Somewhere between the Lifebind and the weeks spent in forced proximity traversing the Seven Gates... the Lifebind was not the only thing holding us together any longer.

Yet in more dangerous, more irrevocable ways, nothing had changed.

I was a witch. An immortal.

He was a half-human bounty hunter with ties to the fae court.

The conflict between us subsumed the gates and the Lifebind. I hated half of who he was—the same half that he hated. Witches, humans, fae, our shared presence on Velora had done nothing but lead to harm and curses and death.

Garrick and I were too small to fight that. And even if there was something bigger, something more between us, we were bound to the Seven Gates.

If I made it through the gates, I would be restored to my coven. If I did not, I'd be dead. There were no happy endings waiting for the pair of us. Faerietales belonged where they'd always been—in my long-forgotten past.

I watched Garrick's throat slide as he swallowed at the same time I did.

Neither one of us needed to say the words. We understood each other too well for that. We may be different in every measurable way, but we were both what Velora had made us.

I fought back the emotions and the power, unwilling to let them loose again.

"Why didn't you intervene?" I asked, rocking back on my heels, desperate for any conversation to distract me from my thoughts.

Garrick released my hands, but he did not move to stand. "What do you call this?"

I huffed out a half-laugh. Isanara appeared at my side, tromping through Nash's blood and over his body without any regard for the man whose soul had once resided inside the frozen shell. He deserved none of her regard, anyway.

"I meant before, when Nash attacked. You just..." I wasn't quite sure where he'd been. I had not even thought of him. My focus had narrowed to protecting Isanara.

"I knew you could handle yourself." The corners of his mouth turned up in a smirk, but it lacked something. "And now you know it, too."

I had no answer to that. I thought that had been the purpose of all our sparring and hiking in the mountains. I reached down, caressing the tender scales between Isanara's curved horns. But Garrick reached for me again.

"Not just here." He stroked a hand over my forehead, brushing back the sweaty strands of hair. Then he slid two fingers down my face, past my chin and collarbone, between my breasts. "And here."

I could not bring myself to correct him, to tell him that it was impossible to feel in a heart that no longer beat.

"I don't think I can sleep any longer," I said instead.

Garrick nodded and handed me my cloak. "The storm has passed. Let's go."

CHAPTER 53

temple. Alize was already there. No one asked about Nash.

I imagined I could smell his blood in the fountain at the center of the temple. The Seven Gates had claimed his life. I had been their scythe, and I would carry that with me forever. But more than any other kill that I'd wrought, this was the one I did not regret.

At first light, Varian and her acolytes led us to the Devotion Gate.

The valley behind the temple was steeped in icy mist that cut through the thick layers of my clothing. My linen shift, thick wool dress, and knee-length leather vest had always felt adequate when layered beneath a heavy cloak, even in the mountains. But something about the mist permeated those reliable layers, slipping between the tightly-knit fabric and fur lining with impossible ease.

The hairs at the nape of my neck prickled despite the high neck of my vest and the thick layer of my hair. Not cold, but magic and power. The mist itself was enchanted, I realized. As we walked deeper into the valley, it slid beneath my gloves and into the recesses of my boots. Places that were reliably protected yielded to the frigid mist.

I glanced over my shoulder, wondering if Garrick had come to the same conclusion. But he looked straight ahead, his face flat of affect.

Isanara was silent at my side. I'd learned she wasn't much for mornings. Another unexpected similarity between us. But I was alert despite the unkind hour. I was the one about to go through the Devotion Gate.

Power hummed in my veins, my blood cooling as the frost swirled through me. It had been quiet since Nash. Sated, perhaps, by the output and energy required. That should have unnerved me. But since regaining control on the floor of the rented tavern room, I had not felt that overwhelming pulse of power.

Of all the gates, the Devotion Gate seemed the least intimidating. Mercy and justice were as foreign to me as the curses that Garrick muttered under his breath when he became frustrated. Sacrifice, I understood. Devotion had been the hymn of the three hundred and seventy-seven years since my resurrection. Maura demanded devotion to the coven. I chose devotion to my sister's line. Those two causes had often been in conflict. My stomach clenched.

This is not the Memory Gate.

Remembering was dangerous.

I forced my mind back to the present, to the crunch of the frosted grass beneath my feet and the steady sound of Isanara breathing as she walked at my side.

Devotion had propelled me through the Seven Gates. This was a gate I could face.

The acolytes on either side of us walked in silence. They always had, yet in the mist-shrouded valley it felt ominous. Even Tomin had not cracked a smile.

Was the Devotion Gate really so heinous?

Or was this the first time that most of them had performed this ritual? This Devotion Gate was the fourth of the Seven Gates of Velora. The farthest anyone had ever gotten, if legends told true, was the fifth—the Memory Gate.

Each gate had been its own version of hell. But what awaited us here… maybe it was even worse.

My confidence shuddered.

But before I could try to steady it, the mist parted. We'd reached the far edge of the valley. A small cottage emerged from the mists, nestled between the sloping foothills that led back up into the mountains. The materials were different than Kyrelle and Kyna's cottage on the coast, but the construction was essentially the same. Stone walls, thatched roof, windows covered by wooden shutters instead of glass. But warm light leaked from the cracks where the shutters and door met stone. A steady stream of smoke billowed from the chimney. Two squat evergreens framed the entrance to the gate and the cobblestone pathway that led to the door.

After our long walk through the frozen mist, the cottage beckoned in welcome.

That must be the purpose of the mist—to enhance the cottage's appeal. Garrick moved to stand at my side, putting Isanara between us. I appreciated the subtle offer of protection he extended to my familiar without speaking.

"I do not need protection," she growled, her voice still rough from sleep.

"Of course not," I assured her. She whipped her tail sideways in discontent, but did not harass me further.

The acolytes fell back, forming a line behind us. Varian lingered longer, considering each one of the remaining supplicants in turn. I wondered what her wide, dark eyes saw that the rest of us did not. She'd presumably spent decades in the temple. I'd put her age at around fifty years. Few mortals in Velora reached such an age anymore. But with the bounty of the gods to sustain her, she might live several decades more.

When her eyes landed on me, I stared right back. I still knew disturbingly little about the woman who had shepherded us through four of the Seven Gates. She intimidated Tomin. Garrick did not trust her any more than I did. But Isanara had not declared her stained or immediately react with visceral revulsion the way she had with both Alize and Nash.

But the priestess would remain a mystery for at least one gate more.

"Enter the cottage at will," she said.

No direction as to order or whether we ought to enter together or alone. Then she led her band of acolytes back through the mist.

Waiting would get us nowhere. "I will go," I said.

"We will go," Isanara corrected.

"We go together," Garrick said at the same time.

I rolled my eyes at my bonded and my familiar, who did not even realize they were talking over one another in their hurry to protect me.

"And if I asked you to stay and protect my bonded?" I said to one and then the other— "I'd rather she didn't enter the gate."

"No," they said in unison.

For fuck's sake. "Fine."

I turned to Alize. Garrick and Isanara I could tolerate. But I'd rather freeze off my own arm than expose myself to vulnerability with the treacherous fae female at my side.

"By all means," Alize said, crossing her arms. She dropped her pack and pulled out a bit of chocolate she must have swiped from inside the temple.

That was the least of my reasons to resent her, though it certainly did not help.

"Are you awake now?" I asked Isanara as the three of us approached the cottage.

She answered me with a growl. Moody ass teenager.

Garrick already had his favorite blade in his hand, though he left the greatsword sheathed and still hadn't touched the bow or its arrows. I checked the two blades in my belt as we walked, but I knew my most effective weapon lurked beneath my skin.

Thick emerald ivy curled over the cottage's door, its color more verdant than I'd seen in Velora's foliage in years. When we were halfway between the gate and the cottage, the doorway swung open and a blast of heat rolled over us. A buttery scent floated on the wind. Everything about the cottage was meant to invite us in. Maybe I should have reached for one of my daggers after all.

The sensations only intensified as we entered the cottage. The heat was hotter, the scent thicker. They pressed in on me, whipping my power up from a low hum to an anxious whine.

Without thinking, I reached for Garrick's hand.

Once I saw who waited inside the cottage, I realized that was a mistake.

CHAPTER 54

Xyta took the form of my mother once again.

They stood before a massive hearth, the flames licking high enough to reach my shoulder. I could have walked into the stone mouth without bending. The rest of the cottage was bare, the scent an illusion.

The warmth was not. The flames threw off an unnatural amount of heat. From the corner of my eye, I could see the sweat already beading on Garrick's temple. My own temperature remained steady, the frost rising in my veins to counteract the brutal heat. But that was not the only oddity. As I watched, they shifted color. They were at once blue, then bright gold and red before shimmering purple. Beautiful and dynamic, like Isanara's scales. But while I felt drawn to every detail of my familiar, my instincts warned me against those enticing flames.

"You are looking well," Xyta said, and though they'd met Garrick at the Sacrifice Gate as well, I knew their greeting was aimed at me.

I lifted my chin. "I did not expect to see you again so soon."

"You owe me two sacrifices," they said, crossing my mother's arms across their chest.

"I did not imagine that gods were so given to mortal vices like impatience." I forced my hands to remain at my side, but my fingers curled in on my palms. "This is not the Sacrifice Gate," I reminded them.

Xyta smiled, apparently delighted by my impertinence. "My twin is always happy to share."

The flames behind them surged, transforming into a vivid red as another figure emerged.

Ramkael.

The God of Devotion, doomed lover of Pava, the Goddess of Peace, and twin to Xyta, the Deity of Sacrifice.

His appearance gave hints as to what Xyta's true form might look like. Ramkael was tall and thickly muscled, his arms left unclothed by a sleeveless tunic. But they were not bare. Every inch of his exposed arms and neck was covered with swirling dark tattoos. I thought I saw runes, like the ones on my forehead and wrist, but they shifted before I could decipher them. His brows were dark, but there was no hair on his head at all, only more shifting marks that followed the curve of his skull.

Despite all of that, his eyes were not unkind. They glowed bright red, like the enchanted fire he'd emerged from. If anything, I thought I saw sympathy in those unnaturally bright orbs a second before he began to speak.

"Devotion and sacrifice are irrevocably linked."

"The only meaningful sacrifices involve those people and things that we are most devoted to," Xyta finished for their twin.

Realization landed in my stomach, heavy and painful. I should not have brought Garrick with me. I owed two sacrifices. And this was a tidy trap that Xyta had laid. If I refused to sacrifice Garrick, my own life was forfeit, and he would die anyway.

"He should not pay the price for my mistakes," I said the thought aloud.

"Koryn." Garrick stepped closer to me, as if he would intervene. As if he could possibly stop the gods from taking whatever they wanted from me.

"That is precisely what the Lifebind means." Xyta laughed. "Did you think it was a gift? Seraxa certainly does. But the rest of us know better."

Ramkael shot his sibling a reproving look. Apparently, siblings were just as fractious even when they were both deities. Though Xyta stopped laughing aloud, their smile still showed all their teeth.

"This is the Devotion Gate," Ramkael said. "Your Lifebind is not our concern. It belongs to Seraxa."

Even as he said it, the tattoo on the inside of my wrist burned. I looked to Garrick, but if he felt it too, he did not react outwardly.

"I do not understand," I said.

"No matter what decision you make, the bounty hunter will face his own trial and his own consequences," Ramkael said, the tattoos on his neck moving in time with his words.

I exhaled slowly, shakily. "You are not asking me to sacrifice Garrick in order to pass through the Devotion Gate?"

"No," Ramkael confirmed.

But Xyta's smile chilled my blood more than my ice ever had. "I want your dragon."

CHAPTER 55

IT HAD TO BE A NIGHTMARE.

I was still asleep in the barracks of the temple, my mind conjuring up horrifying visions of the Devotion Gate to haunt me. I had already passed through the Sacrifice Gate.

I was every bit as foolish and desperate as the humans whom I'd looked down on with condescension. I'd made a deal with a deity, and now that would be redeemed.

The Seven Gates were as much a punishment as the curse leeching life from Velora. Those of us foolish enough to attempt them, to hope, were punished for that again and again and again. That was why no one had ever made it through all the gates. Supplicants were not saviors. We were martyrs.

Isanara flared her wings out wide behind me and Garrick, then snapped them together. I thought it was a show of pride. I wished I'd known her long enough to understand all of her nuances.

"I will protect you," she said, holding her elegant head high.

The ice in my chest threatened to splinter me from the inside out. *"No."*

"A familiar chooses her witch. I chose you, Koryn." She flicked her

tail above her head, the spike at the end daring the two deities to come closer.

"You did not choose to die before you even reached maturity," I said aloud. I wanted them to understand what they did. If deities were capable of feeling guilt, I wanted them both to ache with it. Both Xyta, for asking this reprehensible sacrifice, and Ramkael, for letting his twin do it.

"Maybe there is another way," Garrick said, his voice low, just for me. We both knew the deities in front of us could hear whatever they wanted. But the secret, special tenor of it was a caress I did not deserve.

I still held Garrick's hand. How had I not realized that? His steady warmth had held my power in check, allowed me to anchor myself and remain in control. Now it helped me make my decision without my senses overwhelming and distorting my thoughts.

"I'm sorry," I said to him, just as softly.

They'd said that whatever happened at the Devotion Gate would not interfere with the Lifebind. That had to mean that Garrick would not die. I had to believe that, because if saving Isanara meant damning him, I did not think I could make the choice.

"I can't..." My voice broke. I forced myself to stop and breathe. I inhaled, counting slowly, and then exhaled, counting again. I would not face my fate in a panic. "I cannot give her up."

Garrick's eyes flashed, his grip on my hand tightened. He looked at me, then to the two deities watching, then back my way again. "You cannot do this."

"You've made your decision?" Ramkael asked.

I'd made the only one I could. Isanara was a part of me—the best part. Not the broken, scared, and scarred part, but the courageous and funny and sarcastic. I'd walked this cursed continent for four hundred years and committed heinous crimes in the name of loyalty to my coven. But I also committed some of them for myself.

If it had to end, at least I was not alone.

I nodded to the twins, one of whom wore the face of my mother. I had no illusions that I would see her in the afterlife. But that did not change my decision. "I have."

"You will not!" Isanara roared. But even a dragon was not fast enough to defy the gods.

Xyta ripped me away with a wave of their hand, sending my body crashing into the stone wall of the cottage behind me. Isanara thrashed, but a wall of red power encircled her and Garrick. My head collided with the floor as I fell, but I was able to make out a rough understanding of what was happening. Xyta would punish me. Ramkael would ensure that my bonded and my familiar did not interfere.

My head ached from the impact, but I managed to get my hands underneath me and push myself up. The cottage spun around, and nausea rolled up from my stomach, but I fought it down.

"Please, Garrick. You have to conquer the gates. Promise me you will get through them, whatever it takes." I would never be reunited with my coven, but that was not my only responsibility. I had not trusted Garrick with her name before, but now I had no choice. "Kyrelle. Her name is Kyrelle. She is my sister's great-granddaughter... I cannot even tell you how many times removed. But please. Please. Save Velora for her." I coughed up blood. "Save Velora for me."

Pain shot through my wrists and calves. I screamed, falling on my side. Blood spurted from the four points, but my eyes saw no blades. Xyta did not need mortal weapons to kill me.

But I wasn't concerned with Xyta. They'd have their sacrifice. Some part of me felt a surge of satisfaction—they'd only get one from me, rather than the promised two. So, in the end, maybe I had triumphed over the deity.

I spared them no more of my dwindling consciousness.

Any remaining fragments of my soul belonged to Garrick and

Isanara. My mouth moved around their names, but an invisible force drove into my stomach, stealing my breath before I could get them out.

Garrick burst through the wall of red that encircled him, past Ramkael's power. It was impossible. I must have already begun hallucinating. He threw himself at me, even as a blast of red from Ramkael sent him sprawling. Then he began to crawl.

"You will not interfere."

The last thing I saw was Garrick's face as bands of bright red power encircled his midsection and legs, binding his arms to the sides of his body and holding him in place. I could not bear the pain in those features I'd come to know so well in such a short time. That must have been why I closed my eyes.

The last thing I heard was his plea. But it must have been a hallucination conjured by the blow to my head, because Garrick the Red would never beg for me.

PART V
MEMORY

CHAPTER 56

"Koryn. Koryn. I need you to keep breathing."

But breathing hurt. Everything hurt. It was so much easier to just stop...

"Koryn! No, you can't go! I will not let you!"

So much pain. Pressure on my chest, a mouth on mine.

Cinnamon. I could taste cinnamon.

"Koryn, you must not give in," a voice chided, gentle and distant. It was familiar, that melodic female voice. I'd known her in another life, or was that this life? Was I still alive at all?

No, I was dead. I died alone in a frostbitten forest.

A life governed by rules and cruelty. That was where the voice belonged. It had never sounded gentle before.

My mouth formed around a name, but even moving my lips hurt. I tried to think it instead. Dark God, how my head ached.

Auri... Auri... Aurienna.

"Do not slip away, frost witch," she urged, her voice gentle. But

Aurienna had never been gentle with me before. She was never a friend, never truly a sister, either. She belonged to Maura, to the Midnight Coven, but not to me. Never to me.

"Do not slip away," she said again. But it was she who was slipping away, her voice coming to me from somewhere distant. Not real, not like the hot words that he begged over my skin. Or was the heat from me? Was I burning? Was I sick?

I think I am dying.

That could not be. I was already dead.

"Fight it, Koryn. You have always fought so hard. Do not give in now," the green witch said. I felt her vines curling around me, holding me like a sister.

A sister I'd never had.

The sisters who had died.

The sisters I had doomed. And the one I killed.

MY BODY BURNED. The frosty cold of my power deserted me, consumed by the kaleidoscope of colorful flames. I could not lift my arms. Nor my legs. But still I moved, floating through the air. A flash of shimmering, iridescent lavender flickered somewhere overhead.

Isanara.

She was alive.

The sky was an unrelenting sheet of white, a sharp contrast to the Dark God's frigid hell and what awaited me there. Only darkness. When I closed my eyes, there was darkness.

Opening them was getting harder and harder. Soon I would not be able to at all. Soon I would surrender to the darkness.

But at least Isanara was alive.

COLD TOUCHED MY NECK, then my cheeks and my stomach. My clothing was gone—had probably been burned away by the flames licking at my flesh. But gods, that was snow against my skin, and it felt like ecstasy. Maybe I had not been damned to hell at all. Maybe someone had relented and granted me access to eternal paradise.

A dark laugh filled my head until it throbbed, until I could not see at all. Darkness flooded my vision. I dragged in a breath, but my lungs did not want to work.

More cold. More snow.

A faint whiff of cinnamon mingled with sweat and terror.

"You cannot have her!" he screamed into the night.

I knew him. I dreamed about his face, his shimmering silver hair, the impossible glowing ring in his eyes.

But that voice belonged to a stranger. It raged with emotion. "She has suffered enough!"

Heat subsumed the cold. I was moving without moving myself. A force more powerful than my understanding pulled me to him, against him.

"This was not the sacrifice that was demanded!"

I could hear his heartbeat.

MY SISTERS CAME to me hand in hand with my mother. Janessa with her freckles, Rylynn with her high cheekbones and elegantly styled hair. My mother wore the pendant that Rylynn had secreted away from my father and the golden circlet armband I'd taken the night I died. That was how I knew it was her and not Xyta.

But I had no words to give to them, no apology that would compensate for everything that I had done.

So, I turned them away.

"STAY WITH ME, WITCH," he whispered against my neck.

But staying was hard. Going was easy.

I have failed everyone in my life.

I could hear his heartbeat. I could feel it in my bones. "Did you ever consider that they were the ones who failed you?"

I did not choose to leave my coven. I was cast out.

"You told me that before." His heartbeat sped up. He pressed something cool to my forehead. "But you did not tell me why."

I did not have the words, not even now as I danced the line between life and eternal death. I had only the weight of my own failures in my chest. I longed for the block of ice instead.

More than anything, I longed for him.

What made you attempt the gates?

He would not answer. He could not. After all, this was nothing more than a fever dream. I was not even speaking. My voice had ceased working days ago. Or maybe weeks.

But cinnamon and destiny burrowed into my senses as he exhaled against my neck— "Duty."

CHAPTER 57

"Living shouldn't hurt so much."

"You deserve it for scaring us like that."

I couldn't turn my head. That was how badly it hurt. Or maybe it was the exhaustion. They felt pretty damn similar.

I opened my eyes enough to see that it was evening. The tree-tops overhead were bare. We were no longer in the thick fir forests that characterized the central part of Velora's only mountain range.

I had no idea where we were. After the endless fever-driven delirium, I was surprised that I knew my own name.

Footsteps crunched through the frost to my left, only to be replaced by a soft swish of air. *"Where are you going?"*

"To get your bonded. He is the only reason you are still alive."

My bonded.

His face came before his name. I could see it even with my eyes closed, the lines of him etched somewhere deeper than I cared to acknowledge. But swift footsteps followed the beats of Isanara's wings, and then he was there, more than just a memory.

He searched my face, his eyes moving too quickly for me to

make eye contact. I blinked up at him, afraid that if I tried to use my voice, I might break him. Despite the fact that every muscle and tendon in my body ached, it was the agony lining his face that hurt the most.

He knelt down, moving each limb with a deliberate slowness that confirmed I really was as badly injured as I thought.

"You scared me, witch," Garrick said. His voice awoke the parts of me that still lingered on the precipice. That telltale divot appeared between his silvery brows, but I lacked the strength to reach up and smooth it, even though, in that moment, the feeling of his skin against mine was the only thing I desired in the world.

Garrick seemed to know.

"May I touch you?" he said softly.

I opened my mouth, knowing this next part would hurt. "If you don't, I think I might die," I said, my unused throat burning as I forced the words out. Garrick flinched away—at the words or the sound or both. I cringed. "Too soon?"

"It will never be time for jokes about your death."

But he did not admonish me any more than that. He reached out. I imagined his hand trembled, but that must have been my own wobbly vision, because when his fingertips stroked my cheek, they were warm and steady.

"I am already dead," I reminded him.

I felt his sigh on my skin. "You know what I meant."

My pain was physical, but Garrick's was mental. Of the two, I'd have chosen the physical burden every single time. I'd spent hundreds of years watching those I cared for dwindle away until only one remained.

I could not presume to know who else Garrick had in his life to care about. We hadn't shared those sorts of secrets. But I knew that he felt something for me.

The least I could do was show him that I'd survived. I commanded my muscles to move, determined to raise myself from the ground under my own power. I made it to one elbow before my body collapsed beneath me and I was back on the layered furs.

And that divot was still between Garrick's brows.

"Do not try to sit up. Stay exactly where you are. I will heat you some broth." And then to my familiar, "Watch over her."

Isanara snorted as she settled in at my side. I didn't try to lift my head to see, but I felt her lay hers across my stomach. *"As if I haven't been doing that for the last two weeks."*

"Two weeks?" My tortured throat thanked me for confining that exclamation to my mind.

"Your wounds were—are—severe. But it was the infection that nearly took you."

That accounted for the delusions of burning alive. But not for everything else. *"How did we escape the Devotion Gate?"*

Isanara did not respond immediately. My stomach hollowed out, dread competing with hunger.

"Xyta was going to kill you. But then... Ramkael stopped them. Neither of them offered an explanation. Then Garrick carried you through the fire."

She was withholding something. Not quite lying—I did not know if she even could lie to me, nor I to her. Not with the unequivocal access that our bond as witch and familiar granted us. But there was more that she was not saying, and I suspected it had to do with Garrick.

I remembered the enchanted fire flashing in different colors behind my tormentor. But everything that happened after Xyta threw me into the wall was nothing but a haze of feelings and sounds.

"And then what?" I asked. I let my eyes close, the effort of keeping them open frustratingly noticeable.

"And then he carried you..."

But I fell asleep before she could finish her sentence

I woke to two strong hands braced beneath my arms, pulling me up with more gentleness than a man his size should have been able to manage. Warmth encircled my back and my sides, and those strong hands released me only to encircle my arms.

I tried to stifle the groan, but my lips and body and mind were not all back on speaking terms yet. Muscles that had not done their jobs in weeks protested by sending spasms of pain through my body.

"Don't try to hold it back," Garrick said, the warmth of his breath sweeping over me. There was the hint of cinnamon that had lined my dreams for weeks. "I've heard it all."

"That is not comforting." Thank the Dark God that, positioned behind me as he was, Garrick could not see my cheeks as they burned red from embarrassment. My keen sense of smell informed me that my clothes were unsoiled and my skin was clean. Which meant Garrick had seen to my *every* need.

If he had not been there to hold me up, I probably would have melted into a puddle of embarrassment right there on the ground. A frozen puddle. But a puddle, nonetheless.

Garrick ignored my comment, wrapping one hand around my waist so the other could retrieve something beside him. He balanced a steaming bowl of soup carefully in our laps.

"Do not knock it over," he said over my shoulder to Isanara.

"As if a dragon could be so clumsy," she hissed. But she did remove her head from my lap and settled beside me instead, her body half on the furs.

I tried to lift my hand to reach for the spoon Garrick balanced on his thigh. But my body refused to obey. Garrick did not even seem to notice the effort. He reached for the spoon, dipped it into the bowl of broth, and then smoothly raised it to my lips.

My hunger overwhelmed my pride, and I opened my mouth.

Garrick the fucking Red was feeding me soup with a spoon. It was the most delicious thing I had ever eaten.

Several steaming bites later, the ache in my throat had dulled enough for me to ask a question that had plagued me since I'd opened my eyes and noticed the change in the trees overhead. "Where are we?"

Garrick dipped the spoon back into the bowl. "A week away from the Memory Gate."

I jerked my head back. Given my current state, the motion was feeble, which saved us both from having searing soup spilled across our laps. "How is that possible?"

"After what happened at the Devotion Gate, I thought it best not to risk angering the gods by drawing out the time between the gates." That still did not answer my question. If I'd had the strength, I'd have sunk an elbow into his stomach. But as it was, I could only tilt my head slightly and try to level a reproving look at him.

"I carried you," he admitted.

I'd dreamed I was floating.

Garrick lifted another spoonful of soup to my mouth. I took it, but swallowed it too quickly as my mind tumbled over its own thoughts. I coughed, trying to dislodge the misplaced soup from my airways. Garrick rubbed circles on my back until I stopped.

"You are the one who needs rest. I am not exactly waifish," I finally managed to say.

The hand that he'd wrapped around my midsection to keep me upright curled into my stomach, caressing the soft rolls beneath the fabric of my shift and dress. "Do not insult either of us by implying that your weight is anything but perfect, or that I am incapable of carrying you whatever distance is required. I would not change a single thing about you, witch."

The embarrassment I'd felt before was instantly replaced with a different sort of heat.

But Garrick spared me from having to think up a reply that wouldn't end with both of us buried in the furs by slipping another spoonful of soup between my lips.

I finished the bowl, but Garrick did not move, and I lacked both the capacity and the will to do so myself. I slowly made note of our surroundings. We were tucked in against a wall of shale, the ground beneath us compacted clay that had frozen into permafrost. The clearing was small, barely wide enough for Isanara to spread her wings or Garrick to lie down all the way. As I'd noted upon waking, the trees were slimmer here, deciduous and ever-barren thanks to the curse. We were tucked away from the world. Even our fire was small by the standards I'd come accustomed to as we hiked through the mountains.

Were we… hiding?

I knew Isanara had not told me everything.

Would Garrick do the same?

"How did you pass through the Devotion Gate?"

Now that my body had seen to its first need, I was becoming aware of the places where I'd bled. I counted four wounds—one above each wrist and one in the fleshy muscle of each calf just above my ankle.

Garrick exhaled slowly. I felt it against my back. "It must have been the same as you. Taking care of her." *Her*—Isanara.

He had offered her his protection more than once. He'd taught me how to use my power in tandem with fighting maneuvers to defend her. If the gods had granted the familiar as a way to test us both… but that did not make sense. Varian herself had admitted that the dragons predated the gods. They were not answerable to them. Dragons answered to no one.

The hairs at the nape of my neck stood on end in warning. I ignored them and every other instinct screaming inside of me. Between the sore wounds, my aching muscles, and a stomach that was full for the first time in weeks, I did not stand much of a chance. Sleep was coming for me.

"No matter what decision I make, it turns out wrong," I said. Exhaustion loosened my tongue and muddled my thoughts. "I lost my coven. Failed my sister and Kyrelle. Even Isanara…"

Garrick's hand closed over my own, the bowl of soup set aside. "Koryn. You saved Isanara. You saved me."

"But only because of the Mercy Gate, and because of the sacrifice that I owed to Xyta—"

Garrick lifted my hand. I tipped my head back against his shoulder, watching as he stroked the calloused pad of his thumb over my knuckles.

"I think you have tried so hard, for so long, to be bad, that you do not even recognize when you are doing good." He lifted my hand to his mouth and pressed a kiss to my knuckles.

A new part of me began to ache. "You said before that there is no such thing as a good witch."

He kissed the next knuckle. "I did say that."

"Have you changed your opinion?"

His face answered, even if his mouth did not.

But I did not need Garrick to think I was good. I only needed him to see who and what I was, and stand by my side anyway.

It took all the remaining energy I had to lift my lips to his. My head swam, and I thought I might lose consciousness from the effort. But then there he was, his lips so soft against mine, brushing over my mouth for the barest second before drawing back.

A strangled little sound escaped my throat, even as my eyelids slid closed. Garrick began to rock slowly from side to side. His strong thighs anchored me in place, one hand caressing my stomach while the other laced with mine.

I wanted to kiss him forever, but instead I let him rock me to sleep.

CHAPTER 58

ON THE FIRST DAY AFTER WAKING, I MANAGED TO SIT UP, WALK THE perimeter of our small camp, and relieve myself without assistance.

On the second, I walked for an hour before Garrick decided he did not care about my pride or my protests and scooped me up in his arms.

By the third, I was ready to strangle my bonded or take a knife to my wrist and scrape out the Lifebind tattooed there. They both seemed like perfectly viable options.

More frustrating than Garrick's insistence that he carry me whenever he detected I was wavering was his absolute refusal to touch me at all other times. He cooked all of our meals—not a new circumstance—but once I proved I could feed myself, he sat on his side of the fire while I remained on mine. Every time I moved closer to him, he found an excuse to move in the opposite direction.

But when he carried me in his arms, I knew I wasn't wrong. He wanted me as badly as I wanted him. Maybe he was still hindered by the unspoken understanding we'd shared in the tavern. An outcast witch seeking redemption and a half-fae mortal bounty hunter were not bound for happiness. That had not changed. But something else had.

In that liminal space between life and the second death, a new understanding had emerged. Garrick and I were bound for as long as Seraxa saw fit. The Seven Gates were a microcosm of the rest of Velora, a strange and ubiquitous shadow that held us in its thrall until we emerged victorious or died trying.

What happened between the Seven Gates was separate from the rest of the world. For this brief moment in time, amid centuries of pain, we could have each other.

If he did not realize it yet, I would make damn sure he did before we reached the Memory Gate and had to share a barracks with Alize.

But every time I turned my face up to his while he carried me, hoping to distract him or press a kiss to his jaw, Garrick avoided my gaze. My strength grew by the day, as did the unsated desire that ratcheted up every time I looked at him.

Isanara took to flying off for extended periods that she called patrols. *We* were annoying the teenager. What a mortifying turn of events.

The mountains in this part of the range were more spread out, with large valleys and meadows dipping between them. It gave her the opportunity to spread her wings and soar. Watching the pale gray light from the overcast sky shining through her wings was the only relief I felt from the tension building with every step that I—or we—took toward the Memory Gate.

"We should reach the Memory Gate tomorrow morning," Garrick announced as I rinsed out our bowls and he snuffed out the night's fire. I'd managed to walk under my own steam for the entire previous day. And then I'd fallen asleep approximately two seconds after lying down on my bedroll. But that was beside the point.

I was healed.

I reached up to pull my unbound hair back over my shoulder, a little tremor of pain emanating from the star-shaped pink scar on my forearm. *Mostly healed.*

"I'll scout ahead. I have not yet seen the stained one." Isanara did not wait for a response before launching into the air. I flinched as she swerved sharply to the right to avoid the top of a barren alder. But a few blinks later, she was out of sight.

I knew she could still hear me, a new bit of information we'd gleaned over the past few days. No matter how far she went, her voice remained clear in my mind. But we both knew that when she flew off, it was because she *didn't* want to be exposed to my lust-filled brain.

I tucked the bowls inside my pack but did not reach for the strap to heft it over my shoulder.

"She'll be gone for an hour, at least," I said.

Fire reduced to smoldering coals, Garrick straightened. "We can make good headway on that mountain in an hour."

That mountain was over my shoulder, and while it wasn't as tall as those we'd crested between the Justice and Devotion Gates, I sighed audibly. I immediately regretted the sound. It would not help the point I was trying to make.

Garrick mistook it as worry for Isanara.

"She always seems to find us," he said, shouldering his own pack but still avoiding my eyes.

Instead of pulling my fur over my shoulders, I tossed it on top of my pack.

Garrick was too busy scanning the camp for any last items to notice. So, I sent a wave of ice toward him. It hissed as it consumed the remains of the fire, melted and then reformed into spikes that hemmed him in with a half-circle that I commanded to stop well before they posed any real danger.

It felt good to release my power after so many days. It had been building inside of me, waiting. I'd formed snowballs and thrown them for Isanara, but all that did was dull the edge of the frost coalescing inside of me.

Garrick froze. Pride surged within me that had nothing to do with the ice in my veins.

"What are you doing, witch?"

This time, I was the one who avoided his eyes. It was damn hard when all I wanted to do was look at him. Even with his eyes pulled together and his mouth turned down in a suspicious frown, the rugged lines of his face called to me. It was slightly warmer here on the southern edge of the continent, and he'd unknowingly done me the favor of packing away his traveling cloak, which meant I could truly enjoy the breadth of his shoulders and thickness of his arms.

"Sparring." I rolled my shoulders, testing my muscles and trying to loosen the last of the previous night's stiffness. Too bad I hadn't had the foresight to leave the neck of my gown unfastened. I'd seen the way he stared at my breasts when he thought I was not looking.

He stepped around the wall of jagged ice. "You should save your energy for the Memory Gate."

"You were the one who taught me the importance of building my endurance." I pulled out the smaller of my two daggers. The blade was shorter, but it fit better in my hand.

He did not put down his pack, but he did not begin hiking for the mountain, either. His frown did deepen. "I am also the one who spent the last three weeks keeping you alive, against all odds. Driving yourself too hard, too fast, is a poor way to repay my devotion."

My reply caught in my throat. Surely he hadn't meant—

"I will not fight you, Koryn."

Except that he was, just on a different front. But I suspected that more than me, Garrick was fighting with himself. Even from across the camp, I could see the way his eyes shifted and brightened as he watched me caress the hilt of the dagger in my hand. I saw that glow in his eyes now for what it was—desire.

Finally, after torturing him for several more long, drawn-out moments, I slid the dagger back into my belt. Garrick's throat slid, his chest heaving. He was as affected as I was.

I held his gaze as I spoke. "I am in full possession of my mind, Garrick." I echoed back his words from the tavern. "I know what I want. And this time, there is no chance I am going to forget."

CHAPTER 59

WE CLIMBED IN STRAINED SILENCE. THE FEW TIMES I CAUGHT Garrick looking my way, he turned away just as fast. Even Isanara's reappearance was not enough to loosen the tension between us.

The quiet gave me time to plot.

I set up my bedroll while Garrick pulled out our food supplies and began to prepare the evening meal. He'd augmented our stores before departing from the tavern on the other side of the Devotion Gate, but it had taken us longer than it should have to travel between the two gates, even with Garrick carrying me. If the Memory Gate did not await us the next morning, we would have gotten to try our hands at hunting.

As I watched Garrick's competent hands at work, I felt certain they'd have been up to the task. But I wanted them otherwise occupied.

Wingbeats overhead signaled Isanara's return. She'd joined us around midday before taking off again. The tiniest barb of regret formed inside of me at what I was about to ask of her.

"The stained one has already reached the temple," Isanara reported.

"We expected as much," I replied, though I did relay the confirmation to Garrick. He nodded. Apparently, talking to me was too dangerous now, too.

"Have you eaten today?" I asked my familiar. She circled the campsite we'd set up at the edge of a valley, flaring her wings in and out in a series of movements she always seemed to repeat after extended periods of flying. The dragon equivalent of stretching, maybe.

Her head snapped up, yellow-green eyes finding me instantly. *"I gorged myself on a vein of iron,"* she said. *"I will tell you if I need your help finding nourishment."*

"That was the agreement," I agreed. *"In order to get you to stop rooting around my pack like a toddler."*

She snapped her jaws in my direction.

I responded with a smile. *"Not a fan of the comparison?"*

"Are you being irritating intentionally?"

"I often wonder the same thing about you," I shot back. But she'd caught me. *"I thought if you were in a huff, maybe you would fly off for another few hours."*

Her neck swerved to the side, scales glimmering teal and then violet, then back to lavender in the dying evening light. *"And why would you want me to do that?"*

I looked pointedly past her curved horns to where Garrick knelt over the fire, turning the roasted potatoes.

Isanara blinked up at me. I knew that dragons could not smile. Her muscles did not quite work that way. But the swish of her tail from side to side said enough—Isanara was enjoying herself immensely.

When I did not speak, she planted herself on the ground and curled her tail around her hind legs. *"I guess I will just settle in for the night, then."*

She was going to make me say it.

"Isanara." My cheeks flushed, but I ignored them. I had almost died at the Devotion Gate. There was every possibility I would not survive the remaining three gates. I was not about to be bullied by a teenager. *"If you choose to stay, I will not be held responsible for whatever emotional scarring your precious adolescent mind might have to endure when Garrick and I—"*

"Disgusting!" Isanara hissed, flapping her wings wide. Garrick rocked back on his heels, eyes darting between us.

My familiar launched into the sky in a blaze of iridescent scales, spikes cutting through several thinner branches that got in her way. Garrick blinked at me across the fire.

I shrugged. "Teenagers."

Garrick served dinner an hour later. I lingered over every bite, humming suggestively as I savored the spices he'd used to season the potatoes and cured bacon he'd sliced into bits and sprinkled over the top. The creamy cheese melted on my tongue, marrying all the flavors together. I'd never learned to cook, but I was usually more than happy to eat.

Tonight, I ate every bite of food in my bowl. I did not want to hear a single word from Garrick the fucking Red questioning my strength for what was to come.

Night fell fully around us as we cleaned out our bowls and Garrick stacked enough firewood to last through the coldest hours. Now was the time of night when Garrick usually retired to his furs to brood, while I argued with Isanara from mine on the opposite side of the fire.

But Isanara was gone, and the only person I would be arguing with tonight was Garrick. It was an argument I intended to win.

I unstrapped my belt first, tossing it down alongside my furs. That should have been his first clue. Usually, I tucked it underneath the spare linen shift I used as a pillow.

Next was my knee-length leather vest. Just like every night, I loosened the trio of metal buckles that held it closed over my stomach and just below my breasts. Sleeping in layers was the only reasonable way to stay warm in the frigid cold of Velora nights. At least when you were sleeping alone.

As I shrugged off the vest, the cold night air rushed in, seeking the covered parts of me that had been nestled beneath its thick insulating layer. My sapphire blue wool gown, embroidered with purple and silver thread, provided some protection. But it worked best sandwiched between linen and leather.

I unfastened the ties that cinched the fabric in on either hip and then dragged the garment over my head. At the same time, I kicked off my boots.

Something heavy hit the ground.

I licked my lips, but forced myself to continue in slow, deliberate movements. I tugged on the neckline of the dress until it popped loose over my shoulders, leaving my unbound hair drifting down over my collarbone, the corners curling around my breasts.

Breasts with nipples that instantly rose to attention beneath my shift.

"What are you doing?" Garrick's voice was rough, like the stubble on his chin and the calluses on his hands.

"I am undressing for bed," I said as I turned. I bent at the waist and made a fuss of adjusting my furs, giving ample time for Garrick to admire my backside.

Was it brazen and a little backhanded? Absolutely.

But I was not forcing him. Garrick the Red was a legendary bounty hunter and seasoned warrior. Although I could read his tells and expressions now, he was a male in control of his own body.

I was simply making his choices *very* clear.

"Witch," he groaned. "This is not a good idea."

I flipped my hair over my shoulder and nodded. "That is what you told me before." But I wasn't about to agree with him.

I reached for the neckline of my shift.

"You are more than welcome—"

I pulled the bow apart, and the linen fell away to reveal my shoulders and the soft upper curves of my breasts.

"—to let the fire go to ashes—"

I flicked my fingers, and the fire extinguished, plunging us into darkness.

"—and go to sleep."

I pulled the shift over my head and tossed it onto the ground between us. The sound of the fabric hitting the snow should have been nearly imperceptible. But I felt the reverberations, and I knew Garrick did, too.

For a moment we stood frozen in absolute silence.

I reached my arms overhead and stretched, my breasts lifting with the motion. If Garrick possessed the keen eyesight that the half-fae blood in his veins promised, he could not help but see. Then I rolled my shoulders one final time before lying down on the furs.

It was cold. Of course it was cold. It was Velora at night, in the middle of a cursed, perpetual winter. But I was a frost witch. The cold had already killed me once. My second death would be at a different hand.

For several beats of silence, I thought his better judgment might win out. I even slid my hand down the center of my body, prepared to see to my own needs. It would be Garrick's name I called out when I climaxed.

"I am the only one who will be touching you there tonight."

My fingers fluttered around my belly button.

"Is that so?" I breathed, my voice shaking. I had not lost my confidence, but the pure eroticism of him speaking to me like that, his voice heavy with command, knocked loose something primal within me.

Every footstep he took across the campsite was a physical sensation within my body, thrumming with the anticipation of him coming closer. But he did not reach for me or take off his clothing or join me in the furs. He stood at the edge of my bedroll, fully clothed, staring down at my naked body.

Even in the dark, I could see the faint glow of his remarkable turquoise eyes.

"Get on your knees, Koryn."

Gods help me, I did as he commanded.

My lower lip pouted out, but Garrick was there to catch it. He scraped his thumb over the sensitive skin, his callouses drawing out a tingle of pain. I slid my tongue forward, eager for everything he'd give me.

He caught my wrist, lifting it to his mouth. I expected him to press a kiss to the palm or the fresh pink scar on the inside of my arm. Instead, he dragged his tongue over the Lifebind inked on my skin. My back bowed, my entire existence centering in on the feeling of his hot tongue against my cool skin.

He cursed under his breath in that foreign tongue he only used when he was at the edge of his control.

"You can say no at any time," he said, his voice rough as the words scraped out. He was as affected as I was. I nodded. Of course I did.

"I need to hear you say it, Koryn. You need to say aloud that you will tell me to stop if that is what you want."

There was such power in his voice, barely restrained. Every line of his body was corded with muscle, his voice lined with strength, but I understood what he meant. He might tell me what to do, but I held the power in this exchange.

"I can tell you to stop at any time," I said. I would have said anything if it got him to keep touching me.

"If you ask it, I will stop." He dragged his tongue over my Lifebind again. "Even if it fucking kills me."

I licked my lips, remembering how it had driven him to distraction in the tavern. "Are you going to stand there with all your clothes on? It seems impossibly unfair."

"Everything about this is unfair," Garrick said, but he was

already shedding his leather vest. The layers of wool and linen followed until he was bare-chested before me.

I could see well in the dark, but it wasn't enough. I needed to touch him.

"Oh no, witch." Garrick caught my wrist again. This time, his hold was much firmer. "First, you have to watch."

I rocked back on my heels, a frustrated huff escaping my lips as he released me and then hooked his thumbs into the waistband of his fitted leather breeches. I sucked in a breath as he tugged them down. There was not enough air in the clearing, probably not in the entire world.

His cock was bigger than I'd imagined even in my wildest fantasies. The hard length that I'd felt through his trousers in the tavern was nothing compared to the reality of him, erect and throbbing a few inches from my face. I'd never particularly enjoyed taking men in my mouth, but with Garrick it felt like a *need*. All I had to do was bob my head forward, and I could drag my tongue down the glistening seam…

"You are a wicked thing, aren't you?" Garrick growled.

I tipped my head up, meeting his eyes in the darkness. I could not help it—I licked my lips again. Garrick's entire chest moved as he groaned. But instead of leaning forward and giving me what I was certain we both wanted, he reached between us and pumped his cock several times.

"Everything about you seems designed to torture me," he said as he stroked.

My pussy clenched as I watched the motion, wishing it were my walls that clung to that rigid length instead of his fingers.

"It seems to me that you are torturing yourself," I said, my throat sliding.

"Fitting repayment," Garrick bit out. But his hand stilled, and he clenched his eyes closed. Dark God help me, he was close already.

A newfound sense of power flooded my veins that had nothing

to do with frost or the Dark God's gifts. This was all my own, and it came from somewhere deep inside of me that I had never fully explored or acknowledged.

I could not keep my hands still any longer. I reached down to tweak my breast while the other hand slid over the soft roll of my stomach to my—

"I have not said you can touch yourself, witch."

This time I was the one who growled, but my hands fell away.

"Garrick," I moaned. We both saw it for what it was—a plea.

His chuckle was low and appreciative. He stroked his cock once more before leaning down and pressing a kiss to my forehead. "Lie back."

I did as he said, waiting while he shed his boots and breeches so that he was fully naked when he joined me in the furs. The bedroll was made for one, and my full body took up the entirety of it. But Garrick did not try to slide in beside me. He nudged my legs apart with his knee, planting it between mine. He held himself above me, one hand braced on the side of my head, the other free to stroke down my face.

He brushed his fingertips down the curve of my chin, past my throat. He drew a circle around each nipple, then down over my belly button. He paused to caress my stomach, running his finger along the rounded curve, then out to my hips where my silhouette waved and dipped before finally—finally—sliding his fingers lower.

Garrick groaned when he found me slick and ready. "So wet for me. Have you been like this all day?"

"I've been like this for weeks," I gasped out as he found my clit.

He skimmed his fingertips over the sensitive bundle of nerves, his touch so featherlight it was half in my mind. Then he flicked the bud hard, and I screamed. Light flashed behind my eyelids, impossible in the darkness and yet totally consuming.

He flicked my clit again, then alternated with light, teasing touches.

"Garrick," I moaned to the night, the sounds of my pleasure echoing off of the trees. My release loomed closer and closer, ready to crest at any second.

"I told you that when I made you come, you would remember every moment," Garrick reminded me. "Will you remember this, Koryn? How you writhed beneath me? How you screamed my name?"

There was only one answer. "Always," I gasped.

He nudged apart my legs and slid inside of me. That was all it took. I careened over the edge, my climax stealing my breath and every coherent thought from inside of my head. But Garrick did not relent. He continued to circle my clit, applying alternating pressure as he slid his cock slowly out and then back inside of me, until I was coming again in a second wave, my pussy clinging to him with every tremor.

My legs shook. Hell, my entire body might have been shaking. But I kept my hands at my side, just as he'd commanded. It took torturous minutes for my body to come down, for me to be able to reorient to the world around me. To Garrick—still inside of me.

I cracked open my eyes, expecting the intensity of his clover and cerulean gaze. But what I was not ready for was the longing etched in every line of his familiar face. His hair had come loose from the half-knot at the crown of his head. It shone in the sparse moonlight. How had I ever thought of it as blond? No, his hair was silver, an ode to the fae blood in his veins. But for once, I did not recoil at the connection. It was just Garrick, and he was perfect. He was everything I'd never even known I wanted.

He leaned down and kissed me, his mouth gentle. He explored every corner of my mouth with his tongue, my lips with his teeth, until I was not sure where I ended and he began. After this, separation would be impossible, and we both knew it.

But it was his words that undid me, when he pulled his lips away but pressed our foreheads together, his cock still buried deep and hard within me.

"Touch me, Koryn," Garrick breathed.

I needed no further encouragement. I was a star of raging need about to explode, the heat in me rekindled by those three words.

I slid my hands up his arms, my fingernails scraping into the skin as I went. I'd let the points come back, and now I used them to map the network of scars and muscle. Up his arms and then over his chest.

Garrick shuddered as I spread my fingers across his pectorals and paused. I wanted to feel the pounding of his heart. There it was—strong and true.

With a low groan, he began to move inside of me again. Before, he'd thrust in time with his hand on my clit, intent on dragging out my orgasm. But this was about his pleasure, and I felt his control slipping away as surely as I seized it with my own hands. I raked my fingernails down his chest, desperate to add my own mark to the others I could feel beneath my fingers. Two decades of bounty hunting on Velora had left him riddled with scars. I wanted to know every single one, to memorize them and map them like the stars in the sky.

His pace increased as I slid my hand lower, tracing the tight muscles of his abdomen.

"Koryn," he groaned, my name a prayer on his lips. No one had ever said it like that, not in four hundred years.

Realization clicked inside of me, like the last piece of a puzzle sliding into place. But before I could examine in, the pressure between us overtook me as well.

Garrick increased his speed, driving us both closer to the edge. I slid my finger between us to my clit, but he batted it away. He leaned into the space between us and sucked my nipple into his mouth. One swipe of his tongue, and then he had the sensitive bud between his teeth. That was all it took. My breasts had always been the most sensitive part of me.

I threw back my head, arching into the furs and crying out. Above me, Garrick roared, my climax driving his. My legs shook as he emptied himself inside of me, waves of heat that felt like coming home.

Garrick's chest pressed down into mine, his heart thundering so hard that I felt it as if it were my own. As if three hundred and seventy-seven years after my death, some part of me had finally come back to life.

CHAPTER 60

After holding ourselves apart for so long, we could not seem to stop touching one another. We lay awake for a long time, stroking and caressing. Garrick was fascinated with exploring the curves of my stomach, the dips and swells that he'd personally seen to with his cooking skills. I twirled his silvery, silken hair around my fingers. It was even softer than I'd imagined.

I dragged my fingernails lightly over his jawline, where a sheen of silver stubble was just starting to appear. I could still feel his heartbeat. The blood in my veins surged to match its tone and tenor, though I had no heartbeat of my own.

"I need to ask you something," I murmured. The realization had been flitting at the edge of my consciousness for the last week, ever since I'd awoken from my feverish stupor. But it had crystallized in the moments before my climax crashed over me, when we'd joined not just our bodies, but our souls.

"The Devotion Gate," I said.

Garrick's hand paused, halfway up my stomach on its way back to my breasts. He lifted one brow.

I swallowed past the tightness in my throat. "Isanara is not the reason Ramkael allowed you to pass through."

I waited for him to deny it. There was still a chance, however infinitesimal, that I was wrong, that my emotions had betrayed me. But I forced myself to tip my head back and meet the intensity of his turquoise gaze.

"Say it."

I inhaled the cinnamon and wine scent of him to give me the strength to say the words that would change everything. "It was because of me. You did not prove your devotion to Isanara. You proved your devotion to me." A shaky exhale. "Why?"

Garrick's throat slid. He was as vulnerable as I was. "You know the answer."

My heart no longer beat. It did not pump my blood. If anything of the organ remained inside of my chest, it was long dead and shriveled. But with Garrick's chest pressed to mine, his own heart beating rapidly, I felt a shift inside of me. If not in my heart, then in my soul.

I knew what he meant, but the words scared me more than the realization.

Garrick did not press me. He leaned down and brushed his lips against mine in a silent, gentle answer that it was okay to keep the words inside, for now.

My hand shook as I reached up and tucked a strand of silver hair behind his ear. A tiny stud sparkled in his earlobe. I'd noticed it before. I turned it gently with my fingertip, a small smile curving the corners of my lips.

"It is so at odds with everything else," I said softly.

Garrick's mouth quirked. "My mother insisted. She had it pierced when I was a boy. There is a legend among her people that amorite can protect young men from evil. I wear it to appease her."

Human legends from distant continents. But it was sweet—and it was only the second time he'd mentioned his mother. That bit of himself felt as precious as every other secret we'd shared. We knew one another in the present, in the crucible of the gates. But maybe we could share the other parts of ourselves as well.

"What happens if we pass through all of the Seven Gates together?" I wondered aloud.

Garrick's brow furrowed, that familiar divot appearing. "What do you mean?"

I reached up and pressed my thumb to the mark, determined to smooth it. "No one has ever made it through more than five, and by that time, they were attempting them on their own because all the other supplicants were dead."

I tried very hard not to stumble over the last word, even though I'd seen its truth again and again. For hundreds of years, I'd been a front-row witness to death. I'd wielded it myself, even here in the gates. But saying it felt personal—a reminder that the fifth gate loomed. And if we passed through it successfully, we would join the ranks of just one other. And face what was perhaps a certain death.

I dug my nails into my palms as I forced the words out. "There is no rule that states only one person can conquer the Seven Gates." And then, even more dangerously, "We could make it together."

Garrick turned his head into my shoulder, pressing a kiss to my collarbone. "You wish to rejoin your coven."

Yes, that was why I'd entered the temple. To save Kyrelle and to save myself. Despite the coven mark and my lingering power, a witch by herself could not survive forever. But if we made it through all the Gates, if we broke Velora's curse… we would find ourselves in a world remade.

Why shouldn't we remake it to suit ourselves?

"First, we must survive the Memory Gate," Garrick said. Another kiss. A distraction. I was not ready to name the feelings between us. Garrick was not ready to hope.

For now, just having one another was enough.

Wingbeats overhead announced Isanara's arrival.

Garrick pressed a kiss to my hair. "Later," he promised.

Because we would have a later. For as long as the gates permitted, for as long as we could make it so. And even then, even if the inevitable, probable end came... after that night, I knew that I would never be alone again.

CHAPTER 61

I WOKE IN THE HOUR BEFORE DAWN, COCOONED IN WARMTH ON BOTH sides. Garrick at my back, his larger body enfolding my own, and Isanara at my front, her steady breath moving her glimmering scales. Up and down, and up and down, and up and down. The sight was so mesmerizing I lay there as the minutes passed, just watching her, almost forgetting why I'd woken at all. But eventually the pressures of my body got the better of me. I sidled carefully from between the two of them, and they both did me the courtesy of pretending to still be asleep as I slipped into the forest to relieve myself in privacy.

I cushioned my footsteps with fresh snow, not out of necessity, but because I did not want either of my companions listening in. I'd had precious little privacy before my beating at the Devotion Gate. Since then, one of them had dogged my every step. The least I deserved was to take care of my normal bodily functions in peace.

I was returning through the forest when something rustled overhead. Wind moving through leaves, my mind told me. A sound I'd heard thousands of times. Except that, held in perpetual winter by Velora's curse, none of the trees in this forest had leaves.

But I knew a witch who could summon them.

"Aurienna."

At first, nothing changed. The leaves overhead continued to rustle, deceptively harmless as they moved in the breeze. I glanced up, noting that only the few trees nearest to me bore leaves. It was too dark to see their color clearly, but the scent of lush new growth came to me on the wind.

The red-haired witch stepped from between the trees, her black cloak swaying in time with the trunks. My power swirled beneath my skin, a mixture of frost and ice that formed and then melted and reformed again. It felt as if my power could not quite decide how to react to my sister witch's presence. She had been there at my resurrection, and because of that, our power would always be linked. But she had also chanted in unison with the rest of my coven when they cast me out.

The moon had already begun its descent, but I could see her clearly enough thanks to my heightened eyesight. Just like she could see me.

She examined me openly, starting at the feet I'd shoved into my boots and the cloak I'd thrown over my shift to go relieve myself.

"I am glad to see you walking under your own power once again," she finally said.

My mouth fell open. I may have gotten better at controlling my power, but I had yet to master my own face. "How did you know I was injured?"

An echo sounded deep in the recesses of my mind. I'd heard Aurienna's voice in my fever dreams. But I could not quite recall her words.

She did not answer my question. Nor did she plan to. Instead, she jerked her chin side to side, her fringe of copper hair swaying across her forehead.

It was just so typical of Maura to send another witch to check up on me and then to be evasive about it. She'd played mind games with me from the beginning, encouraging me to use my power and then leveling my fragile nerves with condescension when I failed.

In four hundred years, not a single one of my sister witches had tried to figure out why I struggled to control my powers. Only Garrick had reached out, giving me the stability to anchor myself. Only Tomin had offered concrete strategies for quieting the endless overwhelm from the heightened senses I'd been gifted by the Dark God.

I had conquered four of the Seven Gates without any help from my coven. But now that I stood on the precipice of the fifth, about to do what only one being in all of Velora had ever managed, now Maura wanted to interfere.

Fuck that.

"Why are you here? Does Maura have another message for me? Am I not conquering the legendary Seven Gates of Velora quickly enough for her?" Anger rose in my chest in time with my power.

I'd gotten this far on my own, despite everything Maura had inflicted upon me over the centuries. Not because of it. Loyalty to coven—but when had the coven ever been loyal to me? They'd risen me from death, but even that I had not asked for.

The frost threatened to burst out of me, but I forced it back down. I imagined Garrick's warm hands curling around my own. I anchored my feet into the ground, inhaled a deliberate breath of cold air, and grounded myself like Tomin had taught me.

Meanwhile, Aurienna opened and closed her mouth. The expressions on her face were impossible to discern because they changed that quickly. There even appeared to be—was that pain?

"Maura does not have a message for you," she finally said, her throat sliding visibly. It looked like she was about to cough or choke.

My hands went to my hips, power still present but palatable. "Then why are you here?"

She exhaled slowly. I noticed the vines curling around her feet, spreading across the ground thick as a carpet.

"Nothing is as it seems," she choked out, the harshness of the words cushioned by the greenery sprouting up all around us.

Dark Lord fucking spare me. "Helpful as always, Aurienna."

I'd had enough of this. I did not bother softening my footsteps any longer. If Garrick or Isanara wanted to come save me from the green witch, I'd welcome it.

"I prefer Auri."

I paused, and not only because of the vines that curled around my boots. I waved my hand as I turned, and the vines withered as I froze them to death. "What?"

Her lower lip quivered, but the words seemed to come more easily than they had before. "I've always preferred to be called Auri."

A hysterical chuckle bubbled out of my chest. This was ridiculous. What a conversation to be having in the woods in the middle of the night, with barely any clothes on. "In three hundred and seventy-seven years, I have never once heard one of our sisters refer to you as Auri."

She blew out a breath between her lips, lifting the fringe of red hair from her forehead again. "No one ever asked."

Something about the way she said those words made me pause. The contrast in her face, in her voice and throat…

An idea formed inside of me, cold and confusing and just barely possible.

"Why are you here?" I repeated, watching her closely.

Aurienna looked to the side, then up at the sky, just beginning to change as dawn edged closer and closer.

Her lips trembled as she repeated herself again, word for word, each syllable strangled as she forced it past her lips. "Nothing is as it seems."

Cold surged inside of me, power and realization competing. Those were the only words she could say in response to my direct question because she was under a binding spell that prevented her from saying anything more.

The only witch left in Velora capable of casting one was Maura —and she would have needed help from other members of the coven because Maura was a fire-bound witch, and such a spell was not within her bind.

"Nothing is as it seems," I said softly.

Relief flooded Aurienna's eyes. She knew that I understood. Even those five words had been difficult to get out. She was bound from answering certain questions, most likely, or from giving certain information. That was how I'd seen binding spells used. *Nothing is as it seems*—that was just vague enough not to violate the terms of the spell that bound her.

What could it possibly mean?

We were weeks away from where Alize, Garrick, and I had stood outside the faerie ring. But the weighted looks the two of them had exchanged were burned into my mind.

Only three gates remained—Memory, Peace, and the Unknown Gate that belonged to the Dark God. Three gates and three supplicants.

That could not be significant, could it? Witch lore spoke of the power of three. The triskelion and the triquetra were among our most powerful runes, linking the power of maiden, mother, and crone, and of past, present, and future.

Maybe it was a warning about the gods themselves. Xyta had tricked me, using their twin's gate to call in the sacrifice I'd promised. Perhaps Ramkael and his lover, Pava, the Goddess of Peace, had some similar trick waiting for us. But the Peace Gate was more than a month's travel away, whereas we would reach the Memory Gate tomorrow.

The leaves around us rustled again, drawing my attention back to the green witch.

With a wave of her hand, she withdrew the vines from beneath my feet. She left the ones on the trees, even though I knew they would wither and die in a matter of hours, no match for Velora's cold without Aurienna's power to sustain them.

She pulled her cloak around her, covering her hands once more. "I cannot linger."

Whether that meant that Maura was nearby and expecting her to return soon, or she did not want to risk encountering my companions... I was not sure I wanted to know.

She inclined her head, but did not try to offer any more words, if she even could.

But before she disappeared into the night, one more question burst out of me.

"Auri... why did you come?"

She might not be able to answer, not if the question violated the parameters of the binding spell. Even then, she might not want to.

It had been at Aurienna's urging that my power had exploded out of me at the guild hall on the night of my Rylynn's engagement celebration, permanently injuring her betrothed.

Our intertwined power would always tie us together, and to the Midnight Coven. But beyond that...

"I am your sister," she said quietly. "I always have been... and I always will be."

She melted away into the rising dawn, the trees answering to her command as they whisked her away.

I watched until I could not hear or see or sense her with any of the Dark God's gifts.

You must not give in. That is what the Auri in my dreams had whispered. But it was only a dream, brought on by infection and riddled with nonsensical hallucinations.

But paired with her words tonight... it made an ominous warning.

CHAPTER 62

BEFORE

I should have waited another year or two. Maura was going to find out. She'd only sent me over the mountains to fetch the palmarosa that the priestesses and priests grew in their gardens for use in the temples. The temples were the only place where the plant still reliably grew.

Instead of harvesting the plant and slipping back across the mountains, I'd journeyed south. I carefully kept out of sight of the southern road and did not encounter any humans.

But with every footstep, the words echoed in my ears.

I should have waited.

I should have waited.

I should have waited.

Another prolonged absence from the coven lands, less than two years after my last, was too suspicious. Maura was going to find out, and then I would have doomed not only myself, but Kyna as well. Maura would kill her to teach me a lesson and finally separate me from my past.

My chest ached with the effort as I climbed the last bluff between me and the sea. Once I reached the top, I would be able to see the cottage. I counted out the months on my fingers, pressing each one into my thigh as I ticked them off. The child should be nearly a year old. If it had survived.

I should have waited.

I should have prayed to the Dark God for Kyna's baby to be healthy. Instead, I'd begged him to carry her away from Velora by whatever means necessary. If that meant losing her husband and the life growing inside of her, at least she would be safe from Velora's curse.

But what I should have done did not matter, because with my next step, I crested the hill that overlooked the sea. There was the little cottage, perched on the bluff. Sand blew between the golden grasses. Once, they'd been green and thick with seabirds. For someone who had never seen the landscape in the time before, I knew the mixture of gold and blue must seem beautiful. For me, it only ratcheted up my worry.

The cottage looked the same. The thatched roof was in good repair, as were the walls. I was too far away to see the decorative seashells tucked into the grooves of plaster between the stones. But the walls themselves looked straight and sturdy.

Every window was closed tight.

Kyna liked them open, even before she'd met the man who'd chained her to this continent. I summoned up his name from the dredges of my memory. Merrick.

I walked faster. The chorus in my mind shifted. I should not have waited so long. To a witch, two years was nothing. But humans were so fragile.

Merrick's boat bobbed in the harbor, the deck conspicuously empty. Why wasn't he out fishing?

I should not have waited so long.

Ice filled my chest, sending shivers down my limbs. I broke into a run.

I was close enough to see the seashells.

I forgot to knock on the door. It wasn't locked.

I blinked into the dark interior, my senses struggling to sort out the details as they flooded over me. A fire blazed in the hearth —unnecessary with the spell I'd placed on it to keep the water and ice out. Kyna knew that.

But Kyna was not there.

She was not at the worktable slicing bread, nor in the chair that faced the window. My throat closed as I spun to the bed in the corner. The curtain was closed. I ripped it aside, but there was no one there, either. Just a rumpled pile of blankets.

Then I heard the cry.

"Please, I just got her to sleep."

I turned slowly, not sure I wanted to see. How had I missed the rocking chair before the fire? Maybe I had not wanted to see it. It wasn't Kyna there in the spindly creation, slowly rocking back and forth. The man, Merrick, held a bundle of blankets across his lap. A chubby little leg dangled out, kicked free of the covers.

I had not spent much time around babies in my life or death. But the child looked about the right size for her age. He had said *her.*

I did not move any closer, hovering near the bed in the corner. But it was a small cottage, and my gifts from the Dark God ensured that I noted every bit of sensory information as it pressed in.

My pointed nails dug into my palms as I curled my hands into tight fists.

"Where is Kyna?" She must have told him about me, for him to be sitting there so calmly when a stranger burst through the door. But to not react at all... I should not have waited so long. The ice in my chest became a weight so heavy I struggled to stay upright.

"Gone," Merrick said softly, his eyes fixed on the child in his lap.

"Gone where?" Even though I knew. Kyna would never have left her child. A daughter, her thick hair already the same shade as her mother's and my sister's and my own.

Ice formed in my palms, crystallized in my veins.

"She did so well," Merrick said. His legs stopped moving. The rocking motion of the chair slowed. "Carried her all the way to term. There was no midwife, but she delivered her just fine. She nursed her. Got up and walked around."

I did not dare to hope. But I also could not fully believe what I saw before my eyes. The chair stopped moving.

"But she never really recovered, not fully. She grew weaker and weaker. Until one night she just slipped away." Tears tracked down his cheeks. He leaned down and pressed a kiss to the head of dark hair. "Now it is just the two of us."

Hope—I'd been foolish to ever have it. Hope was for those more fortunate and deserving than I. I'd spent a lifetime helping Kyna, readying her for the journey across the water to safety. Even now, I stood there knowing that if Maura found out, I would be punished brutally for my insubordination. My two allegiances, coven and family, always in conflict. But I'd been so close to getting Kyna away to safety, to finally resolving the terrible tug on my resources and my hea—

"It was supposed to be the two of *us*," I bit out.

This was his fault.

He'd convinced Kyna to stay. He'd gotten her with child. This poor, useless fisherman had ruined everything.

"You were the reason she stayed. She should have been safe. She had enough money to buy passage across the Southern Fate. If it weren't for you, she would still be alive," I raged. My power wrestled free, ice coating the floor. The cloying heat tried to melt it, but my anger was a visceral thing, feral and untamable.

But Merrick did not react. He sat in perfect stillness, staring down at the sleeping child in his lap.

That made me angrier still. Ice climbed the walls. "You have nothing to say for yourself? No defense? You know you are to blame!"

"A spell for the child," he said softly. "That is all I ask."

So, he did know everything.

A spell for the child—for Kyna's child, for Rylynn's last living descendant in Velora. But I could not find the words.

The ice on the floor and walls cracked, thrashing against the spell I'd cast years ago to keep the moisture out of the cottage. My power surged, trying to find escape, then turning back in on me. I was going to combust. I had to get out.

I could not give her a spell. I could not save Kyna. I had failed.

If I stayed a moment longer in that sweltering hell, I would doom us all.

I crashed through the door, ice crackling in my wake. I did not make the conscious decision to climb the bluff rather than descend toward the water. But what did it matter? Kyna was dead.

It was not Merrick's fault. It was mine. I should have gotten the coin together sooner, gotten her across the water to safety before she was old enough to learn about men and love. She should have borne her child in safety, in a land of life and beauty.

She did not deserve to die. None of them had.

It was all my fault.

The golden grass turned brown beneath my feet, withering and dying as my frost murdered the last vestiges of life. It would never regrow, not in Velora. Everyone and everything that remained in Velora died.

Except me. I would live forever.

I stumbled, knees crashing to the frozen ground, then my elbows. I did not try to spare myself. I flattened my hands against the ground, curling them into the dirt. I couldn't hold back the power a second longer. Part of me did not want to.

Velora was already in her final death throes. If my power could speed the process, then so much the better. I poured my frigid power into the ground, freezing the grass and the dirt and the tiny creatures that burrowed beneath it.

Maybe if I tried hard enough, I would reach the Dark God's hell, deep beneath the ground like the humans believed.

The Dark God was supposed to be my patron. The creator of the witches, I'd prayed to him for help. I'd prayed for him to help Kyna escape Velora.

"This is not what I asked for!" I screamed down at the ground, even though I knew the idea of the Dark Lord dwelling beneath it was a fallacy. Human minds were too limited; they could hardly imagine the infinite realms occupied by the gods, so they assigned physical locations to heaven and hell.

I clawed at the ground, the sharpened points of my nails tearing as the dirt hardened, colder the deeper I went. But I welcomed the pain. It was the least that I deserved.

"I asked you to save her! What chance will her daughter have with that useless human! I asked…" A sob tore from my chest. "I should not have waited so long to come."

I hunched forward over the ruined ground, sobs tearing through me, shaking my shoulders, my arms, until I was a ruined shell myself. Just like Velora.

"What do I do now?" I whispered. To the Dark God. To myself.

The air around me shifted, a change so subtle only my enhanced senses allowed me to perceive it. I felt it on my skin, the slight charge of power.

A tendril of wind caressed my cheek, sliding over the sensitive skin of my throat and beneath my ear. It seemed to linger at the back of my neck, almost like a hand brushing across the sensitive, exposed skin of my nape. It lingered there with me for hours as I tried to rearrange the broken pieces of my life into something recognizable. It whispered the words of the spell that I could not summon earlier in the cottage.

When I finally stood, it followed me back across the mountains and into the coven lands.

CHAPTER 63

UNLIKE THE MYSTERIOUS SACRIFICE GATE, CARVED INTO THE mountains themselves, the temple that guarded the Memory Gate stood in the shadows. The stones were the same color as the mountains on either side, clearly sourced from their ore.

Nearly two months had passed since I'd thrown myself over the threshold and into the temple in Canmar. In that time, I'd acquired both a Lifebind and a familiar. My power was somehow, inexplicably, still strong and more under control than ever.

But all of it could be ripped away by one cruel turn of fate at the hands of the gods.

I still owed Xyta one more sacrifice.

Who knew what awaited at the remaining three gates?

Auri's warning echoed in my head. I had not told Garrick or Isanara about the nighttime visitation, though the latter had unfettered access to my mind, so she probably already knew.

I moved through the temple's rituals by rote—eating, visiting the altars, avoiding Alize and Varian. My body demanded an afternoon nap. As night fell beyond the stained-glass windows, I found my bed in the dormitory while Garrick saw to his evening ablutions in the attached washrooms.

There were only ten beds now, though the barracks could have accommodated three times that number. Alize chose one near the exit. I chose the one farthest away from her.

Isanara hissed at Alize and then tucked herself underneath the bed. I let my chuckle of appreciation go free as I unstrapped my leather vest and then unbuttoned my gown, draping them both over the end of my bed. My weapons and belt I tucked beneath my pillow, within easy reach. Even with only two other supplicants left, even with Garrick sleeping in the bed across from mine, even with Isanara coiled beneath me like a snake.

The gates were not places of safety; neither were the temples. The guards who stood in the doorways were part of the deception.

A gate is always near. A god is always watching.

I settled beneath the blankets, adding my fur-lined cloak over the top for an extra layer of warmth and weight. Another illusion of security.

Garrick returned from the washrooms, dousing the torches along the wall as he crossed the barracks. I watched him with open admiration. Alize had already rolled away to face the wall.

He'd left his tight leather breeches unfastened, the charcoal-colored linen shirt hanging off of his shoulders unbuttoned as well. I sank my teeth into my lower lip to keep my little growl of appreciation inside. The muscles of his stomach were so sharply carved I would have thought I could slice my hand on them, if not for my thorough exploration the night before. They curved downward, pointing to the parts of him still concealed beneath the leather.

But the leather could not conceal the glorious length of his—

A snarl ripped from my lips as he doused the last torch, throwing us into sudden darkness. He met it with a low chuckle. I pouted my lips out even though I knew he couldn't see them. How dare he steal away my last good look at him? I couldn't have him tonight, but at least I could sear his body into my memory so I might have pleasant dreams.

My eyes adjusted quickly, made as they were for seeing in the dark. But my mind struggled to make sense of what my eyes communicated. In front of me, directly by my bedside, was a wall of hard muscle.

Garrick hooked his thumbs into his breeches and pulled them down.

I swallowed so that I would not start drooling.

Then, to my utter and complete shock, he reached for my hip.

"Alize is right there!" I hissed, certain she could hear me even from the other side of the room.

"Move over, witch."

He did not wait for me to comply, sliding my heavy body over as if it were nothing and climbing into the bed behind me.

"If this bed collapses down on top of me, I will eat your bonded. I don't care how disgusting humans taste."

I shivered at Isanara's threat. Or maybe it was the warmth of Garrick's breath against my ear as he settled in behind me. Or his cock stroking against my backside. Fucking gods. He wore nothing but his linen shirt, and with the buttons undone, he might as well have been wearing nothing at all.

I shivered again.

"Do you need me to warm you up?" Garrick breathed into my ear, his lips brushing against the shell.

One arm slid beneath my head, creating a little pillow and tucking me in tight against his chest. But the other one… wicked, hateful man. It slid around my stomach, drawing circles around my belly button and caressing the soft rolls. I was so wet that soon the entire temple would be able to scent me—humans and fae alike.

"We are not alone," I said as quietly as I could manage, hoping the thick furs would muffle the words, if not the sound.

Garrick answered by sucking my earlobe into his mouth. "Then you'd better be quiet."

I opened my mouth to protest, then slammed it shut again when his hand slid down my stomach. He paused to tangle his fingers in the dark forest at the apex of my legs, drawing tiny circles that tickled and teased.

I was going to die. For the first time in my life or death, it was not the frost that would be the end of me, but the heat. Holding in the reactions he drew from my body was torture on a level I'd never experienced, not in four hundred years.

Desperate to relieve the pressure, I slid my own hand back over my hip to his harder one. If he could torture me, I could certainly return the favor.

But he pushed my hand away before I could curl it around him. "Not now. Tonight is about you."

"You are being ridiculous." I could feel how hard he was—like the fucking stones that had been hewn from the mountains to build the walls that enclosed us.

My legs pressed together, eager for that hard length of him inside of me. But it was his hand that slid down, urging my thighs apart. He lingered for a moment, stroking the insides of my thighs beneath the blanket. I'd been with many men and women over the centuries, but none of them had ever shown such reverence for my body. Garrick touched the parts of me that I'd never considered to be erotic—my soft stomach, my thick thighs—with as much interest as my breasts or pussy.

My hand began to tremble. I dug my fingernails into Garrick's hip to steady myself. This time, he didn't push me away.

He nipped at my throat. "Be a good girl and keep your hands right where they are." Then he plunged a finger inside of me.

My back arched, hips driving into him. Gods, he was so hard. My mind could hardly process the heat of his cock pressed against my back in tandem with his thick finger stretching me. No matter how I moved, he was there.

There was no way I could keep myself contained. Alize was doomed to hear every sound. I refused to let myself think about Isanara. Hopefully, she was blocking me out, if that was even possible.

Garrick cradled my hips within his own while his finger set a steady, rhythmic pace. I'd admired those fingers for months. I knew their girth, the competent strength in every inch. When he pressed a second one inside of me, the darkness around me exploded into stars.

"Garrick," I groaned, turning my face down into his bicep to stifle the sound.

He took that as an invitation to press his lips to the nape of my neck. "Has no one ever worshipped you, Koryn?"

My answer was another helpless mewl swallowed by his thick muscle.

No—that was what I would have said if I were coherent enough to form words. No one had ever worshipped me like this. At best, sex had always been an exchange. At worst, my partner found satisfaction while I took care of myself or fell asleep disappointed. But Garrick did worship me, every single part.

My pussy stretched around his fingers, my body desperate for every sensation. The slight burn only made me wetter. I sank my teeth into his bicep to try to relieve the building pressure.

But Garrick was merciless. While his mouth made love to the column of my throat, he increased the speed of his strokes inside of me. Then, just as I was about to combust, he curled his fingertips and scraped them across a bundle of nerves I'd only ever dared to tease.

There was nothing teasing about Garrick's touch. He curled his fingers with each stroke, driving me to a place I'd never even seen before. Ice crystallized in my veins, then shattered and melted in a torrent of fire.

A surge of wetness flowed between my legs, coating Garrick's hand, the insides of my thighs, and the furs and blankets we'd pulled over us. Heat bloomed across my cheeks. I rolled to my back, my head still resting on his arm, chest heaving. My mouth opened and closed, but there were no words. Where before I couldn't keep the sound in, now I was too shocked to make one.

Garrick pressed his forehead to mine. "That was incredible." His voice shook. Why was his voice shaking? I was the one who'd just come in a literal flood. "You are incredible."

"I… I've never done that," I said. Too loud—but also too late.

"No one has ever done that for you," Garrick corrected. "I'm honored to be the first."

My hand trembled slightly, but I still reached for him. His cock was still hard against my thigh. He caught my hand, lifting it to his mouth, and pressed a kiss to the palm.

"Absolutely not. Go to sleep, witch." He leaned down to press a matching kiss to my lips. "You deserve it."

I didn't know about that. But I certainly was not about to argue with him. Not when he could make me feel like that. It was easy to surrender to the warmth of Garrick, his breath on my neck, his leg curved over mine. I reached up and brushed aside a wave of pale hair that fell forward across his cheek.

Maybe he was right. Maybe I was incredible. Maybe together, we were unstoppable.

WE WERE ALREADY DRESSED and waiting when the acolytes came for us at dawn. I was not about to be dragged through another gate without having a chance to rinse out my teeth and relieve myself. Whatever Garrick and Alize's reasons, they were ready as well.

I refused to acknowledge Alize at all. She looked the same as she had every other time I'd seen her. Her cropped brown hair curled slightly around her face, complementing her golden skin. A faint luminous glow seemed to emanate from her, even in the darkness of the tunnel, as the acolytes led us out of the temple. I knew it was the fae magic beneath her skin.

Aurienna's warning echoed through my mind as we walked. I was no closer to deducing what it meant, but some halting instinct told me that it had to do with Alize. Or maybe that was just my well-honed hatred for the fae coloring my judgment.

Still, I found myself hanging back, taking up the last position of the three supplicants. Garrick frowned at me, but with Isanara at my side, he let it pass.

I rolled my eyes. Welcoming him into my bed did not equate to granting him any sort of hold on me.

"Keep telling yourself that."

"Hush. I need to speak with Tomin."

Isanara must have approved of that, because she didn't argue. I slowed my steps until I fell in line with the grinning acolyte. We'd never explicitly been instructed not to speak during this ritualistic march from temple to gate. The need to speak to him superseded any reservations about how Varian might react. She was all the way at the front of our little procession, anyway.

"Any tips?" I asked, returning Tomin's grin with a smaller smile of my own.

His smile dimmed slightly. "I have never been to the Memory Gate," he admitted.

The words he did not say hung in the air between us. In his twenty years serving the Seven Gods, no one had ever made it this far. I'd suspected as much, but hearing it confirmed made my stomach drop a few inches.

"If it is anything like the other gates, I would guess that it will have something to do with my worst memory." I'd had plenty of time to think about what the Memory Gate might entail while Garrick carried me through the mountains.

Tomin did not argue the point. His emerald green robes shifted as he moved, tentatively reaching out. I did not flinch away. "In the oldest texts, Zeph is not just associated with memory but also with change." He laid a hand on my shoulder and squeezed gently. "We cannot alter the past, but we can determine how our memories impact the future."

That was a lot of wisdom for someone who had not yet finished their third decade.

I blinked back the surge of moisture that flooded my eyes. When that did not work, I settled for freezing the tears before they could fall.

I lifted my own hand and covered Tomin's, squeezing him back. "I was the youngest of three sisters. I never knew what it was like to be an elder sibling. But if I'd been gifted a younger brother, I would have hoped for one like you."

Tomin's honey-cold eyes widened, then it was his turn to blink back emotion. He was much better at it than me. I recognized the cool mask of composure that he slid into place not as a rebuke, but his way of managing the wave. I did us both a favor and released his hand and turned my attention forward, fixing my gaze on the center of Garrick's back.

A few minutes later, we emerged into a narrow gorge. The two mountains that had framed the temple now rose up on either side of us, leaving a narrow, flat pathway between them. But even that ended a few yards farther on, the way blocked by a swirling, sparkling black mist.

It reminded me more of a nightmare than a memory. Maybe it was because that is what most of my memories were.

"You enter together," Varian instructed.

We moved into place, the steps now well-rehearsed. Alize wore her mask of beautiful, unbreakable composure. Isanara wove between my legs, reminding me that no matter how much I begged her to wait outside of the Memory Gate, we were inextricably linked.

Garrick did not bother with subtlety. He curled his hand around mine, drawing me closer to his side and leaning down. I rose on my tiptoes to meet him, our mouths finding one another with an ease that should not have existed after only two months.

I expected a brief kiss, a touch point to anchor us as we headed into the unknown. But Garrick's mouth was fierce on mine, his tongue diving deep inside of me, claiming me with each broad stroke. I matched him. If he claimed me, then I claimed him as well. For this brief moment in time amid the centuries, for seven gates, we belonged to each other.

We would survive the Memory Gate.

Alize grumbled in the background. But Garrick did not relent. Only when he had explored every curve of my mouth did he finally retreat, the fervor ebbing to slow, savoring licks. He nipped at my bottom lip before pulling away just enough to speak.

"Are you ready, witch?"

My power surged in answer. "Yes."

Hand in hand, we stepped into the abyss.

CHAPTER 64

We did not walk. We fell.

It felt like a blow to the stomach, all of the air suddenly ripped from my chest, my limbs too light and then suddenly much, much too heavy as we crashed to the ground.

Garrick's hand was immediately on my back, trying to steady me. But it was too late for that. I was already on my knees, my stomach doing violent somersaults as I gulped down air. Beside me, I saw the toes of Alize's boots. She'd landed on her feet, of course.

"Isanara?"

"I have wings," she huffed. How dare I ask such an inane question.

I splayed my hand across her back and used it to push myself back to my feet. My first impression was of overwhelming light. Born in the year of the curse, I'd never seen such brightness.

We stood at the threshold of a balcony where it adjoined a cavernous room. The entire structure was built out of a pale golden stone that reflected the light flooding from behind us and almost glowed. Massive pillars rose on either side of the balcony, framing the luxurious suite. Expansive cream and gold rugs covered the stone floors, connecting arched doorways with geometric carved patterns cut out from stone itself. There was an elegantly appointed bed, a table and chairs, and several bookshelves. They all looked like something out of a dream, so bright and beautiful they could not possibly be of this world.

Because they weren't, I realized.

"Where are we?" I whispered, even though we were alone.

"Balar Shan," Garrick said. He was not holding my hand anymore.

My mouth fell open as he reached over his shoulder, freeing the bow and nocking an arrow. But before I could ask what had caused him to draw the weapon he'd avoided even mentioning for the entire time I'd known him, a figure appeared in one of the arched doorways.

Even as a child, Alize was instantly recognizable.

Her hair brushed her shoulders. Two braids started at the center of her forehead before hanging down to frame her face and expose her pointed ears. Her skin was the same luminous gold. But it was the way she moved that alerted me to the likeness. There was confidence and grace in every step, in the tilt of her head as she glanced back over her shoulder, checking for something.

At my side, the present-day Alize sucked in a breath.

She watched, her eyes unreadable as the younger version of herself crossed to the center of the room, where a cradle carved of pale wood rocked gently back and forth.

My stomach clenched.

Garrick slowly lowered his weapon, arrow still conspicuously ready, but at his side instead of pointed at the young fae female.

Young Alize reached the cradle. She stood beside it, gazing down at what I presumed to be a sleeping infant. She waved her hand behind her, and one of the pillows from the bed floated to her on a phantom wind. Her magic had already been strong, even from a young age.

She clenched the pillow in her hands, tension stiffening her body.

Dark God, no.

She leaned over the cradle and shoved the pillow down. The infant wailed, but the sound was muffled by the pillow. I knew it was a memory, I knew it had already happened. But I still stumbled forward, Isanara between my legs. Garrick grabbed my arm, jerking me back.

I opened my mouth to protest, but before I could, young Alize flew backward through the air, crashing into the pale stone wall. My head whipped side to side, looking for who had intervened. But it was just the younger fae female, the infant, and us four spectators.

Before the young Alize could stand up, a bright light flashed, encompassing all my senses.

Then, just as suddenly, it receded, and sensations flooded back in. The light shone over my shoulders, gilding the golden stone. The wooden cradle swayed gently. Young Alize appeared in the arched doorway.

The memory played out exactly as it had the first time. The only difference was that I knew what to expect, and when young Alize flew backward, I thought I saw tendrils of curling white smoke above the cradle. But by the time I blinked, they were gone.

I expected the flash of light. For a second, all of my senses were deprived. It felt something like relief, except that it was too brief, and once again, we were back in the nursery in Balar Shan while young Alize attempted to kill her younger sibling.

I'd heard her crime at the Justice Gate. I now knew which one belonged to Garrick. But this was not the time. If this was Alize's worst memory... which one of mine would the Memory Gate select for me to relive? And how many times?

When young Alize appeared in the archway again, the adult Alize at my side tensed.

I'd seen her composure falter once, but this was far beyond

that. The cool, beautiful mask was completely shattered, leaving behind anger and rage that transformed her lovely face into something terrifying.

"Garrick," I said softly, trying to draw his attention.

But he was already watching present-day Alize. His eyes were bright with sympathy, but he did not offer her any comment or solace.

Young Alize crossed to the cradle. But before she could summon the pillow, present-day Alize intervened. She shoved her younger self aside. The young female's body did not even hit the carpeted floor. As soon as the real Alize shoved her away, the younger version evaporated.

Alize stood over the cradle. A single tear tracked down her face. Her hand twitched, and for one horrible moment, I thought she was about to summon the pillow herself and finish the job her younger self had failed to complete.

Instead, she reached down into the cradle and lifted the infant out. His hair was much darker than hers, nearly black, but I could see that his golden skin matched hers perfectly. Just as suddenly as the other Alize had disappeared, the baby in her arms morphed, and in its place stood a fully grown fae male. There was the same dark hair, the golden skin, but the face was fully formed into the lines of adulthood. Alize leaned into him, resting her head against his shoulder.

He did not reach for her, but nor did he push her away. He looked over her shoulder, beyond her and beyond us, not seeing us at all. He wasn't real. I knew that. But the feeling was still unnerving. His eyes were a deep, familiar blue-green, thick with intensity that—

The swirling black mist ripped me away before I could finish the thought.

CHAPTER 65

EVEN THE SECOND TIME, THE FEELING WAS HORRIBLE. ALL THE AIR fled from my lungs, leaving only a painful, gasping emptiness. This time I landed mostly on my feet, though Isanara was braced underneath me, so I could hardly take full credit.

I felt Garrick at my side, though the frigid darkness and balancing on a slant made taking in the details of him more difficult.

"Where is Alize?"

Garrick scanned me from head to toe, found nothing imminently wanting, and moved on to adjusting his bow. "She passed through the gate."

She'd relived her worst memory and been deemed worthy by Zeph, the God of Memory.

Garrick, Isanara, and I were still trapped in the Memory Gate.

And this memory was mine.

I recognized the barren street and the decrepit buildings. I'd lingered in the tavern at the end of the street for three nights. Too long.

Garrick and I watched from atop the old general store, crouching on the slanted single-story roof as I emerged from the tavern. A different, previous version of myself, though I looked exactly the same. My brown hair was darkened by the night, the blues and purples and browns of my clothing all muddled to black.

When I stepped into the ring of salt, a visceral cry tore from my lips—my present-day lips, not the ones of the witch frozen in the street. She could not move a muscle.

My attackers emerged from the alleyway and began their debate. Guilt swam in my stomach at the same time that power crystallized in my veins.

It was strange to watch the memory unfold from this angle, raised up above the entire scene. In Alize's memory, we'd been closer to the action as it unfolded again and again.

Again and again. She'd been forced to relive the memory again and again, exactly as it was—until something caused it to change.

"We cannot alter the past, but we can determine how it impacts our future." Garrick's eyes swung to me as I repeated Tomin's words. Whether he'd meant to or not, the acolyte had given me a clue. "I have to intervene. I have to change it. That is how we get out of the gate."

But before I could move or decide what to change, Garrick angled his body and slid down the roof. He landed hard in the snow, the sound echoing across the street, but none of the three occupants reacted.

I turned, ready to mimic his movements.

"Let him do it," Isanara whispered into my mind.

If they hadn't heard Garrick's landing, they certainly could not hear my familiar speaking into my mind. But I did as she said. Despite her age and her moodiness, she had yet to lead me astray.

Garrick reached the trio in the street just as the last spark fell on the snow, melting the ring of salt. But instead of exploding with power, he was there to catch me. I watched as his hands closed over my own. I watched my eyes flicker with confusion, then recognition. Even this memory of myself seemed to know him.

The power that had surged inside of me in that street calmed. So did the ice surging in my veins. Warmth filled me instead. I had only a second to savor it before the darkness took us once again.

CHAPTER 66

I landed on my feet with Isanara at my side. She shoved her head into my hand, her horns scraping against my palm. Victory flooded my chest. I'd survived the Memory Gate—done what only one other before me had ever achieved. There was truly a chance that I would make it through the Seven Gates, lift the curse, regain my coven, and save Kyrelle like I'd been unable to save her mother. I reached for Garrick—

And there he was.

At my side.

But that could not be right. He should still be inside the Memory Gate, inside his own memory. Unless the Lifebind had somehow altered things and bound us so that we could not leave without the other—

Familiarity came in brutal, merciless waves.

First was the smell. The cave was always thick with herbs, burned to strengthen spells or stewed to add to potions. Then came the contrast of temperatures. Cold along the walls where our beds were placed, but burning hot at the center where Maura's ever-burning fire blazed. But worst of all had always been the noise. Trapped together in that cave, there was always too much noise echoing between the sloped walls. The other witches in my coven always seemed so unbothered, but I had never learned to manage the gifts the Dark God had granted me. The cacophony of sensory input overloaded me, just as it had for centuries.

Garrick's hand curled around mine.

I took a deep breath, nearly choking on the thick scent, but I managed to count to five and then exhale. I did it again.

But there was no further respite. This was the Memory Gate. And this was my worst memory.

"These are the coven lands," Isanara said from my side. She'd twined between my legs, a movement of protection.

She did not need me to confirm it. I could not speak, even within my mind.

I watched, helpless, as the commotion unfolded at the entrance to the cave. A beautiful blonde witch appeared, clothed in close-fitting trousers and a vest. McKean, the final member of the Midnight Coven. She dragged a limping young woman behind her. It was nearly midnight, but none of the other witches slept.

Aurienna and Elodie sat with Maura around a cauldron, chanting a protection spell. They had to be renewed more and more often as the power in Velora weakened. There was hardly a point. With the fae gone, the witches had no natural enemies. But Maura insisted we be prepared, that our borders be strong and fortified at all times.

Maura spoke obsessively of the day the curse would be broken. That was the true duty of the coven—to be ready for when it was, to assume power. All the other covens had fled Velora, but not Maura. She bided her time, waiting for the moment when the curse would lift and the Midnight Coven would be the first to grab that newfound power. We were immortals. We could afford to wait.

Maybe McKean had foreseen it. She was the coven sister I feared the most, Maura's right hand.

Even with Garrick's hand around mine, ice surged in my veins. There were some things beyond even his comforting reach.

McKean threw her prisoner down on the ground, her blonde hair swirling around her like a sun-kissed halo. I knew what was coming, and still it made me sick to watch—to see the young woman's body, thin from her long journey north, bruised from the beating McKean had given her upon discovering her in the coven lands.

"Intruder," McKean hissed.

"Please, please, I am not an intruder. I came… I must speak with… I need… I need Koryn."

My coven turned as one to where the past version of me stood frozen by my bed.

Ice cracked inside of me as I watched the horror on my past self's face, the pleading in Kyrelle's eyes, the realization of how truly terrible whatever happened next was going to be. Isanara moved toward the other me.

"No," I said to my familiar. *"Not yet."*

I knew what happened next on the night that Kyrelle stumbled into the coven lands, hungry and desperate. This was my memory.

"Sister," Maura said, moving to the center of the cave. There was no doubt she spoke to me—the past version of me, the one that existed in the memory.

My coven sisters fell into place around her, moving to the five points of the pentagram carved into the stone floor. We'd acted out this ritual dozens of times over the centuries, any time there was an intruder on the coven lands.

"You cannot know this human, can you, Koryn? That would violate our sacred covenants," Maura said, her eyes never leaving mine.

I watched the blood drain from my face, watched my hands curl into fists as I tried to quell the power that rose up uncontrollably inside of me. I saw firsthand just how terrible I was at masking my emotions.

"Koryn," Kyrelle rose up to her knees. McKean had bound her hands with a length of rope. "Please, Koryn. My father is ill. We need a spell—"

"A spell?" Maura's voice rose an octave.

"And she will give another," McKean said. Her voice was deceptively smooth, even as she unraveled the secret I'd held close to my decaying heart for nearly four centuries. "And another and another. So long as her sister's descendants walk the continent of Velora, she will continue to betray our covenants. I have seen it."

There was no greater condemnation she could give. McKean's power was foresight, ironically gifted to her by the Dark God when she'd defied her parents' warnings and died because of a lack of it.

Maura's dark curls bounced as she stepped into her place on the pentagram. She did not wait for me to take mine. Maybe she knew that I wouldn't, or couldn't. "Then we will do what is required to save our sister. We will remove the temptation."

McKean pulled a dagger from her belt.

"Koryn," Garrick said softly. He was still at my side. I'd been so caught up in the memory that I'd forgotten. But my power hadn't. It swirled beneath the surface, ready but waiting, soothed by his warm hand around mine.

But I could not let him intervene on my behalf this time.

The only hitch was that there was nothing about this memory that I wanted to change.

My past self stepped forward, moving like I was going to take my place on the pentacle, like I was going to let them murder Kyrelle. I threw out my hand. Power crested inside of me, inside of us, in my chest, in the present. But in the time it took me to move forward, to step in front of the memory of myself, Kyrelle's form changed.

It was no longer my sister's descendant bound at the center of the pentagram, but Garrick. He was no longer waiting at the edge of the memory with his bow in his hand. He was on his knees before McKean and her dagger.

No. No, please, no. Not now.

Xyta's second sacrifice.

This was more than a memory. That was the real Garrick, the one who'd kissed me and worshipped me. The man who'd stood at my side, protected me even beyond the demands of the Lifebind. The warrior who'd awakened parts of me I'd long thought dead.

If I did not stop McKean, she would kill Garrick.

If I intervened, I would betray my coven again. There would be no hope of redemption.

Xyta's laughter filled the cave. It reverberated off the walls. It was more than a sound. I could taste their derision, scent their triumph. Frost swirled in my veins, over my skin. I fought to keep it contained. But Garrick was gone—bound, trapped, at the mercy of every bad decision I'd made over the past four hundred years. There were no breathing rituals that could keep this power contained. I was going to fracture.

"Please." My voice broke. Even this part of the memory was doomed to repeat itself. I fell to my knees and begged. "Dark God, please, help me."

There was no flash of light as the memory was wiped away, only sudden, complete darkness. No cave, no witches, no Isanara, and no Garrick.

Only the dark, frigid hell I had visited once before. He materialized before my eyes, unspeakably beautiful, eternally terrible. There was only one way to greet the God of Death.

I kneeled before the Dark God's throne.

"Welcome home, wife."

CHAPTER 67

"I am not your wife," I bit out as I pushed up to stand. The less time I spent kneeling before this particular god, the better. "Not yet."

"We have a bargain." His voice was exactly as it had been before, the first time he'd ripped me from my world and brought me to his dark, frigid hell. Too melodious for a god of death and darkness. A siren's call in the night.

I'd begged for his help and he'd answered.

The scar on my inner thigh burned. The ancient runes inked there were a constant reminder every time I invoked his name. Garrick had not seen them—I'd been careful. The darkness before the Memory Gate, the heavy furs in the temple, they'd hidden the Dark God's true claim on me. More than witch.

Bride.

"I am well aware of the bargain we made." It haunted me every night when I went to sleep. But I would not take it back. My worst memory was that night in the cave when Kyrelle was captured, but there was nothing I wanted to change. Until Xyta got involved.

The Dark God leaned forward on his obsidian throne, dark

hair falling over his brow. "You seem to have developed a fondness for bargaining with gods. Are you regretting your dealings with Xyta yet? They are not as straightforward and trustworthy as I am."

He did not smile even as he made what could only be a twisted attempt at a joke. The most powerful being in existence did not need to indulge in such mundane human niceties.

I exhaled slowly, biting down on my tongue to keep it in check. I'd learned the first time we'd played this game—he loved to hear himself talk.

"Our bargain was simple. You killed your coven sister to protect your blood sister's descendant. I did exactly as you asked. I spirited the human woman away to safety."

But as usual, even in the most fraught situations, I could not keep my mouth shut. "They would have killed her if I had not asked for your help. I could not defeat them all." I advanced on the throne as I spoke.

He was right—and I hated it.

I'd killed McKean. That was the part of the memory that Xyta wanted to compel me to change. The vengeful Deity of Sacrifice wanted me to kill Garrick instead. Not that either choice would bring back McKean, dead almost a year now.

I'd killed McKean to stop her from killing Kyrelle. But that had still left me to defend an injured woman against three other witches. And while I'd always struggled with my power, Maura, Elodie, and Aurienna had perfect control over theirs.

So, I'd begged the Dark God for help. He'd offered his terms, and I'd accepted them.

He saved Kyrelle. I was cast out from my coven for my crimes.

And when that second death finally came for me, I would spend my eternity here—in hell.

"The terms of our bargain have not changed," he said, drumming his fingers on the arm of his throne.

"I want to make another bargain."

The Dark God stilled.

I refused to let myself flinch as he stared down at me. His dark eyes, black as his crown of hair and the throne on which he sat and the kingdom around us, watched me for any change. He'd gifted the witches with their heightened senses. He must possess them too.

Could he hear the blood thundering through my veins? Smell my desperation?

"You wish to save your bonded."

More than anything.

But if he could not read my mind, I was not giving him any extra insights. "If you save him from Xyta, I will… I will come to you sooner."

His mouth twisted in a sneer. "How much sooner, Koryn? A year? A decade? A century?"

My life was the only thing I had to bargain. Maybe I should have been more careful with it. But I had to get through the Seven Gates first. If I got through the gates, I would be reunited with my coven and restored to my full power. I would be able to save Kyrelle not just for a few weeks or months, but for the rest of her natural life.

But to bargain away a decade or a century, when I did not know how many remained to me… *it doesn't matter.* Not if it saved Garrick.

It mattered to the Dark God.

He stood from his throne, descending the stairs that separated us in three easy bounds. His thick brows curved slightly above his deep-set, dark eyes. He advanced until I was close enough to see the stubble on his upper lip. What a ridiculous affectation for a god.

"You will sacrifice for him, even knowing he will always be beyond your grasp?"

My stomach clenched at the threat. But if he could have undone the Lifebind, he already would have. And the terms of our bargain stated he could not bring about my second death to hurry me along to the place that waited for me at his side.

"I am not promised here until my death," I said.

"I am not a forgiving god, Koryn," he sneered. "For the well-being of your bonded, you had best remember that."

"I did not choose the bond." But I would protect it and treasure it for as long as I could.

"No, it was gifted to you by Seraxa." His dark face curled with revulsion.

I did not care about his petty infighting with the other gods. I cared about Garrick and the future of Velora—not for its own sake, but for the ones I cared about who were cursed by it. "You have not given me an answer."

He lifted his chin. "I cannot interfere with the bargains you make with other gods. If Xyta demands your bonded's life as their due, then that is what is required."

Anger rushed in, cold as the ice that this very god had gifted to me. "You are supposed to be the most powerful of them all. Yet you won't do it. You won't bestir yourself to help me."

I did not hold it back. I couldn't kill or hurt him. I let the ice flow from me, coating the floor around us. I hated that his dark hell made my frost glitter. Like they belonged together, like I'd been made for this place.

The Dark God closed the space between us, leaning down so that I could not avoid his dark eyes as they bored into me. "Haven't I been with you, through all of the gates? How many times have you whispered those words... *Dark God, help me. Dark God, be with me.* And I was. I always was."

"I got through the gates on my own," I said through my teeth.

"Of course you did. I would expect nothing less of my future queen."

It physically pained me, but I forced the words out. "Help me."

"No," he said simply. "You must choose between your lover and your coven."

Lover was worse than bonded.

I remained rooted to the spot as he walked around me, his black eyes dissecting me as he went. I would have felt less exposed if I'd been naked. If I thought he'd accept that offer, I'd have removed my clothes right there. But I knew his answer in whatever remained of my soul. My heart.

Just like I knew not to flinch away from his touch as he lifted the curtain of hair away from my neck. As he pressed his lips to the hollow of my throat.

"I will see you again soon, sweet Koryn. Very soon."

CHAPTER 68

NO TIME HAD PASSED, MY EXCHANGE WITH THE DARK GOD LITTLE more than a flicker of flame. But my skin still tingled where he'd pressed his lips to my throat. I'd begged for his help for a second time, and he'd given his answer—a resounding *no*.

My past self was gone, her form merged with my own. My coven sisters stood on the points of the pentacle, all except for McKean, who advanced on Garrick with her curved dagger.

Choose, Xyta whispered in my ear.

Coven—power—life.

Or Garrick—Lifebind—lover.

Without my coven, I would eventually waste away. My power would dim. I might save Garrick, but eventually, the second death would come for me. When it did, the Dark God would be waiting.

McKean lifted her hand overhead, so caught up in her bloodlust that she did not even realize as she sliced through several strands of her own golden hair. Isanara growled. I recognized the sound of her wings flaring wide. But she could not intervene—I would not risk her incurring Xyta's wrath.

Xyta demanded a choice. Zeph, the God of Memory,

demanded a change. But unlike those first two flashes of the past, it was not the memory that needed to change. It was me. I had already changed. When I killed McKean to save Kyrelle, I'd been driven by guilt, by a heart that I refused to embrace. But now, standing between my coven sister and my bonded, I could not lie to myself any longer. The organ in my chest might be dead, but my heart was very much alive. I could recognize that because of the dragon at my side and the man kneeling before me.

Choose.

I'd made my choice standing before the Dark God's throne, with his lips pressed against my skin.

I threw out my hand, daggers of deadly ice spearing through the air. They impaled my coven sister through her throat, her abdomen, her chest. Before the blade she held could clatter to the ground, the memory dissolved around us.

We landed hard on the rock-strewn pathway between the mountains. Garrick kept me upright, his hand digging into my upper arms as my body pitched sideways. I clung to him, curling my fingers around his leather tunic, desperate to feel his heart beating, his breath against my face.

We'd survived. Both of us were alive on the other side of the Memory Gate.

Garrick pressed his forehead to mine, breathing me in the same way I was him. I savored the slide of his silken silver hair against my cheeks.

"I am so sorry. You should not have had to—"

"It is done," I said, cutting him off by pressing my mouth against his. I needed to taste him, to reassure myself that we were both still here, still alive, if only for this moment in time, for the space of seven gates.

He caught my face in his hands, holding me in place as he drew away. His eyes met mine, the turquoise irises as intense as ever.

My throat tightened, but I did not try to talk. I let myself get lost in his eyes, the otherworldly mixture of clover and cerulean that formed a pattern as unique as any fingerprint. I'd never seen eyes like them, except… except maybe I had.

Gods, my mind was a frazzled mess. I was misremembering memories that did not even belong to me.

"I am so sorry," Garrick said again.

I nodded, releasing my grip on his chest to curl my hands around his wrists. I leaned into his caress where he cupped my cheeks.

I could never return to my coven. But if limited time remained before I was summoned to the Dark God's side, I wanted to spend it with Garrick. For as long as the Seven Gates would allow.

"It was my choice," I choked out. And in the end, it had been an easy one once I realized how I truly felt about him. "I would make it again, because despite everything that is going to tear us apart, I lov—"

Pain ripped through me. Visceral and instant, like someone had ripped a limb from my body. All thoughts but one were eclipsed by the sudden emptiness inside of me. I stumbled out of Garrick's arms. He let me go.

"Where is Isanara?" I choked out, reaching for the nearly vertical wall of rock behind me to steady myself.

"Do not worry, sister. I have your familiar well in hand," the head witch of the Midnight Coven said as she stepped into view.

CHAPTER 69

MAURA.

She waved her hand, and the others appeared just as suddenly, like a curtain had been pulled back.

Garrick and I were not alone in the gorge. Far from it. Behind us, the narrow passage that led back to the temple was crowded with a line of acolytes in emerald robes. Varian stood at their center, her jewel-toned purple stark against the grays of the stone cliffs that sloped upward on either side of the gorge.

The Memory Gate was gone, no hint of sparkling black mist left behind.

Just me and Garrick, trapped on one side by the priestess and the other by witches.

Maura was not alone. But the others—those I recognized and those I did not—were all secondary.

"Where is my dragon?" I demanded, forcing my legs to straighten under me.

"Isanara!" I screamed into the shared space of our minds. *"Isanara, where are you?"*

Maura waved a dismissive hand, her halo of tight, dark curls bobbing around her. "She is perfectly safe. Though I admit, figuring out how to dim the bond between a witch and her familiar was quite difficult. It would not have been possible at all without our combined power and magic."

Power *and* magic.

It was not just Elodie and Auri who stood with Maura, flanking their head witch on either side. There were several more figures, clad in rich, shimmering garments that looked completely out of place in the barren gorge. It was not their clothing that snagged my attention, but their ears.

Fae.

Ice crystallized in my veins. I could not kill them all, but I could do considerable damage, especially with Garrick at my side. He hated the fae, and rightfully so after what they had done to his mother.

But it wasn't Garrick that moved at the periphery of my vision. A swirl of emerald caught my eye.

I threw out my hand, releasing my power in a torrent until it formed a wall that reached my waist. But Varian had already yanked Tomin back. I did not know her motivations, but at least she agreed with me on that—neither of us wanted Tomin anywhere near this encounter.

"We are stewards of the Seven Gods and the Seven Gates. We do not interfere with what happens beyond the temple walls," Varian said.

"Liar," I breathed, even as relief slid down my spine. Tomin was safe. The priestess would keep him safe. But after all she had done, to stand down now... "You lying hypocrite. You intervened before, more than once. Why, if it was just to let it come to this? Unless you are in league with..."

Varian had remarked on Isanara when she first saw her, but she had not been surprised. Had she been in communication with Maura all along? Had this all been some twisted plot to get hold of a dragon?

It seemed too far-fetched. How could any of them have known that a mythical creature whose species had deserted Velora centuries ago would magically reappear and choose an outcast witch as her familiar? The pieces just did not fit.

Maura clucked her tongue, the sound dripping with the condescending disapproval that had haunted my nightmares. "I do not consort with humans," she said.

But she was standing among a troupe of fae.

Three males and two females, plus Alize. Alize, who was not restrained. Alize, the fae female bitch who stood with her arms crossed, a scowl on her face, and deception in her cursed fae heart.

A tall male moved to stand beside Maura. Like the others, he was clothed in layers of rich silk and velvet embroidered with golden thread. But the pretty clothes could not disguise his hardened warrior's body or the distinctive breadth of his shoulders.

An elegant fae female stood at his side. Though I did not recognize her, the diadem atop her head was seared into my memory.

My stomach turned violently. I grabbed for Garrick's hand. I was going to be sick.

"It is unnatural to separate a witch from her familiar. Return her to me, now," I ground out, pressing my other hand to my chest, trying to do something to relieve the growing ache. Every minute I was separated from Isanara, the pain grew.

The fae male ignored my demand, addressing Maura. "This is the witch you promised me?"

Maura's lips twitched, her nearly white skin shimmering in the gray light, before she inclined her head a fraction of an inch. "Indeed, Your Majesty."

Maura had not just entangled herself with the fae—but the fae king. The same greedy, self-serving monster who'd allowed his people to run rampant across the continent, to grasp at power until they angered the gods and brought down their wrath on all of Velora.

I had to get Isanara back. I had to get away from whatever this was unfolding around me. I squeezed Garrick's hand, desperate to communicate with him.

"You even managed to find my runaway daughter in the process," the king said. But he was no longer looking at Maura. He'd shifted his attention, his look of displeasure, to the golden female leaning against the stone wall.

"I knew," I breathed. "You lied to us about the faerie ring. You… he trusted you."

It was all happening too fast. I'd let Alize get too close. I should have trusted my instincts about her. I should not have let Garrick make excuses for her.

But Alize was shaking her head, and she looked… she looked sorry for me.

None of it made sense. But the weight in my chest was getting so heavy I could hardly breathe. I splayed the hand that did not hold Garrick wide, letting power flow from me, releasing the pressure building inside of me, trying to maintain some sort of control as the world around me spun faster and faster.

Maura laughed, the deep sound echoing off of the walls that pressed in on us from either side. "You stupid, foolish girl. You've always been so caught up in your own feelings that you can hardly see what is happening around you. Here you are, so busy clinging to that dead heart that you have chosen the wrong fae to blame."

But I'd only met one fae—just Alize.

The fae king had helped Maura mute my bond with Isanara, and he had more than my hate for that. But I still did not know why he'd aligned himself with Maura, and I'd never seen the male before now. The only other fae I'd encountered…

…was half-human.

When the infant in Alize's memory had transformed, his eyes had struck me. I'd been too caught up to realize why they seemed so familiar. Stupid or foolish or both, because I had been looking into those eyes every day for the last two months.

When the Memory Gate had thrust us into reliving my

encounter with the two men outside of the tavern in Canmar, I'd been confused. The entire memory had seemed off—because it was not my memory at all. It was Garrick's.

I jerked away from him, but there was nowhere for me to go.

Varian and her acolytes blocked the way back to the temple, watching as she'd instructed. Two other acolytes restrained Tomin. The wall of ice I'd erected still stood.

In front of me, witches and fae intermingled in an unnatural mixture that turned my stomach. We were enemies, not allies.

At my side stood the man for whom I'd been willing to sacrifice everything—my coven, and thereby my own life.

Maura and Elodie began to chant. *"Heed the call of earth and bone, shift his form, return him home."*

Alone, Maura could not have done it. Shapeshifting was an earth-bound power, like the many faces that Elodie could wear. But when she lent her fire, they were able to do the impossible.

Garrick's body twisted, contorting as he fought the power of the spell. My stomach lurched, my twisted feelings rebelling at the sight of him in pain. Every muscle in his body stiffened, and then all of the fight whooshed out of him. He transformed in an instant. One moment, the man so familiar I could outline his face with my eyes closed. The next, a ruggedly beautiful black raven.

There had been a crow on the roof of the general store the night I was attacked in Canmar. In the woods over the past few weeks, whenever Garrick and I were separated.

Not a crow. A raven. I'd never paid much attention to the difference, though it was plain now that I saw his shifted form. It must have been how he beat me back to our camp that night I'd snuck up to listen to him and Alize argue. He had not walked— he'd flown.

Not just the halfling bastard of a human mother, raped by the fae, but a shifter. A half-fae whose eyes matched those of the brother that Alize had tried to murder in his cradle.

I forced myself to look at the fae king. I did not bother to beg the Dark God for a different outcome. I already knew what I would find.

Cold turquoise eyes stared back at me.

No. No, no, no, no.

This could not be happening. Not to me... not after I'd been so careful for so long, after I'd spent lifetimes alone and—

"Koryn," Garrick choked, landing on his knees. His shirt was gone—how that worked for a shifter, I did not fucking care. But I did care about the tattoos that I could see, the ones he'd hidden from me just as effectively as I'd hidden the one on the inside of my thigh.

A series of rings looped around his left bicep. I did not know their meaning or significance. But there was no mistaking the dark wings etched across his back. They were beautiful, those raven wings. In a different time, I might have pressed my lips to each one of those elegantly wrought feathers.

But in this reality, betrayal was burning up my throat. Frost swirled in my mouth.

"I am so sorry," Garrick choked out, his chest heaving as he tried to drag in breaths, still recovering from the force of Maura and Elodie's spell.

That's why he'd apologized over and over again. Not because choosing to save his life had cost me my coven and my future—but because he'd betrayed me.

"It was real," he said between breaths.

Maura was not the only one laughing now. The king chuckled, a cruel, cold sound that put my own ice to shame.

"You said you had no magic. You lied to me." I'd known there were secrets between us. But I'd thought that we understood each other, that even if there were secrets, there were not lies.

I'd thought a lot of misguided things.

Now I knew better.

I was alone, just as I always had been.

"I said none manifested while I was in Balar Shan," Garrick

said, dragging himself to his feet. "My *abilities* appeared long before that."

He didn't look at Maura or at his father. His father, the King of the Fae. That's what those eyes told me. Garrick was not just any half-fae bastard. He was a half-fae prince.

He reached for my hand, but I jerked it back. He huffed out a breath, but he did not retreat. "It was real, Koryn. I promise that it was. How would I have gotten through the Devotion Gate if it was not? And after… when we…"

But I shook my head. I wanted to believe him. I didn't want to be alone. I wanted him to be the man I thought he was, the man I thought I knew.

"I don't know what deals you made with the gods," I whispered.

Garrick opened his mouth to argue, but Maura cut him off.

"Give yourself credit, young man," Maura interjected. "You did exactly as we asked."

I closed my eyes.

"You risked your life, and she saved you, just like I knew she would. She's always been afflicted by the remnants of her human heart."

Thank the Dark God my human heart was no longer responsible for keeping me alive. In that moment, it would have broken in two.

"You used the Lifebind to get close to her, to get her through the gates. Exactly as we asked. And now…"

The fae king finished Maura's sentence. "And now you shall have your reward, as we agreed."

Everything had been stripped away from me. I'd only made it through the gates because Garrick had seen to it, not even because of the Lifebind, but because of some deal he'd made with Maura and the fae king. The man I'd been willing to sacrifice for saw me as nothing more than a tool. A means to some unknown end that he'd never trusted me enough to tell me.

Maura and the fae king had plotted from the beginning. The

king must have been responsible for the faerie ring we'd stumbled upon in the forest. Garrick and Alize had known, even then. They'd shattered not only my trust, but my illusion of agency.

They'd even taken my familiar.

I fell to my knees. This time, there was no one there to catch me.

Garrick tried, but Aurienna was faster. Vines sprang up from nowhere, encircling our arms and holding us in place. Garrick thrashed against them, but then Elodie was murmuring a spell, and the fae king waved his hand, and suddenly I could not move anything beneath my neck. I could not even look at Garrick, though I could hear his snarls of frustration.

It was for the better. I never wanted to see him again.

Maura withdrew three cinched bags from within her cloak. She passed off one each to Elodie and Aurienna, who both began to move, sprinkling ash from the bags as they walked.

"Where is my familiar?" I demanded.

Nothing else mattered anymore. At least, nothing that I could see or feel. My chest ached terribly, but there were too many causes to blame just one.

Maura waved away my concern. "You will be reunited with her eventually." She stepped around the lines of ash that the other two witches carefully laid out. "You have been so helpful, Koryn. Do hold still for this last bit."

"Why, Maura." A demand, not a question.

She took my arm, grasping it in the same place she had on a dark, frigid night three hundred and seventy-seven years before.

"Why do you think I have lingered in Velora all of these years? I will not be just the head witch of this coven, but of all the covens. A queen of witches."

"Vassal to a fae overlord," I seethed. Keeping my mouth shut had never been a particular strength of mine.

"You are so shortsighted, Koryn. You are ruled by your emotions rather than your mind. It is why you never mastered your active power." She dug her pointed fingernail into the tender skin of my forearm, ripping open the wound that had healed only days before.

She squeezed until several drops of blood spilled across the ground. The lines of ash burst into flame. I did not miss the irony —a frost witch, imprisoned in a pentacle of blood.

"Koryn, I need you to listen to me."

Garrick's voice hit me with the sharpness of a knife. I felt it in my gut.

I did not turn my head. I refused to look his way. But that did not stop him.

"They are going to take you away from the gates. No matter what happens, you must remember the oath—"

"Enough!" Maura ordered. "That should be enough blood to pacify the gods for now."

"The Dark God will punish you for this treachery," I breathed.

Maura licked her lips. "Not even the Dark God can save you now, Koryn."

Then she snapped her fingers, and the world went dark.

EPILOGUE

GARRICK

You cannot have her.

The words screamed through my head as I opened my eyes. I felt them with every beat of the heart that no longer belonged to me.

You cannot have her. That was what I'd tried to scream at my father and the evil witch whose favor he'd courted. But he'd stolen the words from my mouth, cutting off my ability to speak. Cutting me off at the legs, the way he'd been doing for years.

Why waste time on a bastard when you finally have a legitimate son?

But all grievances against my father faded in comparison to the one that truly mattered. *He'd taken Koryn.*

I would kill him.

I'd dreamed about it since the moment my magic awakened. But concern for my mother had always stayed my hand. Our deal was now done—my mother was free. And I was free to make him pay.

Night had fallen while I lay unconscious in the gorge. The

priestess and her acolytes were nowhere to be seen. She'd decided to take that vow of impartiality seriously all of a sudden.

I did not need their help. Not yet. But if I did, I would have no scruples about going into the temple and begging for their allegiance. I would prostrate myself before the altars of each of the Seven Gods. I would do whatever it took to get my bonded back.

Nothing mattered now except for Koryn.

I scrubbed a hand down my face, trying to clear away the cobwebs of unconsciousness.

A twinge of pain came from my mouth as I scraped my hand over it. My lip was split. Someone had gotten in a few kicks while I was unconscious. But already it was half-healed, the fae blood in my veins doing its magical work.

They could kick me and beat me, split my lips and break my bones. They could peel my skin from my body. But if they laid a hand on Koryn, I would kill them all.

I'd entered the temple to save my mother. I'd played their games at the Mercy Gate. But despite the head witch's rantings, things had not gone perfectly according to their plan. They had underestimated my frost witch.

They saw her emotions as weaknesses. I knew it was her indomitable spirit. They waited for her power to fail. But I'd only seen her grow stronger.

Koryn was going to tear the fae court at Balar Shan apart—and my place was at her side while she did. That was what it meant to love someone.

She may never forgive me. I hardly deserved it after what I'd done.

But I would reunite her with her familiar, hand her the tools to break their shackles, and applaud while she dismantled the ancient powers of Velora brick by brick.

I ignored the bruises that peppered my body and the wound they'd used for their blood magic. They'd heal. In the meantime, they would be a reminder through every wingbeat that carried me north to Balar Shan. I'd broken the heart that Koryn believed dead. I would spend the rest of my life—be it mortal or immortal—repenting.

I checked my weapons. They had not taken my bow—arrogant fae fools. Everything was in order, despite my entire world being completely twisted on its axis. But it had been like that ever since I'd watched Koryn wield her frost power in Canmar. My world had shifted, and now it revolved around her. That was my worst memory—the one where I'd known that I would hurt her and I moved forward anyway.

I'd watched her in my raven form from atop the general store as she subdued the two men. Then again, as she'd faced off with her sister witch and retreated to a cold hay loft. By the time she entered the temple, shoving aside the girl and taking her place, I knew their plan was doomed to fail.

Koryn was an immortal witch with a human heart that had never forgotten how to love. She was a light in the darkness of Velora. If three hundred and seventy-seven years had not been enough to corrupt her, they would not turn her now.

The Lifebind on my wrist burned, protesting the distance between us. I'd be faster in my raven form.

But before I could shift, the air around me changed. I felt the pulse of power and magic, a unique combination that belonged to neither witch nor fae, but to the creators themselves.

The Dark God appeared before me in a swirl of sparkling night. They called his gate the Unknown Gate, for who could begin to fathom the dark, eternal vastness of hell itself.

He stood before me, arms crossed over his chest, dark hair waving on a nonexistent wind, glaring at me with the force of a thousand brutal, gruesome deaths. There could only be one reason for this god to appear.

She'd tried to hide his mark. But I'd seen every inch of her in those torturous weeks after the Devotion Gate. My knowledge of runes was rudimentary, but I knew Koryn. I knew the shape and power of her heart, more meaningful than the frost that lived beneath her skin.

There was only one reason for the Dark God to mark her in that way. Among all of his creations, he'd singled out the witch whose power to love was even greater than the power he'd bestowed upon her. He knew just how remarkable she was.

Good. So did I.

I'd chosen to love her even knowing what she owed to the Dark God. I would always choose her.

"I am going to get her," I said.

His cruel black eyes did not shift, his countenance truly impenetrable. Nothing less than I would expect from the king of hell.

The temperature around us dropped, the darkness of the night pressing in from every direction. The shadows themselves answered to him, I realized.

He lifted one brow at me. "Tell me more about how you plan to save our bonded."

THE END

Not quite ready to leave this world behind? Sign-up for my newsletter to receive the first exclusive excerpts, cover reveal, and all the other official release details for The Halfling Prince, Book 2 in The Covenants of Velora.

PLEASE CONSIDER LEAVING A REVIEW! Reviews are essential for independent authors. They help new readers find my books, set the stage for translations, and build excitement for future releases. Thank you!

AUTHOR'S NOTE

After more than twenty published books, no heroine has tested me more than Koryn. Her story came to me in fits and bursts and endless rounds of revision. It took me a long time to find her voice. Now that this book is in the world, I think I finally know why. Writing her meant exploring the most vulnerable parts of myself, parts that hurt. She is deeply conflicted. She has looked for family and love in all the wrong places and suffered because of it. She has contorted herself to fit into what she perceives others want and has lost herself in the process. If you've ever felt any of those things… well, welcome to womanhood in 2025. It is fucking hard. I don't have any of the answers, but hopefully reading Koryn's first book gave you some company as you sit in those feelings.

Writing the men who would love her was challenging in a different way. I absolutely refuse to write a love triangle. So why choose it is, folks. Feeling tortured by the slow burn? Me too. Don't worry. We'll burn the place down in the next book.

ALSO BY EMBERLY ASH

Secrets of the Faerie Crown

A complete fae romantasy series

Crown of Earth and Sky

Throne of Air and Darkness

Court of Vines and Vipers

Queen of Blood and Vengeance

ABOUT THE AUTHOR

Emberly Ash stole her first romance novel off her mom's bookshelf at the age of ten and never looked back. The author of 12 romance books under her first pen name, Emberly craved something darker and steamier--enter the world of fantasy romance. Her books are dark, twisty, and not for the faint of heart. In the real world, she manages a fire-breathing five-year-old and a grumpy mage of a husband. But you'll most often find her in her hot-pink writing cave, dreaming up your next book boyfriend. Spoiler alert: he's fae.